ACCLAIM FOR
THE NOVELS OF NALO HOPKINSON

SISTER MINE

"The future is always eventually bright in Nalo Hopkinson's fictitious universe. The author of sci-fi classics *The Salt Roads* and *Brown Girl in the Ring* conjures up another hit with SISTER MINE."

—*Essence*

"Like much of Hopkinson's work, SISTER MINE mixes Afro-Caribbean and European mythology, elements of horror, a snappy wit, and astute psychology." —*Los Angeles Times*

"Hopkins writes in the tradition of African-American science fiction authors like Samuel R. Delany and Octavia Butler, but her approach is singularly expansive, a mythography of the black diaspora. (There are parallels with fellow Caribbean native Junot Diaz's work, not to mention *King Rat*, China Mieville's similarly musical urban fantasy.)...Hopkinson's prose intermingles the quotidian settings and cosmic mysticism with sly, assured ease."

—*National Post* (Canada)

"The comingling of the fantastical and the real world in this urban fantasy is seamless and surprisingly credible...complex relationships and knotty family ties, all with a tasty supernatural flavor."

—*School Library Journal* blog

"Is this really Hopkinson's first adult novel since 2007's *The New Moon's Arms*? It feels like an eternity. We heard her read from this story of twins, one with magic powers and one without, recently, and we were left dying to hear more." —io9.com

"Hopkinson's most wildly imaginative novel since *Brown Girl in the Ring*...and some of her most accomplished prose to date; at one point, she conveys the multivalent perceptions of Makeda through stunning passages of pure synaesthesia." —*Locus*

"Novels and stories by the Jamaican-born Hopkinson have won just about every sci-fi and fantasy award there is. She throws together Afro-Caribbean myth and pulpy, urban drama for something that is as audacious as it is addictive...a must read." —*Toronto Life*

"SISTER MINE explores kinship, twinship, and the intense rivalry and intimacy unique to sisters...a fast-paced, slyly transgressive, satisfying supernatural adventure." —*Cascadia Subduction Zone*

"Hopkinson has lost none of her gift for salty, Caribbean-Canadian talk...And the relationship between Makeda and Abby always rings true: resentment and anger enduringly intertwined with love and loyalty." —*Kirkus Reviews*

THE NEW MOON'S ARMS
Sunburst Award for Canadian Literature of the Fantastic
***Locus* Recommended Reading List**

"A significant figure and a singular talent...A most impressive work, *The New Moon's Arms* has everything a reader could want: a compelling storyline with mysteries at its heart; a firm rooting in myth and history; keen social sense; and, most importantly, a focal character it is impossible not to fall in love with. It is a novel that sweeps the reader into its world: vivid and richly nuanced, utterly realistic yet still somehow touched with magic. Hopkinson's writing is lush and note-perfect...The dialogue crackles, and Calamity's narrative voice is direct and winning...one is left with a sense of wonder." —*Toronto Star*

"*The New Moon's Arms* is a dance of lost-and-found. Hopkinson knows not to get too sentimental, thanks in large part to her heroine's unsinkable sense of humor. It let me hear the mermaids singing."
—*Washington Post Book World*

"Considerable talent for character, voice, and lushly sensual writing... her most convincing and complex character to date." —*Locus*

"Hopkinson has had a remarkable impact on popular fiction... [Her] work continues to question the very genres she adopts, transforming them from within through her fierce intelligence and her commitment to a radical vision that refuses easy consumption... With sly humor and great tenderness, [she] draws out the hope residing in age and change." —*Toronto Globe and Mail*

"Shows new depths of wisdom, humor, and insight... Like life, Hopkinson's novel doesn't resolve every mystery. But Hopkinson has answered the essential questions in *The New Moon's Arms*, and she's wise enough to know we need nothing more."
—*Seattle Times*

THE SALT ROADS
Nebula Award Final Ballot
Shortlisted for the Hurston-Wright Legacy Award

"A book of wonder, courage, and magic... an electrifying bravura performance by one of our most important writers."
—Junot Díaz, author of *The Brief Wondrous Life of Oscar Wao*

"Sexy, disturbing, touching, wildly comic. A tour de force from one of our most striking new voices in fiction."
—*Kirkus Reviews* (starred review)

"Succeeds impressively as a powerful and passionate meditation on myth and survival."

—*Locus*

"A brilliant and multilayered tale."

—*Black Issues Book Review*

"Whirling with witchcraft and sensuality, the latest novel by Hopkinson is a globe-spanning, time-traveling spiritual odyssey...The novel has a genuine vitality and generosity. Epic and frenetic, it traces the physical and spiritual ties that bind its characters to each other and to the earth."

—*Publishers Weekly*

"Rollicking, sensual...Required reading...[from] one of science fiction's most inventive and brilliant writers."

—*New York Post*

SKIN FOLK
Winner of the World Fantasy Award for Best Collection
New York Times Best Book of the Year

"Vibrant...stunning...Hopkinson puts her lyrical gifts to good use."

—*New York Times Book Review*

"Hopkinson's prose is vivid and immediate."

—*Washington Post Book World*

"An important new writer."

—*Dallas Morning News*

"A marvelous display of Nalo Hopkinson's talents, skills, and insights into the human conditions of life...everything is possible in her imagination."

—*Science Fiction Chronicle*

"Highly recommended." —*Library Journal* (starred review)

"Employs Caribbean folk elements to tell a story that is by turns fantastic, allegorical, and contemporary." —*Washington Post*

BROWN GIRL IN THE RING
Winner of the John W. Campbell Award for Best New Writer
Winner of the *Locus* Award for Best First Novel
Shortlisted for the Philip K. Dick Award and the James Tiptree, Jr. Award

"Excellent...a bright, original mix of future urban decay and West Indian magic...strongly rooted in character and place."
—*Sunday Denver Post*

"A wonderful sense of narrative and a finely tuned ear for dialogue...balances a well-crafted and imaginative story with incisive social critique and a vivid sense of place." —*Emerge*

"An impressive debut precisely because of Hopkinson's fresh viewpoint." —*Washington Post*

"Hopkinson lives up to her advance billing."
—*New York Times Book Review*

"Hopkinson's writing is smooth and assured, and her characters lively and believable. She has created a vivid world of urban decay and startling, dangerous magic, where the human heart is both a physical and metaphorical key." —*Publishers Weekly*

"Splendid...Superbly plotted and redolent of the rhythms of Afro-Caribbean speech."
                                                              —*Kirkus Reviews*

"Utterly original...the debut of a major talent. Gripping, memorable, and beautiful."

                                              —Karen Joy Fowler, author of
                                                  The Jane Austen Book Club

S·I·S·T·E·R M·I·N·E

NALO HOPKINSON

SISTER MINE

•••

GC

GRAND CENTRAL
PUBLISHING

New York   Boston

For David, who brings me joy

———————

Copyright © 2013 by Nalo Hopkinson
Excerpted poetry is from "Goblin Market" by Christina Rossetti,
first published in 1862.
Reading Group Guide copyright © 2013 by Hachette Book Group, Inc.

Grand Central Publishing
Hachette Book Group
237 Park Avenue
New York, NY 10017

www.HachetteBookGroup.com

Printed in the United States of America

Originally published in hardcover by Hachette Book Group.

RRD-C

First trade edition: November 2013
10 9 8 7 6 5 4 3 2 1

Grand Central Publishing is a division of Hachette Book Group, Inc.
The Grand Central Publishing name and logo is a trademark
of Hachette Book Group, Inc.

The Hachette Speakers Bureau provides a wide range of authors for speaking events. To find out more, go to www.hachettespeakersbureau.com
or call (866) 376-6591.

The publisher is not responsible for websites (or their content) that are not owned by the publisher.

ISBN 978-1-4555-2840-0 (pbk.)

1

❖ ❖ ❖

"Good folk, I have no coin;
To take were to purloin:
I have no copper in my purse,
I have no silver either."

S CORE!" I SAID to the scruffy grey cat sitting on the building's loading dock. "She'd never even think to look for me here!"

The cat replied with a near-silent mew, and set about cleaning its face. One ear was ragged from a long-healed injury.

I double-checked the scrap of paper I'd torn out of the Classifieds section of the *Toronto Star*. Yup, this was the place that was looking for tenants. It didn't look like much, sitting there on a downtown corner. It was a blocky, crumbling cube of a warehouse. Looked like it had a basement below, two storeys above. It was wedged between upscale high-rise condos and low-rise co-op town houses.

There were buildings in this city that went to hundreds of floors. Your ears'd pop from the altitude change just going up in the elevator. But those sparkly new structures, they needed the reflected gleam of sunlight off their chromed and mirrored surfaces in order to shine. This building, it sucked in light, and the glow it gave back couldn't be seen in daylight or in Toronto's overlit night; not by purely claypicken eyes, that is. I could see it, though. One of the few perqs of being a crippled deity half-breed; although I had no mojo of my own, I could sometimes get a glimpse of the glow-on that some things and people had. Not as strongly as Abby could. Still, if I squinted exactly the right way, for just a split second, I'd see a flash bounce off Shiny people and things. Like the green flash on the horizon just as the sun sinks into Lake Ontario. That warehouse had some Shine to it. Inanimate objects can get that way when they've rubbed up against the ineffable for a long time. The building's faint burr of Shininess was my first clue that I might like living there.

The exterior paint job was something else, in a wacky way that I liked. Probably years before, someone had slopped teal green paint onto the raw brick. They'd used a dark, muddy purple for the exterior window rims and sills and the edging around the roof. Then, for good measure, they'd lined the inner surfaces of the windows' rims with dark yellow, kind of a mango colour. Made the windows look like the insides of baby birds' beaks when they gaped them wide and demanded food from their exhausted parents.

When he'd realized he was slipping, our dad had signed our childhood home over to me and my sister. Since Abby and I had to live in the world, it was best if we had claypicken legal documents to prove that the place was ours. But I'd had it with living under Abby's wing. She could have my share in the house. I was going to go it alone from now on. My pulse leapt at the thought.

"I think a tree talked to me today," I told Abby, hating myself for doing this again, for coveting mojo so badly that I kept trying to talk myself into believing I had it. I'd never been able to read trees before, so why would I

suddenly now have developed a knack for it? I waited, toying with the food on my plate, sitting at Abby's expensive mahogany table, eating off her hand-made plates from some artists' studio over in the Distillery District, staring at the graceful young oak tree in Abby's front yard through the leaded panes of Abby's antique stained glass living room window. In my own house, I cotched like a boarder.

Teal with purple edging and yellow accents; Abby would hate the place. She would especially hate that it was crass enough to have a name. Hand-painted in toppling white letters over the entrance were the words "CHEERFUL REST." Abby's lips would curl at the inept lettering, the building that looked like a squat for homeless people. Me, I thought it was neat. Plus it would intimidate her. Even low and funny-looking as it was, even in broad daylight, Cheerful Rest managed to loom. Abby would be able to see that, probably more clearly than I could.

The old cat had finished its ablutions. It sphinx-sat on the loading dock in the springtime sun, watching me through half-closed eyes. I could hear it purring though I was a good few feet away. Its body swayed a little to the rhythm of the vibrations.

Abby didn't reply right away. I looked across the table at her. She was staring out the window, slowly and carefully chewing. I'd made us an excellent dinner: stewed guinea hen and manioc with batata dumplings, and an arugula salad with crumbled blue cheese. No wonder Burger Delite wouldn't let me do anything but bus tables and wash dishes; I was too good for them.

The building's Shine wasn't a flash, but kind of an aura. But it felt like mojo, or tasted like it, or something. How had it come by that Shine? Would it somehow spell trouble for me if I moved in there? I had a bad track record of not getting along well with the Shiny, the Family on my dad's side, my haint. Abby.

"Abby, I'd swear it really did talk. A crab apple tree in that park at Queen and Sherbourne. I think it asked me where Dad was. Said it hadn't seen him in a long time."

Abby whipped her head around from the window to glare at me. "Stop it. Just stop it. Why are you always saying things like this? You're embarrassing yourself. And me."

"But—" Why did I say things like that? Because I couldn't help myself. Because I craved more than anything else to have a little mojo of my own.

"Makeda, I don't care whether it's desperate wishful thinking or a stupid little trick you play to impress, but it's really cruel of you to play it with Dad lying helpless in palliative care."

Oh, gods, why couldn't I ever stop doing this? Abby was right. I was only shaming myself.

A lean black guy came round the corner. He was wearing faded black jeans rubbed thin at the knees and a black Revolting Cocks T-shirt so worn that it was almost grey. The left shoulder seam had split open. He had a big, wild 'fro. His left foot was shod in an orange high-topped canvas sneaker, his right foot in a purple one. He smiled at me before unlocking and yanking open the heavy back door that led inside the building, letting out a grungy roar of miked rock drumming. Sounded live, too, like a practice. The guy made an apologetic shrug. He spied the piece of torn classifieds in my hand. He smiled. Over the racket, he shouted, "It's only this noisy on the weekend!"

If I moved in here, there would be music, and musicians. Plus there was a brother, apparently living here, who liked punk. So it wouldn't be like I was trying to single-handedly desegregate the place, either. Nice. I smiled back at him and relaxed a bit. Music was the most fun part of living with Abby.

He said, "Hey, Yoplait!"

Yoplait?

The cat twitched one ear in his direction.

The guy jerked his chin towards the open door. "Come on!"

The cat looked over its shoulder at him. Stood. Went over to him. The door was hydraulic, and took a few seconds to shut behind the guy and his cat; long enough for me to hear the drumming clang to a halt, someone saying something muffled into the mike, a laugh, the drumming starting up again. Looked like the guy had gone up a short flight of stairs. I'd gotten a brief whiff of stale beer from the open door. There were empty two-fours stacked outside. Some kind of club space in the building?

The door closed completely, and I was left with only the endless Toronto traffic sounds.

Longing tapped me on the shoulder and enclosed me in its arms. I wanted to live here, be fully independent of Abby and Uncle, start learning how to exist as the mortal I was. I bet Cheerful Rest was some kind of claypicken artists' space, where people used scavenged milk crates and bricks and wooden flats to customize their units. There'd be flyers stapled to the walls, advertising bands and readings and gallery openings and dance performances. Would they even let me into a place like that? I wasn't really an artist. I was just an artist's hanger-on who liked to tinker. I'd always wanted to live in a warehouse. A real warehouse, with high ceilings and exposed brick and pipes. And best of all, Abby wouldn't know where I was if I didn't tell her. We'd quarrelled last night, and again this morning. I'd told her I was moving when I stormed out a few hours ago, but I always said that when we fought. Today, though, I meant it. Standing outside Cheerful Rest that warm spring afternoon, sensing its warm-blooded Shine and waiting for the guy who ran it to show up, I meant it. I was finally going to break free of the hold my sister Abby had on me. She could get kinda clingy. We'd always lived together. She lost her shit if I didn't attend a performance of hers. And to tell the truth, I missed her if I didn't see her for a few days. But she really got on my freaking nerves all the time! Today, I was cutting the tie that bound us, locked together like the conjoined twins we used to be. I'd get my own place, tell Abby in a few months where I was living, and by then, she and I would have gotten used to being a little less intertwined in each other's affairs. I could begin to figure out how to live my own life.

It was partly my own fault. Abby'd been so dependent on me in the first years of our life, and I'd gotten used to it. They'd separated us physically, but emotionally, Abs and I couldn't seem to let each other go.

"Abs, can't you even give me the benefit of the doubt? Why in hell can't you accept that maybe you're not the only special one?"

Abby slid her cane off the back of her chair and pulled herself to her feet. "Because you don't hear trees talk. You never did. You started pretending you could after you overheard Cousin Flash calling you that silly name."

"The donkey. Yeah. But that's not when I started doing it."

"When you started to make believe you could do it."

"I started it after you called me the same name to my face." Too late, I realized I'd just practically admitted I was talking shit about speaking to trees. My cheeks flaring with embarrassment, I pressed on, *"The sister I shared all my secrets with. The sister I looked after until she could do it herself."*

She swallowed. Took a breath. "Children can be cruel. They say mean things to each other, play nasty tricks. How about that time you shortened one of my crutches?"

"That's not fair!"

"Just a half inch. And me so used to being uncomfortable in my skin that I didn't notice it for a while. My shoulder ached that whole day and the next, and I couldn't figure out why."

"It was just a prank. A stupid kid prank."

"And me calling you 'donkey' was just a stupid kid thing. Get over it, Makeda."

I folded my arms, looked out the window. "That tree could *have been talking to me," I muttered. I sounded about five years old. I detested myself for it. I hated my compulsion to go on about this stuff. The wind in that tree, it had sounded almost like words in a different language. I just figured maybe that's what Dad heard when plants talked to him. Maybe it was just like a different language, and I could learn it. Or maybe I was just being an ass. I knew how to do that.*

A grey-beige hatchback, new, pulled into the building's three-car gravel parking lot. I moved out of the way. The door whispered open. The man who rolled out of the car was a big guy, white-looking, with straight, light brown hair that stopped just short of his jawline. He was wearing a two-piece suit the same colour as his hair, white shirt underneath. Brown dress shoes, their leather creased across the toe box. He was sweating even though it was a cool spring day. He gave me a distracted glance. "You Mak... Makky...?"

"Makeda," I said, moving forward and extending my hand to shake his. "And you must be Milo?" He was about as Shiny as day-old bread. So he wasn't the source of the building's glow.

"Yeah." His hand was cool and meaty. "Come inside," he said.

As I turned to follow him into the building, I fretted. Didn't have any references to give him except Abby, and I didn't want to bring her into this. I'd been fired from or left the last four jobs I'd had. They hadn't felt real to me at the time. Even Burger Delite was just something I did to prove to myself that I could, until today. Abby made money from music-related gigs here and there, I knew that. I'd never been too clear on the specific details of everything she did. Me, Dad, and Abby, we'd never been wealthy, but if things were getting too lean, Uncle would glean some valuables from the dead for us. Never anything that next of kin might be needing. Lots of people died in ways that made the cash in their pockets or purses inaccessible to claypickens. Today, though, my ignorance could bite me in the ass. When Milo did his credit check on me, it'd reveal a tendency towards bouncing cheques—not all the time, just a lot of the time—low earnings, and a spotty work history. It'd never been a problem before. I did some quick math in my head. Paying my own way was going to be tight. The rent on a run-down place like this would be low, wouldn't it? Fact was, I hadn't really thought my grand storm-out through.

Milo walked me around to the front of the building and unlocked that door. From here, the drumming was muffled. He frowned. "You won't have that noise all the time," he said. "If they have a weeknight show, they stop by eleven p.m."

Weeknights, too, huh? That could get a little rigorous. "That's fine," I lied. "I'm sure it'll be okay." Maybe it wouldn't be so bad.

"They practise during the days a lot, but most people are out at work then."

"I usually work the evening shift. But I'm used to sleeping through the sounds of music practice."

"Yeah? You know some folks in the biz, then?"

"A few."

Milo led me into a tiny, stuffy office on the main floor. One scuffed desk, dark brown Formica with a fake wood grain. No chairs; Milo perched on the edge of the desk while I bent over it to fill out the application form with the chewed ballpoint pen he lent me. "It's a good place," he said absently. "I gotta get another super, but that won't take long."

"A super what?" I was only half listening. *Three* references?

He laughed. "Superintendent. I'm not here every day, so if you need anything, just ask Brian or one of the other tenants. They'll help you. Only not the chick in 213. She's a little crazy. Nothing to worry about! She gets nervous around strangers, is all. If she stays on her medication, she's just fine. I'm giving her a break on her rent till she's back on her feet. In any case, Welfare sends her rent cheque right to me, so no worries there. Anybody else can give you a hand if you need anything, and you have my number."

Yeah, sure he was doing it out of the goodness of his heart. Sweet deal for him, guaranteed rent.

Whatever. He was talking as though I already had the place. That was a good sign. Nervously, I handed him the completed application form. He glanced at the badly photocopied sheet of paper. "No references?"

I guessed I could use Aunt Suze as a reference. I took the form back from him and scribbled down her name and contact information. Thought about it some more, then added the name and phone number of my boss at Burger Delite, even though I'd already written that in the employment section. I couldn't put my uncle's name down; Death didn't exactly have a physical home address or phone number. Or a reliably corporeal body, for that matter.

Maybe Milo would be satisfied with two references. I slid the form back across the table to him. He started reading it again. He said, "You have any pets? No pets allowed in here."

So did he not know about the grey cat I'd just seen? "No pets."

"You don't throw loud parties, do you? Or have loud hobbies, like woodworking? Had a guy in here once with a table saw. Disturbed the other tenants."

I laughed. "No, nothing like that." He was worried about one person having a party, but he had a rock band practising on the main floor? "I make little windup toys. You know, from discarded nuts and bolts. Just something I do to pass the time. Give them to people as gifts. It's not noisy. Mostly I use glue and a screwdriver."

"No soldering? Can't do anything in here that's a fire hazard. You won't even have a stove in your unit."

"What? How do people cook, then?"

He frowned irritably, as though I'd asked him something bothersome and insignificant. "I think there's a microwave in that vacant unit. And there's a kitchen down the hall, with a shared fridge and stove. It can get a little skanky in there, but it's okay."

I bit my lower lip. Store my meds in a communal fridge, where anyone could walk in and help themselves to them? I didn't think so.

"And by the way," said Milo, "the unit doesn't have bathroom facilities, either. You'd have to use the shared shower and toilet down the hall." He saw my face. "Most of the units don't have bathrooms. Only the supers' units do. This is warehouse living, remember? It's pretty bare-bones. But you can fix your unit up any way you like. Paint it, whatever. Brian, he built an honest-to-God loft in his. It's like he has a two-storey apartment. Has these heavy stage curtains running along rods he put in the ceiling. Uses them as movable room dividers. It's the darnedest thing. Girl downstairs is a dancer. She built a sprung wood floor in hers, so she can practise."

"Okay," I said doubtfully. This was the experience I'd wanted, but now it wasn't sounding so hot.

In my pocket, my cell phone buzzed. Probably Abby, calling for the umpteenth time today. I ignored it. Let her fret. "And how much is the rent?" I asked Milo.

He named a figure. I swallowed. It was decidedly more than I'd been contributing to the joint household fund that Abs and I split between us. "That's fine," I said, lying through my teeth. I'd have to see about picking up another shift at the restaurant. And about trying to subsist on the free food I got there when I was working. In a pinch, there was always Uncle.

Milo was still peering at the sheet. "What do you do at Burger Delite?"

"Dishwasher." I looked down at my feet. I'd been so proud

about holding down a claypicken job, but today, in the face of how inadequate my salary was going to be for just the basics, it felt as though I were confessing to some sort of character failing. I made myself meet Milo's eyes. "But they say they're going to move me up to waiting tables soon. I'll get tips then." Gods, that was even worse. Like I was begging him for shelter.

He pursed his lips, studied the sheet once more. "You've been living at your last place of residence since you were... what? Sixteen?"

"Yes, but—" All my twenty-four years on this Earth, actually, but I'd fudged that part of the form.

"And the owner has the same surname as you? Who is that, your mother? You still living at home?"

"No! Not exactly. Abby's my sister. We're co-owners."

He raised an eloquent eyebrow. "So why are you leaving your own home? If you don't mind me asking."

"She and I, well, we aren't getting along. I'd rather she didn't know where I was living." Damn. I hadn't wanted to get into this. I'd hoped he'd think that I'd been renting my previous place and just happened to have the same surname as the owner. Guess that was dumb of me.

"But it's your house, too? I don't get that. You walking away from your own property?"

"She can have it." His prying was starting to make me a little cranky. Was this how it would be, living whole-hog in the claypicken world?

"You don't owe her money or anything, do you? I don't want to take on an unreliable tenant."

I laughed, trying hard to sound like someone who would never, ever "forget" for two months in a row to pay into a household fund. "God, no. That's not why I'm leaving. She's just always up in my business. Nosy."

He frowned. "Can't have any drugs in here, you know."

Oh, no, he did not just say that. I growled, "I'm black, so I must be a dealer? That it?"

He laughed an easy, non-defensive laugh. It threw me. "Hell, no. I was one at your age, though. And when my first wife started to get too curious, I told her to stop being so nosy. She didn't like that one bit, I can tell you. We were divorced within a year. So the word 'nosy' kinda sets me off sometimes."

Nonplussed, I said, "Don't worry. Dope's not my thing. Bottle of Guinness with dinner is more my speed. And early to bed when I can. Those shifts at the restaurant are brutal."

He perked up even more. "You drink Guinness? That's the good stuff. Not like the dishwater the rest of the guys in here swill. You drink it cold?"

I shook my head. "No. You hide the flavour that way."

"Good girl."

The word "girl" made me feel bristly all over again, but I wanted this place. If he wanted to make patronizing small talk, I could play along a little. Milo looked me over, considering. "Mak... Makeda? Listen. Ordinarily, I wouldn't rent a place to someone..." He put the paper down on the table, pushed it away from himself. "I mean, no references, minimum-wage job. I notice you didn't put down any previous employment, either."

"I've had other jobs! I just—"

"Here's the deal." He sighed, set his shoulders as though he'd just come to a decision. "You seem like a nice girl. I'd like to make you an offer."

Now it was my turn to raise an eyebrow. "You would, would you?"

He smiled. "Oh no, my dear. Nothing like that. Nothing at all like that. I need a new assistant superintendent to help Brian out, fill in when he's not around. Sounds like you're pretty handy?

Know one end of a hammer from the other? It's easy work, doesn't need more than an hour or two a week, sometimes not even that."

"So, how would this arrangement go?" This could work out after all. If Milo let me have the unit in return for replacing the occasional washer, I could maybe drop down to one shift at Burger Delite instead of two, still be making enough to get by. Not take handouts from Abby and Uncle for every little thing. Make a real go at having a claypicken life, since I was never going to have the other kind.

"I'd reduce your rent by a couple hundred," Milo said.

My happy bubble fantasy popped, leaving a sting like liquid soap. "Two hundred? That's it?" That wasn't even a quarter of the rent he was asking for the unit. Which, it suddenly occurred to me, he hadn't shown me yet.

Milo nodded. "One-fifty, two hundred, something like that. You'd have your own bathroom."

Did the fool think I hadn't noticed how the "couple hundred" reduction in the rent was turning into one-fifty? "Can I see the unit?" I asked coldly. Might as well, since I was there. But no way was I falling for this guy's penny-pinching con job. There had to be plenty of apartments in this city, if you weren't too fussy.

He led me up the flight of stairs to the second floor. Iron railings, painted in peeling black enamel. The stairs were steel-reinforced slabs of concrete, worn down by years of foot traffic, each step canted at a slightly different angle from its neighbours. I liked that. I liked things that had been solidly made and that wore the evidence of hard use, of survival.

The second-floor hallway was cool and dark. The walls were the same colour as the outside of the building. There was a musty, old-building smell. Only to be expected. Not like I was going to be living in the hall, anyway, right? There were doors lining the hallway on one side, an open doorway halfway down on the other side, leading to what looked like some kind of common room. There was a battered couch in there, an old Formica table, a couple of rickety chairs. And sure enough, posters tacked to the walls: some band playing at the Vault last week, old cartoon film fest at the library this weekend. That room was painted a deep pinkish red. The paint on one wall wasn't just flaking, it was bubbling. Moisture beneath it. Milo noticed me looking at it. "Had a bit of a leak in there last week. Spring rains, you know? I'm having it fixed."

I'd heard about his kind. He was just your average slum land-lord. I kissed my teeth in disdain. Milo blinked at the sound, but clearly didn't know what it meant. Any one of my relatives would have, on either side of the Family. Hell, any black person pretty much the world over would have known it.

Milo unlocked one of the units on the other side of the hallway. "Just had it painted," he said proudly. "This is where the previous assistant superintendent lived."

He pushed the door open and went in ahead of me. "Oh," he said, "I guess Brian hasn't gotten around to painting it yet. Looks kinda cool though, right? Artsy."

A faint scent wafted out of the room. Spices? Was that nutmeg? And some kind of fruit? My mouth watered. I stepped inside. I asked, "Did the previous tenant like to burn incense? I can smell—"

"No incense burning allowed in the units. No burning of any-thing." He clearly wasn't the least bit interested in what the previous tenant used to do in here.

The space was big. The walls were a creamy white, reaching up and up to the high ceiling. A previous tenant had painted curling vines climbing up the corners. Probably the same someone who had painted the Styrofoam ceiling tiles in a sky-scape of blue and massing white clouds. "That colour," I said to Milo, delighted. I pointed at the ceiling. "It's haint blue."

He squinted up at the ceiling. "Is it? I scored a lot of tins of it in a closeout sale a while ago. Don't think Brian's used it all up yet."

I smiled. "No, it's okay. I kinda like it." More than that; I felt oddly at home. The blue of the ceiling was the same colour as the porch ceiling of our— of Abby's house. Dad had done that for me ages ago. Ghosts can't cross water without help. Plus they're stupid. Get the right shade of blue, paint your floor or ceiling with it— doesn't matter which, 'cause ghosts don't have a right way up—and they'll mistake it for the glint of light on water and be unable to pass. Paint your porch ceiling that colour, and your door and your window frames, and you have a haint-proof house.

There was more. The nubbly concrete floor had been coated with a semi-gloss St. Julian mango yellow, layered on so thick it was like enamel. The building had looked a bit creepy from the outside, but looks could be deceiving. Now that I'd seen this part of its insides, I loved the place. "It's cute," I said, trying for nonchalance. The window in the opposite wall was open a crack, letting in birdsong on a ribbon of cool, sweet air that leavened the unit's damp, musty smell. The street noises were a distant background rumble. With the vines, it was like a picnic in the park in here. My bed would fit nicely right over by the window, give me a bit of a view of the outside. Abby'd just bought a new microwave. I could take the old one off her hands when I went to pick up my chest of drawers. Hooks on the walls for any clothes that needed hanging, my workbench and chair. Maybe a card table and a couple more chairs once I could afford them. For when guests came over. I could have guests! That was the kind of thing that claypickens did, wasn't it? But the rent, ouch. Boldly, I asked, "You said three hundred off the rent?"

He frowned. "Two hundred."

Gotcha. I'd tricked him back up to the full discount he'd promised at first and then tried to welsh on. It was still more than I could afford, but I was enjoying playing with the bastard now. Lead him on, make him think I was going to take the place, then shake my head and walk out of there. "Two hundred. Could I get that in writing?"

"Sure. And there's a bar fridge around here somewhere you could have. I'd get Brian to put it in here for you."

That'd solve the problem of where to keep my meds, at least. If I were going to take the place. Which I wasn't.

"So. You like it? The bar fridge could go over there." He pointed to a wall with an electrical socket.

"I don't know about this…"

The hint of fruits stewed in honey and nutmeg intensified. Cinnamon, too? And maybe a bit of orange zest? It was like the scent was seeping from the walls. The Shiny building was flirting with me! Sometimes Shiny objects developed self-awareness, and something a bit like personalities. I smiled regretfully, shook my head. Milo looked at his watch. "Miss, I have to go. No rest for the wicked, and all that. Would you like the place or not? You're not going to find a deal this good anywhere else."

Couldn't I? I opened my mouth to tell him no.

"Like hell you're moving out. You know you're going to stay right here, where the living is easy."

Abby thought she knew me so well. I said, "I'll take it."

> *"Nay, take a seat with us,*
> *Honor and eat with us,"*
> *They answered grinning;*
> *"Our feast is but beginning."*

It felt weird to hand over a cheque for first and last months' rent. That was a lot of money for me. I hoped Milo wouldn't try to cash it today; my bank account was a few hundred short of the full amount. I'd have to figure something out about the balance.

It felt weirder to be heading back into the bright sunshine after the redolent darkness of Cheerful Rest. I hesitated in the doorway, midway between darkness and light, blinking like Orpheus exiting the land of the dead. My skin prickled. I looked back. No one behind me.

Then the second-floor fire door banged open and the black guy I'd seen before came clattering down the stairs with Yoplait the cat beside him. I waved. "Hey."

He had the most wonderful grin. The guy, not the cat. "Hey. Milo says you're my new assistant? Rockin'."

Yoplait slid past me, out into the world. I stepped back inside. The door sighed shut. "Looks like a neat place. You're Brian?"

He stuck his hand out. "Call me Brie. It's my stage name."

I giggled as I shook his hand. "You're Brie, and your cat's called Yoplait?"

He did a half-smile, shrugged one shoulder. "Yeah. It's a thing."

"A dairy thing," I deadpanned.

"Uh-huh."

"Funny. My si— I mean, I know someone with a cat named Butter." I didn't have to mention Abby just yet, did I? Keep her out of my life a little bit longer.

Brie asked, "Want a beer? Me and the band are taking a break for a few minutes."

I hesitated. I didn't know Brie well enough to take alcohol from him. How would a claypicken woman handle this? But shit, I could handle myself. He tried anything, I'd just sic my uncle on him. I nodded. "Sure."

I followed him back up the stairs to the second floor. Over his shoulder, he said, "Milo give you the gears about no pets, no cooking in your unit, blah, blah, blah?"

"Yeah. And no table saws."

Brie snickered. "He says that stuff so that if anything goes down, he can tell the cops he told you, but you broke the rules. I got an extra hot plate if you want one."

"Cool. Thanks. Your cat gonna be okay out on the street like that?"

"Yup. Where I found him. Swear I've seen that mangy old brute hitchhiking. So, whaddyou do?"

"Nothing. I'm not like my...oh, right. You mean for money, don't you?"

He nodded, looking a little confused.

"I work in a greasy spoon."

He glanced back at me. "And for kicks?"

He opened the fire door on the second-floor landing. I followed him through it. "Today? Moving out of my sister's place for the first time ever." My heart jumped. I was letting Abby have the place all to herself. I was really moving out. So what if I'd just outed myself as having a sister?

He chuckled a little. "Rockin'. Gotta break those chains sometime, right?"

"Oh, *hell* yeah."

His voice had the rich timbre of a singer's. I figured him for a tenor.

Now that the band wasn't drowning out the other sounds in the building, I could hear evidence of the other people who lived here: TV show theme music from behind one closed door, a rhythmic creaking of bedsprings from another. Brie grinned. "Hallam's got himself a new boyfriend. They've been going at it since Thursday evening, I swear."

All those lives, separated from each other by nothing but the walls between the units. And was that hot dogs someone was boiling? I wrinkled my nose up. Didn't living in each other's laps like this make them crazy sometimes? Last thing I wanted was to move from one claustrophobic situation to another.

A doorway a little farther down the dark hallway opened a

crack. I squinted. I could just make out a pair of eyes, peeping over the jamb.

"Oh, hey, Fleet," said Brie. "Come meet the new super."

Four fingers crept over the doorjamb, but the person still didn't leave their unit. A soft, sexless voice said to Brie, "But you're the super."

"I know that, babe. Makeda's going to be my backup."

"Like Gus is?"

Brie gave a little sigh. "Gus quit the band, Fleet. Remember he moved to Berlin? And Makeda's not in the band." At his words, my heart thumped, dejectedly, once. "She's going to be my assistant superintendent, though. Like Gus was. Got it?"

After a couple of seconds, Fleet replied, "Gus...moved."

"Exactly. So now we have Makeda. She's going to be your neighbour! Come out and meet her, okay?" He strode over to Fleet's doorway and reached a hand out. "Come on, hon. She's really nice. And she's pretty." He glanced at me, ducked his head away shyly. Sweet. I checked out the number on the partially open door. Two-thirteen. Where the crazy girl lived.

Fleet opened the door a little more and shuffled out into the hallway.

Wow. Why in the world had Milo called her a girl? She had to be in her fifties. She was pale and shrunken. Her head looked too big for her body. Her hair was a little thin on her head, some of it brown, some of it white. It had probably been curly when she looked after it. Right now, though, it frizzed out around her head like thistle fuzz. Her face was broad, her nose narrow. Her cheekbones stood out like razor blades. Her eyes were rimmed with pink. She was wearing low-slung jeans so big for her that she kept having to hitch them back up. Her shirt was a long-sleeved flannel pyjama top with mushrooms and brightly coloured toadstools on it. It was half-tucked into the waistband of her jeans. She peered at me, her eyes narrowed.

I stuck my hand out. "Hey there, Miz...Fleet, is it? Pleased to meet you."

She looked at my hand. There was no expression on her face; none. She put her hands behind her body, leaving mine hanging. Flushing, I lowered my own hand to my side. My smile, un–responded to, had frozen in place.

"I'm just Fleet," she told me. Her voice was so quiet I had to strain to hear it.

A head stuck out of another door farther along the corridor, right across from my new place. Short pink white-girl braids going every which way. A little impatiently, she beckoned Brie. "Dude, you coming, or what?" she called. She was signing as she spoke. Difficult to see with her hands moving that quickly, but it looked as though every fingernail was painted a different colour, all of them bright. "There's almost no beer left," she said. "Bring your friend."

"Be right there," Brie replied, also signing as he spoke aloud. Hot damn. I was already impressed, and I hadn't even heard the band yet, except for some of the racket from their practice session. Brie turned back to Fleet. "We gotta go. Catch you later, okay?"

Fleet stared at Brie. Swallowed. "Are you playing tonight?" she whispered.

"Yeah, hon. Every Saturday night, you know that."

She nodded. "Can I play with you guys this time?"

"Not tonight. But come and see us, okay?" He grabbed my hand and drew me over in the direction of the girl with the braids. He said, sotto voce, "She calls herself Fleet 'cause she used to be a flute player, back in the day. BC, you know?"

"British Columbia?"

He looked sad. "No, Before Crack." His hand was warm, almost hot, and dry. It covered my whole hand so entirely that one of his fingers was curling almost the whole way around my wrist. I looked over my shoulder, but Fleet had already closed her door.

The girl who'd called us over nodded at me. It made her braids bob. "Maturity," she said, while fingerspelling it. She giggled. For a split second I thought she was teasing me for being immature. Or Fleet for being old. Then I understood that it was her name. What was it with the single-barrelled names in here?

I nodded back. "Makeda."

She stepped out to hold the door open for us. "There's some pizza left," she told us, and I remembered that I hadn't eaten breakfast this morning. Maturity was plump and pink and beaming. She wore a crisp white gauze tutu over a pink-and-white crinoline, over striped pink-and-black tights tucked into black Victorian-style heeled boots. She was popping out of the tops of the two old nylon slips she was wearing, one black and one burgundy. She'd slit them both up the sides, presumably so she could get the froth of tutu and crinoline on under them. She looked like the topper on an angel food cake.

Brie held the door open so that Maturity and I could go in first. Gentlemanly and well-spoken; nice combo. I had to brush close to him in order to get through. He smelled of lemons and coffee.

As I walked in, the first impression I got was of a black yawning mouth of space. It dwarfed the four people sitting on the floor in front of the stage, eating pizza out of the box and sharing a two-four of Blue. A stage took up about half of the black-painted room. The rest was bare, black floor. There was room enough for an audience to stand, maybe do a little dancing. There was a stack of iron folding chairs leaning against the stage. Brie opened his arms to indicate the whole space. "This is where we practise," he said. "And these guys are"—he silently counted them off—"most of the band." The three guys and the chick stopped scarfing down pizza long enough to nod in my direction. Maturity curtseyed.

The next few minutes were a flurry of cold pizza, warm beer, and meeting the members of Soul Chain that were present. Maturity, go figure, did sign language interpreting. The other woman, Raini, was dark brown with long, straight black hair. She wore faded jeans, a plain black T-shirt, a rainbow-coloured metal bracelet on each wrist. She played drums. Jeff, a pudgy, light-skinned brother with freckles and cornrowed red hair, guitar. Solaris looked to be about fifteen, but was probably older. White. Thin to the point of transparency, but with a strong handshake. Bristle of blond hair. Piercings everywhere, seemed to be wearing a brace on one leg, under the jeans. Mid-range, androgynous voice. I first thought that Solaris was a guy. Then a girl. Maybe. Then I gave up trying to figure out which. It would become obvious at some point, or not. Andy, an older guy with black earplugs and a sleeve of tats on both arms, played button box. Brie, of all things, tambourine. Brie sang lead, the rest of them backup vocals (Maturity signed as she sang), though they all teasingly accused Andy of only mouthing the words. Hallam (he of the thumping bed) and Cleveland would show up later. They were dancers. As people introduced themselves, I wolfed down a slice of cold pepperoni pizza and knocked back a beer that Brie brought me. Turned out that most of them lived in this building. Like family. Yikes. Warily, I asked, "You guys eat together like this for every meal?"

There was an astonished silence, then they all fell out laughing. "As if!" said Jeff.

Solaris gave Maturity a gentle slap on the shoulder. "If I had to listen to this one complain about work every time I sat down to eat, I'd probably go postal."

Raini said, "Got lives. Know how to use them."

Was she making fun of me? I studied her face. Oh, of course not. She didn't know me at all. I grinned like a fool, contemplating beginning a life in which my pariah status didn't figure in the least.

"And you...live in here?" I asked Brie, looking around the

bare, open space for where he might have a bed, someplace to stash his clothes, stuff like that.

He laughed. "No, but sometimes it feels like it."

Jeff shook his head. "Yeah. Slave driver there only makes us practise most weekends. But I swear he's in here 24/7, trying out new songs—"

"—testing the lights—" Brie explained.

Jeff continued, "—wanking, God knows what else."

Raini and Solaris grinned. Maturity and Andy had their heads together over the button box. I heard Maturity say, "So, you come in on the third note?"

Brie gave a big, theatrical sigh. "These guys, nothing but abuse I get from them. But yeah, I have two units side by side, made them into one. My room's over there." He gestured vaguely at the light-swallowing corner of the space. "I'm afraid you're going to find it loud in here on Saturday nights, especially with you living across from me and all. And you get to help me clean up the mess on Sunday mornings. Plus side is, I give you free beer!" He beamed at me. Nice smile he had. It had slowly dawned on me that it was his band. He wasn't just a member of it. I suspected I was going to like living here.

"Hey, wanna see the rest of my kingly domain?"

I hesitated. Maturity looked up from her confab with Andy. "It's all right," she said. "Brie's cool."

"Jesus, of course I'm cool! Why would you even talk like that?"

"Oh, get the knot out of your panties." She smiled to take the sting out of it. "Girls gotta watch out for each other, jeez. Try thanking me for letting Makeda know that you're not a skeez." She turned to me. "So he's okay, but watch out for that bloody ankle-biter of a cat. It'll try to slash you if you get too close to it, or to Brie."

Brie smiled ruefully. "Yeah, she would know. I'm still apologizing to her for that."

She waved the concern away. "Not a big deal."

I said, "I would like the grand tour."

"Sweet." Brie took me over to a door hidden in the shadows. He pulled a key fob out of his jeans pocket and used one of the many keys on it to unlock the door.

"Am I going to get a set of keys like that?"

"Sure, I'll cut you a set."

Me, in charge of a building. I could just imagine the astonishment on Abby's face when I told her.

The door opened. Brie went in ahead of me. From just inside the doorway, he said, "Come on in. And leave the door open, okay?" Smart of him. No matter what Maturity had said, I still didn't know this guy.

I stepped through the threshold into the unit. I blinked as my eyes adjusted to the dimness of the room. Naked lightbulb, high up in the ceiling. Tiny LED bulbs in the sconce lights lining the walls of the entranceway. The sconces themselves were black mesh in the shape of small pouched triangles. "Those seem kinda Martha Stewart for you," I said, pointing at one of them.

"So I have a gentle side. I made those things out of screen door mesh, though, all manly-like." He made fake bodybuilder muscles.

His room was a big, open space, like mine. Old couch against one wall, with some kind of fancy embroidered cloth thrown over it. Slab of a wooden table in the middle of the room. It was oval, long enough for two people to lie on it head to head. Mismatched chairs all around it; everything from a pilfered park bench to woven plastic lawn chairs. Through the legs of the chairs I could see that the table legs were scrolled iron. The loft that Milo had described to me was built into the far side of the unit, complete with wooden stairs slanting up towards it. Underneath the loft was a computer, sitting on a warped piece of particleboard balanced on two sawhorses. The upper floor of the loft held an honest-to-God four-poster bed, complete with a translucent white canopy. "You have got to be kidding me," I said, pointing to it.

He smiled. "I like to be comfortable."

"Decadent, more like it. How come you can have two adjoining units? You make enough as a musician?"

"Hell, no. We have a lot of regulars that come to our shows and buy a lot of cheap beer, so Milo cut me a deal."

"You, too, huh? What is he, some kind of philanthropist?"

Brie smirked. "Hardly. He gets the bar tab. Unofficially, that is. This place doesn't have a liquour license."

The cat stuck its head over the side of the loft and gave me a questioning yowl. Brie said, "Hey, Yoplait."

"How'd he get back inside?" I headed up the steps towards the cat, remembered my manners, stopped halfway up. "May I?"

"Sure, I'll wait down here." He pulled out one of the chairs and plopped himself down onto it. "Careful, though. Maturity wasn't kidding. He bites."

Yoplait didn't let me get too close. He scowled at me, leapt off the bed, and disappeared below it.

"He's pretty wild," said Brie. "I'm guessing he has lots of reasons not to trust human beings."

"That's sad." I came back down the steps, sat on the lowest one.

Brie replied, "Funny thing about that old cat."

"What?"

"He's a dead ringer for a cat I found as a boy. Maybe that's why I'm so taken with him. Lord knows it's not his winning ways. The one I found when I was a kid, I think a car must have hit it, or something. It was half-dead, lying on the side of the road. Back legs and jaw broken."

I winced.

"Which didn't stop it from trying to sink its teeth into me when I went to pick it up. It was so scared."

"What happened to it?"

"It was bleeding, and its legs were hanging all floppy." The memory was making him sound like the kid he used to be. "After the first try, I couldn't bear to touch it. Made my stomach squirmy. But I couldn't stand to leave him there, either. Street was full of people, too. When I got older, I wondered whether the poor thing might have gotten helped quicker if there hadn't been a fourteen-year-old black boy with his hair in cornrows on his knees crying beside him."

"Me, I would have called my dad. He has a way with living things."

His face set into a hard look. "I didn't have a dad to call. I had a foster home that, let's just say, wasn't working out too well."

"So what happened?"

"White lady came by who wasn't afraid of me or of an injured cat. She sat right down at the curb beside me. Called Animal Rescue and then waited with us both until they came." He smiled a little. "She was a little confused at first when she found out it wasn't my cat, but she dealt."

"Did you ever see the cat again?"

Yoplait had stuck his head over the edge of the top step and was staring at me wide-eyed with what looked like combined curiosity and alarm.

He shook his head. "The lady who'd helped us called me the next day to say that his injuries had been too extensive. He died."

"That's awful."

"That afternoon, I was walking by the place where I'd found him, and there was a torn-up cat collar lying there. No ID on it, but it showed somebody must have loved him at some point, right?"

"I guess."

"I kept that collar for a while. Wore it on my wrist, doubled. But I lost track of it in the many moves from foster home to foster home. Then Yoplait here just wandered in off the street one day. Got into the kitchen, was helping himself to our bacon when I caught him. He was nothing but fur and bones. I let him finish the bacon, and he just stayed. Finally let me get close enough to him to touch him. Nowadays I have to watch where I put my feet when I roll out of bed in the mornings. Yoplait has a way of leaving four or five still-bleeding mouse torsos right where I'll step."

I grimaced. "Gross."

"I know. Scared me shitless the first time it happened. Maybe it's his way of paying rent, I dunno. He arranges them neatly in a row for me. Just their front halves. Their heads and their little front legs. I guess the back halves are meatier. I think he eats those. At least, I've never found any hairy mouse butts hanging around."

"My dad used to bring live mice into the house. I mean, they would come looking for him." I realized my slip-up when I saw Brie's startled face. I tried to think up a reasonable explanation.

"Brie!" yelled a voice from outside. "We're starting up again!"

Brie called out, "Okay, just a second!" He stood up.

Whew. Saved by the bellow. I was going to have to keep a close watch on what I said.

Brie said, "Right; here's what you need to know about this building." He ticked off on his fingers. "If it's raining on the outside, it'll be raining on the inside, so get yourself a bunch of tarps and use them."

"Oh, shit. Now I find out."

"Don't leave your soap and shampoo in the bathroom, unless you really want to share. Ditto with your food in the kitchen."

"Got my own bathroom in my unit."

"Oh, yeah. I forgot. Anyway, garbage and recyclables go out onto the curb every other Thursday morning before seven a.m. Organic waste goes out every Wednesday morning. The big bins for all that stuff are downstairs. Wheeling them out to the curb every week is my job and yours. Got it?"

"Got it."

"Now, you wanna watch us practise?"

Why not? I wasn't working that night. "Okay."

"Great. If you're gonna stay for the show, you can leave your jacket and purse in here. Safer that way."

"Thanks."

As we were walking out into the performance space, I checked my phone: six messages, all from Abby. I turned the phone off and stuck it back into my pocket.

Soul Chain started practising again, and that's where it stopped being romantic. They were struggling. Jeff didn't seem to know half the set tunes. Brie kept forgetting the words to the songs and jumping in either too early or too late. And when he did, his voice wasn't great. Guess I had been spoiled by Abby's perfect pitch. Man, this was going to be one clunker of a show. I got glimpses of raw talent from them, but with no finesse behind it.

But let's be honest; they all sounded better than I did. Abby and I were twelve the first time I saw her perform live. After that, I didn't want to even sing in the shower ever again. Maybe Soul Chain would get it together in the adrenaline high of playing live. So I stayed right through the practice, piqued by the twinkle in Brie's beautiful brown eyes, and the brief seconds where they all came together and sparkled before crashing again in a tangle of notes. The walls of the building exuded ghosts of all the smells it had absorbed over the centuries. Ashes, stale beer, pot, a brief hint of perfume; tantalizing hints of the stories that had played out inside it, and promises of the ones that were yet to come.

◆ ◆ ◆

Like two pigeons in one nest
Folded in each other's wings,
They lay down, in their curtained bed:
Like two blossoms on one stem.

We'd had to be cut free of our mother's womb. She'd never have been able to push the two-headed sport that was me and Abby out the usual way. Mom was still human at the time. My dad's family hadn't yet exiled her to the waters. After the C-section, just for a few days, she was kind of sidelined while she recovered. That gave Dad's family the opening they needed to move in and take over. 'Cause from their perspective, things were a mess. Abby and I were fused, you see. Conjoined twins. Abby's head, torso and left arm protruded from my chest. We shared a liver and three and three-quarters legs between us. We had two stomachs, two hearts and four lungs, and enough colon for us each to have a viable section, come to that. Abby and I could have lived as we were, conjoined. Between us, we had what we needed. But here's the real kicker; Abby had the magic, I didn't. Far as the Family was concerned, Abby was one of them, though cursed, as I was, with the tragic flaw of mortality. Abby and me, my mom brought us that gift.

You might say that my dad married outside the family. To hear some of them tell it, outside the species. Most of his family would barely give Mom the time of day while she was still around, despite the fact that she and her kin had done steward service to them for centuries. Or rather, because of it. Dad's family could have stood it if she were just some dalliance of Dad's, a bit of booty call. Even love might have been okay, if they'd kept it to a dull roar. Wouldn't have been the first time that a celestial had knocked boots with the help. But no, Dad and the help had to go and breed.

With Mom unable to interfere for the time being, Dad's family decided that obviously, the human doctors of the hospital where we were born had to surgically separate Abby and me. They put pressure on my dad till he agreed to it. They're not really venal, that lot, just too big for their britches. They've been emissaries of the Big Boss for so long that they forget they aren't gods themselves, just glorified overseers. But overseers with serious power. Mom's kin didn't say boo. They knew damned well that they didn't have the cash to buy that much trouble.

The second we were separated, Abby began to die. There was something vital she needed that my body'd been supplying. No one could tell exactly what, but we were losing her.

There's a guardian that attends births and deaths. He keeps his eye on the young and on the old; the former having so recently left the other world for this one, and the latter soon to depart that way again. That guardian, you might say that he's a border guard. It's his job to send the living on their way, and the dead on theirs. If it's not your time, you're not going anywhere. He was there, ready to do his job, when Abby and I were born, the semi-celestial child and her human donkey of a sister. Now it was time for him to escort her back across the barrier between the quick and the dead. He lingered over our cribs in Intensive Care for an instant. He smiled at us both, chucked us under our tiny chins. He thought we were kinda cute. Then he kissed us each on the forehead and gently picked Abby up, cradled her in his arms. My dad, grieving, watched him. The guardian gave him a rueful look. Have I mentioned that the guardian is our uncle? Dad's brother? He took Abby, leaving my dad to weep at my bedside.

The guardian should have carried Abby to the crossroads right away. Instead, he took her to my mom's room. He'd taken a shine to Mom, Uncle had. A real shine. The kind that sets brother against brother, starts family feuds.

Mom was still dopey from the anaesthetic, but Uncle took care of that. Plain ol' unconsciousness was no challenge for the being who shuttled humans from life to death like beads on an abacus. Even in her half-sleep she'd been begging to see her babies, and now she was fully awake. This was her first time seeing Abby, but when she clapped eyes on my uncle carrying a gasping bundle whose little mouth pursed like my dad's, she figured out pretty quickly that the baby was one of hers.

The guardian's impartial. He has to be. Normally he wouldn't be put in the position of herding family across the borders between life and death, since the rest of that lot don't die. Not permanently, anyway.

Mom begged him for Abby's life.

He replied, "There isn't enough of her to survive on this side of the gate."

Mom was having none of it. She began to make promises. But what does a human have to offer a demigod? She tried to swear her lifelong obedience. Uncle shook his head. In a way, he already had that, from every mortal on this plane and the next. But he didn't leave with Abby. Mom's arms ached to hold her baby. She promised sex, the best he'd had, and he's had some good stuff. He's not just Lord of the Grave, my uncle. All that borning and dying business has given him a taste for some of the sweetest gifts of the flesh. My mom was fine, they tell me. All blackberry sweet juice. And she knew what to do with what she'd got. How d'you think she managed to catch the eye of not just one celestial, but two?

Thing is, Uncle, for all his lechery, is pretty professional about his job. He shook his head, turned towards the door. But Mom spied the tear twinkling in his eye, and she knew she'd underestimated him. Sure, he liked doing the nasty plenty well, but— "Save her," Mom said wildly. "And I'll love you."

Uncle stopped, one hand on the door's crash bar, the other supporting Abby's one-and-three-quarters-legged little rump. He knows lies, Uncle does. There's a propaganda machine that makes him out to be the prince of them, but that's some bullshit. Those are the same people that won't let their kids borrow fiction from the libraries. Stories aren't lies, people. Some of them are truer than any autobiography. But Uncle does know how lies taste; refined sugar-sweet, not molasses-sweet like truth, with its sulphurous backbite. Mom was telling the truth; the room was treacly with it. If he saved her daughter, she would love him. She would love Death itself, fiercely and hotly. What parent wouldn't, under the circumstances?

Uncle looked down at the child he was holding, at her piecemeal body and oddly canted face. Her jaundiced skin going blue. She had my mom's eyes.

We both do. Uncle turned. Mom reached her hand out, took his in it, her eyes brimming with hope, with love enough to fight for her child, and more.

Uncle whispered, "I can't do it. She needs organs, tissues that I can't give her. I'm a ferryman. I can't make her live."

"Allyou need me for that," said my dad. He walked into Mom's room. Uncle tried to snatch his hand away from Mom's, but she held on and looked Dad full in the face. A mother's love is fierce with pride, and Mom was never one for regrets.

Dad read the signs of what had gone on between them, like spoor in the room. "You want this?" he asked Mom.

"Yes."

"Brother mine," said Dad, "give me my child." His two eyes made four with Uncle's. In that moment, Dad's eyes in his bark-brown face were green, the bright green of new spring leaves. Gently, Uncle handed Abby over. Gently, Dad took her. His first time holding his baby. That was the moment that Uncle violated the border between this side and the next, for once he had taken a soul to himself, he wasn't ever supposed to hand it over until he had delivered it to its destination.

If Uncle is a ferryman between the worlds, Dad is a gardener. His talents are growing, grafting, and pruning. "Lewwe go then, nuh?" said Dad to his brother.

"What?" said Mom. "Where're you taking her?"

Dad replied, his voice full of loss, "Can't fix her up here. We have to go to the next side. You stay and see to Makeda." He tried on a smile. "We going to bring her sister back to you before you could say Jack Mandora."

Uncle embraced Dad. Their circled arms protected Abby. Mom had to look away from the brothers then. Their aspects were already changing, preparing to cross over to the other side. Mortals cannot look upon that celestial shift for long. It's like looking directly into the sun. Between the glory that was the brothers, dying Abby was a fleeting scrap of dull flesh. Then the three were gone. Mom clambered back into her bed, closed her eyes, and prayed for both

*her children. No point imploring the Big Boss. He has more important things
to look after. As so many claypickens do, Mom prayed to the celestials more
directly involved in the affairs of this plane; in this case, to her lover and to
his brother.*

◆ ◆ ◆

I was right; when fuelled by audience energy, Soul Chain was
the fucking bomb. They had a full house that night. They'd been
playing for maybe a couple hours. Brie stepped up to the mike,
grabbed it and screamed into it, fast and angry:

"Suck all the juice this life will give!"

The crowd roared a refrain back at Brie. I couldn't make the
words out. Maturity's signing animated her whole body, a silent
explosion of tough. She punched and clutched at the air, snarled
at life, kneed and kneaded it, sucking its juices. Jeff's axe kicked
in again with a rubber-burning road rage of riffing. The dance
floor exploded for the umpteenth time into people bouncing and
body-slamming to the music. Cleveland and Hallam were doing
some crazy mix of go-go dancing, tutting, and turf. They were
all over the stage and it was all, as far as I could tell, improvised.
Brie played call-and-response with us. I finally heard the words of
the response when a brush-cut white guy not much taller than me
spat it out right into my ear:

"The pretty ones are too good to live!"

It was all incredible. The mass of people, pulsing simultaneously
with one heart and with many. The competing whiffs of sweat,
cologne, weed, beer. The body heat, the sheer aural assault of the
music. I'd pushed my way to the centre of the room, where I wasn't
so much dancing as being shoved back and forth by the tide of
bodies as the crowd contracted rhythmically around me. My feet
ached, I needed to pee, and there was sweat running down the

crack of my ass. I didn't give a fuck. Brie was pushing his voice to the limit, screaming and roaring at us, playing chicken with that knife edge that could do permanent damage to his vocal cords. Abby would have been wincing if she had been there. Which she wasn't. I pumped my fist in the air and shouted triumphantly along with everyone else, "*The pretty ones are too good to live!*" The stage lights picked up verdant highlights on Brie's face and hands.

I worked my way over to the side to give my empty beer bottle back. I caught a glimpse of frizzy brown hair flecked with white; Fleet, swaying drunkenly through the crowd, clapping sloppily in time to the music and slurring the words in a spitty howl. Her face had that damp, bleached-out look that pale people can get when they've been running too hard and too long. It could have felt weird, seeing someone her age body-slamming in a mosh pit full of twentysomethings, but she wasn't the only middle-aged person here. Asian guy over there, wizened as a walnut, belt pulling in a good eight inches of slack on the waistband of his jeans. Stylin' jeans, too, for an old man. And cool haircut. Bobbing along like everyone else. As I watched, he slowed down, panting. He wobbled his way over to the side, where he crouched with his hands on his knees, sucking in air. Man, what if he flatlined right here? I chuckled to myself. At least it'd mean I'd get to say hi to Uncle. Bet he'd be surprised to see me in this place. Even Milo my new landlord was here, rocking a screaming Hawaiian shirt, jammers, and rubber flip-flops, staggering around the periphery of the crowd and occasionally bopping along for a few seconds. Man was an embarrassment to himself, fashion-wise. I bounded back into the fray, fought my way front and centre to give Brie and the rest of the band a thumbs-up. Brie looked down and saw me. He came forward, leaned down, and grabbed me by the wrist. He was strong. I shook my head, laughing, but I didn't fight too hard as he pulled me up onto the stage. But then he put the mike in front of my mouth. I batted it away. He laughed, put the mike back in its stand. "Okay, then," he shouted, his mouth close to my ear. His lips buzzed pleasantly against my skin. He was still holding my hand. He took me to the front of the stage again. "Jump with me!" he said.

I threw myself into the air right away. "Hey!" he yelled, surprised. I caught a glimpse of him leaping to join me. Then I landed in the arms of a bellowing, happy crowd. I'd always wanted to do a stage dive. I thought it'd be like flopping onto a bed of springy green boughs. Not so much. More grabby, ouchy, and confusing. Hands squeezed my arms and ankles too hard, pulled me in too many directions at once. Someone's searching fingers slid between my be-jeaned thighs. "Hey!" I yelled, inaudible under the music. The hand withdrew, grabbed my thigh instead and helped to body-surf me along the top of the crowd. Hands took my shoulders and supported my head. A voice murmured a friendly, "Here you go, love" as I was passed on. Hands patted my bottom. I tried to swat them away, but my arms weren't my own. They had become handles for people to use to propel me along. Fingers tweaked a nipple. I probably shouldn't have liked that as much as I did. Briefly, my knee twisted painfully. I pulled my leg out of the hold. It hung for a second at an uncomfortable angle until more hands lifted it level with my body. I took a light punch to the kidneys. Felt like I'd connected with someone's bobbing head. I thought I heard the person yell, "Sorry!" but I was already many body-lengths away. A stranger's sweat flew into my eyes. I blinked the salt sting away, laughed, and gave myself up to it all.

Brie was being wafted along nearby. Fizzy bubbles of excitement danced in my veins. I giggled. Brie grinned back at me. I yelled, "What a freaking high!"

He yelled back, "Fucking right! See why I love this stuff?"

The rest of the band kept kicking, driving the energy higher, faster, more frenzied. A guy the size of a bear hollered happily at me, grabbed me by the waist, and lifted me over his head, even higher than the reaching arms of the crowd. I hallooed with glee at the roller-coaster feeling of being swooped aloft. I bellowed, "We're flying!"

Brie gave a triumphant howl as he was spun through the green aura of the stage lights. "You're amazing!" he yelled at me. "You just jumped right in!"

I felt amazing. I threw my head back and let the caterpillar hands of the people below me propel me where they would. The blood in my veins carbonated with a wild, diving joy. I yelled, "Higher! Take me higher!"

And then there was nothing.

2

◆◆◆

THE BABY WOULDN'T STOP CRYING. Nothing Suzy tried was working. Winston's diaper was dry, he was fed, he didn't have gas, there was nothing poking into him, he wasn't teething, he didn't seem to be sick, and he certainly had all Suzy's attention at the moment. But still he kept up a disconsolate sob, his little hands curled into angry, helpless fists.

Naima stuck her head around the corner. She'd been happily playing some kind of six-year-old game in the living room. "Mommy, the crows are cawing," she said.

"That's wonderful, darling." Suzy rocked the baby. The baby cried. "Mommy's kind of busy right now."

"But what's wrong, Mommy? The crows are cawing, and Wheedle's crying."

"Call him Winston, sweetie. It's his real name. You wouldn't like it if we made fun of your name, would you?"

And Wheedle cried.

"The crows are unhappy like Wheed— like Winston's unhappy," Naima responded. She stood and twiddled one of her plaits for a bit. When Suzy didn't reply, she wandered back to the living room. Not a minute later, there was a huge crack, then a slushy crashing sound from outside. Suzy rushed out. On her way, she checked to make sure that Naima was still safely in the living room. She was.

The crows had gone silent now. Suzy realized she should have listened to Naima. Cawing crows; around here, that meant something bad was coming. When the crows *stopped* cawing, now; that meant something worse. It meant the bad thing had just happened and the crows had hightailed it out of there.

Suzy couldn't quite get out the door. The way was blocked by branches. The big old tree in the yard had cracked near its base and fallen over onto the house.

Which meant that something had gotten loose from the cage of the tree's roots. And Suzy could guess what or who it was. When you were a steward to the celestials, you saw a lot of family secrets.

"Oh, dear," Suzy said to the baby, "this isn't good."

Winston abruptly stopped whimpering. Instead, he stared, mesmerized, as a tendril of kudzu whipped around one of the branches closest to both of them, lengthening as it went. Suzy's scalp crawled, fright winning out over flight. With the speed of a striking serpent, the kudzu reached for Suzy's wrist. Suzy shouted. She took a step backwards and slammed the sliding door shut. Her heart leapt in her throat like a live frog, desperate to escape.

The kudzu vine pressed itself against the glass, its frustrated leaves spread flat and handlike against it. Suzy managed to croak out, "Papa B.? That you?"

A rope of kudzu, nearly as big around as Suzy's wrist, thumped against the glass. The door rattled in its track.

Suzy fought herself back from the brink of panic. She was a mama. She had these little ones to keep safe. She knew who could do for that kudzu for her. "Naima," she shouted, "get over here!"

Naima whined something back about wanting to stay and have

tea with her dolls. Tiny curls of smoke began rising up from the outer glass of the door where the kudzu was touching it.

"Girl, don't give me your lip right now; get over here, I said!"

Wheedle—Winston—peacefully sucked his thumb and watched the rampaging kudzu. He pointed at it, looked up at Suzy's face to see whether she had noticed the fascinating new thing, too.

"Yeah, baby, I see it. Don't worry, I won't let it hurt you." Winston wasn't the one who was worried.

Naima came pouting around the corner. The clip had come off the end of one of her pigtails. The braid had begun to unravel, her springy hair blowing out into a puffball at the braid's tip. Her pink Dora the Explorer T-shirt had a smear on its chest that clearly showed the imprint of Naima's hand where she'd wiped it clean of heavens knew what; Little Bit was always getting her curious fingers into one thing or another. Suzy'd pay mind to that after they got this bigger mess cleaned up. Naima was so small! Suzy's heart ached for her eldest. She hefted Winston closer to her body and said to Naima, "Sweetie, you gotta call Mister Cross. Now."

"But Mama—"

"Hush. *Now*, I said. And I'll let you have a cookie after."

Naima brightened up. "If I call him real real quick, can I have two?"

A giant kudzu tentacle was curling up the glass. What if it got in the upstairs window? "Baby girl, if you can get him here lickety-split, I'll give you one for each finger on your one hand."

"Okay," replied Naima. "Fetch me a pillow please, Mama. And the bones."

She plopped down right there on the floor, suddenly all business. She was an uncanny child; some part of her six-year-old self understood that her job as living telephone was serious. She tucked her feet under her and rested an upturned palm on each knee, ready to receive the bones. Suzy scurried to fetch them from the carved, lidded calabash on the side table in the living room. There was another thump from the direction of the sliding glass door. Suzy yelled, "Old guy or not, don't you break that door! Do you want broken glass to hurt these children?"

The kudzu left off its raging. Maybe there was enough of Daddy Wood left in there to remember to step careful around growing things when it wasn't their time yet. Please, let it not be anyone's time in this house today. Her cell phone was on the table next to the calabash. She ached to call Roger, to hear his voice, but other humans couldn't help her and her children in this moment.

One-handed because of the baby, Suzy took the lid off the carved calabash and put it down on the side table. She fumbled around inside the calabash until she felt the smooth, warm bones. She snatched them up quick. Small aerial roots were growing, white and twisty as maggots, from the kudzu limb. They were tugging at the tiny space between the sliding door and its jamb. As Suzy pulled her hand out of the calabash, Winston playfully yanked on her hair. She jostled the calabash. It tilted, rolled. With an armful of Winston, she wasn't able to move quickly enough to stop the calabash from teetering, then falling over the edge of the table. She gave a little cry. The calabash hit the ground and shattered. The sound made Wheedle jump and start to cry. For a second, Suzy just stared at the mess of calabash shards on the floor. She wanted to cry, too.

"Mama, hurry!" called Naima.

There was a gleam of white in among the beige and brown pieces of broken calabash. Suzy opened her hand that was holding the bones and did a quick eye count. Ah. Mister Cross had had Winston do her a favour by making her break the calabash, because in her haste, she'd gotten the two hand-carved bone dice, but not the all-important third bone. Nearly sobbing, she muttered at Mister Cross, "If you know you're wanted, why don't you just show, then?" Seemed like everything had to be a production around the old guys. The kudzu had taken to thumping over and over on the glass. No time to soothe Wheedle; Suzy bent and picked the thin, bleached bone from a black cat out from among the calabash pieces. She dashed over and put the two dice in Naima's right hand and the cat bone in her left. Naima had already closed her eyes and begun the breathing that Suzy'd taught her: slow and careful, in through the nose, letting the breath fill and expand her tummy, then out through the mouth. Dandling a sobbing Wheedle, Suzy asked, "You doing your picturing?"

Naima opened her eyes long enough to roll them at her mother. "'Course." She closed her eyes again. Suzy'd taught Naima to visualize the twin crossings her body made in that position: the lowercase-t shape traced by her upper body and two arms, the x shape of her crossed legs. Two roads, crossing each other, twice for good measure.

Crap; a pillow! Suzy's boomerang-shaped nursing cushion was over on the couch, where she'd last fed Winston. She snatched it up and went back to Naima. She bent carefully with the baby in her arms. He chortled; he loved being upside-downed. Suzy fit the cushion around Naima's body. Just in time, too. Naima's head snapped back and her eyes rolled up. She began to shake and foam at the mouth. Winston shook his head from side to side and tried to imitate the garbled sounds that Naima was making. Suzy hated this part. Her Little Bit, her baby girl! She bent to cradle Naima's head as best she could, the way it was bouncing around like that. Her eyes on Naima, Suzy yelled to the kudzu, "Your brother's coming! You just talk to him, instead of damaging any more of our property!"

Naima stopped convulsing. She sat up and wiped the foam from her mouth with the back of her hand. Her eyes were still showing only their whites. She said, "You rang?" in her best mock-deep Lurch voice. Then she giggled.

The racket outside had quieted. Wheedle made a surprised noise. Suzy looked to where he was pointing, at the door.

The kudzu was clean gone, as though it had never been.

An actual silk-cotton tree wouldn't have been able to survive the Toronto climate. When Suzy's neighbours looked at the huge tree in her yard, they saw an ash tree, or sometimes a graceful spruce with needles that gleamed golden from certain angles. The tree was both those things as well as a silk-cotton tree. From what the neighbours told her, Suzy had deduced that its ash tree presence (she'd heard one of the old guys call it Yggdrasil), dutifully shed its leaves in fall and sprouted tiny buds in early spring. Kiidk'yaas, its golden spruce form, was resplendent in its coat of gleaming needles and produced pine cones for those who saw it as a spruce. For Suzy and her family, the tree was covered crown to base in small thorns, shed its leaves in the dry season and then sprang big, scarlet flowers that gave way to fluff that blew everywhere. The kudzu that used to cover it had never seemed to spread. If it had, old Daddy B. would have lost his shit. He was fussy about letting invading species loose in vulnerable ecosystems. Now, if you were the type to see the tree as an ash or a spruce, you didn't get fluff or kudzu. Mister Cross jokingly called his tree the Castle of the Devil. He seemed endlessly amused at being constantly misidentified as said Devil.

Today, whatever else it had been, the silk-cotton tree lay heavily on the ground, as down as a giant felled by a brash young boy with a slingshot. "It's a goner this time," said Suzy.

"Sure is," replied Mister Cross. "'S fucking snuffed it." The ancient being's grin seemed perfunctory; he looked worried. His words came out in young Naima's voice, issued forth from Naima's small body. Naima's eyes were still rolled back, though she could apparently see where she was going just fine. And the way she carried herself was different, more studied and somehow older than the carriage of a six-year-old girl. She'd walked out here with measured steps, clutching the bones firmly in her two hands to maintain the connection between her and Mister Cross. Suzy sighed. Such a big job for such a little 'un, to be Mister Cross's ridden in this generation of their family. But the duty chose whom it would choose.

Centuries her family had been in charge of the hoodoo tree. It was their old guys' branch of the eternal tree, the spine of the world's soul. She'd heard tell that accidents had happened to parts of the world tree before. So long as the world still existed, the tree always mended itself eventually.

Suzy shone the flashlight down into the hollowed-out place where the tree's roots had been, now ringed around with jagged teeth of rotten wood. Something shifted away from the beam of light.

"There's something down there!" she told Mister Cross.

He raised an eyebrow, a gesture too elegant for her little girl. Underneath all the preciousness, his movements were careful, his face too still. That's how he got when he was pissed and biding his time. That worried Suzy even more than the lightning-blasted hoodoo tree. Was he mad at her for letting this happen?

Mister Cross got down on his knees and peered inside the hole. He said, "Something there? So there is." Talking down into the hole like that made his voice echo, only it sounded like two people saying the same words; Naima and a deep-voiced man. "Not the one I'd hoped to see, though. That pigeon has flown the coop." Mister Cross looked up at Suzy. "Stop fretting, Sis-in-law. I know you weren't careless."

Suzy felt her shoulders lower in relief. She'd heard that Mister Cross could carry a soul halfway across the border between life and death and strand it there for as long as he chose.

Mister Cross sighed. "Someone took entirely too much care

over this escapade." He reached a hand down into the hole. "Come out, little earthworms," he cooed. His voice was shaking with suppressed anger. "You know I won't hurt you."

From the hole, a woman's voice replied, "We know that, sir. But it was just finally getting quiet in here again after all that commotion that one was making last night. We were trying to enjoy the peacefulness."

Suzy knew that voice. Hearing it brought on a fever-shock, like someone had doused her in warm water. "Ma?" she said. "Is that you?"

"Susanna? How're you hearing me? You never have before this. Not since I crossed over."

Mister Cross said, "Come on up, Pearl, if you want to chat with her for a bit. She can see and hear you while I'm here." He said to Suzy, "Some of your kinfolk choose to hang around for a while after they've passed over."

Suzy had known in theory that the ghosts of her family's dead gathered around the exposed buttress roots of the silk-cotton tree, but she'd half decided that was just a story the adults told to frighten children away from the tree. Heaven knew she'd told Naima the same story herself. "Ma was here all this time, and you never told me?"

He shrugged. "Not my business. You're already living, and she's already dead."

The old guys could be so cruel, without scarcely knowing they were doing it! Suzy found she was shaking; she wasn't sure whether it was with anger for lost opportunities long past, or with longing trepidation for what was about to happen. What would Ma look like? By the time she'd died, the illness had burned all the plumpness from her body.

A man's voice from the hole, trembly with age and speaking

with an accent Suzy didn't recognize and could barely understand, said, "Tell her that baby of hers is coming down with a cold."

"A cold. Figures," Suzy said to Winston, chucking him under his chin. "You have to go and do everything your big sister does, don't you?" Naima was just getting over a cold.

Then Suzy remembered her manners. She called, "Thank you, sir!" down into the hole. Her voice echoed with only one person's voice.

The ghost down below continued, "You should give him catnip tea, then grease him all over with camphor and lard."

Suzy blinked in surprise. The hell?

"For heaven's sake, Peter," said Ma, "you're confusing curing a child with pickling it!" And then there was Ma, standing right there in front of her. She wasn't wearing the black skirt suit in which she'd been buried seven years ago, the one they'd had to pin in the back because she'd lost so much weight. Instead, she had on the comfy, wash-worn jeans she'd preferred for hanging around the house in, and her pale blue T-shirt with "Foxy Mama" on the front of it in rainbow glitter. It had the same old coffee stain on it over the second *m*.

Ma winked at Suzy. "Him and his old-time cures," she said. "He still thinks he wouldn't have died of gangrene if they'd washed his leg in warm turpentine." Wheedle chortled and thrust a pudgy brown arm in Ma's direction, squeezing his fist open and closed. He still confused the signs for "hello," "goodbye," and "milk." But it was easy to tell which one he meant this time.

Ma wiggled her fingers back at Wheedle. "Hello, darling! Yes, I'm happy to see you again, too. You're the only one who seems to know I'm there when I come over to the house." She looked Mister Cross sternly up and down. He, wearing Naima's body, was leaning against one of the huge exposed roots of the old tree. Ma said to him, "I know that you're the boss of me and I have to mind my manners. But there's a thing I'm going to say; don't you let any harm come to my granddaughter. Wearing her like an old suit."

"Harm," he scoffed. "As if. You know better than that, Pearl."

It was Ma! Right there! Looking like she'd never died! "Oh, my goodness, Ma; can I hug you?"

"You can try," Mister Cross told her, "but you'll be grabbing air."

Sadly, Ma said, "He's right, honey. I've tried hundreds of times to put my arms around you. And to read you the riot act for calling that poor child...what is it? Naima? Is that some kind of Black Power thing?"

Like a wheel sliding into a comfy old rut, Suzy snapped back, "You would know, I guess. That Black Power stuff was from your time, not mine."

"Pearl?" said Mister Cross. "Did any of you see what happened here?"

"Lightning strike," replied another man's voice from down in the hole. "Not long after sunrise. Out of nowhere. And Himself that you had in here with us was mighty agitated all last night."

A woman's voice said, "It was Flash that struck the tree."

Mister Cross scowled. "Really? Why am I not surprised? Did you see him? Did he say anything to you?"

A younger woman's voice said, "Weren't Flash. She just wants it to be, because she has her cap set for him something bad."

"Oh, yes, it was!" said the first speaker.

"Yeah? What do you know about it? There wasn't any thunder! Flash always comes with thunder."

Mister Cross raised that eyebrow again. "There wasn't, huh?" Angrily, he stamped his foot. Looking up to the sky, he said, "Crap and damn, Cathy! Why can't you stay out of this?"

"Told you it was her; nyah, nyah."

From the hole came a drawn-out, echoing kiss-teeth of vexation. Suzy had to smile. She'd never met a black person who didn't make that noise when they were exasperated. Apparently even the dead ones did it.

"And what about the kudzu? What happened to it?"

Suzy said, "I was so busy watching over Naima while she called you that I didn't see what happened to it." She looked at Mister Cross. "I told it I was on its side. I told it I was calling you. I figured it'd want to see you."

Mister Cross sighed. "Seems not," he said.

A child's voice came weebling up from the depths of the tree: "Sir? Can you cover us again, please? The sunlight's coming in and bleaching stuff out. We can't see the numbers on our dominoes."

"Gotta go," said Ma. "I'm winning that dominoes game, and if I don't watch the little dickens, she cheats."

"Ma?"

"Yes, sweetie?"

"Why do you stay here?"

"On this plane, you mean?"

"Yes. And in the tree. I mean, come on; you're living in the roots of a tree? You hate dirt!"

Ma smiled. "I wanted to make the acquaintance of my grandbabies, and to see how you were getting on." Ma had passed while Suzy was pregnant with Naima. "Besides, it's not forever. I'll move on along presently. Won't I, sir?"

Ma glanced meaningfully at Mister Cross, who smiled and blew her a kiss. "In you go, Pearl." For all that he was tooth-gnashingly pissed off, he was being gentle with his charges.

Ma mimed blowing three quick kisses: one at Suzy, one at Winston, and one at Mister Cross. "That's for Naima," she told him, "not for you."

"I'm not jealous, honey," he said. "Like any claypicken, you were mine from before you were born."

She cut her eyes at him and turned to Suzy. "Naima's a pretty name," she said. "You and Roger are doing a fine job." Then she winked out, like a star.

Suzy felt a tear trickle down her cheek. Wheedle touched it and baby-talked something at her. Mister Cross put a finger to his lips. "Don't tell her too much, now," he said. And Wheedle hushed, just like that.

"Wow," said Suzy. "I could have used you here this morning, when he wouldn't stop crying for anything."

"Catching a cold will do that to them," he said sympathetically. "Hey, can you cover that hole with some tree branches for me? I can't because, you know." He opened his hands to show the two dice in his right and the black cat bone in the left. In his open palm, the dice had rolled snake eyes.

"But—"

"Wheedle, I'll hold you," he said, "if that's okay with you?"

He wasn't asking Suzy. Winston cooed and reached out to him with both hands. He leaned so far forward that it was easier to hand him over to Mister Cross than to try not to overbalance. "His name's Winston," she said. "I won't let Naima call him Wheedle."

He took the baby from her. "Why not? You do, when you think Naima's not listening. Naima just told me so." He dandled Winston, his fists still closed tightly over the bones. "Besides, Wheedle prefers the name 'Wheedle,' don't you, boo?" He blew a raspberry at the baby, who chortled and bounced, clapping his hands in that hit-and-miss way that babies do.

"You won't drop him?"

"You don't scurry, I just might, not meaning to, you understand. A six-year-old's muscles can only hold up a strapping baby like this for so long."

Suzy scurried. As she was dragging branches over the hole, Mister Cross and Winston were babbling and cooing at each other. At one point Mister Cross said, "Sure, they're particles. But they're also their own antiparticles. At least, the way claypicken perceptions reckon it."

Suzy looked over there to see who he was talking to, but there was only him and Wheedle. Great. Just great. She'd taught the baby to sign only words like "Daddy" and "ball." Suzy was sure that it wouldn't occur to any parent on this green earth that their babe in arms might need to know how to say "antiparticle." What was ASL for that, anyway? Mister Cross called, "That'll do for now, Suzy. But soon's you can, get that hole filled in with dirt."

Alarm spiked Suzy's heartbeat. "Dirt? But how will the folks down there—"

"Breathe?" He chuckled. "Now, why in the world would they do such a thing?"

"Oh." They were dead; breathless and insubstantial. "Right."

Mister Cross's eyes widened. "Motherhumping...do you know what that ignorant chit has gone and done?" He began a flow of impressively inventive invective.

"Hey!" said Suzy. "Quit it with the language, please? I had a hard enough time of it trying to explain when Naima heard the word 'fuck' on television and asked me what it meant."

Right away, he stopped cussing. He smirked at her, though. "Don't know why you're trying so hard; she'll be teaching herself what 'fuck' means anyway in a few short years."

"She needs to learn in her own good time, not in yours," Suzy replied. One good thing Suzy'd figured out over the years was that she didn't have to mind her p's and q's so much now that she and Mister Cross were practically in-laws, thanks to her fool sister. Though you'd think Cora would have had more sense than to take up with Boysie. Look at all the mess it had caused.

Suzy went over and took Winston back from Mister Cross. "Actually, she needs to learn in her parents' good time while she'll still listen to us, 'cause Roger and I have our hands full enough trying to deal with her at six, let alone at sixteen." Honesty scored you points with the old guys.

He smiled that eerie smile. "I feel you, cous, I really do. Kids, eh? One of our kin's trying to rip apart the veils of physics and probability right this minute. What's she want to go and fashion a thing like that for? And all totally innocently, can you imagine? But don't young 'uns all try to rip their worlds apart at some time or other?" He frowned. "Though it might be happening right now, or tomorrow, or maybe a year from now. You folk are so finicky about time, living it in straight lines like that. It's enough to drive a body to drink."

"If that was a hint, I'm not giving you any white rum," Suzy replied. "Not till Naima's of drinking age."

He pouted. "In my day," he grumbled, "'drinking age' was when you were old enough to pick the cup up and put it to your mouth without spilling any."

Oh, but he was starting to get up her nose now. First this business with the kudzu, and such a fright that had given her! And then the tree, and the surprise of Mom. Plus she still had a full day ahead of her before Roger came home to do his child-care shift. She hadn't made Naima's lunch yet, or given her her lessons. She'd planned to start teaching Naima about burnt offerings today. And Wheedle was beginning to fuss for the boob. Suzy said to Mister Cross, "You want to whine for treats like a six-year-old? Fine. You can have apple juice, or milk. Which one would you like?" She said it in exactly the voice she'd use to talk to Naima. She'd lay odds he was only whinging for the principle of the thing. He never hurt children. Sure enough, he burst into a belly laugh. He liked a show of wit.

"Good one, Mama. Point taken. But make sure you give Naima

her cookies, now. She's earned them." He sighed. "This has been pleasant, but I have to go and find out where my dear brother has got to."

With no more warning than that, he closed his eyes. Naima opened hers. Her pupils were back where they should be. "Did he come, Mama?" she asked, then let the three bones fall to the ground, and fainted.

Suzy tutted in exasperation at Mister Cross as she went to see to her child, but she took note that he'd stepped off the hard patio stones onto the soft earth before he let Naima fall. "Thank you!" she called to the open air. He'd know what for. "And thanks for letting me and Ma talk!" She had no idea what he'd been going on about with that stuff about ripping veils, but that kind of business was for the celestials to handle. Her job was to watch over the tree, which meant that she was currently without portfolio. Maybe when Mister Cross returned, he'd have a new job for her.

Huh. Ma hadn't asked after her other daughter. Ah, well. Maybe Ma had her ways of going to visit with Cora, too. After all, it wasn't like a ghost could drown. Though water could get them powerfully confused, if the stories were true.

Naima opened her eyes.

"You okay, Lil Bit?"

Naima looked a little doubtful, but nodded. "I'm tired," she complained. "And my tummy's not happy." The celestial hauteur was gone. Now she was only precious Lil Bit, whiny for her post–Mister Cross nap.

Suzy stroked Naima's springy-haired head, smoothed back some of the naps. "I'll make you some warm milk with honey. That'll soothe your tummy."

"And cookies? You promised."

Suzy chuckled. "Not so stomach-soothing, I think. But yes, you can have five cookies. Real small ones."

Naima sat up. Wheedle cooed something at her. Naima made

an oogly-boogly face at him until he chortled in that full-throated, belly-deep way that only babies can.

Naima said, "Mom? What does 'motherhumping' mean?"

Suzy looked to the heavens, whence there was no comfort. She growled, "It's something I'd like to call Mister Cross."

> *"We must not look at goblin men,*
> *We must not buy their fruits:*
> *Who knows upon what soil they fed*
> *Their hungry thirsty roots?"*

I was standing. And walking. Okay, all that was probably good, even if I felt like shit on a stick, with peanuts. Walking…where? It was daytime. I was on a narrow gravel path, stumbling past thistles with pinkish-purple blowout 'fros, past asters with their star-shaped flowers, past white-belled ladies' tresses. Whoa. That was the lake over there, through the trees. I was walking beside it. I recognized this place. I was on the Leslie Street Spit. I had the feeling—more definite than a guess, not quite clear enough to be called a memory—that I'd been wandering the wetlands of the Spit for quite some time.

What time was it? Man, that'd been some shindig last night. My mouth was dry. I felt light-headed, a little queasy. Well, it wouldn't be the first time I'd finished a night of partying in a drunken haze. There'd been that time with Abby and the Bejis. I'd woken up at home, though, not lakeside.

Shit. Had somebody put something in my drink? I'd heard of that kind of crap.

A red-winged blackbird cussed at me in song from a nearby maple tree off the path. Didn't need Abby to tell me what it was singing; *Get away from my nest, baby-eater!*

"Yeah, cool your jets," I growled at it. "Do I look like a fucking hawk?" The sun was too bright. The trees and exploding spring undergrowth were too green. The path was too uneven, the light dancing off Lake Ontario too twinkly. Everything was too something. The world felt unreal. "Real" was back in Brie's club at Cheerful Rest, grooving on some fierce-ass sounds and dancing with people of all colours, all ages.

Thistle and chamomile bushes poked their way through rounded shards of broken china. I ambled past nipple-height chicory. The underbrush was growing so thickly, so energetically sprung by spring that I couldn't see through it. The Leslie Street Spit was a semi-man-made wetland, a wild mix of junk and nature. It was one of those fascinating borderland places that cities foster so well. It used to be one of my favourite places to go and ramble. Yeah, that was probably the reason I'd come here. Even semiconscious, I didn't want to go back to Abby.

After a few more minutes, though, I was better. In fact, better than better. My tummy was no longer queasy, and I felt as though I could walk for miles more. Even my hunger had faded.

I walked along a narrow dirt bike path that was hidden from the road by maple saplings. I reached down to touch an achingly perfect chicory blossom with crisp, royal lavender petals. The sun was pleasantly warm on my shoulders. Good thing, too, 'cause I wasn't wearing my jacket. I'd probably left it at Brie's.

Through the trees, glimpses of the lake gleamed sapphire-blue. The burgeoning beauty of a perfect spring day took me away from myself. I meandered, outside time, mesmerized by the wilderness around me. Greens seemed greener, the calls of tern and geese more sonorous. It seemed entirely natural to spy through the bush and trees what might have been a panda bear pulling down a length of tasty bamboo, a brown monkey swinging on liana vines from tree to tree, a giant silk-cotton tree with its thorn-studded trunk, an iguana tearing its messy way through a ripe fallen mango, a rainbow-feathered lizard leaping from one soaring branch to another. In the back of my mind's eye, everything had a fuzzy green haze on it, like a brand-new tennis ball. The world was getting its Shine on.

Soon the narrow path veered off from the main road to run closer to the lake. I recognized the low cliff bolstered by big broken slabs of concrete and jabbing lengths of rusted rebar. I reached the edge, peered over the lip of the overhang. The beach below hardly deserved the name. Brown wet sand, and not much of that. Mostly rocks and detritus. I'd been coming down here in vain since I was a teenager. I'd sit down there for hours, hoping to see the mother I'd never met. Wishfully thinking that she might be in the area; maybe she even knew that this was my favourite place and she'd have left me a message in the flotsam and jetsam that littered the strip of shore. Eventually, the disappointment had become too much to bear. I hadn't been down here in quite a few years. But today I was feeling all nostalgic. My Mom place. I decided to go down to the shore, for old times' sake.

I scooched down onto my heels at the edge of the lip. The idea was to get your butt and hands under you as you went over, and sort of slide a couple of feet to the place where the piled-any-which-way concrete slabs thinned out just enough that if you were careful, you could clamber down it to the few yards of narrow, rocky beach there.

I was out of practice. Just as I edged over the low cliff, my foot caught on a small rock that was sticking up. I almost overbalanced. I put a hand out to steady myself, and scraped my palm on a boulder. I began to skid. I'd meant to do this carefully. Instead, in a crabwise panic of skinned palms and scrabbling feet, I half-slid, half-fell over the broken concrete teeth. Good thing it was only a few feet down. I reached the bottom and rolled. Fetched up against a broken jut of concrete. A cloud of annoyed sand flies rose up from beneath the shelter of the leaning slab and whizzed around my head. "Sorry," I whispered to them. I stood and dusted pebbles off my stinging palms. About ten feet away, the lake lapped quietly at the shore, tumbling the rocks and pebbles there with a faint tinkling noise. A flock of geese paddled past, honking irritably at me for being on their beach. Blooms of green algae floated close by, probably enriched by goose guano; you could see smears of it here and there on the rocks. The combination made the lake smell, as always, vaguely rank.

I used to imagine Ma hunting this lake, swirling slinkily through the cold, deep water and surfacing to gobble up the cranky geese. Abby and I loved roasted goose.

Dreamily, I searched the beach. Waterfront dump sites made for lots of driftglass, beautifully weathered smooth into gleaming jewels. When we were little, Uncle had told us stories about Mom, about how much she used to love beachcombing. How she especially adored the scarcest colours of beach glass, cobalt and red and orange. Uncle would give me and Abby small, whorled shells, tell us that if we put them to our ears and listened carefully, we could hear our mother talking to us. *Cipangopaludina japonica* was the name of the molluscs that created those shells. Their common name was *mystery snail*. Some of the shells were scattered around the beach right where I was standing now. I could see the jagged holes in a few of them where gulls had dropped them onto the rocks to break them and picked the tasty meat out with their sharp beaks.

I found a few pieces of beach glass, but only one nicely frosted one, and it was colourless. No Ma colours. In total, my finds were a handful of frosted beach glass pebbles; two black goose feathers and one white one; three of the ubiquitous mystery snail shells, bleached and empty, but unbroken; a small piece of aluminum tubing, surf-tumbled to smoothness; a handful of red insulating wire, tangled as a bird's nest; and a bleached fish vertebra I'd found high up on the shore. It was a good inch across.

Abby used to hear Mom's voice in the shells, she told me. Said Mom sang to her. I only heard a faint whooshing sound, except one time, when a Mom shell had clearly whispered, *Eat your peas.* That had been the first and last time, though. I'd been about nine. Never did start eating my peas. I mean, it wasn't like she could make me.

I put one of the shells to my ear. Only the usual slushing sound. Maybe. Maybe it was more than that?

Yeah, right. And maybe I could understand what trees were saying, like my sister could.

On the bike path above, a motorbike slowly puttered by, idling so low I couldn't hear the engine. Its rider was a comfortably fat black guy. Big 'fro restrained by a bright orange bandana. Cheerful face. He looked like he'd be good to hug, share a doobie with, and just shoot the breeze with about life, the universe, and everything. He'd taken his T-shirt off and tucked its hem into the back waistband of his shorts. Smart. It was a hot day, for spring. I'd been longing to do the same thing, had been wondering whether the occasional hiker or dump-truck driver would be taken aback at the sight of a woman topless but for a heavy-duty sports bra. The Leslie Street Spit felt like the type of place where the social rules could be a bit relaxed.

There was a bright blue knapsack lying on the ground near where I'd made my descent. It was on its side, gaping open. It had a crumb of sand crusting one edge. I went over to it, picked it up. Nothing inside. One strap torn, front pocket half coming off. Not too bad shape otherwise. I put my beachcombed haul inside it.

An ozone effervescence to the air tickled at my nose. I looked up at the sky. I was right at the shore of the expanse of the eerie inland ocean that is Lake Ontario. No way to miss the determined little thundercloud trundling my way, literally out of a clear blue sky. Grey-bottomed, it was waddling towards me like a grimy toddler with a full diaper. A fat, wet drop landed on the back of my neck. The thundercloud was about to drop its load, and soon. It looked as though it only held enough water for a short burst, but spring storms were chilly. Wouldn't be great to be caught out in one for long.

The oncoming squall started herding wavelets ahead of itself to shore. They batted, catlike, at my boots. I said to the thundercloud, "Could you give me just a sec, please?" It was probably a natural storm, but politeness never hurt. Could be Aunt Cathy up there nudging that storm cloud along. Whatever the reason, the cloud advanced no farther while I took my cell phone out of my pocket and dumped it into the knapsack, too. If there was going to be rain, it'd keep drier there. There was a spectacular lightning flash. "Okay," I said, "I'm done now." It was time to rejoin the world anyway. I hauled the knapsack onto my shoulders and climbed up to the bike path. I set off back through the trees towards the main road that led out of the Spit.

I'd barely registered the rustling in the high undergrowth when a large pair of clutching hands grabbed my leg.

I screamed. Terror lent me the strength to wrench my jeans-covered calf out of the handhold. I felt the scrape of claws slicing through the fabric of my jeans as I pulled away. My haint was upon me. Its small, heavy body scrambled, quarrelling, up my side. Hideously contorted baby face, brown as my own, its hair an angry, knotted snarl of black. Now it had those large hands at my throat. It punched small knobkerries of knees against my rib cage, all but knocking the breath out of me. I staggered. Managed not to fall. One of the haint's searching thumbs pushed brutally past my teeth into my mouth. It tasted of dirt, and of nastily salty skin. The skin was looser than skin on thumbs should be. I gagged. I bit down, hard. The haint's snarling became a whipped-dog yelp. More by luck than aim, I got my hands around its ankles. I tore it off me and swung it around, full weight, to crack it with a dull thud against the bole of a tree I hadn't even seen there. The haint crumpled to the ground, its eyes closed, its spine oddly bent in the middle. Then it was up again, though its upper body hung wrongly to one side. It glared at me. Today my haint was wearing the form of a child just old enough to walk on its chubby legs. Its hair framed its anger-contorted cherub's face.

I chanced a look behind me. There was dense chest-high undergrowth barring my way to the paved entrance to the Spit where there might be people. Might; the place was usually pretty deserted. I took off, running pell-mell away from the haint along the narrow footpath. Would the haint recover enough to follow me? Fuck, fuck, fuck. *Daddy!* my brain screamed, regressed with terror. But Daddy couldn't help me now. I took a sharp left over a low patch of scrub grass. *Mom! Mom!* Was that the thump of little feet behind me, or the thud of my own heart? I threw a terrified glance over my shoulder. I know; how many times had Abby told me not to look back at a pursuer? Not that she knew bugger all about running. But she was right. You only lost more time looking over your shoulder. Psyched yourself out and did stupid things. Such as tripping over your own feet, which is exactly what I did, for the second time that day. I tumbled ass over teakettle into the undergrowth. All the rolling made my head spin. I came to a stop with my cheek lying on a thistle. I hissed, jerked my head up off the ground, off the thorns. I was in a thistle patch that had grown so high and thick that it covered me completely. The prickles jabbed into my wrists and against my face where there was exposed flesh. My thick clothing protected me from the rest. But I didn't dare move from my hiding place. I twisted my head away from a thistle that was scraping too close to my eye, and peered through the plants.

My haint was tracking through the tall undergrowth a few feet away. It no longer seemed injured. We'd never been able to hurt it badly enough to stop it, though gods knew we'd tried. Looked like it hadn't seen me. It had softened its appearance, trying to look more like a toddler. It was wearing rugged little baby jeans, turned up at the cuffs in the cutest way. A pair of sweet kiddie runners on its feet: white, trimmed with aqua and pink. They were the kind with a red light in their heels that flashed every time the creature took a step. It always got one thing wrong, though. Almost like it couldn't help revealing itself. Itself or themselves. I'd never known whether it was the same creature hunting me, or whether a different one came every time. Whatever; it always looked different. At the moment, the detail that gave it away—other than the fact that it was, as usual, trying to kill me—was its hands. They were the size of a grown man's. Not a small man, either. With those hands, the thing heedlessly uprooted the underbrush. It pulled up whole thistles, thorns and all, without any sign of discomfort. And here I was, wheezing for breath, watching that eldritch not-child get closer. Damn it, how could I have let Babyface sneak up on me like that? I knew better than to be so absentminded!

Babyface gaped its jaws impossibly wide and stuffed a whole thistle plant into its mouth. Then it fastidiously brushed its hands off on the backs of its jeans. It was even creepier doing something so claypicken-normal. It stood up on its little tippy-toes and strained to scan the shoreline beyond the edge of the incline. I ducked my head down again. Had it seen me? I needed a miracle. I'd learned better than to hope for one. If only I could get back to the lake! I knew what would rout the haint. Nasty brute was persistent, but we'd figured out a few reliable ways to discourage it over the years, Abby, Dad, Uncle, and I. Probably the only reason I'd survived to adulthood. Right now I had plenty of water easy to hand, but no way to go and get it without alerting the haint to where I was.

A drop of liquid landed on a leaf just in front of my eyes. It hung on the tip of the leaf for a second before falling off to land on my hand. Another drop hit my nose. The baby rain cloud! Hope unfurled in my chest, sweet as an inhaled breath. Maybe I was getting my miracle after all.

The haint must have felt the raindrops, too. It flinched as though it'd been stung. It flinched again, yelped, and cast a panicked look upwards. Hallelujah! I mentally cheered for the storm to come on faster.

A few more drops splatted down. The haint yelped. It scanned the underbrush, even took a few steps in my direction, but the rain thickened suddenly. The haint made a snarling face, then ran off, swatting at the air the whole time. I watched until it disappeared into the dump-truck depot off to one side. There was a steady drizzle spattering me now, but I breathed a sigh of relief. So long as the rain continued, I'd be completely safe. What an idiot I'd been, letting my attention slip like that.

I stood up into the spring rain. The fine drizzle was beginning to weigh my hair down. Maybe the rain cloud wasn't a result of divine intervention, but I still said a polite, "Thanks." You never knew.

As though in answer, the rainwater seemed to get a little more sparse. No surprise there; the Family members who could control the weather usually wouldn't give me the time of day. The big surprise would be finding out that it really was one of them who had sent me even a few minutes of rescuing rain. I had to hurry. I was running out of rain cloud, and out of time. I had to get out of the Spit and home to safety. I wasn't ready to go back to Abby's yet, but that's where my haint-repelling stuff was.

A loud thunderclap made me jump. Cathy *and* Flash? Were they both in on this? What the hell was going on?

And suddenly, buckets of water were sheeting down from the

sky. Holy shit; the sky was lead-lined with storm clouds as far as the eye could see. When had they shown up? This was a full-blown spring storm. "Thank you!" I shouted at the sky. Then I hauled ass.

The boiling thunderclouds weren't actually right above me, yet the fists of rain from them were pounding me and the surrounding area for many yards around. Probably something fancy to do with the curvature of the Earth and the speed and direction of the wind. Daddy would have known how that worked. Did know, somewhere inside that softening mind of his, if the gradual smoothing out of the wrinkles of his brain hadn't already taken the knowledge.

Oh, crap. Dad. I'd totally forgotten that last night had been my night to drop in on him. Abby was going to rip me a new one for this. I'd just go see him right now, after I went home and changed into dry clothes. Abby was teaching all day today; with any luck, she'd never find out that I'd missed my visit with Dad. He probably hadn't even noticed.

And shit, I hadn't taken my meds. The little bottle of vileness was also in my room back at Abby's. Stupid, Makeda! I was flirting with liver failure for sure.

I hurried along the path. The ratio of raindrops to air approached fifty-fifty. Rainwater pockmarked the surface of the lake. The susurrus was an almost-comforting white noise. Thunder rumbled and chuckled. A bright stitch of lightning tore the sky in half a few miles away. I wished I hadn't left my jacket at Cheerful Rest. I was chilled through, shivering; the gifts of the gods are two-edged things, sometimes way more than two. The lake had turned an oddly pretty greenish blue. Sort of Ty-D-Bol mixed with almond milk. The rain was sheeting down so hard that it was difficult to make out detail. I only knew I was still on the bike path because of the wet crunch of gravel under my feet. Water trickled from my hair into my ears and down the back of my neck. I couldn't help sucking some of it in from my mouth corners. It tasted so sweet, though I knew the skies were as polluted as the soil. Dad was forever ranting about it, even in his mostly mindless condition.

I walked through the occasional little cloud of tiny flies, hovering unerringly at eye and ear height. I hated the damned things. How'd they stay flying in this downpour? You'd think one good raindrop would easily kill a few of them at one blow. I contemplated being a creature so helpless that a raindrop would kill it. Decided that wasn't so different from being me. The surface of the lake danced crazily, pounded by the bullets of the storm's friendly fire. Then, gradually, the downpour lessened to a light drizzle. Still enough to keep my haint away.

What could I make with today's haul? I hadn't stumbled on any cobalt driftglass just now; not even the tiniest bits. Not any red. It was one of the rarest colours. In all the years I'd been looking, I'd found barely enough pieces to fill a thimble. Someday I was going to save up enough to buy a trip to Puerto Rico. I'd read that the shores there were a trove of ocean-tumbled cobalt driftglass pebbles. Apparently Puerto Rico used to use a lot of cobalt glass in olden times, and much of it made its way into trash heaps there and, eventually, into the water. I'd never been to the Caribbean. Ever since I read about the Puerto Rican driftglass as a kid, I'd had this fantasy image of myself down there, surrounded by an ankle-height circle made up of hundreds of perfectly rounded, frosted pieces of deep-blue driftglass, each one found by me personally. My mother's favourite colour. Of me standing in the middle of the circle, spreading my arms wide, throwing my head back and summoning my mother forth from the depths of the waters. Of hoodooing her back into a woman from the sea monster shape they'd told me she'd been forced into. Of *having* a mother. One whose face I could come to recognize in all its moods, not just the way she smiled for the camera in the couple of old photos my dad had of her.

A man's voice yelled, and I jumped. A couple of cyclists, guys in baggy shorts and loose football T-shirts, came around a bend in the path, going the other way. They were hallooing for the glee of wind and rain, and weather almost warm enough for enjoying both. I relaxed a bit. Whatever form it showed up in, my haint always came alone, and never in the rain. One of the guys splashed his bike through a puddle, holding his legs and feet out straight ahead of him. Got himself splattered in mud, which the rain began immediately tattooing patterns in on his pale skin. He grinned shyly at me. I was still too shaken to grin back, plus I wasn't quite out of the woods yet. They zipped past me. Probably heading towards the beach I'd just left.

I kept going. I was shivering badly. I needed to get somewhere warm soon. Would my cell phone be okay inside the knapsack? I might need to swallow my pride and call Abs for help. The knapsack looked sturdy enough. It hadn't been out there long enough for the elements to rot it or rust the metal clasps. A good brand, too. Fancy hikers' make.

I stopped. There was a snake lying near the edge of the path, half in and half out of the underbrush. It was smallish as snakes went, about nine inches long. Darkly gleaming greyish black. Curled in a figure eight. Melanistic garter snake. Dad had a soft spot for those. My first alarmed thought was that the cyclists had run over it out of spite or ignorance, as we monkeys will. But it seemed whole. It glanced sideways at me, its tongue flickering to taste my air. Why was it there? If it'd been sunning itself on the path, it should have gone back to its lair when the rain started. But there it lay. I looked at it and it at me. For a few seconds we stayed still, cocooned together in the soft sound of the rain. I took a small step towards it. It jerked, twisted its body into a shape that looked uncomfortably rectangular. Then it shook itself loose again, slithered into the new spring thistles and violets lining the path, and was gone.

Something was wrong. Other than the haint attack, that is. I couldn't suss out the snake's exact meaning, but I knew that right angles were mostly anathema to Dad. He was okay with the ones that occurred naturally in the jes'-grew world, but artificial right angles were like nails on a chalkboard to him. If I was understanding the snake correctly, Dad was in trouble. Damn. I should have been there.

I glanced over my shoulder. Nothing coming after me. I sped up. I was only a few minutes away from Lakeshore Boulevard. Hang on, Dad. I'm coming.

From inside the knapsack, my cell phone started to ring. Crap! If I took it out in the rain, that'd be the death of it. I hurried a little farther, looked around for somewhere that'd be shelter. Only saplings, the open beach, water pattering down from the skies. The phone rang and rang. Twelve rings. Fifteen. It was only set for nine. That kind of music mojo meant only one person. "Fuck, Abby!" I said. "I'm trying!"

The hell with it. I reached into the knapsack for the jangling phone. Maybe I'd be able to hear enough of what Abby had to tell me before it shorted out.

"Here," said a soft voice behind me. "Allow me."

It was the guy on the motorbike. He sat the bike securely, as though it were a horse. He was holding up a vast golf umbrella decorated with a swirl of rainbow colours. He smiled and twirled it. The colours appeared to spiral into its white centre.

"Thank you," I said. I stepped into the shade of the umbrella, fumbled the phone out of the knapsack with wet, cold-numbed fingers. "Yeah, it's me."

"Took you long enough," said Abby's voice. "What the hell are you doing down on the Spit?"

I'm on the run from a creepy baby with a mouth big enough to eat the world, I thought. "Abby, what's wrong with Dad?"

"Meet me at the nursing home right away. Lars'll bring you."

"Lars?"

"At your service," said the man holding the umbrella. His voice was quiet, but rumbly. I could feel it in my belly.

"You gonna tell me what's up with Dad?" Please, Dad. Please be okay. I won't do it again, I promise.

"His room is empty. The people at the home haven't seen him in hours, and they can't find him anywhere."

"Shit." Officially, Dad had advanced Alzheimer's. The care home kept him carefully under lock and key.

"You were supposed to be watching him, Makeda!"

Oh, gods. "He's gotta be there somewhere."

"Well, he isn't. I know you're mad at me, but did you have to do Dad like that, just to spite me?"

"I'm sorry, okay? I'm on my way." I dropped the phone back into the knapsack.

Lars smiled at me. "Can you hold the brolly a sec?" he asked. Black man, Swedish name, English accent. And now that I was close to him, I could see the Shine on him like emerald dust. Abby's boyfriends were always interesting, but she'd never dated a Shiny one before. I hadn't recognized him. Which side of the Family was he from?

I took the umbrella and held it over us both. He turned behind him and pulled a couple of helmets and a wad of plastic sheeting out of a bag attached to the back of the bike. One helmet was fluorescent aqua splashed with lemon-coloured lightning bolts. The other was scarlet with beige and purple smiley faces. The words "Voodoo Chile" were splashed across it in a bulbous hippie-style font. The plastic sheeting was fuschia with starbursts of an uncomfortable green, outlined in chocolate brown. Lars balanced the lot between his wide thighs, tucked under his overhanging belly. The plastic sheeting turned out to be rain ponchos. He pulled one on, slammed the red helmet onto his head. Took the umbrella from me. "Your turn." He handed me the remaining gear.

"A poncho's no use to me now," I said. "I'm already soaked."

He smiled. "Maybe it'll delay hypothermia for a bit though, yeah? Got dry sweats in the trunk once I get you out of this downpour." He patted the lidded fibreglass box at the back of the bike. He waited while I put the poncho and helmet on, then snapped the umbrella shut. The rain popcorned down onto my helmet. He slid the brolly into a sheath built into the chassis of the bike.

"Handy," I said.

He grinned. "Hop on." Not many words to him, Lars.

I slipped the good strap of the knapsack over my shoulder, straddled the bike, wrapped my arms around Lars's solid middle. He *was* good to hold, even through the crinkly plastic. I said, "'Voodoo Chile.' That was a Hendrix release, wasn't it? Limited edition?"

He raised up off the bike a bit, gunned it. It vroomed into life, and we took off. As we went by the dump-truck depot, I saw a tiny form huddled under the body of a garbage-encrusted truck. My haint. The wet side of its face glistened and ran a little more than you'd expect from just rainwater. Looked painful. The haint glared at me. I leaned into Lars's bulk and stuck my tongue out at it. Suddenly, it smiled, its mouth too broad for its face. Something spilled, wriggling, from its baby lips. Hard to see through the sheeting rain, but it looked like the snake messenger I'd just seen. The haint bit down, and a writhing length of its snack fell to the ground. It landed, kept twisting as though it weren't quite dead yet. My stomach twisted with it. Lars gunned the motor and the bike sped up. As we hit the main road, he leaned back a little so that his mouth was next to my ear.

"I used to be his guitar," he said in his soft voice. "Jimi's, I mean."

The wind carried his words away. I was too stunned to reply. Make-no-waves Abby was dating an instrument?

We sped on towards the Comfort Zone (I kid you not) Convalescent Home. Where the fuck was Dad?

Me and Abby, we didn't have exactly the same face. It was more like someone had dropped a funhouse mirror, cracking it into two related but uneven pieces. Abby's left eye was about five millimetres farther away from her nose than mine was from mine; she and I had measured and compared once. The tip of her nose tilted ever so slightly to the left. Near as we could tell, mine didn't. She and I had pretty much the same mouth. Her left shoulder hunched a little, hinting at the mild scoliosis that skewed her spine slightly to the left. The skin graft keloid scars on her from our separation operation were on her left flank. Mine, of course, were on my right. And her left leg was shorter, where both my legs were the same length. It was as though, in the womb, my body had been the lodestone that had drawn hers in. A head of boisterous dreadlocks concealed the tablespoon-sized indentation on the left side of Abby's skull, where no hair had ever grown.

She was standing near me in the corridor outside Dad's empty room. She leaned on her crutches. Guilt nipped at my conscience. On bad days she used her crutches instead of her cane. Worry about Dad was taking it out of her today. Her elbows were locked to hold herself stiffer, and she was giving me her famous evil eye. As a kid she'd used the crutches all the time. Right now, she looked just the way she used to when she was a kid and she was mad at me. "Abby's Glare of Hot Death" Dad called it, even now. Old, well-worn memories were the last to go.

Lars had given me a dry sweatshirt and dropped me out front. He hadn't followed me in. Maybe guitars didn't like the smell of hospitals, either. And call it whatever they wanted, Comfort Zone had that unmistakable hospital bouquet. I'd had plenty of time to come to hate it during all the nights I'd spent curled into that bloody orange vinyl La-Z-Boy by Dad's bedside.

On Abby's other side stood a slight, worried-looking man in a beige suit, so elegantly tailored it was practically invisible. Grenville Tankhouse was the currently quite-uncomfortable-looking director of the Comfort Zone Palliative Centre.

"You've checked the grounds, right?" I asked him.

"Ah…" Tankhouse took a quick glance up and down the corridor, as though Dad might be lurking in the doorway of one of the other patients' rooms. "Yes," he said, "we have searched the premises thoroughly. We're going over it again, just in case we missed anything. And the officers—"

"He's not here, Makeda," Abby burst out. "We went over all that while we were waiting for you. And I had a look, too. In here, around the grounds. Didn't see him."

"Crap." I'd tried to sop my hair dry with the wet sweater I'd taken off in the rest home's public washroom. But my black girl's hair held water like a sponge. Though I'd already squeezed my two plaits out once in the bathroom sink in the washroom, that had only slowed the flow down, not stopped it. Water was trickling off the ends of them. I could feel it streaking damply down the back of the sweatshirt Lars had lent me. And my jeans were still sodden. I shuddered. I asked Abby, "So what do we do now?"

"I haven't checked Dad's room yet. Let's do that together. Two pairs of eyes might be better than one."

"Please," said Mr. Tankhouse, indicating the way.

Abs and I went ahead of him. My running shoes made a squelching sound with each step. I was leaving wet footprints behind me. I said to Abby, "Take care you don't slip in my wake."

She grunted an ungracious thank-you.

Mr. Tankhouse said, "Please don't worry about it. I'll have it cleaned up immediately." He chuckled nervously. "Heaven knows, we've had worse things on this floor. The scat of that raccoon, for example. Have I ever told you ladies how grateful I was for your indulgence in that incident? The Health Department could have closed us down in a second."

Abby glared at him. Poor guy, it wasn't his fault. Living organisms liked to be near Dad. Since we'd put him in palliative care at Comfort Zone, they'd been experiencing a rash of little surprises: squirrels clambering down the chimney, alarmed deer in the foyer, roses climbing so avidly up the outside wall to get to Dad's window that they'd had to assign one of their grounds staff to cut the rosebush back every few days. I'd taken to bringing a cage with me at night so I could quietly return the visitors to the outdoors. And after that business with the earwigs—thank heaven, the frogs had snapped up most of them—I'd started carrying a cricket cage, too. Dad had been no help. I would come to see him, and find him cooing at an intrusion of cockroaches, sprinkling a spreading patch of moss with water from the glass on his bedside table, or picking the fleas off a family of scrofulous foxes that was rolling around in his bed. Once he'd tossed his eggplant sandwich into a corner, presumably to nourish the blue fuzzy mould that was creeping towards it. Still, I counted myself lucky. A couple of months ago, Mrs. Block two rooms over had covered her walls with her own shit, screaming wordlessly as she did.

The three of us entered Dad's room. High hospital-type bed, single, with bars along its sides. Those ubiquitous blue cotton hospital sheets, rumpled and flung aside. The awful orange La-Z-Boy. I frowned. There was crumbled dirt on the seat of it. Abby looked around, then stopped dead where she stood. Her mouth dropped open. "What happened here?"

The floor was littered with shattered pieces of black and silver plastic and glass that had been the TV. Something had torn it from the jointed arm that swung down from the ceiling. Snail trails streaked the cheery poster on the wall that showed a boat on a lake or ocean. The handful of snails responsible for the silvery tracings dotted the walls. There was a small brown lizard stalking one of them. Lizards in Ontario?

"Perhaps...," ventured Mister Tankhouse, "some of your father's strays?"

I had him half convinced that the deer and the raccoon had been rescue animals that Dad was looking after until they could be returned to the wild. "No," I said, "something else did this."

"Oh," he said. "If you're sure. I just wondered whether that boa might have returned...?"

I shook my head. "I took her back to her owner." Abby'd made her promise not to come back inside the rest home, but I didn't need to try to explain that to Mr. Tankhouse.

I stared at the mess in dismay. Dad's potted plants were in a bad way. Half of them had been spilled from their containers. It looked as though they'd been dragged across the floor and the bed. I'd brought them for him in an effort to make him be more comfortable. I'd lined the windowsill with some of them, and hung others in planters from the top of the window. The organica broke up the smooth right angles of the room a bit, inserted more of the jes'-grew lines of natural things to conceal the rigid lines and angles of human-made objects. The plants had made it a little easier for him to be in here. That and sedatives. When was I going to stop feeling guilty that Dad had gotten too sick for us to take care of him? I'd been coming here almost every night since he was admitted last year. I'd swallowed the responsibility for his illness as though it were my personal fault.

"Where the hell were you?" hissed Abby. "You told me that you were going to stay with him last night!"

Mr. Tankhouse pretended to be very interested in the pattern of linoleum on the floor.

The bars on the windows were rusted through and broken. "I guess I found somewhere else to stay," I muttered absentmindedly. There was a sweetish smell in the room. I couldn't quite place it.

"You did what?"

"All the nights I've overnighted with him, nothing unusual's ever happened."

"Unless you count the bobcat," said Mister Tankhouse meekly. "That was quite an interesting morning, I must say."

"Abs, Dad should have been okay for one night."

"Well, he wasn't!"

A woman in a baby-blue pantsuit popped her head in the door. I nodded at her. "Hi, Mrs. Pereira. We seem to have caused you even more excitement than usual." I was playing it cool, I always did, but I was itching to get out of there and start combing the city for Dad. The spring nights were still freezing. We had to get him back before nightfall!

She replied, "Hello, dear. I'm sorry you had to have such awful news today."

Mister Tankhouse told us, "The police say he can't have gotten far in his condition."

Mrs. Pereira picked her way delicately through the pieces of smashed television. "Something was upsetting your father last night. Perhaps the break in his routine? He's always agitated when one of you girls isn't there to tuck him in at night. Oh, my, are those snails?"

Abby peered at her name tag. "Ms.—Pereira, is it?—I gather you were on duty last night?"

Mrs. Pereira replied, "Yes, I—"

"Then perhaps you can enlighten me about how my father managed, in his advanced state of confusion and mental deterioration, to make his way out of a locked facility and find himself at large?"

Hoo, boy. When Abby started in on the ten-dollar words and subordinate clauses, there was going to be hell to pay.

Mister Tankhouse ventured, "Perhaps an orangutan?" His smile had more fear in it than jocularity. "I believe there are some in the zoo. They might be strong enough to force those bars open."

Abby snapped, "A kitten could break those bars! Look at how rusty they are!"

I said, "They weren't a couple of nights ago."

Mister Tankhouse put in, "The bars are cold-forged steel, top of the line. We had them installed after the brown bear got in." He shook his head sorrowfully.

"It was just a baby," I said. "I gave it a bit of Dad's salmon and it nodded right off to sleep. Mrs. Pereira, do you know exactly what time it was that Dad disappeared?"

"It would show on the video."

Mr. Tankhouse said, "It most certainly would. Might you ladies perhaps like to see the playback from the camera monitoring your father's room?"

Abby blew out an exasperated sigh. "You keep camera surveillance on the rooms? Well, why didn't you say that in the first place?"

We gathered around the video monitor in Mr. Tankhouse's office. He flipped the playback on. Took me a second before the image on the small, low-res black-and-white screen began to look familiar. It was Dad's room, all right. The spider's-eye view from the camera mounted in one corner of the ceiling was throwing my perspective off. My heart twisted a little in me when I saw Dad. He was sitting upright in bed, the bedsheets pulled up over his legs. He paid no attention to the restraints around his wrists. The bulk of him nearly filled the small twin bed. He picked at the sheets repeatedly with one hand. His blank gaze was fixed at a point somewhere halfway up the wall. It tore at me to see him so absent from himself.

"What's he staring at?" Mr. Tankhouse asked Mrs. Pereira.

Abby frowned. "He likes to watch TV," she replied. "At least, it seems to capture his attention. Not the nature shows, though. Those send him into a fury half the time."

They did. Dad couldn't bear the least inaccuracy in those programmes. He knew the living world too well. He loved watching Japanese tentacle hentai, though. For humans, it was porn. For Dad, it was high comedy. I'd snuck a few DVDs of it in for him once or twice. Watched it with him. He would cheer right up. His laugh still sounded like him. But in the past few months, he'd been losing the ability to keep his attention on the images.

Abby said, "I came to sit with him right after class. Like I was supposed to. Got him to take his dinner and his meds."

We watched our demented dad on the screen, twisting the sheets.

Mrs. Pereira looked at Abby with no expression at all, then took my hand in both of hers and patted it. "You've been very good to him, Makeda."

She was making me uncomfortable. "Abby visits him, too. She's just got a lot more going on than I have." All kinds of people paid to have Abby come and perform for them, teach and lecture. Hers was a small world, but she was queen of it.

Abby frowned. She pointed at the monitor screen. "What's he doing?"

In low-res black and white, the miniature image of our Dad hadn't changed position much, but there was a definite difference; his whole body was at attention now. His hands no longer plucked at the sheets, but gripped the bed railings at either side. Not for very long. Too many straight lines and right angles to them, even though they were rounded right angles. His mouth had snapped shut, and he was staring intently at the window. That was the most shocking shift; everything he was doing now, he was doing with intent.

Whoops. What had just happened on the screen? I jutted my chin at the monitor. "He's trying to get free!" I said.

He was pulling at the strap around one wrist.

"Those restraints are foolproof," Tankhouse told us. "I don't see how he could have removed them."

Dad gave up after a second and looked frantically around the room. The intelligence in his eyes nearly broke my heart. He hadn't looked like that in years. Even though it had prompted him to escape, I was almost thankful for whatever it was that had brought him back into himself, even briefly.

A snaking web of black lines fell across the screen. Behind it, a square white flash fell downwards.

"Did you see that?" asked Tankhouse. As we watched, the lines on the screen thickened—some of them flattening out into trilobed leaf shapes—till we couldn't quite make out what was happening behind them.

"Oh, my," said Mrs. Pereira.

"Oh," said Abby.

A few seconds later the screen jerked, and the web of stuff fell away. Dad was no longer in the bed, and near as we could tell, the room was empty. There were tiny black marks dotting the screen.

"Son of a gun," said Abby.

I'd realized the same thing she had. "Was that—?" I began. Abby flashed me the Look. I didn't finish the question.

"There was nothing covering the camera when we checked his room after he went missing," said Mrs. Pereira. For the first time today, she sounded flustered.

I said, "Mr. Tankhouse, can you go back a few seconds? To just before the television fell? That white square?"

After some fumbling back and forth, he found the spot on the playback.

"Pause it, please."

He did. There was a blur in one corner of the screen. Our view of the television was obscured by what looked like a long, many-fingered shadow about to fall on it. Only slivers of the screen were visible.

"*Monstera*?" I asked Abby.

"Use your eyes. It was *Pueraria*."

Right. The outlines of the stems and leaves that had swelled on the monitor screen had been wrong for *Monstera*. I exclaimed, "Grape hard candies!" The others stared at me. "That's what Dad's room smelled like just now." Abby gave a tiny shake of her head to warn me not to say anything more. *Pueraria*—kudzu—blossoms smelled like grape candies. If he was going to get one of his plants to help him escape, it made sense that he'd ask a *Pueraria*. That stuff could grow a foot a day all on its natural. Even with his mojo as severely limited as it was, Dad could work literal miracles with plants. But it was easier to enhance their natural tendencies than work against them. At least, so he'd told me. Sure, he could sometimes make a bougainvillea thrive in the winter, but a Douglas fir would be much happier with the arrangement, and thus more cooperative. Some people talk to their plants. With Dad, the plants talked back. I didn't know quite what to do with the perilous joy, the hope. Dad hadn't been able to so much as sprout a seedling for a couple of years now. In fact, we'd been regularly bringing him *Pueraria* infusions from the vine of it that grew outside Suze's place. It seemed to have some small effect against Alzheimer's. Dad had taken to fondly calling the vine Quashee.

"Mr. Tankhouse," I said, "you have both our phone numbers,

yes?" He nodded. "Then please call us the minute you have any news."

"Oh, dear," he whiffled, "the temperature's supposed to drop below freezing tonight."

"I know that!" I growled. "Don't you think I know that?"

Abby's voice was already well below freezing, "Our family will find him before then. I consider our contract with you terminated as of this moment."

"Abs, that's a bit hasty, don't you think?" If Dad came back home, I'd be practically on 24/7 caretaking duty. I couldn't go back to that. It filled me with shame that I couldn't, but there it was. Mr. Tankhouse looked relieved at first, then quickly schooled his features to show regret. "I'm so sorry," he said. "Mr. Joli was one of our more *lively* guests. But if you feel you must, I do understand."

Abby stumped out the door of the room. I followed her. Then we had to talk to the police, give them a bunch of details. I'd shivered myself and my jeans dry by the time we were done. As I warmed up, the scent of Lars began to emanate from the sweatshirt. It was like man-sweat with a charged vacuum-tube tang of superheated amps.

I marvelled again that my sis was dating a guitar. I couldn't dwell on that right now, though.

Once we were done with the police, Abby and I took the elevator down to the first floor. My purse with my cash in it was at Brie's place. I borrowed a few bucks off Abby and bought myself a candy bar and a pop from the vending machine at reception. We exited the home in silence. I waited until we were outside and well away from the building, heading for the parking lot. Then I asked Abby, "Why'd you give Dad a kudzu plant?" I knew I hadn't.

She frowned. "I didn't. You know how he feels about stuff like that."

I did know. Dad loved kudzu, kept a small vine of it growing indoors at home. But he had been very careful about not letting it spread. He would incinerate the few blossoms and seed pods that his tame plant produced, even though kudzu rarely propagated that way. The plant wasn't native to Canada. Its vines grew at an enormous rate and would quickly cover and strangle anything in their way, edging out the native flora. The new Dad probably didn't even remember what kudzu was. I said, "So somehow he got some. Is that how he got down three floors?" I banished the image from my mind of my dad, heavy but frail and more than half out of his mind, clambering down the outside of a building on a rope of green vines.

Abby replied, "But how'd he make it grow so quickly?"

She had a point. Sure, Dad was a genius gardener by claypicken standards. But stuck in flesh as he was, he'd have a hard time making a plant grow and move as quickly as that kudzu apparently had.

I gasped. "Abs, do you think they've finally set him free? The Family?"

She gave me an odd look. "No. They haven't."

"But how can you be sure? Maybe they decided that his punishment was over, and they let him out of that body, and now he's a full celestial again and he can do plant magic like he used to!" And if they'd done that, maybe they'd release Mom as well. Maybe that's why they'd helped me back at the lake? All was forgiven? Please, please, let it be so.

"Stop it! They didn't. He can't. I just know, okay? So drop it. We have to find him."

That was just like her. Keeping secrets, dumping ash on my hopes. Keeping me tame. "Fine," I replied. "Be like that. But what do we do now? Gods, I'm so sorry I wasn't here!"

"You're always fucking sorry! Do you know what I was doing last night? Marking about a million papers. Earning the money that pays for keeping Dad in care. We can't depend on Uncle all the time. Don't you think I'd like to have a carefree evening some-times, too? I can't work and look after Dad!"

She saw my crestfallen face. Hers fell to match it. "Oh, Maka. I don't mean to bust your hump. You do the lion's share of looking after him. Let's just find him, all right?"

"Sure." Her too-ready apology had left me still feeling like a shit. I followed her across the full parking lot. I looked around for Lars, but I didn't see him, and I didn't ask. Kinda didn't want to confirm whether the two of them were actually an item. It was too weird.

The sun was out, sprouting tiny rainbows in the puddles of brown water that dotted the parking lot. But tonight, all those puddles would become blocks of ice. If Dad didn't have shelter, his ailing body might not withstand temperatures below freezing. I knew what we had to do. Reluctantly I said, "I guess we should go ask the Family whether they've seen him."

Abby literally started. "What? Why? Can't we just let the police handle it?" She looked scared for some reason.

"What's up with you? I'm the one who doesn't travel there well, not you. And I'm the one they hate." Then I understood. "It's that Lars, isn't it? The tool."

"Hush. Don't call him that." She looked around, probably to see whether Lars was in earshot.

"No problem, my bad. But you know that even if I don't call him that, Dad's folks will. You guys really are dating, aren't you? And you're afraid they'll find out. That's why you don't want to go to the palais."

The fright on her face would have melted a statue's heart. Com-pletely ruined my enjoyment of the moment. "C'mon, Abs. I won't tell them." For all their power, the old guys didn't know everything. It was possible sometimes to keep secrets from them.

She searched my face, then straightened her shoulders. "You know what? *I'll* tell them. I mean, it's not like our paternal relations are the best dating prospects out there, and anyway, they're not the boss of us. Right?"

Had she gone nuts? "Wrong. They totally are. Our uncle is pretty much the Grim Reaper, remember?"

"Will you stop it, already? I'm trying to have a moment here. Anyway, Uncle won't mind me dating an inspirited instrument. He's not stoosh that way. So let's do this, before I change my mind."

I shrugged. "Your funeral."

"Will you stop that?"

I hushed and went along with her. My ears were ringing from lack of sleep, and my heart was wrung with worry about Dad. Plus I had just rented a place on my own for the first time, and had maybe been slipped some Rohypnol by my new neighbour and coworker. This last twenty-four hours had been entirely too full.

Abby's car was parked in the fifth row of the lot. "Taking up hiking?" I asked.

"Some bastard took the last disabled space just as I was driving up."

"His car didn't have a 'handicapped' sticker?"

"Her car. No, it didn't. I fixed her wagon, though. Shattered her brake lights."

"Red glass?" I asked, fancifully imagining the shards being washed into the storm drains by the rain, then tumbled through the sewers all the way down to the lake. A delighted nessieform Mom finding them gleaming on the lake bottom. Mumbling them delicately up with her monster's muzzle and spiriting them to her lair, which I envisioned as a hidden, semi-submerged cave. Adding the pieces to her precious stash of glittering reds, oranges, blues, even a pink or lavender nugget or two.

"Plastic," Abby replied. For a second I didn't know what she was talking about, so lost I'd been in my reverie. "They don't make brake lights of glass any more."

"Oh." I shrugged. Didn't matter, anyway. Took decades for the lake to grind broken glass into smooth, frosted lumps. "Didn't know you could break plastic like that."

"I wish. I used this." She lifted one crutch up and mimed jabbing it at a brake light. "Sure, you can sing anything to splinters if you hit the right note. But some of those notes are beyond the range of the human voice."

We were at her car, the one that Dad had deeded to her along with the house. With the seizures I used to have, he'd figured it wasn't safe for me to drive. I hadn't had any seizures for years now, but chickenshit Abby didn't want to take the chance and let me use the car.

I loved that ride. It was a 1950 Plymouth station wagon, the kind with a body and dash made of real wood. Uncle had found it years ago, in the barn of a solitary old soul he'd gone to collect up in Kapuskasing. Dry rot had gotten into parts of the body, but Dad knew how to handle wood. He pretty much rebuilt the Plymouth, using local woods to replace the rotted bits. He'd left it to me to get the engine working, since I could handle all those acute metal angles without wincing. Dad found the woody wagon easier to ride around in than in other cars. Some day I would get my license, and then Abby would have to share the car with me. Pity I hadn't already done so. If I'd been able to drive, it would have kept my mind off the trip we were about to make. I went over to the passenger side, Abby to the driver's. She unlocked her door and tossed me the keys over the body of the car.

"Why d'you do it that way?" came a quiet, buzzy voice from behind me. Startled, I spun around, fist cocked. I barely managed not to clock Lars. Though I doubt the blow would have seriously connected, seeing the thick arm he'd instantly put up to block me. "Don't *do* that!" I said to him. "Don't sneak up on me!"

"Sorry."

Abby gave him a fond smile. "It's hard for me to let her in from the driver's seat. I'd have to lean over and stretch one arm out to open the door. It's hard for me to lean like that if I can't use both hands to support me."

He replied, "You could just open the passenger door first, then go around and let yourself in after."

"Or," I put in, "she could get me a spare set of keys." I scanned the parking lot for anything out of the ordinary. Second time today I'd forgotten to be watchful. Stupid, stupid.

"Get in the car, Maks."

I let myself in. Lars closed the car door behind me. Abby handed her crutches to me from her side. I stashed them across the backseat as she lowered herself behind the steering wheel. I handed her back her keys. We both knew why we did this particular choreography to get into her car. The first time she'd tried letting me in first, a haint had been after me. I'd made it into the car safely enough, but by the time she'd hobbled around to the driver's side and started putting her crutches in, the blasted thing had broken the passenger side window and hauled me halfway back out again. Sometimes I still dreamt about its claws digging into my upper arms; the heavy stench of its breath, muddy-sweet as stale blood.

Abby motioned to me to roll the window down so she could talk to Lars. "We're going to the palais to ask after Dad. You want to come?" Another person would probably only hear bravery in her voice, but I could pick out the tiny tremolos of trepidation.

Lars said, "Wow. You really think that's wise? I don't fancy being unmade."

She gasped. "Gods, I hadn't even thought of that. Yeah, better not."

Lars was right. There were those in our bloody family who really would kill him if they had a mind to. They considered the likes of inspirited objects such as Lars and Cheerful Rest to be reflected glory, not real life.

Lars went around to Abby's side of the car. When she rolled the window down, he reached in and touched her face. "I'll escort you part of the way. Then I'll see you later."

"Okay." She took his hand and kissed it. The sight unsettled me. No matter how enlightened I wanted to be, I couldn't quite shake the reaction that it was kind of like me pitching woo to my workbench.

Lars strode off to get his motorbike. I said to Abby, "If Dad had become an old one again, would he let us know that he was all right?"

"I told you, he hasn't!"

"If you say so," I replied glumly. "I'm only saying we don't know how he'll act when that happens. I mean, once he's practically a god again, would he bother so much with his human daughters? It's not like the rest of them love us so much. Maybe he would become more like them."

"We don't know that."

Lars roared up behind us on his bike. Abby started the car.

"Abs, stop at a drugstore first. Gotta pick up some Gravol." For travel sickness. The journey to the courtyard was going to turn my stomach, in more ways than one.

"You should try a piece of nutmeg under your tongue. Better for you than all those chemicals."

"Just please take me to a drugstore."

"Yeah, yeah. Did I say I wasn't going to?" We pulled out of the parking lot. I looked back. Lars was following.

"So," I said, "Jimi's guitar, huh?"

"Yeah." She smiled bashfully.

I ignored the spike of jealousy. "How long have you guys been seeing each other?"

"About six months."

"How come you didn't tell me?"

"Didn't think you'd care."

I looked at my feet. "Haint attacked me earlier today," I said.

"*Oh, no!*" she replied in the language that only she and I shared. "*Was it bad?*"

With a will, I kept my voice nonchalant. "*Nah, I handled it. Scary, though. I didn't notice it creeping up on me.*"

"*Christ on a crutch, Maka! Why'd you let your guard down like that? You know you can't afford to.*"

"*Get off me.*"

"*Did you have your medicine with you, at least?*"

"*Come on, Ab. What're you, my mother?*" I didn't tell her that I'd left the bottle at home. It's not like I'd planned to spend a night away.

Abby reached into her jeans pocket, pulled out my vial of tincture, and handed it to me.

"*You went into my room?*"

"*You keep it in the bathroom, remember?*"

I took it from her without another word. I opened it and tried to swallow the requisite two mouthfuls without tasting them. I didn't quite succeed. I swear, the stuff tasted like armadillo scat mixed with swamp water. I made a face. "Gah." When I was young, I used to think that "vial" and "vile" were the same word. "I'm getting low on this stuff," I said in English.

"I know." She managed to look even more worried than before. This was one of the last few bottles of the tincture. Dad used to brew it. No one else seemed to be able to make the ingredients work properly together. Uncle had tried it once, and I'd had the belly runnings for two days.

"It doesn't have to be a big deal," I reassured Abby. "I've figured it out. I'll just go to a claypicken doctor. The science of antirejection meds has probably progressed a ton since we were kids."

"Shows what you know." She sounded almost as though she were crying.

"Well," I said huffily, "forgive me for trying to use my very own brain to solve my very own problems."

She didn't reply for a few seconds. Then she said, "You're probably right. Just try a human doctor. It'll be fine."

"I'm saying. Besides, it's time I start living more in the claypicken world, since I pretty much am one."

"Uh-huh."

Wow. Did she have to agree so easily? Oh, whatever. It was Abs, after all. "Funny thing is, I think one of Dad's kin helped me escape the haint."

"Really?"

"Yeah." I described the fortuitous, strangely responsive storm to her.

"Weird. That sounds like Cathy. Or Cousin Flash."

I nodded. "That's what I thought. But why would any of that lot give me a hand? They hate me."

"They don't hate you. They just—"

"They just don't think I'm worth the ground I walk on. I know. Hey; how'd you know to send Lars down by the lake for me, anyway?"

"Butter told me you were there. Luckily, she made it back before the downpour started. If she'd gotten wet, I'd never have heard the last of it."

"Butter tracked me to the lake?"

"She's been keeping an eye on you ever since I got her."

"Your *cat* shadows me?"

"Yup."

"Did you tell her to do that?"

"No. It was her idea. She likes you. She likes to make sure you're all right."

I flounced back against the seat and crossed my arms. "She's a spy. I am *so* never going to buy her liver treats any more." The hell with this crap. I'd found a home where people saw me for the adult I was.

And where my new neighbour, Brie, had the Shine. Holy crap. That green glow I'd seen behind him. I'd just been too stoned or whatever last night to recognize it for what it was. What the hell was Brie? He wasn't one of the old guys; I'd have recognized him. No matter what human guise they wore, even I could tell who they were. Maybe he was like Lars? If so, what was that last night with the music that sent people into a trance state? Did Brie use mojo on his audiences?

Abby turned into a parking lot. We were at a drugstore. I opened my door, then remembered that I still didn't have my wallet. "Uh," I said, "could I—?"

Abby rolled her eyes, shoved a hand into the pocket of her skirt, and handed me a few bills.

"Thanks."

Lars pulled up behind us. I was glad that he was coming even part of the way. He and I had just met, but he'd been the only person to say anything halfway pleasant to me all day. I went over to him. "Just a quick stop," I said. "Gotta pick up some things I need."

"Sure." To my surprise, he got off his bike and followed me into the store.

I said, "Hey; did you see the thing chasing me earlier today?"

"Yeah. Why I followed you in here. Because it might come back."

"What'd it look like to you?"

"Like something bad wearing a skin suit. The suit was like

a mask, you know? I didn't need to pay mind to what the mask looked like. I could see the Shine coming off your little boggart."

"Interesting. Most people just see my haint as something normal. A kid, a dog."

"I'm not people."

"Fair enough."

Lars went over to a rack of CDs labelled "Summer Tunes." He pulled one of them off the rack and examined it, scowling. "Remastered, my ass," he grumbled.

A claypicken guy who'd been flipping through the CDs, too, said, "I know, dude! Give me an old record any day, right?"

Lars eyed him. "Live was better."

The guy laughed. "I guess." He glanced at the CD that Lars was holding. "But I wasn't alive yet back when that guy was recording."

Lars smiled. "Neither was I."

I grabbed some antinausea meds from a nearby shelf. "I need one more thing," I told him. As I wandered in search of the right aisle, I asked, "So, you and Abby seem to be getting along." I cringed inwardly at the whiff of cattish jealousy in my voice. Dating was complicated for me and Abby. We'd run through all the family members we could stand, on both sides of the Family. It wasn't a huge pool. That pretty much left humans to whom we weren't related. Which was okay for fucking, but for the long term, not so much. Try explaining to your human lover that you're not talking to thin air, but to your uncle, the invisible Lord of Death. It doesn't go down too well.

Lars's giggle when I asked about him and Abby was a creamy cascade of harmonics. It made me want to smile, too. "We're like a house on fire," he said.

I checked the aisles where they sold the seasonal stuff. Sure enough, the summer kitsch was already crowding the shelves. Lawn chairs. Coolers. Giant Super Soaker water guns. I picked out one of the guns. It was a cheery green, reeking of new plastic. "This'll keep the haint away. Once I load it up with water, that is."

Lars didn't bat an eyelid. "I saw gallon bottles of water a couple aisles over. I'll take you there."

As I followed him, I aimed at the back of his neck with the giant water gun. A little girl wearing a jacket with a picture of a Disney princess on it scowled at me and shook her head. She couldn't have been more than seven. Sheepishly, I lowered the Super Soaker. "Damn it," I said to Lars, "I can't pretend. I'm jealous."

Lars was squatting to reach some huge containers of distilled water that were on the bottom shelves. "Come again? Jealous of whom?"

"Abby. She gets the cool life and the hot dates."

He grinned up at me. "And you don't? Nah, that can't be."

"Really, not so much."

"Ah, c'mon. You're just taking the piss. Who wouldn't want to get with you? These three jugs enough?"

"Yeah, those'll do. As to my dating life, you know how it is. When other Shinies find out that I don't have mojo, it's game over."

He stood up with the jugs. "What d'you mean, you don't have mojo? I can smell it on you."

"That's not cute," I growled, "making fun of me like that. I know what I am."

"I'm not kidding. I smell it on you. You've got a sprinkle of fairy dust, all right."

I stopped dead in the drugstore and stared at him. People brushed past us. I scarcely noticed them. My scalp was prickling. My arms had gone cold. The nose of the Super Soaker banged gently against my calf. "What kind is it?" I whispered. "What can I do?"

Lars boggled. "How can you not know?"

"Nobody ever told me!"

"Nobody can tell you what your mojo is. You know how to work it the way your heart knows how to beat." Then his face fell. "Oh, hell, I'm rubbish. I've probably told you something I wasn't supposed to, haven't I?"

"You can *smell* mojo? Can Abby smell it? Can my dad, and my uncle?"

"Dunno. Never thought to ask. Like I said, it kinda comes with the territory. Look, maybe I'd better shut it about this now. You should ask your sister what you want to know, yeah?"

I'd had it. I exploded. "Why does everybody treat me like I'm too dumb to live? I have something this big going on, and people have been keeping it from me?"

"Hey, don't drag me into this!" said Lars. "I only just met you and Abby!"

Other people in the aisle were trying to look casual as they edged away from us. Nothing cleared a room faster than a black man and woman arguing. I took a deep breath. I was so furious, my hands were shaking. "Fine," I snapped. "I'll ask Abby. Let's just go." I turned on my heel and headed for the checkout counter.

Great, just great. I'd had mojo all the time, but I couldn't even figure it out on my own. A freaking *guitar* had to come along and enlighten me. No wonder Dad's side of the Family treated me like an impostor. And my own immediate family hadn't seen fit to tell me. Dad. Uncle, who apparently could lie when he bloody well chose. Abby, literally my own flesh. All three of them all these years smugly flaunting their grand personal magics and watching me flounder, directionless. My heart swelled with the betrayal of it and beat angrily at my chest wall. The pounding climbed up into my throat. It drummed in my ears. A dull, pulsing ache began behind my eyes. I didn't trust myself to speak. It would come out as a roar. I paid for my purchases. Blindly grabbed a candy bar from the display beside the cash register and paid for that, too. Stalked back out to the car with Lars scurrying to keep up.

Back at the car, I told Lars to put the water bottles in the front, where my feet would be. Quietly, he obliged, and then scurried back to his bike. I got in and slammed the door. Abby gave me a curious look. "What's up?" she asked.

"Nothing." I handed her her change.

"No, keep it."

"Fine." I pocketed the money. Abby started the car.

Bloody Shinies were so closemouthed about their pretty, gleaming world. They were the masters of not answering the question. Evasion, misdirection, bait and switch; whatever carrot would distract my dull donkey brain and lead my clodhopping feet away from their golden paths. I pushed a couple of the anti-sick tabs out of their plastic and swallowed them down with a sip from one of the water bottles at my feet.

I knew the city pretty well, but we'd woven through so many back roads that I was thoroughly turned around. And bored. I started filling the Super Soaker from the bottles of water. Not easy to do in a moving car. I'd slopped a fair bit of water over my knees before I was done. I was so over being wet today!

Abby drove with no hesitation about which way to go. No way I could have told where the Family courtyard would be this time, but finding it'd be a breeze for her. Between clenched teeth, I asked her, "Can you smell how to get to the courtyard?"

"What? No, I just know the way. What's the matter with you?"

"But you can smell mojo."

"Yeah, so?" She took a U-turn, went up someone's driveway and across their lawn, then through an alleyway on the other side.

"Lars says I smell of mojo. Why didn't you tell me that it had a smell?"

She started, but kept her eyes on the road. "Maybe the smell's just rubbed off on you from me and Dad and Uncle." Her voice was shaking.

I slammed my hand against the dashboard. Abby jumped. "Don't confuse me with your new boyfriend! I am not some kind of tool!"

"You just watch your mouth!" she snarled.

"All this time, you and Dad and Uncle Jack have known that I have some kind of mojo? What the hell, Abs? Did you guys keep the truth from me as some extra-special torture that the three of you dreamed up to torment me with?"

"You know we would never do that. You don't understand—"

"I can't understand if you won't tell me! Does that mean that everyone on Dad's side of the Family can smell it, too?" My shouting was reverberating off the walls of the closed car. Abby winced.

"Hon, calm down. We can talk about this later, all right?"

"No, it's not all right! What in bloody hell is my mojo, and why can't I work it?" I felt a tear roll down my cheek. "What's wrong with me, that I can't access my own mojo?"

This alleyway was really long. Suddenly, the bottom fell out of my belly, as though the car had dropped into a hole. But we were still on level road, travelling smoothly. I swallowed my gorge back down. "Oh, shit. It's starting, isn't it?"

She nodded. "Yeah, we're getting close. We're gonna have to press pause on our fight for a bit, I'm afraid."

"Fuck." I took a deep breath. I gripped the undersides of my seat hard. "Couldn't you have warned me?"

"Don't need to, do I? You keep telling me you don't need my help."

"Eat shit, Ab."

"Try to relax."

"Easy for you to say." Now I'd have to wait to find out from Abs what kind of mojo I had. She was getting her way, as usual.

My stomach gave another sickening lurch, and the transit into the other world took hold of me.

A white mist enveloped the car. The outside sounds ceased. It was like we were driving through cotton. My senses were fucked up. I smelt chartreuse, heard the light of the sun falling like knives of obsidian. My body turned itself inside out, my skin rubbing against itself, my organs flopping to the outside to bobble like so many lumpy calabashes hanging by their stems from the trunk of their tree. Every time this happened, I swore I could feel the place where the doctors had cut into me to give me a piece of Abby's liver from which to grow my own. Touch was a taste and smell a sight. I groaned, inwardly cursed Abby for doing this to me, cursed my dad for sending us looking for him, cursed all the powers that were.

Nearly there, sang Abby. Her voice ran bright in my veins, multifaceted, like diamonds. Whenever Abby took me through this transit, her voice was the only sense the world made. Only Abby was kinda ticked at me right now. If she should abandon me halfway! Panicked, I reached for her, to hold fast to my lifeline through this horror. My hands, trapped inside the sausage of my skin, scrabbled at each other instead. A torn edge of nail on my pinkie scraped the back of my other hand. Broke skin. The scratch welled blood, which whispered the words to "Michael, Row Your Boat Ashore," except that the first, second, third, fifth, eighth, thirteenth words, et cetera were each baby aspirins, in a synaesthetic Fibonacci sequence of pain relief inadequate to my current requirements. "Abby!" I screamed into my skin. Have you ever yelled with your head in a bucket? I nearly deafened myself. Except that I was tasting sounds, not hearing them. Instead of blowing my eardrums out, I came close to choking on a tsunami flavour blast of wasabi and fried eggs.

Oh, chill already, sang Abby in her crystalline voice, the only sensation that rang true for me in transit. *I'm here.* Plucked electric chords twanged behind her voice. *So'm I*, they said. *We won't lose you.* Lars, accompanying Abby. That shocked me into calm. I'd never heard any voice but Abby's in transit before, not even Dad's. With his circus mind, Lars walked with us through the clouds. For Jimi's guitar, synaesthesia was probably just business as usual. Touch the sky. 'Scuse me. Kiss this guy. My ass. Wherever my ass was at the moment. Effortlessly, Lars plucked notes from the aether like picking ticks from a favourite dog's fur.

I sat—at least, I think I was still sitting—in the car—I hoped it was still a car—and focused on the beacon of sound that Lars and Abby were creating. His music and hers sparred, teased each other, flirted. Even their discords made deliberate, playful harmony. They were at home in this bodiless space between the worlds. Me, I was ever the donkey, needing solid ground beneath my feet to make even poor sense of the world. "Great. That's just wonderful," I grumbled.

"Thank you," rumbled Lars, misunderstanding. I sighed. My grumpy exhalation was soap bubbles popping in my ears.

My senses didn't go back to normal, exactly. It was more like they recalibrated. But that was transit for you. It began to seem normal to smell the sound of the car's engine, to hear the dull navy blue of its interior. The flashing indicator light tasted like lemon juice being dripped onto my tongue, and that was fine by me. My stomach settled. It was no longer misty outside. Or perhaps it was. Perhaps what had been mist a few minutes ago I was now experiencing as a tattoo of drums, filling the space. For we were in a space both enclosed and infinite. That plush fun fur tickle behind my eyes was Lars saying, *Here's where I leave you guys. See you when you get back.*

My ears popped and my perceptions shifted once more. The synaesthesia remained, but now, like the image on a transparency smoothed over a paper page, sight was once more sight, sound sound. But different. It's difficult to explain. Claypicken eyes saw the world as it was. Spirit eyes—well, mine were kinda myopic. Maybe donkeys could only see in a limited spectrum. Everything emerged at me through a gunmetal fog. Perspective was off. An object might be small enough to hold in my hand, or big enough to run me over. I could never tell which unless I got up close to it. And I might be right beside it, or miles away. If miles meant anything in the spirit world. I sort of thought not. For me, the spirit world was always fuzzy, dark. Like a nightmare of nighttime. Abby and I were no longer in her car, but standing beside each other and facing a peristyle, a shout of a pole that extended up and up, drummed as high above us as the breeze of blessing that was the drums could carry it, and higher. I perceived Abby as a shimmering arpeggio, lavender shot through with juniper green and scented with a bouquet of seawater and new shoe leather. I wondered how she saw me.

You know those drawings of the superhero the Flash when he's running? Multiple iterations of him, all spread out in a wavy line? That's how the whole family looked to me, not just Uncle Flash. Except the comic-book Flash travels in a single line. These guys were all going in all directions at the same time. Made my claypicken eyes queasy, so I didn't focus on it too much. They were all so zigzaggy that they were, for all intents and purposes, glowing balls of forever. And glowing lines of forever at the same time. See? I said it was difficult to explain. Their radiant selves filled the fogspace that was the best sense I could make of the infinite. I should have found it bright as daylight in there. Abby once told me that to her it was. To me it was twilight. Full moon on a foggy night. Bright and dark simultaneously, refusing to be distinct. I just knew that if I ever saw it clearly, my insides would turn out and I'd never stop throwing up. Got a headache yet? I sure had. So, to simplify it, imagine a boiling night sky with sheet lightning tumbling out of the clouds. That'll do as an image. Now fill everything you can see in every direction with it. You're not sure whether you're standing on firm ground, falling into nothingness, or floating. You might be upside down, right side up, or, yeah; you might be inside out. Whatever. Deal with it. I had to.

I reached for Abby's hand. Touching her grounded me a little, and gave my poor inner ear a break.

To my claypicken eyes, we both were and weren't in a basement, white-painted brick industrial. Plain. Some nondescript building in the city, then, that rented its space out to these worshippers. Probably owned by someone who was quietly also a devotee. Someone who wouldn't freak at the sounds of drumming, the occasional chicken feather that escaped the cleanup process. The owner might even be part of the congregation I could see right now through earth eyes.

"This isn't a good time," growled General Gun, crouched beside the human drummers: dark men of flesh, their faces stripped lean of anything but music. Abby nodded in acknowledgement at the human music-makers. At the moment, the General was wearing fatigues, a helmet, heavy laced boots. He carried a Kalashnikov. "We're working here." He deliberately addressed his comments only to Abby, not me.

"Dad's missing," Abby said to Uncle Gun. "Have you seen him?"

◊ ◊ ◊

Baby Abby came back to us from the other side a living being who could grow and thrive on her own. Of course the Family knew immediately what the brothers had done. Abby shouldn't have been alive. Those were some big-ass laws they broke. There were to be consequences. Since Dad had been willing to do all that for a human, they made him into one. They stripped his godsoul away from him, leaving him purely claypicken. (You do realize that Dad and his family had been among the first humans of the world? When the Big Boss decided he wanted some managerial staff, they volunteered for the job.) Dad would have to spend a whole human lifetime with only the tricksy pinch of mojo that claypickens can sometimes muster if they chance upon exactly the right charms, potions, and prayers in exactly the right configuration at exactly the right time. His godsoul would return to him when the flesh body died.

After all, Abby would need someone to look after her until she was grown; someone who wasn't too busy looking after every other living thing. Because Grandma Ocean had seen to Mom. Grandma's province is the waters of the world, salt and sweet both. She tossed Mom over her shoulder into one of them, and didn't even look back to see which one she'd landed in. She didn't deprive my mother of life, but of the beautiful form with which, Grandma convinced herself, Mom had bewitched her sons. Loch Ness has Nessie, its monster of fame and fable. Okanagan Lake has Naitaka a.k.a. Ogopogo, a snake demon. As with them, no one has ever found proof that the monster that people began sighting in Lake Ontario just under thirty years ago really exists. She does have a name, though, and it's Cora. I call her Mom, or I would, if I ever met her.

And Uncle Jack? Or John, or whichever of his monikers he chose to use at any given time? Well, his family couldn't do anything incapacitating to him, as they had to Dad. If they did, it would bung up the claypicken wheel of life and death. No one would be able to get on or off, and pretty soon the Big Boss would come looking for the cause of the constipation, and though he (or she, or they, or it) might or might not be green, they say he's a big fella, bigger than all Creation, and you sure as hell wouldn't like him when he was angry.

So for his transgressions against the tabus of death and life, the Family punished my Uncle in the worst way they could think of; they left him unharmed. His curse was to carry the knowledge of the fate he had helped bring down on his dear brother and on my mother.

That's how the story went that Uncle used to tell me and Abby when we *were kids and he was babysitting and had run out of other ways to keep us occupied. He made it sound almost jolly. At least romantic. Because Uncle likes to keep things lighthearted. It's important to him to always have a smile on his face. It keeps his spirits up, and sometimes it prevents people from being too scared when it's their time and he shows up to ferry them over to the other side. Though sometimes his death's-head grin just makes them shit their pants with terror. But, as Uncle says, you win some, you lose some.*

3

♦ ♦ ♦

GENERAL GUN TURNED HIS cold iron eyes Abby's way. "Boysie's gone AWOL, has he?"

"Yes, and he's too sick to be wandering on his own. We thought he might have come looking for family. Part of him probably remembers you guys."

If I were Dad and I remembered that lot, I'd have run as far as possible in the opposite direction.

Gun shrugged. "Do you see him here?"

Apparently he now considered us dismissed, because he turned his back on us and returned to forging red-hot steel on an anvil. In the space between one instant and the next, his chest had gone bare. The sweat beading his dark skin flickered red, reflecting the incandescent metal he was working. Each upper arm was thicker around than both my thighs together. He pounded his hammer on the anvil in time with the beating of the palais drums. The motion made the muscles of his pecs and biceps jump. I was pretty sure he wasn't making a ploughshare.

Over the knell of the hammer, Abby called, "Do you know where he is, Uncle?"

General Gun just shook his head no. He was wearing a beret and army drab now, sitting at a heavy metal desk. He was too busy writing a cover-up of a massacre to pay attention to us. I managed to squeak out, "Maybe you could help us to look for him?"

It was the hunter of the lot who answered. "Why should we do anything of the sort?" Uncle Hunter was carrying a briefcase in this instant. He wore a snappy suit, had a cell phone clipped to his waist in a tasteful leather hard-shell case. "I've been doing his job just fine, haven't I, Ma?"

And there was Grandma Ocean, her godsoul piggybacking on that of a big, beautiful woman who was sitting in the front pew. Grandma nodded indulgently at her son. "You know so, darling." Her horse flipped open a fancy yellow lace fan to cool her face with.

Hunter smirked. He knew he was one of his mother's favourites. He flipped the cuff of the suit off his wrist to check his watch, just as his form changed: leather outback hat, khakis.

In the courtyard a live white chicken, held aloft by its bound feet, was being swung in a huge circle by the officiating claypicken woman. Blood from the chicken's severed neck spattered the chanting celebrants. One of them, a woman who'd been singing the invocation in a high, strong soprano, gasped when the blessing splashed the left side of her face. She stiffened, then began to tremble. Her eyes rolled back in her head. She slumped. The celebrants near her leapt to support her. In overlay, I saw the chicken's flung life-blood cohere into a shape that enveloped her. It dropped when she dropped. When her friends picked her back up again, she seemed much taller than she had been. Her limbs had gone skeletally thin. She laughed, and her voice was deep and hollow. She had offered entrance to the guardian, our uncle Leggy John, sometimes called Jack. "Girls!" came his rattly voice. "I didn't expect to see you here!"

"Uncle!" Abby ran to hug his tall, bony self. In palais space,

Abby could move quicker than thought. I hung back, seething. Never lied, did he? Only all my life, as it turned out.

Uncle John was dressed to party, as he always was. He swirled his cape out of the way, dropped his gold-topped cane, and opened the long reach of his arms to welcome us. In her haste, Abby knocked his top hat off. He just chuckled and reached to pull me to himself, too. Resenting him, resenting myself for giving in to the beloved and familiar, I sank into the dark cave of his embrace. He smelled the way he always had, like the step through a doorway to something unknown on the other side, like the last breath before forever. And like cigars and peppermints. There had to be an explanation for the secret they'd hidden from me all these years. Abby could be spiteful and Dad moody, but Uncle, never.

Uncle said, "I'm afraid I have something awful to tell you. Boysie—"

Abby nodded. "We know. He's gone missing from the nursing home."

Uncle drew back in surprise. "But that's—"

"Jack, we're busy here. Why're you letting the children interrupt us?" It was Aunt Zeely, a vision as usual in flowing blue watered silk that perfectly complemented her earth tones.

Right. As though we *could* interrupt them. As though they weren't all simultaneously doing an infinity of things in an infinity of locations in the present, the past, and the future.

Abby replied, "Like I said, I thought you would tell us where he is. That you might want to help. He's your kin."

"We don't know where he is. We're only multipotent, not omnipotent. Seeing all is for the Big Boss. You know that."

Abs and I shared a look. This was old-time story, but neither one of us had really understood what it meant before this. Abby said, "And the Big Boss won't intervene? Not for his very own kin?"

General Gun hissed. "You want the Big Boss to interfere in the gears that keep the worlds going? You want existence to end?"

"Besides," Grandma Ocean added, "Biggie B. isn't our kin, except in the way that everything in Creation is related. He's our employer."

Abby persisted. "Couldn't you guys, I dunno, ask around? I'm sure you could contact more beings quicker than Maka and I could."

Aunt Zeely replied, "We won't, though."

Abby faced her down. I had to admire her courage. I could scarcely look those folks in the eye without shitting my pants in fear. "You hate Dad that much? Just because he caused us to be?"

Zeely, now a large seal with soft, liquid eyes, honked with laughter. "We don't hate him."

"But he could be in danger!"

"Of what, dear? We're immortal."

"Dad isn't! Not any more!"

Zeely's smile was patronizing. "Of course he is. And the sooner he throws off that hard shell that Ma stuck him into"—she cut her beautiful brown eyes at Ma Ocean—"the sooner he comes back to us whole once more. I, for one, miss him. Not like some here."

Matter-of-factly, Hunter said, "Yeah, I do hate him." Hunter, dressed in denim and wearing a fluorescent orange vest, sighted Abby and me down the length of a modern-day crossbow. I shouted and ducked, pulling Abby down with me. We sprawled on whatever passed for the ground in this space. Hunter smirked and lowered his weapon. "I hate him like poison. If he comes back, he'll be protecting my prey from me, like he used to do. With him tied to a body, I have his domain, and I have free range."

Uncle Jack grimaced. "Killing spree much, Bro?"

Hunter grinned. "Part of the job description."

"By your interpretation, anyway. I'm glad it's only human souls I have to ferry, otherwise you'd keep me jumping."

Hunter's grin went feral. "I can dream, can't I?"

"Never mind that right now. The thing is, the girls are right. Boysie might be in danger. Because it's not just his shell that's missing. His soul's escaped the place where I'd stored it."

The general psychic racket in the palais went silent. In clay-space, it was as though someone had muted the sound. Some of the ridden humans were coming out of their trances. They blinked and looked around, bewildered. The dancers were wheeling to a halt and the drummers were looking distracted. In the palais, the old guys and Abby were staring, openmouthed, at Uncle Jack. So was I. I said, "Hang on; what? You had Dad's soul somewhere that wasn't inside him?"

Uncle nodded. Abby looked horrified.

I couldn't make any sense of this. "For how long?"

"Since you girls were born."

"You pilfered Dad's soul?"

"I didn't steal it, Niece. Boysie knew about it. I had it in safe-keeping."

"Why in all the worlds would you do something like that?"

Abby touched my shoulder. "Maka, wait. Let me explai—"

Uncle said, "Ma ordered me to do it. But this morning, lightning blasted my silk-cotton tree, and Boysie's soul slipped out from beneath its roots."

Hunter chuckled evilly. "Is that where it was? I've been looking high and low for it."

General Gun said, "So, Boysie's soul's been reunited with his body? Then why's the girl okay?"

Abby gave a little cry of dismay. Aunt Zeely said, "And why hasn't Boysie come back to us?"

I tried to ask Uncle Gun what he meant, but Uncle Jack was saying something, and Hunter and Zeely were yelling at each other.

Ma Ocean surged up off the low carved wooden stool on which she'd been sitting. In a fathoms-deep voice she roared, "Flash! Cathy! You get here right this minute!" The palais fairly rocked with the power of that summons.

A bolt of lightning crisscrossed the palais space, blinding me for a second. Aunt Cath showed up concealed in the squirming, crackling column of silver snakes that was her hair. She whipped her head, revealing that her hair was all she was wearing. A rope of lightning-snake dreadlocks snapped way too close to me. The magnetic pull of it set my altered senses jangling painfully. Then a sudden thunderclap made me jump again.

Cousin Flash galloped in on a huge, silvery roan horse—the four-legged kind. He was wearing a red-sequinned jumpsuit. Not big on the fashion sense, Flash wasn't. "Sorry I'm late, Ma," he boomed. He swung down off the horse. By the time he'd dismounted, the horse had become a djembe drum, and his outfit was a red dashiki, white jeans, and leather sandals. He took his place among the claypicken drummers by sliding into the head and body of their djembe drummer, whose eyes rolled back to show their whites and whose drumming switched from masterly to virtuoso. The worship service went back into full swing.

Ma Ocean put her hands on her hips and stank-eyed her two tardy offspring. It was easy to see which side of the Family Abby's Glare of Hot Death had come from. "Which one of you blasted open Jack's silk-cotton tree and let Boysie's soul out?"

The two of them looked at her, surprised. Uncle Jack said, "I'm thinking it was you, Cath. There was no thunder."

She rolled her eyes. "As if. Why don't you ask Flash? 'Cause I'm telling you, sometimes he doesn't have any thunder, either, knahmsayin'?"

"Sure," grumbled Uncle Flash, "make me the bad guy."

General Gun snickered. "Yeah, some undercover villain Flash would make. He can't sneak around. Everyone can see him coming for miles."

Flash kissed his teeth and rapped out a sudden irritable tattoo on the djembe.

Zeely said, "Guys, come on. This is serious."

Through gritted teeth Flash ground out, "Someone please tell Miss Cathy that the thunder can't roar if the lightning don't flash."

Ma Ocean shouted, "Shut up! All of you!"

Pouting, they all fell more or less silent, though Flash first grumbled under his breath, "They started it."

Ma stared at him until he zipped his lips and looked down at his hands on the drum. She said, "I brought the sorry lot of you into this world, and you know for damned sure I'll take you out of it. Now, I am going to get to the bottom of this mess. First of all, Jack; has Boysie reintegrated?"

"I don't think so, Ma. I haven't felt his soul cross the border between the worlds, and since his body's missing, I can't tell you whether it got back together with his soul. There are...signs that it hasn't, though."

He glanced guiltily over at me and Abby. Abby took my hand, as though for reassurance. What the fuck was going on? What had Hunter meant about why was she still okay? I squeezed Abby's hand. If they wanted to hurt her, I wouldn't be able to stop them. Yet I could do whatever I could to not let her go through it alone.

Ma Ocean said, "But why wouldn't Boysie's soul go back and join with his body once it was free? It was supposed to work that way! He can't be lost. I didn't mean for that to happen."

Hunter cooed, "It's all right, Ma. You have me to take his place."

Perhaps in response, Ma closed her eyes. "Give me strength," she pleaded. Her words utterly demoralized me. She was practically a god herself; what did it mean that she needed to implore a higher power in this moment?

She opened her eyes again. "Now, Cathy, Flash; your brother asked you a question. You will both answer him truthfully. You hear me?"

Cathy pursed her lips and Flash scowled, but they both replied, "Yes, Ma." Ma nodded to Uncle Jack to continue.

"What I want to know," Uncle drawled in that lazy way he talked sometimes when he really meant business, "is who blasted the hoodoo tree in Suzy's backyard in half with a lightning bolt?" He turned accusing eyes at Cousin Flash.

Flash shook his head, left the drummer he was riding, and mounted another one. "You know, the truth is, I don't really want Boysie back. Making us all mind our p's and q's, be nicer to the claypickens, blah, blah—"

Cathy interrupted him with, "Flash, if this is a confession, will you just get the hell on with it, already? Idiot."

"Shut up."

Hard to believe those two had once had kids together. Where were Beji and Beji, anyway? I scanned the space. Right. Over there, mounted on two worshippers, teenaged boys, who were sitting on the steps at the entrance, probably hoping no one would notice them and make them take part. I waved at my cousins. I didn't have a beef with those two. They waved shyly back.

"What I'm saying is, no matter how much Boysie gets on my nerves, it still wasn't me who blasted the hoodoo tree! You would have known if it were, right? After all, everyone can see me coming for miles, isn't that so?"

Hunter snorted. Uncle said to Flash, "I'll take that as a no, then. Cathy, Sis, if you'd be so kind as to answer the same question?" Completely hidden by torn motley made from the clothing of the dead, Uncle began a graceful spin to the rhythm of the drums. The strips of cloth woven into his robe twirled in the deadly wind of his passing. We all stood back to give him room. "Cathy, did you strike my hoodoo tree to smithereens?" His voice was ominous.

Cathy sneered. "Please. I don't care enough about you to damage anything of yours."

Her hair grew straight and white and her black eyes faded to blue. Now she was wearing the wet-dream tights and high-heeled boots of a comic book superheroine. There was an X emblazoned on the chest of her outfit, deformed almost to illegibility by the improbable mammaries she'd sprouted. She smirked at Uncle and began her own spin, only umpteen times faster than he had, until she'd churned up a tall, narrow whirlwind in the space that extended upwards to infinity. We were all fighting not to get sucked into the maelstrom of it. Abby whimpered, "I hate this." I put my arms around her and braced myself against Cathy's storm.

Ma Ocean bellowed, "Cathy, you stop that this instant!"

Cathy obediently went still, but not without giving Uncle a head toss and a Z-snap first. I had to give it to her. Her tornado had definitely been showier than his dervish twirling. Even Uncle Gun, he of the arms like thighs, had been struggling not to be drawn in.

Ma Ocean glared at her offspring. "I'm asking for the last time. If neither Cath nor Flash let Boysie's soul out, then which of you did?"

I piped up, "And why was it separated from him in the first place?"

Abby tugged urgently on my arm. "Hush. I'll tell you later."

I fell silent again, seething at the insane family drama playing out around me.

"Grandma?" said Beji.

"Yes, dear?" She smiled indulgently at her grand—I think Beji was a granddaughter right then.

"It was us. Me and the other Beji."

"Yes," said the other Beji, "we let Uncle Boysie's soul out."

Uncle Flash exclaimed. Aunt Cathy cussed. Ma Ocean's jaw dropped open. "But how?" she asked. "It was a lightning bolt!"

The Bejis looked sheepish. I thought I knew the answer. I said to them, "It's because you're the children of lightning and thunder, isn't it?"

They nodded. "Mom, Dad, we figured out how to wield the storm from watching you. We just never told you before. And we're not very good with the thunder part yet. That's why there wasn't any. Not until later this morning, down by the lake."

Light dawned. "That was you guys that chased the haint away from me? Thank you!"

"You're welcome." They looked pleased with themselves.

Cathy said, "Huh."

Flash smiled. "Chips off the old blocks." He and Aunt Cath looked at each other, and if that wasn't parental pride making them both beam so, I don't know what was.

Uncle Jack said, "But why did you do it? Don't you see how you've screwed everything up?"

Beji replied, "We know. We're sorry. But we went to visit Uncle Boysie in the hospital last night, and he was sicker than he'd ever been."

Beji added, "He was dying, Uncle Jack."

A sound rang out that was utterly foreign to palais space. Everyone turned to look at me. It was coming from the pocket of my jeans.

"I'm so sorry," I stammered. "I'll just get this."

I answered my cell phone. It was Mr. Tankhouse, from the rest home. "Ms. Joli, I'm sorry to disturb you, but someone found your father. He's at Saint Sebastian's Hospital."

I couldn't ask the next question, I couldn't. But I had to. "Is he...?"

"He's still with us, but I'm afraid he's in a bad way. You and your sister may want to go there right now."

I hung up. I couldn't remember whether I'd even said goodbye to Mr. Tankhouse. "It's Dad," I told Abby and Uncle Jack. "He's alive, but we need to go to Saint Sebastian's."

Abby nodded. Her face was grey.

"Oho," chortled Hunter. "Things are getting really interesting now." He leaned over and took Abby's hand. He put it to his lips.

Abby snatched her hand from his grasp. She snapped at him, "You will *never* replace our father." She linked arms with me and Uncle Jack and trilled a brassy flourish of notes that made my back teeth shiver. The last thing I saw as we began the shift back to the corporeal world was Hunter, staring knowingly at Abby and sniffing the hand with which he'd held hers.

Transit.

◆ ◆ ◆

Dad swore and threw his pencil. It flew from his favourite armchair by the living room window and bounced off the opposite wall. The skunk that had been crouched adoringly at his feet waddled over to the pencil, mouthed it up, and toddled back to return it to him. I was fifteen, awkward in my body. Alternately sulky and elated. In the moment, definitely sulky. Abby and one of the Bejis had gone to a movie. I was supposed to have gone with them, but I was grounded because I hadn't done my chores for more than a week. Just for a few unwashed dishes! It was so unfair! Curled into a resentful ball on the couch, I ignored Dad's outburst and kept studiously watching some nighttime talk show host talking to some beautiful famous person or other.

Dad sighed and rattled the science journal he'd been reading. He tossed it to the ground and tore off the rubber gloves he'd been using to handle its right-angled pages. He stuffed the gloves between the cushions of his chair. He probably didn't even notice that he was doing it. It was just his habit. If he didn't hide them, his mouse supplicants would take them away to make nests in. "This research is all wrong," he grumbled. I refused to look at him. Louder, he said, "All wrong, I tell you!" He pointed an accusing finger at the journal. "Allyou so close! But when you going to learn that if the results not optimal, you need to try the enantiomer? Eh? Your compound might be chiral! Allyou can't see that?"

I couldn't hear my show over his ranting. "So write them and tell them that, Dad." He spent hours torturing himself like this, poring over medical and science journals and seething about research that wasn't quite on the right track.

"Who going to take me seriously? When I don't have no blasted piece of paper saying I'm a scientist? When I have to write up my research on home-made paper? In pencil?" He flung the offending pencil again. This time, the skunk stood on its hind legs and caught it neatly in midair.

"But you know how to make whatever it is, right?"

"Yes, I suppose I could." He took the pencil from the skunk's patient mouth. "Why?"

"Could you make it here at home?"

He considered. "I don't see why not."

This was more interesting than the talk show. I unfolded from the couch. "Let me use your computer for a second. I want you to see something." I said it in a frosty tone to let him know that I was still mad at him, but I quickly forgot my huff as I introduced my dad to the wonder that was eBay. I called up some auctions for various types of potions, pills, and ointments. "See what I mean? People will try anything in order to stop hurting."

He studied the screen. "Some of these are nonsense," he said. "But some of them work."

"Uh-huh."

His eyes lit up. "I could be doing part of my job, and getting paid for it!"

"I figure." In minutes I had signed him up for an account, and he was

chuckling and making notes. The lab he set up in the basement sometimes
smelled worse than the time that Butter startled the skunk and it sprayed her
and the living room blinds, but soon, Green Man Herbal Online was doing
enough business that Uncle didn't have to subsidize us as often any more.

◆ ◆ ◆

"He looks so tiny," said Abby. She slid an arm around my waist so that
we stood scar to scar, joined at the place where they'd separated us.

"I know what you mean." I would have thought that nothing
could make the three-hundred-plus-pound mass of my dad look
small. But in that hospital bed, wearing only a blue examination
gown, covered with a single thin white cotton sheet, with tubes
coming out of his arm and a respirator hissing softly beneath his
nose, Dad seemed insignificant.

Where had Uncle gotten to? He hadn't shown up to meet us.

A woman had found Dad lying in the alleyway behind her
convenience store. The store was only a few blocks from our—
from Abby's place. It looked as though Dad had been trying to get
home. The woman had recognized him and called 911.

"I'm afraid his higher brain function is gone," said the doctor. He'd told us his name. I couldn't remember it. My brain was
churning. It was a struggle to keep anything in mind but Dad.

"What can we do?" I asked. My eyes were all for Dad, lying
there with his mouth gaping slightly open, hooked up to every tube
under the sun. With my fingertips, I stroked a patch of skin on
the back of his hand where there were no needles. Wide, brown,
shovel-shaped hands with knotty fingers like strong roots. He'd
coaxed food from the earth to feed us with those hands, bandaged
our skinned knees with them. His skin under my fingers was rough,
dry and ashy. I thought, "I must bring some lotion for him, so he
won't be itchy." Then I realized I didn't know whether he could feel

anything in his condition. Unlike his side of the Family, I couldn't perceive his clay form as different from his self. To me, the person lying there was still my dad.

The doctor replied, "I know this is hard to hear, but there isn't anything that can be done. He won't wake up. His organs are beginning to shut down. We can keep the blood circulating in his body, keep filling his lungs with air, but his brain has ceased to function. In every way that counts, he's deceased. I'm very sorry."

Abby gave a soft cry.

I couldn't get any air. I stared at the doctor, fighting to take a breath in. He said, "Joli? Are you all right? Do you need to sit down?" It was just empty sound. It was as though I were seeing him from the other end of a long tunnel. He helped me to the chair at my dad's bedside. The doctor told me, gently, "Put your head down."

I obeyed. For a second, the head rush got a little worse. Then, over a few seconds of forever, it faded. I sat up straight. "I'm okay." The two most ludicrous words in the universe right now to describe how I was. I asked, "Is it...is it because he got out of the rest home?" My mouth was so dry that it was hard to get the words out. "Did he have an accident out on the street, or something?"

The doctor looked at his clipboard. He shook his head. "He had no injuries when he was admitted to the hospital just now. I see that he has—had—advanced dementia?"

Abby was perched on the edge of Dad's bed, sobbing and stroking his shoulder over and over again. Without looking up, she nodded.

"Well, that could be the reason he collapsed. It may have progressed to such an extent that he, uh, developed the condition in which you see him now."

Abby's sobs grew stormier. Blindly she reached for my hand. I grabbed hers and held on. Her fingers were cold in my grip.

The doctor said, "I know this is all very sudden, but we need to secure a DNR from you both, since you're his next of kin."

Abby asked, "What's a DNR?"

I said, "It means 'do not resuscitate.'" The doctor nodded. "They want our permission to turn off the life support machines and let Dad..." I couldn't finish the sentence.

"Absolutely not," said Abby.

My heart sank. "Abs, don't you get it? It's the only way he can be...released." If Dad's body died, he would have fulfilled the terms of his punishment. He could become a celestial again. We could have him back, whole.

The doctor took a deep breath. "Ms. Joli, I know this must be very difficult, but there's no coming back from the state he's in now. The life support is the only thing keeping the body breathing and the heart circulating blood."

"No. That's not how it's going to happen."

I squeezed her hand. "Abs, what else can we do?"

"No, I said!" She pulled her hand out of mine. She turned to the doctor. "Can you give us a few minutes alone, please?"

"Of course. When you need me, just ask one of the nurses to page me."

He pushed his way past the privacy curtain that went around Dad's bed. We were left alone with the relentless rhythms of the machines keeping air and blood moving in Dad's body.

"Abby, we can't keep him chained in this body! Hasn't he suffered long enough for us? Let him become what he was again!" I was desperate for her to understand. I *needed* Dad back.

Abby's face crumpled into tears again. She wailed, "But I'm not ready to lose you!"

She was making no sense. "Why would you lose me?" The headache I'd been nursing all day blossomed from babe-in-arms to full-on, raging adulthood. "I mean, I'm moving into my own place in a few days, but it's not like I'm going to the moon."

She looked at me like I'd sprouted two more heads. "But you can't do that," she told me, her voice despairingly wan. "Especially not now."

"No, it's all right. Look, I know I was pissed at you when I stormed out yesterday morning, but I won't leave you to go through this alone, I'd never do that. I'll visit Dad every day until...I promise. And I'll stop borrowing money from you, and—"

"It was part of his punishment."

I stopped in mid-spate. "Whose punishment? Dad's? You mean the soul-severing thing?"

She nodded. She went closer to Dad's bed. She stroked his balding head. He'd complained so bitterly when his hair started falling out! He'd never experienced aging before.

Abby continued, "It takes a mind and a soul to work mojo. One to drive, one to steer. It's not clear which does which. Granny Ocean made Uncle Jack reap Dad's soul."

My scalp prickled. "She made him take his own brother's immortal soul? Abby, that may be the coldest thing I have ever heard."

Abby's lips trembled. She pressed them together. She bent and kissed Dad's cheek. "Really, it was Gran's way of punishing both Dad and Uncle Jack. Dad's soul can't die. Without it, he just wouldn't be able to work his mojo." She looked at me. "It isn't permanent." She was crying again. "She was going to let Uncle Jack give Dad's soul back to him when you died."

My skin literally went cold. "You mean when Dad dies?"

"No, Niece. When you do." Uncle Jack stood in the doorway to Dad's room. He was wearing a handsome but wasted black man of about thirty. His horse sported flannel pyjamas, blue with yellow ducks on them. The sleeves were rolled up. One of his wrists was bandaged. A pack of smokes stuck out of the chest pocket of his jammies. Uncle shrugged, tapped the horse's chest. "He looks a little like I did, before I was transformed. I wanted to look sort of like my old self when I came to collect my brother's soul." He glanced at Dad's body, then away. "But Boysie's soul is not in that dying clay. It'd be so much simpler if it were. Just pop it on out of there, find another place to store it, and go back to plan A."

Softly, Abby said, "Maka, you asked me in the car why you couldn't work your mojo."

Uncle interrupted. "She knows, then?"

Abby shook her head. "Not yet, but she's about to."

Right then, I badly wanted to beg them not to tell me.

Abby said, "You can't use it because it's not your mojo. It's Dad's."

Uncle supplied the next piece of the puzzle. "I grafted it into you. When you die, Boysie's soul can get its mojo back, and then he'll no longer be locked into just one kind of body. He'll be back to normal."

"Why..." I began. "Why do..." I couldn't figure out how to begin the sentence, how to end it. I fumbled my way to the chair and sat down.

Uncle said, "This is such a cock-up. But we'll figure it out, Maka. Your time to go isn't yet."

Abby stammered, "Now that Dad's...like this, will Grandma, uh, make you take his mojo out of...?" She stopped, a stricken look on her face.

"Of course she will not!" Uncle replied, all indignation. "She can't. She's not allowed."

I leapt up. "But that's it! That's the solution!" Elation was making me light-headed. "Don't you see? Dad's fulfilled the term of his punishment, or he's about to. So here's what we do: Abs and

I issue the DNR, Dad's body shuffles off this mortal, and Uncle, you take his mojo out of me and graft it back onto his soul. It's perfect, right?"

Abby's shoulders sagged. Uncle had his head in his hands. Neither one of them was saying anything.

"It's not perfect?"

To my profound horror, Uncle started to sob. He stared at me, his eyes brimming with tears in his skull-and-bone face. Uncle ferried deaths and births by the thousands, every day, always with a ready joke and a smile. I'd never seen a single one of them make him cry.

An uncomfortable stillness came over me, that sick calm you feel the moment before you know that something awful is about to happen that will change the course of your life forever, and there's absolutely nothing you can do about it.

Uncle got to his feet. He held me tightly. Breath rattled in his horse's chest, and the man's bones poked into me. "I'm sorry," he whispered. "Niece of mine, I'm so sorry."

I took a deep breath. "Tell me. Just fucking tell me."

"It's not as simple as taking Boysie's mojo out of you. If I do that while you're alive, you will return to the way you were when you were born."

"Which is what?" I whispered.

Uncle replied, "Absent."

And he told me the rest. That story? That romantic family saga of tragic, forbidden love and star-crossed lovers? A pile of bullshit, stinking to high heaven. It was maggot-riddled with lies.

Abby had been fine when we were born. Only that shorter leg. Whereas I was all but an empty shell. A living body with a near-inert mind, and a tiny undifferentiated nubbin of aetheric where there should have been the psychic organelle of mojo that all living creatures possess to one degree or another. Whereas Abby's had been working a-okay. And it was Abby's blood and breath that had been sustaining me in the womb.

Dad's kin had cut me away from Abby in order to keep her alive. They sliced me off my precious sister, neatly as paring a hangnail, and left me in my crib to die.

Ma had begged for *my* life. For mine. Abby's continued existence wasn't in question.

It was me that Dad and Uncle had carried across the border, intending to break the chiefest laws of life and death for love of my mother. And there the Family caught them, and Ma Ocean meted out her punishment, forced one of her sons to rip the other into pieces. Without mojo, Dad couldn't transform into his celestial self. With his soul locked away, he couldn't get to his mojo.

Turns out that when Uncle brought me and our newly mortal Dad back over to this side of the border, to their surprise, I began to grow and develop. I had a personality, an intellect. My father's mojo had instilled me with a false life. When it was gone, I might remain alive, but I would return to my vegetative state.

"You put Dad's mojo into me." That information was beginning to sink in, leaving me woozy. I clutched the railing on Dad's bed, for something steady to hold on to. Dad's body inhaled and exhaled, remorselessly.

"Yes. I offered to put it back into Boysie at the beginning of his punishment. If he'd been careful, Ma need never have known. But he said no, you were using it."

There was no me. I was nothing but a living container. I started to shiver. "That bush medicine you drink," Abby said. "Nothing's wrong with your liver."

"My liver didn't come from you?" My voice came out thin and squeaky.

"It did. But you and I have identical genetics. Your body accepted the graft perfectly. You don't need an antirejection drug for it."

I understood. "The medicine is so I won't reject Dad's mojo," I mumbled.

Uncle said, "That graft couldn't take forever. You can't sustain a demigod's mojo indefinitely. It's like a house cat whelping a lion."

Abby told me, "That's why you have the seizures. The tincture keeps them under control. I'm sorry, Makeda."

"Shut up."

A rattly exhalation came from Dad. There was a bit of drool trickling from one corner of his mouth. I took a tissue from the box of them by his bedside table and dabbed gently at his lips. My whole body shook with the effort of being so very gentle. "Guess it wasn't me you were looking after so diligently, huh? I'm just a life-support system."

"Maks, it's not like tha—"

"Shut the fuck up, I said!"

Uncle tried to touch my hand. I yanked it out of his reach. My gorge rose at the brief brush I'd felt of his fingers on my skin.

He said, "I know you're mad at me. You have a right to be."

"I think I'm madder at Grandma Ocean than at you. Or maybe I will be, eventually."

"I could fix all this if I just knew where that kudzu plant had gone to."

Dully, I told him, "A kudzu vine broke into Dad's room last night. We think that's how he got away."

Uncle's eyes went wide. "Really?" It was a disturbing look on the face of his half-dead horse. "Oh, this is excellent news!"

He told us what had happened at Aunt Suze's.

Abby said, "Let me get this straight. Quashee the kudzu vine is walking around with Dad's soul inside?"

I shook my head. "That sentence is too long. Let's start with this, Uncle Jack; Quashee is walking around?"

"More like rampaging, actually, to hear Suze tell it."

"Shit. Did anyone get hurt? Are the kids all right?"

"Everyone's fine. Suze said she reminded Boysie that there were children inside, and he backed off."

"Oh, Dad," said Abby. "You were only trying to rescue yourself before your mind went completely."

I grunted. "Fat lot of good it would have done him without the missing piece that I'm carrying. If Dad has no mojo, what's making the kudzu move?"

Uncle Jack replied, "I don't know."

Surprised, I looked at him. He said, "I don't know everything, remember?"

"How did Quashee even know where to find Dad?"

"That part's easy. Quashee has been visiting him regularly for months."

Abby gasped. "The kudzu tea we've been making for him!"

Uncle smiled. "Smart girl." Then he looked uncomfortable. The man he was riding slumped. When he straightened up again, his eyes were rolled back in his head, and his uneven breathing rattled in his bony chest. Uncle said, "I'll need to take this guy back soon." He smiled weakly. "Can't reap 'em while I'm wearing 'em, can I?"

That did it. I was already hurling into my hand by the time I shouldered through the bathroom across the hall to upchuck into the toilet.

I washed the sour taste out of my mouth and returned to Dad's side. His breath had definitely started to death-rattle, too. Between him and Uncle's horse, it was macabre squared. "Abby? I think we need to get the doctor back in here. It's time to let Dad go."

"Yeah," said Uncle, "they need the bed." He saw our horrified faces. "What? I already told you, that's not Boysie! Don't mistake the doghouse for the dog."

I winced.

"I'm just saying, better we spend our energy finding him than in mourning his suit of clay. He'll make himself a new one once he has his mojo back. Maybe he can hang on inside Quashee until it's Maka's time. I'll figure something out."

Through a clenched jaw, Abby said, "I'll go get the doctor."

He nodded absentmindedly. "You do that. And since I'm already at a hospital, I'll just go about my regular shift." He grinned. "People in here are a-borning and a-dying on the regular. I'm needed."

"Fine, then." Abby patted Dad's shoulder, then left the room, leaning wearily on her cane and walking more slowly than she usually did.

Uncle tried, he really did, but he just didn't have the same perspective on death that Abby and I did. I said, "That was harsh, even for you. And with Dad right here in the room, too."

"What? Where?" A startled Uncle looked around, his face full of hope. "Oh. Right. You're talking about the shell again."

"Stop saying that!" I wanted to put my hands over Dad's ears so he wouldn't have to listen. "And you're not fooling me by saying you have work to do. You're perfectly capable of delivering and collecting souls the world over and being right here at the same time."

He made a face. "It's true. Fact is, I don't have much patience with human grief. I don't exactly understand it."

"How about human anger?"

"You're pissed at me?" His voice was cool.

"I'm furious."

"Why? Because I played god with you? Baby girl, that's what I do. And not lightly, either." He thought about that for a second.

"Well, yes, sometimes lightly. You know what they say about all work and no play." He hacked for long seconds, bent over and wheezing. He spat into the sink by the wall. I looked away, repulsed by my own uncle. He composed himself, straightened his clothes. "All right. Things to do, a brother to locate. I'll bet you that a giant, ravening kudzu vine stomping around Toronto is not going to go unnoticed for long."

"Quashee is probably shedding. Dad's gotta be freaked at all the bits of invading species he's contaminating the city with."

"Your Dad's not in his right mind at the moment. He's not in any mind. I'll find out whether anyone's spotted him. I'm going to check the world's best source for spawning new urban legends, the Internet. What, you thought I couldn't even type? The Web is just another threshold between one world and another." He leaned over to kiss me goodbye, but I pulled back.

"Suit yourself. Let me know if you hear from Boysie." He waved instead as he left. His horse had to hold on to the walls in order to stay upright.

In a minute or two, Abby was back with the doctor, who said, "I hear that you ladies have made a decision about your father's life support?"

"Turn it off," I blurted. I couldn't let myself know how I felt about giving that order, so hard on the heels of what I'd learned about how Dad and Uncle had treated me. I did my best to switch my brain off and do what I knew I should; I bent and kissed Dad's warm, stubbly cheek. The furze of his beard tickled my nose, perhaps for the last time. "Bye, Dad," I whispered.

The doctor looked at Abby. "Ms. Joli, do you give your permission, too?"

She didn't answer him. She was looking at Dad. She drew two quick, shaky breaths. "Could you lower the railing for me, please?"

"Of course," said the doctor, leaping to do as she asked.

She sat on the edge of the bed. She clasped Dad's hand for a second. Straightened his pyjama top. Said, in a quiet, trembly voice, "He would have hated being plugged into all these machines."

"Yes," I replied, "he would have."

She wiped her nose angrily with one of her sleeves. Bent and kissed Dad's cheek. "Bye, Dad." She stood and came to huddle against me. She moved as though she'd suddenly been blinded. Her hand was shaking and cold when I took it. Mine were no better.

She said, "Turn them off."

One by one, the doctor did. In hushed tones, he asked, "Would you prefer to be alone with your father right now?"

"Yes."

"Yes, please."

He left the room, shut the door quietly.

Dad sighed heavily, once. Then twice more. And then no more. As I watched, the faint, Shiny scrim of green around him faded away to nothing. And all I felt was fury.

◆ ◆ ◆

*I need to go, I need to gogogo. Have to find the thing I lost. Lost lost moss
horse. Ride a moss horse to Banbury Cross to find a young lady. Ride the
green growing walking. Thank the green growing walking for offering me to
ride. You see, Boss? I give to my garden, and the garden give back. But this
horse too small. No; the fuse, I mean to say. Green growing brain too diffuse.
Can't spread myself so thin. Can't hold. I might fall off. I might get worse.*

*To find a young lady before she get worse. Thief! She is a arrant knave
and thief. Is she have the rest of me, lock up tight in she pannier. Must find
her, take it away from her. Take it out of her.*

*Max? Mak? Makeda? I sorry, doux-doux. I sorry I burden you. For I
don't know what to say the donkey won't do. Thief! I can smell it out, you
know? Smell out where you hiding me, ride to the hidey-hole. Rip. Oh, Big
Boss, they rip me. Rip me in two, in three. And now two of me in this tree,
and I going to find she. Go, green growing. Go.*

◆ ◆ ◆

Chang and Eng Bunker; those were the very first conjoined twins
I'd ever heard tell about. Born in Siam, which became Thailand.
Where the term "Siamese twin" came from to denote people like
me and Abby. Born joined at the chest, those two guys were, by
nothing more than a "fibrous band of tissue." They each had their
own limbs and their own organs. Their livers were fused together,
but they each had a complete one. Nowadays, it would be a breeze
to separate them. But in 1811, that wasn't going to happen. So they
lived joined together all their lives.

*"The left one's a little too tight." Abby was sitting on our bedroom floor,
between our two twin beds. She was wearing a white cotton singlet and her
baby blue "Wednesday" panties. She was leaning her back against my bed.
She had her crutches across her knees, within easy reach.*

"Okay," I said, "I'll do that one over." I was sitting on my bed in my favourite green nightie, my bare legs hanging down on either side of Abby's body. I'd been plaiting her hair into two. I began undoing the left one. The twined strands of her hair were crinkly and crisp against my fingers. "You don't have to keep your crutches so close, you know," I told her. "I can help you up."

"I know." She hummed a tune.

"What's that one?" I asked. We were only about thirteen years old, but I was already beginning to be jealous of Abby's music, that seemed to be taking up more and more of her time and attention.

"The one from this morning. Remember, I told you about it when we woke up? How I'd dreamed about these happy ghost girls playing dress-up with their mothers' clothes, and dancing to a song they were singing?"

"Yeah, I guess."

Lots of people remember the moment in their youths when someone first enlightened them about sex. People talk about their youthful selves being both fascinated and repulsed by the details of this weird thing they were apparently going to want to do—if they weren't already doing it, that is. If a kid didn't know, suspect, or care anything about sex before they were told about it, I think that the scariest thing wouldn't be the specifics of what bodies did when they slapped their naked selves up against each other in that particular activity. What's really creepy is being told that you, your essential self that went "Ew!" at the very idea of even putting your tongue in anyone else's mouth, was going to change into some unrecognizable creature that would find sex deeply desirable. You were going to suddenly start seeking out opportunities to get some. You were going to cease being yourself, and there was nothing you could do about it.

I didn't have that life-changing moment of learning about the birds and the bees. Abs and I had figured most of it out because we'd been learning about how birds, bees, lions, spotted cranes, leaf moulds, and amoebae reproduced from the get-go. When we were maybe nine, Dad decided we were old enough to be told how humans did it. We kept asking him if he was done yet. He was boring us and *The Simpsons* was on and we didn't want to miss it. But it took only a couple more years for the hormones to kick in and our curiosity to be piqued.

"How about Aunt Zeels?" Abs asked.

"No, she thinks she's prettier than we are. She'd give us attitude."

"Yeah. I think we'd need someone kind. Someone willing to take their time."

"Someone who wouldn't laugh at us for being inexperienced."

Abs giggled. "I guess that rules out Flash, then."

"Yikes! As if!" I mimed gagging.

From between my knees, Abs looked up to meet my gaze, her eyes merry. "He'd tell us we should be making more noise."

"And that he couldn't really date us because our clothes weren't brightly coloured enough."

"I know!" said Abs.

That was the problem with dating and mating when you were one of the Family. The only beings of the same species were, well, Family. Kinda limited your choices, especially for those of the Family who'd been mired in sibling bickering for millennia. The wonder wasn't that Dad had chosen a human being as his partner, but that more of that lot didn't.

Abs chortled. "We could ask Grandma Ocean!"

I whooped with laughter. "Or Hunter!"

We'd been playing this game for a few years now. We knew the basic mechanics of sex, but we had so many questions. We wanted someone more experienced. Someone who could initiate us.

When I was a kid, I wondered what life had been like for the twins and their wives. Wives! Those guys had married sisters. Chang had ten children with his wife and Eng had eleven with his. This in the Victorian era, a time when sex just wasn't spoken about in polite company.

"Aunt Suze?" asked Abby.

"Ew! She's so old! Besides, she's claypicken. You know how weirded out their kind gets about family-on-family nookie." Uttering the word "nookie," I felt so worldly, so sophisticated.

Abs replied, "Hunter's old. Grandma Ocean is older."

"I know, but they're old celestials. Auntie Suze is pure claypicken. They age faster."

We'd already considered and rejected Uncle, or Dad. They used to change our diapers. It would be too strange, even for us.

You would have said, "Chang and Eng's sex life," wouldn't you? Like they were one person, Changandeng, emphasis on the second syllable. When you're a twin, the world has its ways of letting you know that you and your sib are a package deal. Everything I had, Abby either had an identical one, or she and I would share one. It was like we'd never actually been separated at all. As really young kids, Abby and I had been so close that we'd occasionally try to sit on the toilet seat together, laughing so hard that we sometimes fell off, and Dad would have to clean the mess up. Abby's body was as familiar to me as my own.

I said, "How about Beji?"

Abby considered. "Or maybe the other Beji?"

"Yeah."

"Maybe. They're kinda like us."

"And they're nice to me," I pointed out.

Abby sighed, pouted. "It'd be our first time. I just wish there was someone to show us who was really like us, you know? Part claypicken, part celestial."

"Mm."

Then the pick I was using to tease knots out of Abby's spring-coiled hair slipped from my hand and landed in her lap. I leaned down over her to get it. My fingertips brushed against her naked thigh. The texture of her skin was as comfortingly familiar as my own, but in that moment, so new it was electrifying. Jolted, I dropped the pick again. Face flushing, I reached for it once more. Before I could touch it, Abby retrieved it herself. She put it into my hand. Bent over her like that, I was achingly aware of the radiating heat of her, newly woken from sleep. The scent of her breath, like warmed milk on a cold day. I took the pick from her. She let her fingers trail along the back of my hand as I straightened up. Goose bumps rose along my arm. Her nipples poked twin bumps into the thin singlet. Shyly, I made to continue plaiting her hair, but she turned her face upwards to look at me. "We are like us," she said delightedly, like it was a new discovery.

For years I'd been wondering what Eng's and Chang's involuntary threesomes—and maybe foursomes sometimes?—had been like. Could the brothers each feel it when one of them got excited? Did the sights, sounds, smells of sex turn on the brother who wasn't having it? Suppose one of them was doing the nasty, and the other one really just wanted to have some supper and chat with his kids? Before they'd been married, hell, even afterwards, had they ever touched each other?

My heart's agitated fluttering regulated into a fast, excited rhythm. I returned Abby's smile. Simultaneously, we both said, "D'you want to?" then laughed at our twin synchronicity. Then we were serious, searching each other's faces. I wanted this.

Abby nodded; so did she. In a second she had her singlet off and was using her crutches to lever herself upright. She let herself fall, laughing, onto my bed. She reached for me. "C'mon, silly," she said. "Take that thing off."

We spent the rest of the morning giggling and tumbling puppylike over each other, sniffing, probing, and tasting, urging each other on, till Dad knocked on our door and said it was time for breakfast and lessons. We were studying fractions and basic oceanography that week.

For the next few years, Abby and I were each other's eager study partners in things sexual. Abby liked to roughhouse, and the nip of teeth on the sensitive bits of her, except her toes. I liked to have things inside me. Anything that looked likely was fair game. We both liked long, slow kisses. In theory, she liked spooning afterwards as much as I did, but it tended to make her leg crampy and she'd have to wriggle out of my arms. We thought we'd stay partnered. After all, Aunt Cath and Uncle Flash were sibs, and they had made a go of it for aeons. We knew ourselves to be more even-tempered than either of them. And we had Dad's and Uncle's blessings. But by the time we hit our late teens, I was feeling shut out from Abby's life. She had her music. But I was tone-deaf. I could hear musical notes fine, just couldn't sing them for the life of me. Unlike Abby, I had nothing that absorbed me so fully. Except, of course, her. And then I heard her joking with Uncle Flash, both of them calling me the donkey. The word pierced me through like a spike of ice, and I hadn't really warmed to Abby since.

When you abide with someone so closely they might almost be inside your skin, sometimes words aren't necessary. You learn how to signal each other to butt the fuck out. Outwardly, Abs and I were still loving towards each other, but I froze her out bit by bit, with a slight shake of my head no here, a subtle shift there of my shoulder away from her reaching hand. I ignored her looks of puzzled disappointment. I hid my things and my self away from her. I'd lie in my bed at night, hearing Abby's breathing from the bed on the other side of the room. She had to be as lonely for me as I was for her, and as horny. I learned to mostly ignore the shifting of the bedsheets and the occasional quiet groan from my equally pubescent sister. She got the message and did the same for me. I yearned for the easy bond between my sister and me like lungs yearn for air. But if I was to be a donkey, I could go her one better; I could be as stubborn as a mule.

Truth was, I kind of envied Eng and Chang. Yoked permanently together, they had to figure out how to get along, and how to disagree. They had no choice.

◆ ◆ ◆

Stacking plates into the big dishwashers at work was like lifting boulders. I felt feverish from sleep deprivation. I chewed down some Tylenol. It helped a little. I could not come down with something right now.

I was a wreck. My heart couldn't figure out whether to grieve for Dad or not. And I was so angry at my family that I scarcely trusted myself to speak civilly to anyone at work. I kept having to clamp down on storms of weeping and fits of rage. Near the end of my shift I was clearing a table when I lost my hold on an almost-full bowl of hot pumpkin soup and dropped it right into some guy's lap. Boss chewed me out but good for that one. Thank heaven I only had a few more minutes on my shift. I sleepwalked through them. Left on the dot of two a.m. Crawled home. Let myself in, hoping Abby wouldn't hear me and come and try to have a heartfelt talk.

In the dark living room, two dollar-sized silvery green circles floated just above the coffee table. Then they blinked. Butter, the cat. "Stool pigeon," I said. "I'm going to tell Abby that you were on the furniture."

Butter got to her feet and stretched. The light from the street glinted off her fangs. She watched me head down the corridor to my bedroom. I heard the velvet-pawed thump of her jumping down off the coffee table. I slipped quickly into my room and shut the door to keep her out. Let her go sleep on Abby's chilly feet if she wanted company tonight.

I pulled my clothes off in darkness and dropped them on the floor where I stood. I'd clean the mess up tomorrow. Right now, I needed to let sleep muffle the memories of the past day for a few hours. I climbed into bed. I reached to pull the blanket over me and touched warm flesh. I screamed and flung myself out of the bed. I hit the ground tailbone first, hard.

"Maka," said Abby, "don't be scared! It's just me."

My brain had already figured that out, but my body was a hair behind, scrabbling crabwise away from the bed. At the sound of Abby's voice, I jerked to a stop. I rolled into a ball and whimpered.

In a few seconds, Abby was kneeling beside me. "Sorry."

I was still shuddering, but I replied, "It's okay. You startled me, is all."

"I was lying in my own bed and I couldn't get to sleep, and my brain wouldn't stop churning. I could use some company tonight, Sis."

"What about Lars?"

"He's not into threesomes," she deadpanned.

"Not like the Bejis, huh? Though I guess those were technically foursomes. At least, I think so. Sometimes the Bejis are kinda like one person." My breathing was beginning to return to normal after the scare.

Abby said, "Lars offered to stay with me, but I asked him to give me a bit of space tonight. Once I went to bed and I started feeling even worse, I realized I should have let him stay. I kept telling myself that I was going to call him back, but it got to where I was so panicked that all I could manage to do was come and lie here. Your sheets smell like you. Like family." She touched my shoulder. "Please, Maka?"

I sighed. "It's all right," I lied. "I could use the company, too."

"Thank you."

I got to my feet. "There just won't be lots of room." It was a three-quarter bed.

"Look, you don't have to do this. I'll go back to my room. I can take a sleeping pill, or something."

"No, those things always make you woolly-headed the whole next day. It really is okay, Abs. Come on."

We got back into the bed and pulled the blanket up over ourselves. Like me, Abby slept naked. I could feel the warmth radiating from her. Basking in our shared heat, I began to relax for the first time since I'd found myself down on the Spit that morning. My aching muscles relaxed. My eyes began to close.

She'd known all this time that I was toting Dad's mojo, but she hadn't told me.

I came awake with a jolt. I didn't want to be soothed by Abby's presence. I wanted to stay pissed at her. I made myself stiff as a log beam, arms clamped firmly by my sides so that I wouldn't touch her by accident. And there I lay, gritty-eyed with exhaustion, desperate for a few hours' rest before Abs and I had to deal with tomorrow's ordeal of arranging an interment for Dad's body.

Abby made a soft murmur of discomfort. "Ow."

"What?"

"Nothing. My leg."

She shifted and stretched, trying to get comfortable. Her knee brushed my thigh. I nearly jumped out of my skin. She said, "Sorry I'm so twitchy. I usually prop my knee up a little with a pillow."

"I remember. Let me go and get one from your room."

I threw back my side of the blanket.

"Maka?"

"Yeah?"

"You were partly right. About why I smother you the way I do."

"I'm listening."

"I would see you having those terrible seizures when we were kids. I was terrified that they would kill you. Then one day I overheard Dad and Uncle Jack talking. That's how I discovered that Uncle Jack had grafted Dad's mojo into you. They caught me eavesdropping and told me the whole story, how Dad's mojo had helped your brain develop, and how Dad figured it was better to let you hang on to the mojo for as long as you needed it."

"Right. So he was doing me a favour."

"He was. He is. He loves you."

"Hee-haw."

"Oh, Maka."

"What? Did Dad and Uncle Jack downplay the part where they'd made me their mule without giving me any choice in the matter?"

"The living get culled every day, and their souls reaped. What does their consent matter to the likes of Dad and Uncle Jack? We may be their kin, but we're also their subjects."

"Right now, I don't care. They fucked with me. I don't so much mind that, because it helped Dad out. But they've been lying to me about it all my life, and that bites."

"When they told me, what I understood was that if you died, you would go away, so then Dad could have his mojo back, and then he would go all godlike on me, and I figured he would probably go away, too. It made me frantic. Since then, I've been trying to make sure that nothing ever happened to you."

"We're sisters. You and I shared a bloodstream in the womb. Why did you keep the big secret from me for so long?"

"Dad and Uncle Jack said it would upset you too much."

"Abby, you know me better than anyone else does. Didn't it occur to you that I might have felt honoured to know that they'd given me something so precious to protect?"

"It really didn't," she said wonderingly. "But wait; you didn't sound so honoured just a second ago. That was pure resentment."

I sighed. "It was. And then you talked to me, and suddenly it wasn't any more." I lay back down and put my arm around her. The touch of her skin on mine was so right that there were no words for it. Her body untensed. She slid right up against me. My arm fit across her breastbone just as it used to. My hand cupped the curve and weight of her breast, so like my own. I said, "You can prop your knee up on my leg."

"Mm-hmm. That's how I used to do it."

"Before we started sleeping in separate beds."

She took my hand. Kissed it. Put it back on her breast again. "See?" she said. "We'll be fine. You don't need to move out."

She was asleep in seconds, while I was still trying to work out how to reply to that. "Fuck." I listened to her breathing and to Butter scratching at my bedroom door. The arm on which I was lying fell asleep. I wanted to get more comfortable, but Abby was still holding tightly to my other hand, and I didn't want to disturb her.

4

◆◆◆

IF YOU'RE GOING TO ARRANGE A FUNERAL, you probably shouldn't be one of the bereaved. Not that most people have any choice about that. For Abby and me, the next couple of days were a miasma of relentless detail, fatigue so profound we didn't even have the energy to weep from it, and of the myriad emotional jolts of loss. The faint and fading smell of Dad's sweat on his clothes as we cleaned out his closet; the junk mail addressed to Mr. Joli; getting a bill from the rest home that had the word "FINAL" stamped on it. There were kindnesses, too: flowers from the shop owner who'd found Dad in the alleyway, Lars and Beji doing the dishes and the laundry that we'd neglected for days, squirrels raining acorns down on our heads every time we stepped out of doors. Abby said the squirrels meant well. They were trying to make sure we had enough to eat.

No one had found Dad a.k.a. Quashee the kudzu vine yet. There'd been sightings in the city and even one blurry satellite photo, but by the time anyone arrived on the scene, Dad and Quashee would be long gone. Whether or not the two of them understood it, they had good reason to be so evasive; Uncle Hunter was looking for them, too. He was thrilled to know that Dad was so defenseless in his mindless, mojoless state. Uncle Hunter was ruthless with his prey, and he had every intention of turning his position as interim Lord of the Forest into a permanent posting. He was making sure to point out to everyone how seriously he was taking his responsibility. "I'm sorry about Boysie, but he brought this on himself. And now he's spreading an invasive species all over his own daughters' home soil! The entire opposite of what a nature celestial should do. It's unfortunate, but if I find him, I'm going to do what I have to. It's my duty, after all."

Uncle Jack wasn't too worried about that. He figured Hunter wouldn't take the risk of breaking the celestials' biggest tabu: killing one of their own. But Uncle was worried about Dad's well-being. "I don't know how long Quashee can keep carrying Boysie," he said. "Kudzus need to root to live. If Quashee withers away, that'll leave Boysie bodiless. A haint. Haints don't survive on this plane forever, no matter who they were when they were alive."

Dad's body had already been cremated. I was on the phone with Aunt Suze, finalizing details of the wake, when Abby came home with the ashes. She put the container down on the living room table and pulled out a chair for herself. She sat with a groan.

"Auntie?" I said into the phone. "Call you back, okay?"

"Sure. Do you have white Barbancourt on your list, though? Mister Cross says he's going to be drinking a lot of it."

"Got it." The old guys didn't eat, but they sure loved their white rum.

I rang off. The ashes were in a matte coal-coloured urn fashioned, oddly enough, in the shape of an anvil. "Where'd you get that urn? I don't remember seeing it in the crematorium's catalogue."

"Me neither. I think I know where it came from, though. I just didn't figure General Gun for having a considerate bone in his body."

"I dunno, Abs. Suppose it's actually surveillance? Maybe when we fall asleep tonight, an army of teeny-tiny Greek soldiers is going to come out of it and try to conquer us."

The corners of her mouth turned down. "Can you not crack any more jokes today, do you think? Can you at least pretend to be taking this whole thing seriously?"

I put my pen down on my sheets of cross-referenced lists of stuff we needed for the wake the day after tomorrow. "Excuse me? What part of me rolling my sleeves up and pitching in with you to help this funeral happen strikes you as me not taking it seriously?"

She growled, "The part where you act as though you're doing me a favour. He was— is your father, too, you know."

Ouch. I stood up. "I'm gonna make myself a sandwich. Want anything?"

"You're changing the subject."

"You betcha."

There was a big blue bowl on the kitchen counter. It had a wavy raised pattern on it, and it was full of shrimp, scallops, and snow peas in a coconut curry sauce. The blue of the bowl offset the warm yellow of the food perfectly. I could see kari leaves in the sauce, and narrow strips of red sweet pepper. A smaller bowl beside it held a mound of fluffy white rice. There was enough to feed me and Abby each at least twice. The aroma of the steam rising off the curry made my tummy rumble. This morning I'd gotten right to work on funeral arrangements. I didn't remember having breakfast. "Abby? Did you cook?"

"Did you see me cook? I only got in a few minutes ago. What's that smell?"

"Hang on a sec." I put the bowls onto a tray along with a couple of plates and some cutlery. I carried the lot out into the living room.

"Oh, my," said Abby as she saw what I'd brought.

"I know. Who d'you figure made us this offering? Aunt Zeels, or Grandma Ocean?"

"Maybe both of them. Gods in heaven, but that smells good. Put it down onto the table already, nuh? I'll take Dad's ashes elsewhere."

She took the urn over to the coffee table that was in front of the couch and set it there. Butter, curious, got up onto her hind legs and touched her nose to the urn. Then she caught the scent of the seafood. She sashayed over to the living room table, nearly tripping Abby a couple of times on her way. For the duration of the meal, Butter trolled under the table, sliding seductively against our legs and churring hopefully at us. She was the only one doing any conversing. Abby stared down into her plate and chewed and swallowed mechanically. Though the food was so good that it practically made me light-headed, I couldn't enjoy it, either. I might as well have been eating from the urn of ashes on the coffee table.

Abby said, "I'm gonna finish my plate in my room."

"Uh-huh."

Butter went with her. So then the only noise was that of the occasional acorn hitting the front door. Yup, Abs and I sure were getting along well since we'd cleared the air the other night. No need for me to break away from our holding pattern at all, no sirree.

Well, the details of the funeral the day after tomorrow were pretty much all arranged now. And Abs clearly wasn't enjoying my company, any more than I was revelling in hers. Good thing I hadn't changed my plans for moving into Cheerful Rest tomorrow. I'd be doing us both a favour.

I took my plate to the kitchen. I scraped the uneaten food on it into the garbage. Dessert was a couple of painkillers from the bottle of them that I'd taken to carrying around in my pocket. Life was definitely being a big pain in the neck at the moment.

◆ ◆ ◆

When we were little, Abby and I used to have a ball fooling people into thinking I was her. I'd dress in her clothes, use her crutches. Even though our heads were shaped a little differently and she was smaller than I was, most people who knew us would be fooled, unless they were Family or other black folks we knew. But the last time I'd wanted to play pretend like that, Abby'd nixed it. "It's not fair," she'd told me, pouting. "You can be me, but I can't be you." I'd argued with her, tried to convince her. But I didn't fight for it as hard as I could have. She'd looked so vulnerable, little kidney-bean-and-matchsticks body propped up with child-sized crutches.

◆ ◆ ◆

The next day, I woke up late and gritty-eyed with that flu-like ache you can get after too many stressful days in a row. In the bathroom I swallowed a couple of painkillers. I opened a bottle of the nasty medicine from my dwindling supply. Dad needed to get his ass out of Quashee and into a functioning human body so that he could make me some more of it, pronto.

I put the phial to my nose and grimaced at the smell. I braced myself for the taste. I used the dropper to suck up a dose of it. I opened my mouth and squeezed the dropperful of tincture into it. A flash fire of fury grabbed me. Before I even knew that I'd done it, I'd flung the dropper against the bathroom wall, the spat-out mouthful of medicine not far behind. The dropper shattered into tiny pieces, leaving the black rubber squeeze bulb to drop and bounce erratically on the bathroom tile.

"Maka?" came Abby's voice from the direction of the kitchen. "Everything okay?"

"Yeah." Damn. I'd hoped to be packed up and out of there before she woke up. I looked at the half-full bottle of medicine. I didn't want Dad's fucking mojo. But I needed it. I swigged my dose right from the bottle.

As I was on my way back to my room, Abs called out, "Do you want some lunch? I made fiddleheads and bacon."

My favourite. Miss Thing was trying to be nice to me after yesterday. Well, I guessed I could stay long enough for a meal.

"Maka?"

"Yeah, I'll have some."

The smell of greens and bacon cooking wafted at me in a cloud. I retched. My nose was saying yes, yes, yes, but my stomach was saying *hells* to the no. "Did you burn it?" I asked.

"No." She sounded puzzled. "Come and eat."

The smell assaulted me again. "On second thought, maybe later."

"Oh," she replied, disappointment and disapproval clear in her voice. "It's going to get cold."

"That's all right." I went into my room and closed the door before any more of that smell could get in. What'd she done, cooked it in bat piss?

I looked around at my worldly possessions. Not much there. I bet I could get it all packed up in an hour or so. First, though, I needed boxes. And a moving van to load the whole lot into.

Holding my breath against the reek of lunch, I crept out into the hallway. I could hear the sound of running water from the kitchen. Abby was running through her scales as she did the dishes. It hurt my head to listen to her. Man, was the world ever ouchy today.

I crept into Abby's room. Her handbag was on her bedside table, as usual.

My cell phone said the time was 12:32 p.m. Abby had physio at one thirty. I clambered gratefully back into bed. When Abs knocked gently on my door a few minutes later, it was easy to feign sleep. Not long after that, I heard the car pull out of the driveway. I hoped she wouldn't need to show her driver's license today for any reason. Or use her credit card.

I got out of bed and peered out the window. Looked like a sunny afternoon out, though with the crisp cold of a Toronto spring. I dressed in jeans, socks, heavy sweater. In the front entranceway, I dragged on my boots and shrugged myself into my light spring jacket. The ten-minute walk to the subway would probably clear my head a bit.

I was right; the whole thing hadn't taken much time at all. A couple hours later, I pulled up outside Cheerful Rest in the rented van. My few boxes of stuff rattled around in the back. I took two of the smaller ones up the stairs. I put them down and stuck my sparkling new key into the lock. It caught a little as it turned.

When I opened the door, a dark, muscular wad of fluff slid past my ankle and into my unit. The fuck? I stepped inside and felt around until I found the light switch on the wall near the door and flipped it.

Yoplait sat in front of me, watching me with a calm yellow eye. "Cat," I said, "Where's your daddy?"

"Yoplait!" called a voice from behind me. It was Brie, standing in the doorway I'd left open.

"He's in here. Come get him." I moved aside to let Brie in. He was in full dress uniform: black torn T-shirt, et cetera. He looked really good. Still, if I found out that he'd slipped something into my drink that night...I was pretty sure it'd been mojo, though. I was dying to know what Brie was.

"Yoplait," Brie said, "get out of here! What're you doing, bugging Makeda like this?" It was echoey in the empty unit. Living with Abs had taught me to notice things like that. Brie snatched the cat up. From what I'd seen of Yoplait, anyone else who'd tried that would've lost a body part. But with Brie, Yoplait satisfied himself with a brief, disinterested yowl. Point made, he settled himself comfortably in Brie's wiry arms.

"I'm really sorry," said Brie. "I was feeding him, and when he heard you go by, he rushed out of my place before I could stop him."

"No worries," I replied cautiously.

"You finally moving in?"

"Uh-huh. Hang on; is he *purring*?"

"Yeah. He sometimes remembers how." Brie gruffly knuckled Yoplait's head. Yoplait half-closed his eyes and turned his head so that Brie could reach the itchiest spots.

"Wild. Listen, sorry to run, but I gotta empty the van and get it back before the rental place closes." Abby would figure out soon enough that I'd put the cost of it on her credit card. I didn't want to saddle her with a late fee into the bargain.

"Sure. Lemme just put Yoplait back inside, and I'll help you off-load your stuff."

"No. It's fine. Thanks, though." I was going to play it cautious until I could find out what was up with Brie.

He drew back in surprise. "Really?" Then he grinned. "Tough chick, huh?"

"Yup." He left, and I locked the door behind him. I stepped through the entranceway, just to have a quick look at the space. I still couldn't quite believe it was mine. I smiled up at the ceiling-scape of clouds in a haint-blue sky. I had finally broken free. My eyes welled up, blurring my vision a bit. For a split second, the clouds seemed to actually be moving against the sky.

I poked my head outside my unit. Brie hadn't gone into his place yet. He was standing outside its closed door, still cradling Yoplait, looking forlornly in my direction. "It's no trouble to help," he said. "Really."

"I said I didn't need help." I left the unit and locked the door. Pointedly tested the lock by twisting the handle and shoving my weight against the door. It held.

"But that's your van parked outside, right? I peeked inside. No way you're gonna be able to get that mattress up these stairs by yourself." He grinned. "Even if it is a single."

"It's a three-quarter. Why the hell were you snooping inside my van?"

The door to the unit at the other end of the hallway opened. It was the old Asian guy I'd seen dancing at Soul Chain's show. He came towards us and headed for the stairs. Seen in the light, he looked frail and a little shaky on his pins. His B-boy jeans and hoodie seemed to hang even looser on him than they had the other night, and he had a bit of a stoop. Hard to believe he was the same man who'd been pogoing like a twenty-year-old a few hours before. "Brie," he said, "you kicked serious ass the other night, man!" It wasn't just his clothes; his voice sounded like a young man's, too.

"Thanks." Brie replied. "This is Makeda; she's new. Makeda, meet Win."

"Wayne...?" I said uncertainly.

The old man replied, "Win, as in full of. Brie, you doing a show tonight?"

Full of win. Well, check him out, with the youthful hipster references.

Brie, mock-bashful, cocked his head and said, "I dunno. Looks like Makeda didn't like it. I may never sing again, Win."

Win glared at me so fiercely that I actually took a step back. He noticed. He tried, unsuccessfully, to turn the snarl into a grin. "Hah, Brie, such a kidder. No, for real, dude; when next you guys playing? I could really use a lift, knahmsayin'?"

I raised an eyebrow at the black American street slang coming from a Chinese-Canadian octogenarian. Not that I would say shit to him about it. When your elders are millennia-old demigods, you'd best take the injunction to respect your elders seriously. I could no more backchat an old person than I could open a bottle of white rum without pouring the first drops into a glass and setting it aside to feed the spirits.

Brie replied, "Whoa, guy. It's great that we have fans, *knahm-*

sayin'?" Did I imagine a bit of mockery in the way he said that word? "But dude, you gotta give the well time to refill. We can't perform every night."

"But—"

"Seriously, Win." Brie put a steadying hand on Win's shoulder. "Come check us next weekend, okay? That's only a few days away. And stop making like such a fanboy. You're freaking Makeda out. Understand me?"

Win seemed to finally remember that I was there. "Sorry, miss," he said, shamefaced. He shook Brie's hand. For a second, he almost looked as though he were going to genuflect in front of him. "Okay. Next weekend. I can wait."

He hitched his jeans back up onto his hip bones and shuffled painfully down the hallway, holding on to the wall with one hand. He struggled a little with the fire door that was in front of the stairway. Brie called out, "You need a hand there?"

Win mumbled a no back. He made it through the door. I could hear the first few thumps of him descending the stairs until the door whispered shut, closing the sound away. Yoplait jumped down from Brie's arms and stood expectantly at the door to his unit. Brie said, "Just a sec, boy." He turned to me. There. Right by his head, out of the corner of my eye; the green flash again. "Look," he said, "I'm sorry about peeking into your van like that. But it's not like you'd blacked out the glass or anything, right? Anybody walking by can see your stuff in there, just like I did."

"Well…"

He ducked his head. "It's just that I'm really happy to finally have someone in this building I can relate to, you know? I mean, the people in here are mostly fine. But I swear, most of them probably think George Clinton was the forty-second president of the United States."

I laughed. "I wish."

"I'm serious! Last week, Erin from downstairs asked me how long it took me to do my 'braids' every morning."

I gaped at the spiky Koosh ball of his short dreadlocks. "You're serious? Actually, never mind, I know how it is. I was humming 'Sympathy for the Devil' at the restaurant last week, and the other dishwasher asked me if I was singing 'Amazing Grace.' 'Cause you know, a black woman's singing a song, so it must be a hymn. I mean, I know I'm as tone-deaf as a cat with a head cold. I could have been singing anything, but really? His eyes almost fell out of his head when I told him it was the Stones."

"I know, right?"

This was great. If I'd tried to have this conversation with Abby, she'd be falling over herself to point out to me the two black people she knew who'd made the same mistakes. *So* beside the point.

The corners of Brie's eyes crinkled up when he smiled, kinda like Uncle John's. "All right," he said, "I'm offering for the final time, and then I'll back off."

I considered. "All right. You can help me."

He chuckled. "I knew my winsome ways would work their magic on you."

"Seems so." My dad's side of the Family could do shit like control the weather, for crying out loud. I could handle one skinny, overeager brother.

With him helping, moving in was a breeze. He was easy to work with, laid back but not lazy, chatty but not too chatty. It went quickly. Looked like I would easily get the van back before the late fee kicked in.

Out the back door of the van, Brie handed me two knotted garbage bags. My clothes were in them. I slung them over my shoulders. He said, "Only one box and your workbench left. How be I take the box and you and I come back for the bench?"

"Good by me." I went on ahead, with Brie following. Yoplait

met us at the top of the stairs, just outside my unit. "Wow. How does he get out like that?"

"My guess is there're holes in the walls that I haven't found yet. Cat, quit it! You'll trip me!"

Yoplait was weaving around Brie's ankles. I said, "I'll let him into my place. That should keep him interested for a minute or two." I opened the door and reached in to flick the light on. With a tiny, satisfied mew, Yoplait scampered in ahead of us. I stepped through the short entranceway and into the main body of the unit. I yelped and dropped the full garbage bags I was carrying; Butter was crouched on the sill outside, pressed against the glass of my lone window. "Butter," I yelled through the glass, "get down from there!"

"What?" asked Brie, coming in behind me.

I pointed at the window.

"Holy shit," he said, "we're two floors up!"

"She got up there by herself," I said. "She can make it down again." Yoplait, purring, watched Butter with a cattish lack of concern. Moving slowly so as not to startle her, I picked my way through my junk, over to the window. Butter wove her head to follow me as I moved. I mouthed "Stop following me!" at her. She had her face pressed against the glass to see inside better, the tattletale. Her eyes were taking in everything.

Brie said, "If that little guy falls, he's toast."

"Yup. Butter on toast." I sniggered. "Oh, don't look at me like that. I'll bring her inside."

But the window was the type that swung outward from the bottom. Opening it would push Butter off the ledge. "Oh, crap. I have to go outside to get her down. Wait here."

"You sure?"

"Yeah. I'll be right back." I clattered down the stairs to the outside, ran around the corner of the building to where my second-floor window was. I looked up. There was the dang cat, sprawled on the narrow ledge as though she were on flat ground. "Butter!" I hissed. "Come down from there this minute!" I'd left her locked in the basement. Goddamned feline escape artists.

She looked over her shoulder and down at me. In the gathering dark, her eyes glowed. Without any warning, she sprang up and launched herself towards me. I yelped. I tried to catch her, but she slammed right through my outstretched hands. The thump of her body against my chest threw me to the ground on my back. Only the cushion of my hair prevented me from cracking my head against the pavement. For good measure, she dug her claws into my sweatshirt and hissed at me, as though the rough ride had been my fault. I swatted at her. "Fucking hell, Butter! Get off me!"

She did. She leapt and pounced onto the back of something low to the ground and snarly. The something reared up to stand on two legs. Oh, gods. My haint. "Butter!" Today it was a troll. At least, that was the first word that came to mind at the sight of it. If Butter hadn't shoved me off balance, it would have grabbed me by the legs.

Butter had dug her claws into the haint's back. It tried to drag her off. Nothing doing. Then the cat really got busy. She spat, she snarled, she clawed. She had puffed up to three times her size. She nearly took off one of the haint's clutching fingers. I tried to reach for her. A woman passing by pulled her young daughter by the hand and made a pointed detour around me. "Don't look," she told her little girl. "Those people are always brawling in the street, like dogs. It's a disgrace."

The haint turned to face me and opened a fanged maw. I could smell the spice of its breath. I backed away. Butter jumped down, bounded off the ground right back into the fray. She was like a fur ball of pure hell, leaping everywhere, hissing and scratching. She was only about a fifth the haint's size! My water gun was under the seat in the van, just around the corner. Could I make it there and back before that thing bit Butter in two?

Butter decided the question for me. She sank her teeth good and proper into one of the haint's limbs. It yelped like an injured dog. It shook her off and bounded right into the traffic on the Esplanade. Horns honked and brakes squealed. A car fishtailed. Its driver fought for control, managed to bring the car to a halt halfway into the intersection, facing diagonally across both lanes. By the time the dust had cleared, the haint was nowhere to be seen.

Butter rubbed herself affectionately along my leg, then sat to lick her pale yellowish-beige fur clean.

"I suppose you want me to thank you now," I said to her.

She ignored me. She was working hard at getting her right shoulder as clean as possible.

"C'mere, let me make sure you aren't hurt."

Instead, she stayed where she was and calmly waited for me to come to her. I scooped her up and examined her as best I could. She seemed okay, but suppose that thing's claws were poisonous? She might have a light scratch that looked like nothing until the poison worked its way into her body. Crap. "I'm going to have to take you home," I told her. Last place I wanted to go.

Butter yowled something scornful-sounding.

"Yeah, yeah, thank you," I replied. "Thank you very much for saving my life. There. Happy now?"

For answer, she fought free of my arms and jumped down to the ground.

"Fine," I said. I pointed in the general direction of Abby's place. "Go home on your own then."

She glared at me. She yawned, stretched, turned her back on me and pounced on a small yellow maple leaf that was blowing by at street level. She chased it, doing her catly best to look as though she weren't obeying my order. I called after her, "And don't you dare tell Abs where I am!" She pretended she hadn't heard me.

Brie peered around the corner. "You talking to someone?" He looked in the direction I'd been yelling.

My hands were trembling. Aftershock was setting in. Two haint attacks in a matter of days! What was up with that?

Brie came over. "Were you talking to that cat?"

"Kinda," I said sheepishly. "I know her. She's my sister's cat. She's always following me. C'mon, help me find her. I need to take her back to Abby."

But Butter was nowhere to be seen. Bloody cat. "Let's just go back," I said to Brie. "She's probably home already. I'll call Abby to make sure."

Brie and I took the workbench up. Climbing the stairs with the heavy weight made my head throb. But we were done. My bed had gone against one wall, the box with my sole pillow and my sheets—only two sets of them—on top of it. My clothes and shoes were in five garbage bags piled onto the bed. My nightstand. Three boxes of books. Two boxes, spilling open, that held my tools. My Dremel in its hard black plastic case. My workbench. And five boxes of assorted junk. It still looked empty in there. I didn't even have dishes. With an Oof! Brie put his end of the bench down onto the floor. "Ouch!" He pulled his hand away and sucked at the base of his thumb.

"What happened?"

Scowling a little, he looked at his hand. "No biggie. Caught it on the corner of the bench. Barely a scratch."

"I'm so sorry. Maybe I have a Band-Aid somewhere around here…" I looked for my purse.

"Really, it's no thing. But what the hell was in those last five boxes?"

"Materials. I make altered art."

"Whosie what now?"

"Altered art. I turn other people's junk into pretty things. Well, I think they're pretty, anyhow. Sometimes I make them into windups."

"No kidding! Got anything in there that you've made?"

"I'll show you later. Gotta take the van back."

He was giving the room the once-over. "So," he said, "when'd they let you out of the nunnery?"

"I know. I've never lived on my own before."

"For real? You sound like one of those chicks who go straight from Daddy's house to living with a husband."

"No!" I blushed. "I mean, that's not the plan. I've been living with a re— a friend, is all. Most of the furniture is hers."

"A girlfriend?" he asked carefully.

"No. At least, not in the I-date-women sense of the word. I told you, remember? With my sister."

He nodded. "Right, you did. I can be a little spaced for a couple of days after a show."

All right. So we'd established that I was neither a gold digger nor a lesbian.

"Who're these little girls?" he asked, pointing to the image glued onto cardboard that I'd rested on the bed for the time being.

"They were singers. They were called Millie Christine, as though they were one person. But they were two separate people, born joined together."

"Wow." He stared at the black-and-white photograph of the two teenage black girls dressed in beautiful Victorian gowns, each with a ruffle of black lace at the throat. They stood proudly, apparently back to back, in their pretty dresses and black buttoned boots. "I didn't notice it before, but that's just one big skirt for the two of them, right?"

I nodded. "One dress with two bodices."

"They're pretty. How come you have a picture of them?"

"It's just a photo I like," I replied. *Because weaker Millie could lift her legs off the ground and the stronger Christine would carry her*, I thought. *Because Christine was like me, except she, like her sister, could sing.* "They were born in the nineteenth century. They were slaves all their lives."

"No shit. From Canada?"

I shook my head. "From the US. But they were friends with Anna Swan."

"Who?"

"Canadian giantess. She used to be on exhibit with the Barnum & Bailey Circus. Millie and Christine were bridesmaids at her wedding. I have some other pics somewhere in one of these boxes. I'll show them to you when I find them."

"All of Christine and Millie?"

He'd said Christine's name first. Another point in his favour. "Nah. Of Chang and Eng, of the Biddenden Maids, and a few more. All conjoined twins, pre–twentieth century."

"Conjoined? That's like Siamese twins, right?"

"Yeah. They just don't call them that any more."

"You got a thing for freaks?"

Now I wasn't liking him so much. "I guess you could say that. Listen, you'd better go."

"Wait. Did I say something wrong? Your voice got way frosty all of a sudden."

"It's just that...well, it's like a white person calling us niggers, right? Some of us might say that word about ourselves, but white folks had better be careful how they say it."

"Oh. I'm sorry. But it's not like I said it to anyone's face."

"You said it to me."

He stared at me for a beat or two, and then his eyes went wide with comprehension. "No way! You mean, you and your sister...?"

I nodded. "Way. They separated us, though."

"Christ, and now you think I'm a jerk."

"Little bit, yeah." I chuckled at his stricken look. "Which just makes you claypick— human. Don't sweat it." I could finally display my collection openly. Abby thought it was morbid. One by one I took the framed pictures out of the box and put them on the bed. "Radica and Doodica, India, nineteenth century. Rosa and Josepha Blažek, Bohemia, twentieth century. No, wait; they were the nineteenth century. Daisy and Violet Hilton, UK, early twentieth century. Giacomo and Giovanni Batista Tocci, Italy, nineteenth century. Ritta and Christina Parodi, nineteenth century, Sardinia. Eliza and Mary Chulkhurst, the Biddenden Maids, England, twelfth century. Blanche Dumas, nineteenth century, Martinique. Technically, hers wasn't a case of conjoined twins; she had a parasitic twin."

"That sounds creepy."

I shrugged. "Maybe. It's when someone is born with part of another body attached to them."

"How is that not twins?"

"The second body is incomplete and, as far as we know, unaware. They're often born without heads."

He made a face.

"Oh, it gets stranger. Blanche Dumas's twin took the form of a fully formed extra vagina and two tiny extra breasts fused onto Blanche just above her own coochie. Girlfriend was doubly talented, and she loved using what she had. There's even a rumour that she made it with this guy"—I pointed to the picture of Juan Baptista dos Santos—"and you can see why she might have been curious about him."

Brie boggled at the image of the famed "Man with Two Swords." "Holy…"

"I know, right? Ah. Here it is!" I'd reached the bottom of the box, where I'd put my favourite T-shirt to help protect the glass in the picture frames. I pulled the black T-shirt out of the box and shook it open. "This is the pièce de résistance!" I turned the shirt so that he could see what was on the front of it. On it were five small words: "What Would Millie-Christine Do?" Below that, a line drawing of the image of Millie and Christine that I'd first showed him. He burst out laughing.

"You like it? My sister gave it to me on our twentieth birthday."

"You are something else, you know that?"

"I gotta tell you, I do know that." I checked the time on my cell. "Shit. Gotta go return this van."

"Okay. You like beer, right?"

"Yeah, why?"

He smiled. "See you when you get back."

When I dashed into the rental place, the woman behind the counter smiled at me. "Just under the wire! A couple minutes more, and I'd be charging a heftier fee on this card."

I gave her back the keys, and she started filling out the paperwork. Now I just had to work out how to get hold of Abby's next credit card statement before she did, so she wouldn't see the charge on it. That was going to be tricky with me living somewhere else. "All done?" I asked the woman.

"Yup, we just have to do a once-over of the van, make sure you brought it back in the same condition you left it, and then you're all squared away"—she looked down at her forms—"Abby."

I clattered up the Cheerful Rest stairway and into my unit. Oh, damn; Butter! Was she okay? I called Abby.

"What?" She sounded right cranky. This was not going to go well.

"Is Butter there?"

"Yeah, she came home about an hour ago. Why?"

"No reason. Is she all right?"

"Did something happen to her?"

"Maybe, I don't know." I didn't want Abby to know I'd had another haint attack so soon. I thought quickly. "Um, I was at a convenience store, buying a chocolate bar, and when I came out, there she was, following me. You need to get her to stop doing that."

"Just tell me what happened to her, please."

Lessee, another cat? A raccoon? No, that'd mean rabies shots. I didn't hate the dang cat enough to put it through that kind of pain. "A flowerpot fell on her. From a stand outside the convenience store. Some guy jostled the stand as he went by, and the pot was right at the edge. He didn't even notice what he'd done."

"Oh my God! Was she hurt?"

"I don't know. I tried to get a look at her to see, but she ran away. I've been hunting for her all this time. I'm glad she made it back home! You might want to, you know, check her out."

"I'll do that right away." She'd seen my room, I could tell. There was no mistaking the defensive sullenness in her voice.

"'Cause if she has a cut on her anywhere, it could get infected." I was babbling.

"Your room's empty."

"Yeah, well, I meant to call you about that before this."

"At first I tried to convince myself that an exceptionally tidy and considerate troupe of thieves had inexplicably removed everything from only one room of the house. The one that had almost nothing of value in it."

"You don't need to be so sarcastic about it."

"I knew it had to be thieves, because my very own dear sister would never just sneak all her stuff out of her home when I wasn't around and leave me not even so much as a note."

"Abby, I'm—"

"No, she's far too mature for those kind of high jinks. And she'd never, ever think of doing such a thing the day before our father's *funeral*!"

Her voice was rising. Not good. I replied, "But it's not. Not really. You heard what Uncle said; that wasn't Dad."

"Are you really so heartless?" My ears rang with the mojo-powered oomph she'd put into those terminal sibilants. "Didn't it look like Dad lying in that hospital bed to you?"

"Abs, watch it with your voice. Remember that time you punctured my eardrum?"

"Answer me! Didn't it?"

"Yes, I guess." I held my cell away from my ear and frantically clicked the volume control down.

"Did it make you grieve at all to see even his discarded body lying there?"

"Of course I'm grieving!"

"He's still gone, Makeda! And now so are you, and you didn't even leave me your address!" I heard her loud and clear. I dropped the phone onto my bed and covered my ears, but much of the sound was still getting through. "Gods *above*!" she shouted, her volume powering higher on each word. "Sometimes you make me so mad I could just—!"

There was a crackling sound, then my phone went silent. Cautiously, I picked it up. I talked into it, holding it well away from my ear. "Abs?"

Nothing. My phone was fine, but she'd blown hers out. On average, she had to get a new phone two or three times a year. At least she'd saved me from having to finish the conversation. Phew. I plumped myself down onto my bed and waited for my ears to stop ringing. I knew this wasn't going to be the end of it. Abby didn't give up so easily. Maybe she'd be calmer when I saw her at the funeral tomorrow. It really was for the best. She would get that eventually.

I surveyed my new domain. My stuff looked lost in the huge space. I'd never had this much room to myself before! I set about opening boxes and finding places to put things. I needed some shelves. I'd noticed some scrap wood out back. Maybe I could use it to make some.

And where were my sheets? I wanted to make my bed. I couldn't remember where I'd packed them, so I opened a box at random. Inside was a sproingy mess of partially knitted yarn, puce in colour. *Puke* was more like it. A few weeks ago I'd gotten it into my head to teach myself to knit. I was trying to live within my means, and the yarn had been cheap in the local thrift store. It was good quality, too; some kind of fancy wool, like camel hair, or yak underbelly, or some damned thing.

I dragged the mass of it out of the box. The ball of yarn to which it was attached shook loose, hit the floor, bounced, and rolled a few feet. Along with it fell two fat knitting needles that landed on the floor with a gentle clinking sound. I held up the already-knitted part. It was supposed to have been an afghan, maybe for Dad. I hadn't decided. Man, was it ever hideous. I'd given up on the pattern directions when I got bored going round and round in the same raised herringbone in itchy puce wool with flecks of yellow in it. Whoever'd thought to put those two colours together was only slightly less insane than I'd been for buying the yarn in the first place. And there we had it; Makeda dis-completes yet another project.

The afghan flopped, its far edge hitting my feet. Sucker was big. And, now that I looked at it, almost done. Why'd I stopped? But that was me all over. What was the last thing I'd ever seen through to the end?

I was out of yarn anyway. Fucker was heavy, too. The yarn had been thicker than the pattern called for, but beggars couldn't be choosers, right?

It would only take maybe another half hour to finish the thing, and a few ounces of yarn. But no way was I going to spend money on a hobby right now.

I scoped out my stuff. Stacks of tumbling cardboard boxes, crap spilling out of them; the arm of a sweater here, a wodge of paper shopping bags there. I heard the skittering in the walls again. I would need to get big plastic tubs with lids for keeping my stuff from being made into mouse nests. A nature deity's daughter had to be unsentimental when it came to pests, or our house would have been nothing but a big mound of mouse shit and cockroach eggs from all the little critters that wanted to get close to Dad. To my mental list of need-to-gets I added some mouse traps to bait with smears of peanut butter. Plus some peanut butter. A trip to the nearest grocery store was in order.

Knitting. Right. The sweater sticking out of that box used to be my favourite. Aunt Suze had made it for me, the only one like it, just for me. No identical one for Abby in a different colour. I'd worn it to pieces. It was unravelling at the back hem. But I couldn't bear to throw it away.

I went and pulled it out of the box. I hefted it in one hand. It was a thick, soft cotton, and it was a washed denim blue, not puce. I turned it inside out. Yep, I could see that Suze had made it well; knitted each individual piece, shaping it as she went. Then she'd tacked the pieces together by hand. That meant no raw ends; each piece was made of one long, unbroken length of yarn. I rummaged around in my dented, thigh-high red metal tool cabinet. Found a pair of scissors I kept for junk jobs, the cheap aluminum kind with the moulded plastic handles. I sat on the mango-yellow floor. Wouldn't want to get snippets of yarn all over my bed. I spent a few minutes snipping apart the stitches that held the sweater seams together, then cut the knot at the top of the big piece that had formed the back. The yarn began ravelling free pretty easily. I joined the end to the loose end of the puce monstrosity. Then I smoothed out the pattern sheet and had a look. What the hell did "Knit bar from Row 1" mean? I must have figured it out before, to have gotten this far. Already frustrated, I dumped the yarn beside me.

Someone knocked on my door. I opened it. It was Brie. I smiled. "I'd forgotten that you said you'd see me when I got back."

"Forgotten so soon! I'm cut to the quick!" He brought a six-pack of beer out from behind his back. "Welcome to the building. I got some good stuff, not the kind I usually sell at my gigs."

He looked so earnest, standing there with his six-pack of Steam Whistle. This was perfect. A drink or two, he'd be more relaxed, then I could ask him about his mojo. I stepped away from the door. "Come on in."

"Thanks." He craned his neck and had a good look into the unit before he stepped inside. "You don't have company or anything?"

"No one here but us chickens."

"Chickens?" He took a half-step backwards.

"Yup. Where does that expression come from, anyway? 'Nobody here but us chickens'?" I followed him in and plumped myself down onto the floor, beside the bed. "Let's have a couple of those beers, all right? You can put the rest in the fridge."

He knelt to open the fridge door. I glanced at the knitting instructions. Oh, wait; I knew what that instruction meant now! I picked up the knitting and the needles and began working the loose yarn from my sweater into the piece. It was a little less bulky than the puce. I decided not to wonder about what that would do to the shape of the afghan. Knit one, purl one across... w—

"Uh, Makeda?"

"What?" I was frowning at the instructions.

"Why do you have a pair of panties in your freezer?"

"Two pair, actually. Each one in its own ziplock bag." Oh, right. I had company. I put the knitting down. "See how hot it is in here already? This place is going to be a bugger come summer, right?"

"Right." He closed the fridge door, brought two beers over, gave me one. He sat on the floor and leaned his back against the bed. "And this is relevant how to panties in the freezer in spring?"

"You know how stupid-hot and muggy Toronto summers get?"

"God, yes. Days when you feel like you can't even sweat the heat out, because the air already has all the moisture it can hold?"

"Ooh, and he's good with a turn of phrase, too!"

He smiled teasingly. "It's what I do. So. It's hot in summer. What next?"

"Half a mo. Can you reach me my handbag, please? It's on the bed behind you." I took the bag from him and got my medicine out of it. "My uncle told once me that nights when it's too hot to breathe, much less think, if you keep a couple of clean panties stored in the freezer, you can just slip into a crisp, chilly pair."

Brie burst out laughing. "And nothing cools a body down faster than a cold shock to the gonads!"

"Exactly. And this is my first chance to try it out. My sis's place has air-conditioning. When it starts getting hot in here, I want to be ready." I used the beer to wash away the taste of the vile stuff. I wasn't supposed to mix it with alcohol, but it was better than not taking it at all.

"How'd your uncle come by this handy little piece of fashion advice?"

My eyes were sliding back to the knitting. Absently, I replied, "I didn't ask him how he'd learned it. I figured the answer'd either have something to do with his profession, or with his amatory escapades, and either way, it'd be TMI."

"And what's your uncle do, exactly?"

I shook my head. "And here I was the one who wanted to start in with the questions."

He had the oddest look on his face. "Earlier today," he said, "you were fighting with some kind of creature out in the street."

Now he had my attention. I had a sip of beer to buy myself some time. The fizzy bittersweetness tickled my nose.

Brie looked sheepish. "Never mind, I'm kidding. Sometimes I kinda see things when I'm tired. Just forget it. Okay."

"You saw my haint."

"I wasn't imagining it?" he asked warily.

"I knew it! I knew that you were Shiny! What are you? Whose were you?" I chuckled. "Abby's gonna hate this. She's not the only one that can have cool inspirited friends, so there."

Brie was holding up warding hands. "Whoa, whoa." His smile was tentative. "You lost me somewhere around...I saw your what?"

This was exciting! "We'll get to that. You're Shiny. How come?"

"Shiny? Does that mean good-looking, or talented, or something?" His smile had taken on a tinge of puzzlement.

"No, silly. Though you are. But Shiny is Shiny. Happens if you're one of the Family, or if you've been rubbing up against brilliance daily for a very long time. And I know you're not one of the Family."

"Rubbing up against brilliance? As in I don't have any of my own?"

"Well, no, that's not what I mean at all. Some of the old guys on Dad's side of the Family think that way, but I don't. Though in the beginning, you probably didn't have a mind of your own, right? Before you became a person? What were you before that, if you don't mind my asking?"

"Makeda, if this is some kind of extended metaphor for artistic talent, you lost me way back. What are you really asking me?"

"Huh? You can't be serious."

"If one of us is joking, it's sure as hell not me."

Incredulous, I glanced over at him. His posture had gone stiff and defensive, his expression wary. Could he possibly not know what he was? "Brie, when you and Soul Chain play, people get stoned. I seriously tripped out at your show the other night, came to hours later to find myself wandering down by the Spit. You're the only one in your band with the kind of Shine that can do something like that."

"Wow, that sounds awful," he said, all concern. "Holy shit! Maybe someone roofied you?"

"No, 'cause it didn't happen only to me. That whole crowd was high, including the rest of the band. And most of us were drinking beer. Sealed bottles. Pretty hard to dose those. So that leaves the other thing, doesn't it?" My arm came all over little prickles. I'd seen the green flash again, just now when he turned his head. I knew I was right. Which meant he could probably see that I wasn't exactly human, either, so why in the world were we playing out this charade? I said, "You can drop the act, you know. I can see the green flash. What is it, some kind of special talent with music?" I could feel the tiny blossom of familiar jealousy blooming in me.

"That's right, talent. Some people do have it. So I'm good at what I do. So what? I'm sorry that something creepy happened to you at our gig. But don't go making it into some kind of woo-woo psychic whammy bullshit so that you can blame it on us. Fucking groupies." He got up and put his empty bottle on top of the fridge. "I don't know what game you're playing, messing with my head. Don't know what you tricked me into seeing a few hours ago."

"But—"

"But, nothing. Just keep it to yourself, okay? I don't have any patience for that kind of shit."

He stalked out of my unit, leaving me completely confused. What in the world had I said to get him so upset?

Wait. Suppose he was like me and Abby, a celestial's by-blow? I could see why he'd want to hide that from one of the Family. And he had mojo, too, like Abby. I tried not to feel envious. I think I almost succeeded.

Screw it. I'd scored a copy of a new consentacle last week. I'd just take it over to the rest home and watch it...

...with Dad.

Turns out that tears of anger and tears of grief aren't so different from one another.

◆ ◆ ◆

Next morning when I stepped out of Cheerful Rest, uncomfortable in a plain black skirt and sweater and chilly in my dress boots and coat, the wooden car was waiting for me. Abby sat behind the wheel, looking simultaneously tired and disapproving.

An icy breeze ran up under the hem of my coat and skirt, pimpling my thighs. Frost rimmed the edges of the grass blades on the sidewalk verge. The windows of the cars whooshing by on the already-busy street were ringed with icy, crystalline teeth. Hands in my pockets, I walked over to the driver's-side window. "Butter tattled on me, didn't she? Told you where to find me?" I peered into the backseat and sure enough, there was Butter, in her plastic-sided carry case, looking smug. "You see what you get for telling tales?" I asked her. "Locked in a box."

Abby said, "Oh, get in already." When she saw my hesitation, she said, irritably, "I'm just giving you a lift to the funeral. It's not like I'm going to try to kidnap you."

I went over to the passenger side and got in. "Why'd you bring her?"

"Had to. She couldn't exactly tell me your street address. She had to take the cattish route. It involved far too many back alley garbage cans for my liking. Besides, she liked Dad."

"You've told her what's going on? She understands the concept of burying the body of someone who's no longer in it?"

Abby took a jerky breath in and out. "She understands the concept of putting rotting meat into the earth."

Something unhappy fluttered in my rib cage. "Oh." Now I was going to have to sit with that thought for the rest of the drive, if not longer.

Abby reached into the backseat of the car and handed me a giant water cannon, much like mine, except this one was black plastic. "I thought it'd be more appropriate. It's already filled."

I took it from her. "I could have thought of that on my own, you know."

"Point is, you didn't." She checked her mirror and pulled out into traffic.

"You really think I'd be in danger with so many people around?"

"Butter says it seems to be getting more vicious."

I turned to Butter and bared my teeth. I could speak that much carnivore, at least. Butter drew back into a corner of her cage.

Abby began, "Maka, I—"

I wasn't sure I wanted to hear it. I said, "Remember that time you didn't come home from school, and Dad thought maybe something had happened to you?"

Abby cracked a tiny, sad smile. "Yeah. And his bicycle had a flat tyre, only he didn't know how to fix it. Plus he could have just called me. I had my cell on vibrate." Dad could make an apple tree bear lemons, but had never really gotten the hang of most mechanical things. "I'd lost track of the time, is all. I mean, I was *singing*. What'd he expect?"

She'd been in the choir, rehearsing for the school's annual

year-end concert. I chuckled. "He was so freaked out. But no way would he just drive, or take the TTC, like a normal person." Dad hated being cooped up in buses, surrounded by right angles, metal, and engines. He used the car as little as possible, and he sure as shootin' wasn't going to get on the subway and ride underground in a hurtling metal tube.

Abby was full-on grinning now. "Last thing I expected was for him to canter up to the school doors on a freaking horse! In the middle of the city! Where'd he find a horse?"

"He's Dad. He called, and it came."

"Melody Kitchin's eyes when she saw it! She kept saying, 'But he's a stallion!' I guess that was a big deal for some reason. You'd think she'd never seen a male horse before, even though little Miss Rich Bitch was always boasting about going to her parents' farm every weekend and riding her very own pony."

"I never told you the funniest part."

"What?"

"I had a look at that horse's tack later on. It had the OPP logo sewn into it."

Abby risked a startled, amused glance at me. "Makeda, you lie! Daddy stole a police horse?"

"Not stole, asked a favour of. You know that's what he would have said. He didn't make that horse do anything against its will."

"How you figure it got free to come when he called?"

"I don't know. But I've always imagined it rearing and throwing some surprised cop onto his blue serge ass, then galloping off to come and be Dad's steed for a couple hours."

"It was so cool, riding home on the back of a horse! It moved like..." She made a rhythmic percussion in her throat, tapping her fingers on the steering wheel for accent. "And Dad sat on it like he was part of it. Something that big, moving with the grace of all its limbs...look, I'm not going to try to get you to come back."

"What? Okay, I guess." And here I'd been braced for a fight.

"I just want you to know that if you need anything, you can ask me."

I was touched. "Thanks, Abs."

"You may have abandoned me, but I haven't abandoned you."

"Aaand, thanks for nothing," I bit out. "Let's please just get through this. We can resume our regularly scheduled bickering afterwards."

Abby sighed and took the exit to Aunt Suze and Uncle Roger's place. I looked back and saw that Lars was behind us on his bike.

Uncle Jack came to meet Abby and me as we pulled up in the driveway of Roger and Aunt Suze's house. The Bejis were with him, two solemn-looking brown bookend youths in funereal black suits. Lars pulled in on his motorbike and eased it into a sliver of space beside Abby's car.

Uncle opened Abby's door for her and gave her his arm. He ignored Lars, who'd walked up beside the car. I was beginning to get the feeling that Uncle wasn't too sanguine, either, with the notion of Abby dating the help. The Bejis and I followed them. Uncle said to Abby, "I'm so excited! You know, I've never been to an actual funeral before. Plenty of births, but no burials."

Abby replied, "How come?"

"By the time you 'uns are planting the body, my work is long over. But this will be good practice for when you girls kick it." He half-turned to address me. "I decided to appear in this aspect. Leave little Naima free to be here as herself. Besides, it's more tasteful than my undertaker shtick, don't you think?"

"And more grand," one Beji whispered in my ear. "Convenient, that," muttered the other.

I pointedly didn't respond to Uncle. Whereas Lars looked at the ground, his lips working to try and hide his mirth. Uncle was all Angel of Death this morning; night-black, easily seven feet tall, with majestic black-feathered wings twice his height that arched protectively above us.

Beji said, "And by the way, Maka? Nice gun." She nodded at my Super Soaker.

I stuck my tongue out at her. She kissed me on the cheek and put her arm around me. On my other side, her sib took my hand.

Aunt Suze and Roger were waiting for us at the front door of their house. Roger cradled baby Winston in his arms. A shy Naima in a cute bell-shaped black dress and matching hair ribbons clung to the back of Aunt Suze's thigh. So then it was hugs all round, blowing raspberries on Winston's tummy, and Naima-you've-gotten-so-bigs, and how's-by-yous. All the stuff that people say and do at family gatherings. And woven all through it, the sad knowledge of what we were about to witness in the backyard.

Once everyone was present who was coming, we all trooped out back. I didn't know how the Family had managed to work it so that it would be okay to bury Dad in someone's backyard in the suburbs. I didn't know how the Family did a lot of things.

The ragged hole in the earth where the hoodoo tree used to be was a shock. Roger leaned over and said, "I cut the wood into kindling, but I'm kind of afraid to burn it. You never know what'll happen when you mess with hoodoo."

Granny Pearl had the answer for that. "Don't be silly, Rog. It's wood. It'll burn, is all."

Granny Pearl was there! In fact, a bunch of Aunt Suze's dead relatives that even she didn't know. There was a black girl, looked maybe fourteen, with her hair in two plaits, wearing an old-timey navy dress, sleeveless, with pleats in the skirt. An old man with reddish-tan skin, long black hair, what looked like deerskin pants, tunic, moccasins. White-looking guy, grey fedora, matching suit. Real haints, not like the horror that had been pursuing me for much of my life. They milled around, looking mostly solid unless the light caught them a particular way or you tried to shake their hands when they introduced themselves. Good thing Abby had brought all the white rum I'd purchased. Perfect haint food.

We gathered around the hole in the earth. The next part was a blur of words that didn't make sense being said to try to alleviate the mean, implacable horribleness that was the death of someone you loved and the sealing away of their carcass. No matter what Uncle had said, I couldn't see this any other way. Tears. People murmuring the same old platitudes, because what is there really to say about something like that? Uncle's smile appeared thin, painted on. For all that he knew that Dad's noncorporeal self hadn't crossed the border to the other world, he had to admit that this was an awful business; this and everything that had led to it. Uncle's eyes held all the sorrow that he couldn't let out, lest the force of the centuries of it that he was holding back burst the dam and overwhelm us all. Abby held my hand so tightly that she squeezed it cold and bloodless.

Naima and Winston, wide-eyed, watched as Uncle Jack hefted Dad's urn and transported it into its grave inside the hole where the hoodoo tree had been. The hands of the shades that existed below the tree, like wreaths of mist, reached out to stroke the urn and welcome it to its new home. The hole would be sealed afterwards by having concrete poured into it. I asked Granny Pearl, "Are you shades all right with having Dad's urn in there with you?"

"We don't need a lot of space. Could store us all in less than a teacup."

"Is Mom coming?"

Granny Pearl shook her head. "She would come to mourn your father's soul, not his body."

Glad she was so clear on the distinction.

Lars and Abby sang a eulogy. "Pastora Divina," a parang song that Dad had loved. Did love. I tried to imagine what it must be like for Abby to keep her voice under control in these circumstances. I failed. I couldn't even imagine why she thought she needed to be all stoic. I'd already cried my way through two boxes of tissues and was working on a third.

It was my turn. My heart pounding, I went to the centre of the crowd. Poured a circle of overproof white rum on the ground and laid Daddy's bull's horn in the centre of it. I lit the circle of spirits on fire and stepped back. We all waited. Uncle murmured, "Come on, Boysie. Come back."

I craned my neck, hoping for a glimpse of side-winding kudzu. Nothing. When I looked back, Hunter had materialized beside Uncle Jack, in SWAT black with false sympathy plastered all over his face and a short-range rifle tucked under one arm. The non-celestials had all bowed the knee at Uncle Hunter's appearance, even the dead ones. I made haste to do the same. My head swam with the quick change of position. I muttered at Granny Pearl, "Who invited him?"

"Ssh. Don't draw his attention."

I looked up. Uncle Jack had gone all death's-head. He would put on his skull-face aspect when he wanted to hide his emotions. I bet he was pissed as hell that Hunter had presumed to appear the way he had.

Hunter gestured for us to rise, and then there was nothing to do but end the proceedings. Dad and Quashee probably weren't going to show up with Hunter around. Aunt Suze waved us all inside. For those of us who ate there was fried chicken, cornbread, and potato salad. I hung back a bit to wander about the yard. The Bejis had blasted that tree but good. There were silk-cotton thorns and matchstick-sized bits of wood scattered everywhere on the ground, and even the occasional dried-out kudzu leaf. I picked up one of the sprigs, a couple of desiccated leaves with a half-dead purplish blossom. The flower gave off a faint whiff of grape candy.

"Playing the tracker, Niece? That's my job."

I froze. Uncle Hunter reached from behind me and took the leaf out of my hand. Even his hunting gloves were a deadly matte black. He sniffed the leaf, then, smiling, crushed it in his hand. He opened the hand to show me the brittle green crumbled bits, like so much tea. "Don't worry," he said. "If your crazed daddy shows up, I'll protect you."

I managed to squeak out, "From what?"

Again that thin, eagle-eyed smile. "Oh, I think you know what. You hold the thing he needs most. Sure, you're his beloved daughter, but he isn't quite himself right now, is he? He might have forgotten who you are. He might only remember *what* you are." While I was still digesting that terrible thought, he said, "And have you seen your other friend lately? Your, what d'you call it? Your haint? Cute name for something so deadly. But I gather you have some sort of weapon against it?" He smirked and patted his rifle. "Now this baby, she can drop a stag dead in its tracks at two hundred feet. But if you feel a dollar-store water gun is adequate..." He pointedly slung the rifle over his shoulder.

Beji's voice said, "Uncle? So glad you came to honour your brother." He came and slid his hand into mine. "Did Mama Ocean send you? Please do join the rest of us inside. Suze has outdone herself." He calmly faced down the glowering Hunter while I wondered why I kept thinking of the Bejis as youths. Youthful, yes. But millennia older than me and Abby. In this moment Beji was every bit the celestial, and he was making sure that Hunter recognized him as an equal.

Uncle Hunter scowled. "Can't stay. Must be about my brother's business."

Beji nodded. "It is, you know. Your brother's business."

"If he ever comes back."

Beji had no answer to that. Uncle Hunter turned to walk away.

Turned back. "The thing is, *burrito*," he said to me, "I really am glad to see you're still feeling well." He began walking backwards. "The longer you hang on to Boysie's mojo, the longer I get to keep this job. Imagine the trophies I could bag!"

Beji squeezed my hand. I let my world shrink to that; the gentle pressure of a single loving touch.

Hunter faded from sight. When he was invisible, Beji said, "Don't let it get to you. He treats everything as though he's flushing prey from a thicket."

"He did not just fucking call me *donkey*."

"In Spanish. Yes. 'Cause it's just so much classier that way, don't you think?"

His words surprised a snort of laughter from me. I slid my arm around his waist, and we headed to the house. "I'm female, so shouldn't it be *burrita*?"

"My ass."

I swatted him playfully upside the head. He grinned, took my swatting hand and made to put it to his lips. Suddenly shy, I pulled away from him. "Thank you," I said.

"No worries."

When we got inside, Abby asked us, "Is he gone?"

I nodded. "For now."

The living room was full of people and the smell of food and drink, which, frankly, was making me a bit queasy. Aunt Suze was sitting at the living room table with her uneaten meal beside her and two armsful of Winston. I pulled up a chair. "Here, let me take him so you can have a bite."

"Sure."

"Hey, Wheeds; come to Cousin Makeda?"

Wheedle cooed as I put him on my lap, drooled a drop of spittle on my dress, and made an eagle-eyed beeline for a handful of my plaits. By then, Aunt Suze had already downed a forkful of potato salad. She took a sip of juice. "Well," she said, "I'm glad that woman didn't show."

"Who?"

"The one that messed with Cora."

"You mean Grandma Ocean?"

"Yeah, that beeyotch. Oops," she said, with something halfway between a smile and a tear, "that's five cents in the kitty!"

"Say again?"

"Oh, it's just this thing I'm always on about. I sometimes wish I could fine people every time they use black street slang to prove how hip they are."

"Yeah, I know what you mean."

"Just charge them a residual. White people, Chinese people; even those boho Obamanegroes with their braided hemp necklaces, you understand me?"

I opened my mouth to reply that I didn't exactly, but Aunt Suze was on a roll.

"I'm not prejudiced, shit. Fine all their asses, fine myself, even; everyone who isn't actually black, American, and street. It wouldn't have to be a lot of money. If everyone dropped a nickel in the kitty every time they slang-copped black street talk, think how fast that'd add up."

"I—"

"Except for dirt-poor white people surviving the life in some hood somewhere. And those Filipino prisoners you see on YouTube dancing to Michael Jackson songs. I figure those guys have earned the right to drop the occasional "homie" now and then. And maybe those queeny fags that grew up poorer'n shit and had to claw and fight every step of the way. Or Roma people. Or hejiras. Maybe I wouldn't charge people like that. But fucking everyone else. It'd be like a royalty to black people. And I wouldn't keep it all for myself, hell no. Invest it in every black community all over the world. It'd be black Wallstreet on the rise again, only this time as a multinational. Globalize us and we'll globalize your asses right back."

"Yes, Aunt Suze." "Obamanegroes" was a nice touch.

"You would think she would have let Cora at least attend Boysie's funeral."

"It's only a funeral when someone is dead. Dad's still out there somewhere."

"I haven't seen Cora since that woman did what she did to her."

"I haven't seen Mom ever. It's like I don't have one."

"Hmph." She had a few more bites, then said, "Has Mister Cross told you what he plans for us? Me and Roger and the kids, I mean?"

I was confused. "Why would he have any special plans for you?"

She stared down at her plate.

"Aunt Suze, are you crying?"

She met my eyes. Sure enough, hers were damp. "I was just hoping." She swallowed. "Since the hoodoo tree doesn't need so much tending to now, you know?"

"Know what?"

"I thought maybe he'd free us. Not even me and Roger so much, but the next generation. I thought maybe he'd let Naima go." A tear rolled down her face. She wiped it away on her sleeve.

"But you're not slaves, or anything!"

She gave a hard, short laugh. "You've never even thought about this, have you? Girl, to you it may be the lightest of bondage, but we are the help, and there's no escaping it." She saw my face. "Never mind. I shouldn't be talking about it when we're putting your father in the ground."

"It's all right," I murmured. But was it? She was right; I'd never thought about it. Always figured I was the only unhappy one in the family. I bounced Wheedle on my knee. He grinned. A *blurp* sound emanated from somewhere in the vicinity of his diaper, and then a distinctly poopy smell.

"Whoops," said Aunt Suze, "there he goes." She quickly wiped her mouth and stood. "Here, give him to me."

I gladly handed him over. She baby-talked at him, "It's time to go change the stinky baby, isn't it? Yes, it is." Wheedle laughed uproariously as his mum took him in the direction of the bedroom.

"It's so strange," said Beji, making me jump.

"Whoa. Didn't see you there."

Beji shrugged. "Many don't. We're used to it."

"What's strange?"

"All this sadness, all this grief, but in the middle of it, people are making jokes and changing their babies."

The other Beji said, "I even heard a couple people making dates to hook up."

"Okay, I've never been brave enough to ask, whose brilliant idea was it to give you two exactly the same name?"

Beji quirked a smile. "It was our idea."

Beji said, "Do we need separate names?"

It was true. Beji almost never went anywhere without Beji. They pretty much finished each other's sentences. "I guess not. It's just kinda weird, you know?"

"Everything's weird." Beji looked over to where Naima and Uncle were sitting on the floor and playing tea party with Naima's dolls. Uncle had folded his wings tightly around himself so that they wouldn't be in the way. Butter rolled around on the floor between them, occasionally batting a plastic teacup away.

I used to think that I could tell the Bejis apart because one was a he-Beji and one was a she-Beji, but when they and Abs and I had a regular booty-call thing going for a few months that time, they'd showed us that they switched that up whenever they got bored with it.

"I would hate it if people thought of me and Abby as one person split into two separate bodies."

"That's very human of you," Beji replied.

"Besides," added Beji, "so many people will think of you as one person, no matter what you do."

I sighed. "'S true. How do you guys handle it?"

They looked at each other as though they were trying to decide whether or not to say something. Then together, they replied, "Who cares what they think?"

"Huh. That's very celestial of you."

Beji said, "Listen, we're sorry we screwed up by letting your dad's soul out of the tree."

Abby had joined us. "How come you didn't tell Uncle Jack what was going down? Let him decide?"

They looked over to where Uncle, Naima, and Butter were playing. "Maybe you shouldn't be quite so trusting of him."

I burst out, "Aw, come on! First Hunter tells me to be scared of Dad, and now you're telling us to be scared of Uncle Jack?"

Abby threw me a puzzled look. I said, "I'll tell you later."

Beji sighed. "Have you ever asked Uncle Jack for the real story of your birth?"

Abby replied, "He told her a few days ago."

"Yeah, and I'm still pissed at him."

"Have you ever asked him what happened to your mojo?"

My skin got all prickly. "I don't have any."

"True, you don't. It was pretty rudimentary, the little blobby thing he tore out of you."

The word "tore" gave me a small, psychic ache, unplaceable anywhere in my physical body.

"A healthy mojo organ is muscular, like a heart. Adamantine. Solid and lacy. Coruscating and matte."

"Still and restless. Infinite and infinitesimal."

Weakly, I joked, "All that at once, huh?"

"We were there, spying on him when he operated on you and on Uncle Boysie. He threw your mojo away. I picked it up."

Abby was agog. "You did? Do you still have it?"

"No, I lost it," replied Beji, crestfallen.

I stared at her. "All these years. We've known each other all this time, and you never told me?"

She looked puzzled. "It was a useless flap of protoplasm."

"It was a part of me!" I was standing. Everyone was looking at me. I pointed at Beji. At both of them. "You two, I never want to speak to you ever again. Do you hear me?"

Glumly, they nodded.

I turned to Abby. "I'm leaving. You gonna give me a lift home?"

"Maka, are you sure? Is this really such a big deal?"

She saw me jerk my arm in towards my body. I could see in her face that she knew I'd just fought my own impulse to slap her. Her eyes widened. "Okay, then. If you're going to get all crazy. Let me just get Butter and tell Lars."

"I'll be in the car," I growled.

◊ ◊ ◊

"Where's Lars?" I'd looked behind us as we drove along the highway, but he wasn't there.

"He's got marking to do."

"Marking what? Time?"

Abby pressed her lips together. "Papers."

"As in teaching? Lars teaches?"

"Uh-huh. How'd you think I met him?"

"At work? Lars has a job? But he doesn't need money for anything. Doesn't eat physical food. Doesn't need a roof over his head. He can just decorporealize."

"Need money, no. But he might want. For instance, an expensive hog. Took money to buy that bike, takes money to maintain it. Where did you think we'd met?"

I threw my hands up. "Think? Aw, Abs, I dunno. At some mighty magic mojo shindig where Shiny beings stand around in shiny clothes and listen to the heavenly chorus?"

She rolled her eyes. "That's the problem with you. You think that just because you don't have mojo, you've been denied access to some kind of sublime life that the rest of us are living."

"Well, haven't I?"

"Makeda, take a look around you! You're living that life! You know many claypickens that have a demigod and a lake monster for parents?"

"No," I mumbled.

"So get the fuck over it already. Would you really have hit me back there?" There were tears in her eyes again. Had been on and off since she'd gotten into the car to drive me home from Dad's interment.

"No, probably not. It was touch-and-go for a second, though."

She sniffed. "That's not like you."

"I'm sorry. I don't know what came over me. I've been pretty edgy."

"Like I haven't been under a lot of stress, too? And this last tantrum of yours was over…what? A piece of offal?" She shook her head. "Thank heaven you never had your appendix out."

I hung my head. "Yeah, I know that was over the top. I've been feeling weird, too. Headaches, food smelling off."

"You have, huh?" She turned off the highway.

Something wasn't right. I checked to see which exit we'd taken. "Hey, this is taking us back to your place!"

"Well, you yourself just said you weren't feeling well. Don't you think that a night at home would do you good? Just one night?"

"Will you stop trying to manage me!" It took a lot of shouting for me to get her to head towards my new place instead. She said some things, I said some things, just the way those kinds of fights go. Upshot of it was that I made her let me out of the car so I could make my own way home. Who the rass did she think she was, trying to tell me what to do?

I headed down the steps to the subway. A woman coming up the stairs widened her eyes in alarm when she saw me, and ran the rest of the way up the stairs. She flinched away from me as she passed me. "What?" I called up to her. I sounded as cranky as I felt. She didn't answer, just kept going to street level. Then she scurried away.

I thought about it. The giant black water gun could look kinda like a machine gun to people who didn't know. And I, toting it, looked exactly like the glowering black woman I was. I didn't feel like putting the glower away anytime soon. And I was about to get onto a subway train with a bunch of claypickens, many of whom would see their fears, not me.

But I didn't dare toss the Super Soaker away, lest my haint show up again. My mind shied away from the thought of the damage it could do in a closed subway car full of people. So, with a sigh, I ended up walking in the biting cold as the day darkened gloomily towards evening. More than one passerby twitched at the sight of the Super Soaker. One guy actually yelped. I growled, "Water gun, man. Big, scary water gun." I strode away from him while he was still stammering out some lame excuse. I started to watch out for cop cars as I walked. In gun-controlled Toronto, it was mostly the cops you could count on to have real guns. And the same fears as the people who blanched at the sight of me.

Oh, I was in a mood, all right. Frigging Abby. And Uncle Hunter, what the fuck was that about I might not be safe around my own dad? Would the essence of Dad really go all Audrey II on my ass?

Even if Hunter was wrong and we found Dad and everything

was copacetic, Uncle Jack said that Dad would never consent to live out his days in decomposing loaner bodies. That did sound like Dad. He was more about the living than the dead.

What would it be like, having a Dad/Quashee hybrid? Could a kudzu vine Dad keep a house pest-free by politely asking all the mice, rats, and roaches to please take audience with him out in the backyard, not inside? Bellow out the rudest words to the Sparrow calypso about never eating a white meat yet, while rolling out the dough for the lightest, flakiest buss-up-shirt rotis ever to grace the world of clay? Throw a party for all the neighbourhood dogs? Could a kudzu plant persuade crabby, depressed old Mr. Weller from down the street to try his hand at growing roses, and then persuade him into bed, show him how to smile again? A stroke took Mr. Weller the next year, and Uncle came to reap him. Uncle told me that he'd died in his garden surrounded by a riot of blushing Sexy Rexy floribundas. And that there'd been a giant three-quarters-empty bottle of lube on his bedside table. How could Dad manage, stuck inside that plant? How long did kudzu even live? Would it stay alive until I died and gave Dad's mojo back to him?

I grimaced, cracking a tear that had frozen onto my cheek. The tear fell away. My skin stung where it had been. I plunged into the melee of bright television billboards, street music, and general rambunctiousness that was the corner of Dundas and Yonge on any day of the week.

My lips were too frozen from the cold to cuss. It'd taken me almost two hours to get to Cheerful Rest. My face and hands were aching from the cold, and I was madder than spit. Of course I hadn't brought any gloves with me. Grumpily, I yanked the outside door of the building open and stepped inside.

Warmth caressed my windburned face, soothing where it touched. My hands began to tingle as sensation returned to them. I climbed the short flight of stairs, opened the hallway door. Was someone baking cookies? A divinely seductive aroma of sugar, vanilla, and butter made my tummy rumble, never mind that I was still full from the spread that Suze and Roger had put on at the funeral. Home. I was home.

I put my key into my lock to open my door, but underneath the gorgeous smells, so faint it was difficult to detect it, there was that same sour note I'd smelled before from the ancient drains in the building, like a hint of meat beginning to go off. I started to sniff up and down the corridor, trying to trace the source of the smell, but I lost the thread. Whew. Wouldn't want that to get worse. I turned to walk back to my unit. Could we fix the drains without dragging in a plumber? From what Brie'd told me, Milo would never go for the expense. Dad used to use...was it boric acid and hot water? Or maybe lemon juice and vinegar? I couldn't remember. Maybe Brie would know. If I could ever get him to talk to me again. I glanced at his door. It was closed. I shrugged and let myself into my unit. I hung my coat and Super Soaker on their hooks just inside the door. At least I couldn't smell the mouldering drains in here. As I was on the way to the fridge to get myself a beer, something snared my ankles. I tripped and stumbled. *Oh my God oh my God haint where's my Soaker.* I struggled to keep my footing, to twist to see what was attacking me, but I sprawled headlong. One elbow cracked down onto the concrete floor. I cried out. The pain was a white-hot brand, implacable and explosive. I stole enough attention from it to check what was holding my ankles. Nothing important. So then, for most of a minute, all I could do was rock, lying half on my side, nursing the elbow, sobbing and cussing. Slowly the pain eased off. I sat up.

I'd caught my feet in my half-finished afghan. Served me right for leaving it lying on the floor like that. Lucky I hadn't impaled myself on one of the knitting needles. I sat, remembering how to breathe, until my heart was done yammering out a tattoo of panic. I clambered to my feet. Wincing whenever I bent the whacked elbow, I laid the bumpy, uneven throw out as flat as it would go. It was ugly as poison, lying there trailing an umbilical cord of denim-coloured yarn that attached it to the sorry-looking remains of my old sweater. Poor misshapen thing.

It looked warm, though. If I finished it, it'd make a good throw for my bed. My window wasn't insulated. It rattled when the wind blew, and on an icy evening like tonight, the little thread of air that seeped in through it might as well have been a needle.

I hunted around until I found the instruction sheet for knitting the afghan, crumpled into a ball and tossed under the bed. I smoothed it out, found the place where I'd stopped. The direction after that read, "Next st on left-hand needle together, K3." The hell?

I picked up the needles and sat back down on the floor with my back against my bed. I pulled the unfinished side of the afghan onto my knees. *Next st on left-hand…?*

Oh, whatever. I stuck the needles into the weave and started improvising the best I could.

When I looked up a few hours later, I realized that I had reclaimed and used up the yarn that had made the back of my sweater, both sleeves, the neck ribbing; apparently even the front piece of the sweater that had had the hole in it. If I looked closely, I could see where I'd knotted the broken yarn ends from the damaged sweater front together every few inches and knitted it right into the afghan. That must have been a bitch to do. Good thing I'd zoned out during it. I frowned, trying to remember what I'd done, what stitches I'd used. Nothing. I was probably still bushwhacked from the roller coaster that this past week had been.

I laid the working end of the piece down on the floor, stuck the needles into it. My forearms ached from bearing even part of its weight for so long, and my insulted elbow had settled into a dull, whiny throbbing.

I creaked to my feet. I worked the kinks out of my neck. My spine and the backs of my thighs were crampy from sitting hunched over like that. And boy, did I ever need to pee! So I went and took care of business. Then I grabbed one of the beers Brie had brought from the fridge. I popped the tab and took a gulp. The crisp cold of the liquid tasted so good that I overlooked that it was both sweeter and thinner than I liked my brew. I drank it slowly, standing right there beside the fridge, while I considered the monster afghan. It needed something else.

I tossed back the rest of the beer, and got to work opening boxes. I knew exactly what I was looking for. Where'd I put them? I looked through box after box, and even in the garbage bags where I'd stashed my clothes. Didn't see them. Perhaps I'd thrown them out after all? I mean, it wasn't as though I needed one and a half strings of— Ah. There they were. In the bottom box of a shaky stack of boxes, wrapped up in a shredding garbage bag and stuffed into a milk carton. When I finally got to that box and opened it, I could only tell what was in there by the glint of a small aluminum wing that had torn its way through the garbage bag.

Inside the milk carton was one whole string and part of another of patio lights in the shape of origami birds, made with thin folded sheets of aluminum. For years, they'd been wrapped around the head of a store mannequin that used to be propped up at one end of the bar in Sally's Bar in Kensington Market. I'd always been fascinated by the little birds, by the combination of metal and delicacy that had gone into making them. When Sally redecorated the place, she'd offered them to me. I'd always meant to make something with them, but hadn't worked out what.

As I unwrapped the birds from the tattered green garbage

plastic, one of them jabbed into my finger. "Ouch!" I exclaimed. I sucked the blood away. "I guess I deserved that," I said to the patio lights, "for neglecting you. And you might hate me even more after I do what I'm about to do with you now."

The birds had begun to develop little rust spots from sitting wrapped in humid plastic, but something about them still pleased me. Beauty and ingenuity beat perfection hands down, every time.

I set the string of them down on the floor beside the monster afghan. Yes, they'd cheer it up. It wouldn't be an afghan any more, but I'd figure that out when I got there. I could weave the birds' wiring around the edges of the piece; unravel what remained of the sweater and use that yarn to attach them. I began to try that. It was slow work, and the birds' tiny wire claws were tearing through the yarn. I needed something tougher to tie them down with. Found the box in which I had put the seven balls of twisted nylon twine. Yeah, that stuff would do. I returned to the afghan.

I suppose I should have measured the circumference of the piece, figured out whether the birds would fit all the way around it, but I hated that kind of finicky shit. Got me discouraged and over-whelmed before I'd even begun. So I just plunged. I found the end of one of the balls of nylon; electric blue, it was. Discovered in half a mo that knitting needles weren't great for attaching the birds. So I used my fingers instead. I wove and knotted and tied—whatever seemed like it would fix each bird solidly in place. It kinda worked, but my fingers were mostly too thick for pulling strands of nylon through the dense weave of the afghan. Ordinarily that would have stopped me right there. I was hungry, and I needed to check in with Abby. But I had a yen on, for some reason. And a few bucks in my pocket, left from the money Abby'd lent me. There was a craft store not far away, in the Eaton Centre. I grabbed my jacket and hightailed it to the bus stop. I made it to the store minutes before it closed. Had enough cash for two crochet needles, one big, one smaller. What the hell did I know about what gauge I needed? Home again, jiggety-jig. On the way, it occurred to me that I'd already begun to think of it as home. But I didn't spare too much time for the thought. The image of the birds attached around the edges of the afghan, standing sentinel, filled my thoughts.

The crochet needles were exactly what I needed for pulling the twine through the afghan and the claws of the metal birds' feet. Took me a few tries to figure out how to attach them so that they would stand along the edge, looking out, their wings held open. Watchful. For some reason, that pleased me.

Of course I ran out of birds before I got all the way around the piece. I stared at it, grumbling, "Right, that's me all over. Start shit without a plan, get discouraged, never finish it."

Hang on; there was that piece of melted aluminum I'd found on the shore of the Spit the other morning. Turn it the right way, it'd sort of look like a beak, or like tail feathers.

I got up and rifled through my half-unpacked boxes, throwing stuff out at random when it got in my way, until I found the knapsack I'd put my beachcombed jetsam in. I peered inside it, rummaged around in there. There was the fish bone, the few sad pieces of driftglass. And yup, there was the piece of dull, sand-tumbled aluminum, its edges scoured smooth by wind and waves. I pulled it out. It did look like a beak. And it had that handy hole worn into one end. If I attached it to that springy little coil of red insulated wire from that morning...

I carried my knapsack over to the afghan and emptied the contents out onto the floor beside it. I sat down and picked up my pliers.

◆ ◆ ◆

I was sitting cross-legged on the floor, with a section of the afghan draped over my knees. Something scraped lightly along my arm as I got to my knees. The fabric I had to push off me in order to stand was heavier than I'd expected. I glanced down. It was huge; way too big to be called an afghan any more. Almost big enough to carpet a third of the room. And what was all that stuff clattering around on it? It was dark. I couldn't see. Had I been working in the *dark*? I flicked the light switch on the wall and took a look around. The door of the tool cabinet was hanging open. I rocked to my feet and went over there. Needle-nose pliers, hammer, brass shank buttons; where'd those come from? I piled a bunch of tools under one arm. A pair of pliers slipped out and fell on my foot, exploding my brain with a sharp, bright pain. I cussed and hopped around the room for a bit until the pain was only a sullen throbbing. I put all the tools back and wheeled the tool cabinet over to the afghan. Then it dawned on me that there had been knocking on the door and yelling for some time now.

"Maka? You in there? Makeda!"

"Yeah! Coming!" God, I was hungry!

"Makeda!"

Shit. Abby. What'd I have to do to get her to stop bugging me?

"Coming, I said!"

I stumbled to the door.

"Makeda, open up! You all right?"

"Just wait, okay?" My fingers were so cramped, it took me a couple of seconds longer to turn the latch and open the door than it usually would have.

Abby stood out there, Brie beside her, Yoplait sitting beside him. Brie said, "You weren't sleeping, were you?"

"No. Why?"

"You were in the dark. I saw the light come on under your door."

"Oh, right. Hang on, let me make it a little brighter." I reached over beside the door and turned the entranceway light on. I squinted at them.

Abby said, "Butter's been yowling your name for hours now. You in trouble?"

"Butter can say my name?"

"Well, her name for you, anyway."

I jutted my chin at Brie. "And why're you here? Again."

He frowned. "I'm not sure. There's something...it's coming from your unit. And I heard your sister knocking forever."

I asked Abby, "How did you know which unit it was?"

"Butter doesn't know from numbers. But once I got inside this place, I could hear why she was upset."

"What's to hear? I wasn't making any noise. At least, I don't think I was."

Brie, so much taller than me and Abby, was peering over my shoulder. "Holy fuck," he said. "What *is* that?" He pointed into my room.

"What? Did a rat get in?" I turned to see what he was talking about.

Abby wailed, "A *rat?*"

Brie, mesmerized, was already moving past me into the room. I said, "Brie, get out of the way. Can't see what you're on about."

He exclaimed, "Makeda, this is amazing!" I still couldn't see past him.

Abby looked as miserable as a wet cat standing there. "Oh, just come on in, then," I said. "Since you're here." Our kind had a thing about being invited into places before we would enter. Grudgingly, I stood back to let her past me. Bad enough she knew where Cheerful Rest was. I hadn't wanted her to see the inside of my unit. Didn't want the whole rant/wheedle/shaming thing to start again: *Come live with me, Makeda, let me take care of you, you can't manage on your own, why can't you be more responsible?*

As I started to close my door, Yoplait slid inside. "Sure," I grumbled at him, "why not you, too?" From where I stood, I saw Abby step out of my entranceway into my main space. She pulled up short. "*This* is where you're living?" She peered around in horror.

"It was tidier than this." Lock was sticking. I'd have to see to that. I went to see what Brie was talking about. I really had to do some grocery shopping. A sandwich would go down well right about now.

My first thought was that someone had somehow broken into the place while I was tranced out and doing what-the-fuck-ever I'd been up to in the dark. The room had more wrong with it than the things I'd first noticed a few minutes ago. Tools scattered on the floor everywhere. Boxes torn open, clothes upended onto the floor and on the futon. Noodle-y piles of unravelled yarn everywhere. The drill press set up on top of the fridge. Under the drill, a shallow bowl with what looked like water in it.

"Did you make this?" asked Brie, his tone reverent. Standing beside me, Abby just looked stunned. That's when I saw what he'd been talking about, lying in the middle of the room.

"I guess I did make it," I replied. I picked my way through the debris to have a closer look. Yoplait sat sphinxlike at the edge of the afghan to watch the to-do.

"What do you mean, you guess you made it?" asked Abby. "Don't you know?"

"Not exactly." You couldn't really call it an afghan any longer. Not sure what you would call it, though. Looked like I'd run out of nylon twine, so I'd taken apart a whole bunch of my sweaters—my good sweaters!—for more yarn.

"What are those things around it?" asked Brie.

"Birds. Had a couple strings of about twenty-two of them. But they weren't enough. I ran out."

"There's way more than twenty-two there."

So there were. Apparently I'd created some more out of aluminum foil. I'd made it to about ten of them before I ran out of foil.

My homemade birds were lumpy, vaguely birdlike, with none of the elegance of the ones I'd gotten from Sally's. I could see clear stuff seeping out from under their mitt-shaped feet, yarn wound around their ankles on top of that. Had I *epoxied* them on? But that wasn't all. The original metal birds were now only the inner ring. I'd knitted more rows, and added more birds as I went. I'd strung them together out of my precious hoard of beach glass, the flat pieces. I knelt on the floor to get a closer look. I'd drilled holes in the bits of glass. "I thought that drill wasn't working," I whispered. The glass birds got smaller with each row I'd added; some of them so small I could scarcely make out their bird shapes. I guess I must have been getting the hang of it by then, 'cause I'd even given them eyes by gluing tiny pieces of brown, green, or blue glass to the colourless, frosted glass of the bodies. One of the birds had red eyes. Shit. I'd searched forever to find those two red pieces. And sitting smack-dab in the middle of the thing? The fish vertebra from down on the Spit. I yanked at it. It stayed stuck to the rug. I knelt and tried to look under it. "I can't even see how I attached this. More epoxy, I guess."

Abby put her crutches together, began to use them for support to lower herself to the ground beside the rug. Reflexively, I reached an arm to help her. Reflexively, she took it. She knelt beside me, peered at the rug. She ran her hand over the rows on the outside, still empty of birds. She cursed and pulled her hand away. She sucked her finger. "How'd you do this?" she asked me. "How long have you been working on it?"

"Just this evening," I replied. "The last two-thirds or so of it, anyway."

Brie exclaimed, "No way, Mak! There're about two hundred birds here!"

"No," said Abby. "More like thousands."

"Don't be silly," I told her. "Maybe if I finished it, added more birds to the empty rows—"

"Run your hand along the empty rows," she told me. "Carefully."

Brie's face was a picture as he watched us. I did as Abby said. "Ow! I got a splinter!"

"Not a splinter," Abby replied. She gave Brie a measuring stare. "You heard something, too, right?"

"Not exactly heard." His eyes were only for the rug. "More like I felt it somehow."

Abby began to hum. The metal birds resonated with the notes, vibrated back at her. She added a second tone, a third, more. The glass birds picked up the pitch and echoed it back, like when you wet your finger and run it along the edge of a crystal glass filled with water. Softly, Abby looped higher and higher tones into her humming. A tickle began in my ears. Yoplait leapt to his feet, bristling and hissing. Brie's eyes went wide.

The empty edges of the rug were vibrating.

I clapped my hands over my ears. "Stop it!" I yelled. "Stop making fun of me!"

Abby hushed. She looked at me. "I'm not."

"There's nothing there! The birds aren't singing! It's just you! Or Brie!"

"Not me," said Brie. "It's like you put hundreds of invisible tuning forks on that thing!"

"It's Abby's voice, then. She's always doing things like that."

He shook his head. "It's not coming from her. Though I dunno how she gets multiple notes like that. She was just finding their pitch. The pitch of whatever it is you put into that blanket thing."

"Twenty-two birds and a handful of scrap. That's all."

Brie looked puzzled, but he didn't contradict me. He just shrugged.

Yoplait poked his nose at the rug, then leapt backwards, his ears flattened and his fur bristling. Abby had her hand held over the rug, a look on her face that I couldn't interpret. Was that what respect looked like? "How could I make something like this?" I asked.

Her voice weirdly calm, Abby replied, "I don't even know what this is."

"Am I learning to...you know, do the *thing*?" I didn't want to talk family troubles in front of Brie. I switched to our sister tongue. "*Am I learning to work Dad's mojo?*" Brie, hearing the unknown language, politely became very interested in the unfinished windup toys on my workbench.

In English, Abby replied, "I don't know. Help me up." I got her standing. She plopped herself down onto my only chair.

Brie was holding a limbless plastic doll. "What'd it feel like?" he asked. "Making that rug, I mean." There was reverence in his voice.

I'd gone light-headed, as though I wasn't exactly in my body. I deliberately stared at the doll, not at the rug on the floor between us. I was afraid that I'd look down and it'd be gone. I pointed at the doll and said, "Someday, I was going to build her a tin army tank, put her inside it with only her head sticking out. Make her a spiky helmet out of curls of tin." I was trembling. Not with fear. I looked down. The rug was still there. The aluminum wings of some of the birds flickered in the slight flow of air through the space. They were set on thin springs I must have found from somewhere. Light twinkled off the shiny metal, stabbing into my eyes. I laughed, a short, hysterical bleat. "If I can do something like this with some yarn and patio lights, I'd better be careful when I make myself a sandwich!"

Making it had felt like the trance I went into when work was going well on one of my tinker toys. Except to the power of one thousand. It was like the difference between snorkeling and what it must feel like to dive, naked and gilled, right down to the bottom of the deepest, bluest ocean. No matter what fate might be rolling down upon me like a freight train, I would know that at least once in my life, I had made magic. It was lumpy, funny-coloured and misshapen magic, but it was whole, and bigger than the sum of its parts. It had come from me. It existed because of me. It made my heart full to look at it, to remember the divine trance that had come upon me and taken me out of myself as I wove it.

I was vibrating with excitement. I met Brie's eyes. I said, "It felt like magic."

He smiled uncertainly. "Because magic exists."

"Don't bullshit me. You know that it does. I've heard Soul Chain perform."

He gave me an odd look. Abby made an unhappy sound, then said, "You do realize that Dad would hate that thing."

Her words were like a blow to my solar plexus. "Fucking hell, Abby! I finally work one little piece of mojo, and all you can do is tear it down?"

Now my shaking was from fury. I held a hand up for her to stop for a sec. "Brie," I growled, "Abby and I need some time alone."

"Yeah, I get it. Should be turning in, anyway. Catch you later?"

I was so consumed with rage that it took me a second to realize that he'd asked me a question. "What? Oh, yeah, right. Later."

"I can let myself out." He padded over to the door. A second later, I heard the soft click of it shutting.

Abby got in first licks. "I'm sorry, but don't you get it? Those birds are still singing, right now! Everything about that rug sets my teeth on edge. It shouldn't be able to exist, shouldn't be *allowed* to exist. Can't you feel it? That thing is the entire opposite of jes'-grew! Dad would call it abomination."

"Yuh rass. You just jealous." Resentment was sour in my belly.

"Not a bit of it," she snapped back. "You've used Dad's mojo to make a thing that can't be. And you're proud of it."

I stood there for a second, stunned. Then I went and got my jacket, shrugged into it. Abby watched me, perplexed. I came back. Bent and started rolling the rug up, trying to avoid the myriad pointy bits that I couldn't see.

Abby yelled, "What the hell are you doing?"

It took me a couple of tries to pick the mass of the rug up. It was scratchy and smelled like wet wool. It weighed a ton. I wouldn't be able to carry it for long. "I need you to give me a lift somewhere."

"Where?"

"You're right, okay? You're fucking right." The words wriggled like worms in my mouth. "So you gonna take me, or what?"

She sighed. "Oh, screw this. Screw you and your sulking." She stood up. "Come on, then. I'll take you."

Yoplait scooted out the door with us. I hadn't even noticed that he'd stayed behind when Brie left. He padded down the stairs alongside me, nearly tripping me a couple of times. "Open the front door, please, Abs."

"Won't the cat get out?"

"He has ways of getting back in. Just please open the bloody door."

◆ ◆ ◆

Abby squinted through the windshield at the slushy freezing rain that was splatting down onto Toronto's nighttime streets. It was pretty. A part of me noticed that, even though shame and anger were making my blood roar in my ears. Streetlights and lit-up shop signs threw smudged light through the fat, wet flakes. The snow muffled the usual harsh city sounds, giving the whole thing an urban fairy landscape quality. But it made the roads a slippery bitch to drive on, and as it froze on the windshield, it made a thin scrim of obscuring ice. Abby flicked on the defogger to melt it. In the close quarters of the car, I could smell the lanolin in the wool of the carpet I'd made. I said, "Turn left here." With an exasperated sigh, she did. I still hadn't told her where I was going. I didn't trust myself to speak much to her right now.

We were nearly there. I unclipped my seat belt. Abby glanced over at the sound, but said nothing. I turned and wriggled over my headrest to the backseat. "Hey, watch it!" said Abby. "What the fuck, Maks? What're you doing?"

The afghan hadn't fit in the trunk, so I'd stuffed it into the backseat, where it took up most of the room. Couldn't sit on it; I'd get a bird bite, or epoxy burn, or something. So I eased myself down into the tiny space left beside one door. I reached over and yanked up the lock on the opposite-side passenger door. Abby eeped and locked it again from the driver's control pad. "You're gonna make me crash the car!" she shouted. The car slewed about in the lane. Drivers leaned on their horns.

"Unlock the door. Right now." A tsunami of anger washed over me again. I didn't bother to tell her that we were only feet away from where I wanted her to take me.

"But—"

"*Now*, Abby, or I'll fucking kick the window out!"

"All right! Just let me pull over!"

"By that dump bin over there." The bin was one of those tall steel ones with hollow ridges at the side so a dump truck could pick it up.

Abby asked, "What're you doing?"

"It won't take long."

Cursing a fiery mix of Trinidadian swear words and down-South imprecations, Abby pulled over and coasted till the car was just in front of the Dumpster. She stopped. The locks on the car doors thunked upwards. I leaned over to open the door. Something scratched my tummy. "Fuck!"

"Makeda, this is crazy!"

I shoved the door open. A curtain of cold rain blew in on me. Abby snapped, "You're getting water on my leather seats."

I sat back down on the opposite side and pushed the afghan. Dang thing weighed a ton. Abby, obviously seething, watched me in the rearview mirror. I ended up putting my back against the door on my side and pushing the afghan out with my feet until all of it had flopped to the ground in the downpour. I kicked it out of the way of the door and crawled out beside it. Icy rain kettle-drummed on my skull. I leaned in through the open car door. Abby had twisted around to watch what I was doing. I said, "There. Since it's such an abomination, I got rid of it. Happy now?"

Abby glared at me. "You think this makes me happy?"

"I don't care. And I'm walking home."

"Oh, for fuck's sake! Fine, then! Do what you want. And you know what? Don't bother coming home at all any more. To our home, I mean. I don't need the aggravation."

"Suits me just fine." I slammed the door shut. Abby didn't try to stop me. Her wet tyres screamed as she pulled out into traffic and sped away.

The rug was too heavy for me to lift over my head and into the Dumpster, so I made do with rolling it underneath.

My thick hair was soaking up rain like a sponge. I brushed a hand over it. Damp snowy slush was already caking in my braids. It was going to be a miserable walk home, and for the second time today, too. I needed to find some other way of ending a fight than stalking away in high dudgeon. But tonight I'd made my exit strategy, so there was nothing to do but lie in it. I turned up my collar, stuck my wet hands in my pockets and got on with it.

The rain cried my tears for me. I wasn't going to give the world the satisfaction.

Fucking Abby.

5

◆ ◆ ◆

"Do you not remember Jeanie,
How she met them in the moonlight,
Took their gifts both choice and many,
Ate their fruits and wore their flowers
Plucked from bowers
Where summer ripens at all hours?"

AH, HELL, dunno whom I thought I was kidding. I'd barely walked a block before I turned back in the direction of the Dumpster. My boots made a hollow thump on the pavement as I walked down the dark side street lined with construction lots. The rain thinned to a drizzle, then stopped. I stopped and squeezed my hair out.

Crap. My Super Soaker. I hadn't brought one with me. It'd been raining buckets when I left, after all. The back of my exposed neck prickled.

I tried to reassure myself that usually haint attacks were few and far between, so maybe I'd seen the back of the fucker for a while. I tried not to think of the fact that it'd jumped me twice in the past couple of days. I made myself stop and turn in a deliberate circle, scanning the darkness as best I could. Not so difficult, really; Toronto streetlights kept the city from ever being truly dark at night. Diamond patterns of tall chain-link fencing lined each side of the street. On the construction sites behind them loomed scaffolding and excavation machines, black on black against the darkness. As far as I could tell, there was nothing coming for me. Probably too damp and drippy out for the haint's liking. But I still felt like a mouse at a hawk convention. Looking over my shoulders every few seconds, I scuttled to the place where I'd left the rug. When I reached it, I bent and dragged it out from under the Dumpster. There must have been a puddle under there. The rug was a bit damp. I rerolled it and picked it up. I'd only walked a few steps before my arm and back muscles began to burn with the effort of carrying it. My fingers gave out and the rug dropped to the ground with a thump and a faint clinking of the metal and glass inside it. "Sorry," I said to it. I hoped I hadn't broken anything.

It was now the wee hours of the morning. I wasn't going to get it home on foot. I contemplated lugging it onto the twenty-four-hour streetcar that ran along Queen Street. Not enough room. Someone would probably trip over it and damage it, or themselves. Besides, Queen Street was a good half mile away. I probably wouldn't even be able to carry it that far. Taxi, then. Or thumbing a lift.

The street was busy enough, but I stood there in the damp for about an hour with my thumb out, and cars just kept zooming on by. It could have been usual Toronto caution around strangers, or the effects of Hitching While Black, or just the weirdness of a woman standing by the side of the road at three a.m. with a wet, rolled-up rug that looked as though it could have a body inside it. Whatever the reason, no one stopped. "I might have to leave you here after all," I said to it, though the thought made my heart wrench. "Wouldn't be the oddest thing that ever got dumped on this road."

It lay there, looking suspicious.

I bent and began to unroll it. I wanted to have one more look at my wondrous creation. I might not find it there when I came back, and I might never be able to make the mojo work again. I jabbed my hand on it as I unrolled the last bit of it. I hissed with pain and held my hand up to the streetlight. It wasn't the tiny pinprick the others had been; there was blood dripping from a stinging slice along the side of my palm. I sucked on the cut, then held my thumb out to an SUV that was coming along the highway. It zipped on by me. I sighed. "Guess I'd better get going," I said to the rug. "I'm really sorry. Tomorrow I'll see if someone in the building has a car. Maybe I can get a lift to come back for you." If the donations people hadn't picked it up by then.

The rug undulated. I swear every hair on my head stood up and saluted, especially when the rug raised itself into the air and stopped at just about knee height.

"You aren't serious." I watched it warily. It stayed where it was. I knelt and looked under it. Nothing there but air. It really was floating. I looked around. No one nearby. The high beams of an approaching car lit the rug up. The wings of the birds on the rug were whirring, so quickly they were a blur that Dopplered into a sidewise-figure-eight trick of the light.

I murmured, "Holy flying fuck and a bag of chips." If the visible birds were flapping their wings, did that mean that the invisible ones were, too?

A flying carpet. My heart was thrumming so hard I could feel it pushing blood through my veins. Wow. I'd made a fucking flying carpet! "For real?" I asked it. It hovered silently. I was going to step onto it; I knew I was. "Can you lower yourself back to the ground? I don't want to cut myself on the birds again."

The rug sank gently back down and hovered just above the pavement. It undulated invitingly. And I was catching my death out here, and I really needed some sleep. The rug was mine, and it wanted me to ride. Would it be able to carry my weight? I said to it, "Wait till I sit down, okay?" I stepped gingerly onto it. It wobbled under me like a loosely strung trampoline. I sat down so I wouldn't fall down. How fast could it, hypothetically, go? What would people do if they saw a chick go zooming past on a flying carpet? Feeling like many kinds of fool, I took a deep breath and sat down. "So far, so good," I said. "You can lift up again. Not too high! Let's say, oh, twelve feet." Did a flying carpet know how high twelve feet up was?

Gently as kissing your baby good night, the rug lifted into the air. By my guess, I was probably exactly twelve feet up. "Holy. Wow. Wow! Uh, let's head home, okay? I mean, go that way." I pointed. I felt like an idiot, giving driving instructions to a rug. But without even a lurch, it smoothly took off, heading in exactly the direction I'd asked it to. Could it see? Or did it read my mind or something? Did I want a rug knowing my innermost thoughts? And suppose I hadn't known the route? Had I woven some kind of mojo GPS into the thing while I was being so brilliant? If I told it where I wanted to go, did it consult its inner MapQuest to find the way there? Oh, man. No wonder Abby was so smug all the time, if she had power like this flowing in her.

The rug was going at a fair clip, making the crisp spring air downright icy. I didn't care. I laughed. If Dad had been there, I could have taken him on a magic carpet ride. Maybe Abs was wrong. Maybe Dad would have loved my creation.

There was a honking of horns and a screeching of tyres behind me, then that awful metallic crunching sound you never want to hear on a busy street full of cars. "Holy shit!" I went onto my knees and turned around to see what was happening.

A car had swerved out of control. Had I startled the driver? The car was still sliding diagonally across the road. As I watched, it crashed into a tree on the sidewalk and stopped, canted over onto its two left-side wheels. The crumpled hood popped open. The second car was in the slow lane, upside down and spinning giddily. Other vehicles were slewing to avoid it. I saw three more near-misses as I watched in horror. "Stop!" I yelled at the rug. "Put me down!" It ignored me. It turned onto Queen Street, and the accident scene shrunk out of view. With trembling hands, I took my phone out of my pocket. It took three tries before I was able to dial Emergency.

"Police; what is your emergency?" said a mellifluous man's voice.

I babbled out what I'd seen, where the accident had happened.

The man laughed. "Look underneath the rug," he said.

"What? Is this the right number? This is serious!" Oh, hell on legs. I knew that voice. The deep laugh had piped its way upwards into a silly giggle. I crawled to the side of the rug, lay on my stomach, and peered beneath it. There was Uncle Jack, wearing the aspect of that bald black guy in the old 7UP commercials. He was holding the rug aloft, giggling to beat the band, and covering yards at a stride. He grinned up at me.

"Hey, girl."

"Uncle, stop it this minute! You put me down!"

Instead, he flung the rug on ahead of himself, like a paper airplane. I was heading, at speed, right for a telephone pole. I abandoned ship. But Uncle snatched me around the waist before I could hit the ground. Time and space went *pop* and next thing I knew, he and I were both back on the rug, which was still flying. While I retched from the swift transit, the rug banked expertly around the telephone pole. Uncle reclined, cocking himself up onto one elbow. Now he was wearing a long black leather coat. Its hem flapped loose behind him in the breeze of the rug's passing. "That was great! Now I know how Old Scratch felt, playing Flying Canoe."

"Will you be serious for once?" I screeched at him. "There may be people dying back there!"

"Now, why do you want to go and throw cold water on my little joke like that? Besides, thirty-five people had already called Emergency before you even remembered you had a cell phone on you." He reached a long arm over and chucked me under the chin. "Don't fret. Nobody in that accident is at their time to cross over yet. Not from that little fender-bender." The grin got even broader. "Though they won't thank you for their insurance bills. And that little boy in the blue car, poor thing, he's escaped this time, but he's not long for this world. He's going to choke on a spoonful of peanut butter."

I stared at him, openmouthed. He continued, "Eighty-one years, nineteen weeks, and one point two three seconds from now."

I swatted at his shoulder. "Big meanie, scaring me like that." I tailor-sat beside him. I was beginning to calm down. As much as a person who was sitting on a flying carpet with Lord Death by her side could calm down. "By your standards, none of us have long for this world."

"Because you don't. Mayflies, the lot of you." He turned the smile off like a light. "Even you and Abby."

"But people got hurt in that pileup, right? Maybe even badly injured."

He shrugged. "Probably." The manic rictus was back. "Did you see that orange Volvo? Spinning on its head like a B-boy?"

"Don't you even care that people are broken and in pain because of your little joke?"

"Have I ever? Health care was Boysie's department, not mine." He rolled over onto his back, hands clasped behind his head. "Hunter's pinch-hitting for him, but that boy wouldn't know his own ass if you gave it to him right in his two hands. Boysie's going to have a hell of a backlog when he reports for duty again."

"You're sure that's going to happen, then?"

"Of course not."

"Uncle, can I ask you a favour?"

"Anything. You know that."

"Set Mom's family free."

"Oh, but I barely ask them to do anything for me!"

"Do you? Ask, I mean? Naima has no friends her age. Suze and Roger have to homeschool her, because they know it's too much to expect a six-year-old to keep quiet about being handmaiden to a demigod. Do you ask them to do all that, or do you just know that they're too terrified to say no to you?"

He pouted and looked up at the stars. "You know what the really important thing is?" He fixed me with a gimlet eye. "What the fuck were you playing at, making this thing?"

"What do you mean? You're the one making it fly." Maybe I hadn't worked any great mojo after all. I swallowed back the bitter taste at the back of my throat. Envy is an organ of the emotional body. Just like your gall bladder, it squirts out bile.

"No, I'm not. And there's no way that *you* should know how to make an abomination like this fly. If Ma found out about this, the shit would really hit the fan."

"Wait, let me get this straight; I finally figure out how to exercise a little bit of my birthright, and both the relations I'm closest to call it an abomination?"

He didn't rise to the bait. He gazed at me calmly. It's how he'd kept me and Abby in line when we were kids and he was babysitting us. If we acted up too badly, we'd get the Look. You know how every black mother the world over can put fear in her child's heart with one look? Well, none of them can hold a candle to Uncle Longleg Jack. The long seconds of his gaze would give me and Abby time enough to think about just how foolish it would be to piss off Lord Death, and we'd stop whatever it was we'd been doing that we shouldn't have. But I was grown now, and he didn't scare me. Mostly didn't. Bravely as I could, I set my jaw and glared right back at him.

He sat up. "Here's the thing; you know how I'm like the ultimate firewall, yes?"

"Say what?"

"Think about it, baby girl. I guard the transfer point between this world and the next. I make sure nothing gets in that shouldn't get in, or out that shouldn't get out."

"Oh. Yeah, put it that way..."

"Well, when you gave this thing the life of your blood," he said, making a nasty-smell face at the rug, "and whoever else's blood I can smell on it, and then invested it with your love, you probably inspirited it. You gave the energy of life to a construction that shouldn't be able to hold it. And every perimeter alarm I ever set or will set started hollering, all the way back to last week. This thing shouldn't be here. It's toxic to this world. It's a virus."

Suddenly, I wanted to not be sitting on that rug as fervently as I've ever wanted anything. "I'm sorry," I said. "What should I do?"

"You?" he replied cheerfully. "Nothing. This is my department, after all. I'll get rid of it. Just don't ever do anything like this again, okay, sweetie?"

I sulked. "All right. Only I don't even know how I did it the first time."

He frowned. "Neither do I. Something weird's going on."

"You don't think I'm finally growing into Dad's mojo?"

He looked doubtful. "Maybe. We'll see."

"And shouldn't we get off this thing now, if it's dangerous?"

He shook his head. "Not yet. It's such a sweet ride. Might as well let it take us to where we're going."

"We? Where're we going?"

"Oh, I'm coming back with you to your place. Just so happens I have an appointment there." His toothy smile made me shiver.

I shuddered, and not just from the cold. "Uncle, is it me you're coming for?"

"Don't be ridiculous; if it were your time, I'd just take you from right here. By your standards, you're nowhere near..." He trailed off. He blanched right down to his bones, and now there was a chattering skeleton sitting beside me. "Well, it could be soon, at that. Not tonight, though. I don't think. You know I can't see these things too clearly when it's family involved." His grin was more like a grimace.

"Oh, stop your kidding around. Your jokes get more macabre the more worried you are."

Casually, he pulled a fat cigar out of the brim of his top hat. It hadn't been there before. And it was already lit. He puffed on it for a second or two, not meeting my gaze. "Sorry," he muttered around it.

I tried to wave the cloud of cigar smoke away. "Man, that thing stinks."

"It should. It's made of bonemeal and cinnamon."

I rolled my eyes. "Since when? I thought you preferred the ones made of dried blood and graveyard ash."

He shrugged. "A change is as good as a feast, they say."

"What's on your mind, Uncle Jack?"

He took the cigar from his mouth and tamped it out against the back of one hand, adding the hissing smell of burned bone to the charnel perfume that hovered around him. "You know I can't interfere."

"Yeah, you lot and your celestial Prime Directive, I know. Can't interfere in what? Never mind, I know this one; you oversee life and death, so you're not allowed to affect anything that might lead to either one."

His smile was wry. "There are two forty-year-old claypickens in a parked car over the next ridge. One man, one woman. They're both divorced. From each other. They're indulging in a bit of angry breakup sex. Neither one of them has made out in the back of a car since they were teenagers. They're mature adults and they know what's what, so they're using a rubber, but wait for it…" He held up a bony forefinger, looked up and to the side as though listening for something. "Ah. There it goes. The condom just broke."

"And what's going to be the result this time? Birth, or death?" He was a two-way ferryman, after all. Sometimes it wasn't so much fun, getting a peek into Uncle's job.

"It'll be birth. Two births, in fact. When she learns that she's pregnant, she's going to tell her shrink, who's going to go out that same evening and knock his girlfriend up. Bim-bam. And now a mile over yonder, a man has just beaten his dentist to death with a frozen fish. Happens more often than you'd think. It's a kind of ludicrous situation. Almost as ludicrous as if your Dad's soul was trapped inside a large climbing plant."

My mouth had gone dry. "Is it Brie you're coming for?"

Uncle gave me his best death's-head grin. "How 'bout them Jays, huh?"

"Stop it! You don't even like baseball!"

"You know I can't talk business with you. And anyway, who or what is Brie? Hell of a name." He stood up, balancing shakily on the flying carpet like on a water bed that hadn't been filled enough. "Gotta go. Woman with a crossbow just walked into a gas station in Bogotá and boy, is she pissed."

He was gone. I sat there seething while the carpet drifted slowly downwards. He was only using the woman with the crossbow as an excuse to get out of the conversation. His quantumate selves could be here, there, and everywhere people were borning and dying, every millisecond of every day, world without end, amen. But off he'd hustled, leaving me alone with the knowledge that tonight, someone in my building was going to breathe their last. You've heard people say they have the family from hell? Well, I have the family from heaven. And I honestly didn't know which type was worse.

Just like that, Uncle was back. "Whew. That's done. Let's bring this hunk o' junk in for a landing, shall we?" The rug hovered in front of my window. Uncle would have crashed right through it, only I made him stop and help me to pry the window open. We sailed into my unit. The carpet settled with a squelch, and promptly began leaking the rainwater it'd soaked up all over my floor. We got to our feet. Uncle said, "Pity I have to confiscate this thing. You did a really good job on it. Anyway, there isn't much time. You'll have to mop that water up later if you want to watch me work. Meet me outside Room 213, there's a good niece."

And I was alone again, with my feeling of dread, even though it wasn't Brie. Room 213 was where old lady Fleet lived.

◆ ◆ ◆

Fleet came around the corner from the direction of the kitchen. She was wearing a balding, pink chenille bathrobe, cradling a small blue bowl in one hand and swinging a spoon about in the other. Conducting with it, actually. And humming breathily along as she did so.

Uncle literally did a double take when he saw her. "That's not her," he said.

"Sure it is. Hey, Miz Fleet. How goes?"

She turned towards me, ethereal as the planets in their spheres. She waved at me with her spoon. "Hey, girl. Whoever you are. How's it hanging?" She walked right through Uncle to get a little closer to me. Unless he chose otherwise, he wouldn't be real to her until she crossed over. She said, "So who are you, and what day is this?"

Thrown, I mumbled something like, "Uh, I'm...Makeda... new neighbour...assistant super...today's Sunday."

"So almost another week to the next Soul Chain gig. I wonder if I can wait that long?"

Uncle mumbled, half to himself, "It *is* her. Why is it her?"

"I like listening to Brie play," Fleet told me, her voice reverent. It was as though she were lit from within. "When he plays, my soul thins out, like oil on water. Sometimes I think I feel myself float. I swear I can vibrate my molecules and pass right through walls." She gasped and put a hand to her mouth. With her teeth, she worried at the knuckle of her index finger. She pulled the finger out of her mouth with a popping sound. She leaned in close to me. "It doesn't work so well any more, though. Even though I go to all his shows. Why is that man looming over us?" She waved a hand at where Uncle was standing. She could see him! She averted her face from him, but her eyes kept sliding in his direction. "Tell him to go away!" she hissed at me.

"Tell her I haven't come for her yet," said Uncle gently, his voice cold as crushed ice being shovelled over a corpse. "It's not quite her time."

Fleet turned and looked right at him. "It's not?" Oh, but she sounded so very weary! "It'll be soon now though, won't it?"

Uncle nodded. "Soon."

"I'll be brave."

He nodded again. "I have a feeling you will be."

"I don't want to go yet, I don't think. But I guess I've thinned out so much that there's almost none of me left."

"That's true. And when it's time, I'll come and help you pass through one last wall."

Fleet nodded. "That'd be nice. Now I have to go and have supper." Her face broke into a crazed smile. "Oatmeal. It's good for the blood!" She floated away in a haze of chenille and incense. Uncle John, one eyebrow raised, watched her go. When she reached her door, her trembling fingers dropped the keys three times. I called out, "You need a hand there, Miz Fleet?"

"Do it myself!" she shouted, face to the door. "I'm sorry. I mean, no thank you." She giggled in hemidemisemiquavers, a concatenation of hyena-mad notes that put Uncle's manic laugh to shame. She bent to the floor, managed to pick the keys up the third time. With a shaking hand, she jabbed the key once or twice in the general direction of the keyhole until it slid home. As she let herself in, I could hear her muttering, "Do it myself. Do it myself." She slipped inside and slammed the door behind her.

"That was weird," I said shakily.

Uncle John murmured:

"She pined and pined away;

Sought them by night and day,

Found them no more, but dwindled and grew grey;

Then fell with the first snow,

While to this day no grass will grow

Where she lies low."

"Say what now?"

There was a thud from behind Fleet's door, a soft cry, then nothing. Instinctively I rushed towards the door, scrabbling at my waist for the master key. Uncle stopped me before I got too far. "Uh-uh. I've already taken her across the threshold. Nothing you can do now." He made a wry face. "People *will* walk with spoons in their mouths. If they trip and fall, it's not pretty."

"But I can't let her just lie there!"

"Sure you can. Her body'll be just fine where it is for a bit."

Whenever I managed to half fool myself that Leggy Jack was just my eccentric old uncle, he did or said something that reminded me that he was so much more. He asked, "Do you have any idea who scraped that poor child all hollow, like pulp from a grape-fruit?"

"They told me she was in and out of the psych hospital, that she'd done a lot of crack and was on a crapload of meds. That what you mean?"

Tasting the air with his tongue, he tracked a few steps in the direction that Fleet had gone. Always creeped me out when he did that. Made him look like he'd been inhabited by a snake. "Drugs aren't what did this," he said. "And she was no crazier than you or me. I know that's not saying much. But it wasn't anything of the physical world that made a girl of twenty-three look like a woman of ninety-two. She's been emptied."

"That old lady was only twenty-three years old?"

"Yuppers."

This was beyond crazy. And why was he asking me for the answer? "How come you don't know stuff, huh? Like where Dad is, and what happened to Fleet? You used to tell me and Abby that you knew everything we were getting up to!"

He was still sniffing around. "It's what you tell children. It only keeps them in check for so long, though. Then they grow up and figure out that the adults have been lying through their teeth."

I couldn't take my eyes away from Fleet's door. I couldn't make myself stop imagining what she looked like, lying there, her soul fled.

Uncle shrugged. "I don't want omnipotence. That's the Big Boss's burden. He runs with the throttle full open, all the time, no filters. He receives all information, always."

"Sounds like autism to the power of infinity."

"Something like that." He inhaled deeply. His lips pulled back in distaste. "You need to get out of this place. Something's not quite right."

"But I like it here! There are cool people, and one really hot one, and besides, the building likes me."

He nodded, narrowing his eyes. "The building's inspirited. A little. I think. And that's lovely and all, but the hag that was riding that child's back has tried to sink its claws into you, too. Whatever it is, I'm pretty sure that it's drained a sip or two more out of you than you probably reckoned on. You need to leave here, Makeda."

Fleet had been only twenty-three years old? My skin went all creepy-crawly as I remembered the high I'd gotten from the Soul Chain performance. Fleet had liked them, too. A lot. When she talked about them just now, she'd sounded like an addict, not a fan. "But I don't want to leave," I said.

"You have to. Every second you stay here brings you closer to my having to reap you prematurely."

"Uncle, I want this to be my home now. I don't want to run away from it. Besides, I have you to look after me."

He caught my gaze and held it until I looked down. I really hated it when he put on the aspect of a maggot-ridden corpse. "Oh, so now you're all grown?" he said. "Well, I guess you won't be needing me to babysit you any longer." His half-eaten lips mangled the words. His breath stank like rotting beef jerky. "Makeda child, please do as I ask. Your mother will never forgive me if I have to take you before your time."

"Mom? You talk to Mom?"

Quick as a blush, his face flipped to whole, and human. It bore the vulnerable, melting look of a young man in love. The change seemed to surprise him. He smiled shyly. "All the time," he replied.

"You never told me that!"

He was in control of himself again. "You might want to call someone to collect that shell in there." He nodded towards Fleet's door. "You know they get smelly if they hang around for too long."

I shuddered.

"If I let you keep the rug, will you get the hell out of here?"

My heart leapt. "I can keep it?"

He was fading away, Cheshire cat–style. "Yes. So long as you get out of here tonight. And so long as you don't use it any more. To, for instance, go for one last jaunt. Because you know there's no way I would ever, ever encourage you to do something so rash as that." He winked out, leaving his smile behind.

I chuckled. "Sure. 'Cause it's not like you're a trickster deity, or anything."

The smile said, "Your mother would be so proud if she could see what you'd made. And I'll talk to Suze and Roger about their servitude." Then it was gone, too.

I could keep the rug! Abby would be pissed enough to spit bricks. Now I just had to convince her to let me come and hang for a few days until I found somewhere else.

Halfway to my unit, I remembered Fleet. Crap, crap, crap. I had a hard time summoning up the courage to go to her door. Despite my uncle's profession, I actually hadn't seen a lot of death in my time.

I knocked gently. "Miz Fleet?" Could Uncle ever be wrong about whether someone had died? He said he'd already carried her over to the other side, but how did I know what that meant? Suppose she was only sleeping? If so, I wouldn't want to disturb her. I knocked again, harder. Nothing. I looked around to make sure no one was coming, then got to my knees and peeked under the badly hung door. The light was on in there, and just in front of the door I could see something that looked a hell of a lot like pink chenille. Gods, suppose she'd been lying there unconscious, needing help, while Uncle and I jawed?

I made myself open Fleet's door. I peeked inside, then closed it again. I got my cell phone out of my pocket and called 911; told them I'd heard the thump as I went past Fleet's door, and gone in to investigate when she didn't respond to me. And I kept my supper down.

When they came, the paramedics told me unofficially that she'd probably died on impact. By the time all that kerfuffle was done, I'd been awake almost twenty-four full hours. Very full. I was nauseous with fatigue. I needed sleep, pronto. And I knew how to get to Abby's place in mere minutes.

This time, I had the rug fly high in a route that took it over as many parks as possible until it deposited me at Abby's. When she opened the door, bleary-eyed, to my ringing, and saw the rug floating six inches above the ground beside me, she only said, "Holy fuck," and stood back to let me and it in. An acorn pinged the back of my head before she closed the door behind me.

Abby began, "What—?"

"Uncle says it's okay." He sort of had, anyway. I'd give her all the details tomorrow. "I'll tell you everything in the morning. After I've slept for, oh, a week." I put the rug down on the living room floor. Butter, her eyes wide in alarm, crouched in a guarding position beside it.

My bed was at Cheerful Rest. "I'll take the couch, Abs."

"Okay," she said, her voice modulated with unspoken questions.

I fell asleep to the quiet whirring sounds of the birds on the rug, and Butter chittering back at them.

Lake Ontario is the smallest of the Great Lakes, clocking in at a mere 19,000 square kilometres, or 7,300 square miles. It's nearly the size of New Jersey. It's about 244 metres at its deepest point. It's roughly the same length and breadth as Lake Erie, but holds about four times as much water, due to being much deeper than Lake Erie. It has 726 miles of shoreline. I know all this because for a while, I was obsessed with Lake Ontario. I did so many homeschool projects on it that Dad finally told me I had to pick other topics.

I don't care how small it is by Great Lakes standards; 104,000 cubic miles is a lot of lake. I used to dream about finding her there, the mother I knew only from a couple of photographs that Aunt Suzy had. I had fantasies of setting sail on Lake Ontario, like the owl and the pussycat, in a beautiful pea-green boat. (For years I thought it was a pee-green boat. I once asked Dad what was so beautiful about the boat in the poem, and then grumbled, "Besides, who pees green, anyway?" He fell out laughing for a good five minutes before he could collect himself enough to explain my mistake.) I would imagine myself lost somewhere on the lake with no land in sight, on a warm, sunny day. And my mother would hear my frightened sobbing and would arise out of the depths. With her nose, she would gently nudge my boat to a safe shore.

Since I was forbidden to do any more projects on Lake Ontario, I fell instead to looking up everything I could find about legendary freshwater monsters. No one had ever gotten a clear look at one, so I was free to theorize. In my childhood imagination, my mother looked something like a cross between a dolphin and a mermaid, with a bit of dragon thrown in for good measure.

When I learned that the Saint Lawrence Seaway connects Lake Ontario to the Atlantic, I wondered whether maybe Mom had found her way through it to the ocean. I looked up the dimensions of the Atlantic Ocean. The number crushed me. I couldn't fathom it, figuratively or literally. I couldn't look for my mom there, I just couldn't. I pestered Dad and Uncle Jack with questions about whether Mom might accidentally find herself in the ocean and not be able to get back. About whether lake monsters could breathe in salt water. In desperation, Dad started taking me and Abs to walk along the Spit, where we could at least be close to the lake that had swallowed our mother. But after the first few times, Abby didn't want to go any more. So it would be just me and Dad and the water, and a little pea-green boat bobbing in my imagination's eye. Those walks along the Spit relieved a little the helpless lostness I felt whenever I thought about my mother.

6

◆◆◆

GOT IT!" Sitting at the living room table, Abby threw triumphant hands in the air. "I've been trying to work out this arrangement for three days now. Couldn't make sense of it for the life of me."

"That's the new blues suite?" I asked. "For your gig at the Music Gallery?" I had unrolled my rug on the floor nearby and was repairing some sloppily laid adhesive on a few of the visible birds.

"'Weeping, Not Gently.' Yeah. The theremin needs to come in on the upbeat after I start singing, not the downbeat. And the whole slide guitar part needs to go up a fifth in the final movement."

"I like that suite a lot." I used the tip of a toothpick to put a dab of epoxy on the bottom of a clawed wire foot, then pressed the foot back into place on the rug. "The bit where you harmonize with your own recorded voice sounds so ghostly. For some reason, it makes me think of old, scratchy records. Hey, you have any thoughts about how you want to cook that salmon you have thawing in the fridge?"

But Abby had gotten a faraway look. "Ghostly..." she murmured.

"'Cause I'm getting hungry, and I bet you've been sitting in that chair since this morning with nothing but a cup of green tea."

"What? No. At least, I don't think so. I can't remember..." Her voice trailed off into silence.

I wasn't going to get anything intelligible from her for a while. I went and rummaged around in the kitchen. There was fresh kale, and ginger, and garlic. "Abs?"

No answer. My tummy grumbled. Next thing you know, I was baking the salmon for dinner, and tossing the kale in the frying pan with some olive oil, lemon juice, and ginger, and using the rest of the ginger to make self-saucing ginger pudding for two for dessert. At some point during the cooking, I heard Abby exclaim, "Candy wrappers! Maka, you're a genius!" I smiled and looked for sour cream to go on top of the pudding.

When I put a plate of hot food under her nose, she started, then looked up at me with a tired smile. "Cellophane candy wrappers. If I crumple them while I'm singing, it'll evoke that old record sound." Then she saw her dinner. "Oh, Maka, thank you! You didn't have to do this."

"Enlightened self-interest," I joked as I put my own plate down on the table. "You know I won't be having any salmon dinners with my salary from Burger Delite."

Her face hardened. "You're going back to live in that place, then?"

"Sure," I lied. Cheerful Rest had me seriously spooked. More truthfully, I continued, "Or somewhere else. I really think it's for the best, Abs. 'Bout time I started learning to live like a claypicken, don't you think?"

"But you're not a claypicken."

"Might as well be."

She shrugged. "Your choice, I guess." She tucked into the food.

She slowed down somewhere around bite three. She closed her eyes. Chewed. Sighed happily. "Really, Sis," she said, "thank you."

I hated myself a little for how wonderful that simple thanks from my sister made me feel. Trust me to be able to simultaneously feel good and to feel shitty about feeling good.

Abby asked, "We still on for tonight?"

"Uh-huh. In about four hours." I'd promised her that once it was good and dark, I'd demonstrate my flying carpet for her. "Where would you like me to take you?"

"I don't know. You choose."

"Okay." In the meantime, I would keep trying to reach Brie. I'd been calling all day, but he hadn't answered and he wasn't returning my calls.

When we were done having supper, I did the dishes; if I left them unwashed, Abby probably wouldn't notice until the bits of salmon stuck to the plates and the baking pan started to rot. Then I went through the living room into the hallway and pulled on my jacket, which was hanging on the peg there, and my boots. I would have a little more privacy for a phone call if I was out in the backyard; along with a supernatural talent for music came excellent hearing.

Abby didn't notice me leaving. Butter did, and tried to follow me, but as she came to the door, I gently pushed her back inside with my foot and closed the door behind me.

When I turned around, a flung acorn almost blinded me. "Stop that!" I hissed in the general direction of the oak tree. "Thank you, but we're not hungry, all right?"

It was that hour of magic light when the setting sun and the rising night painted the world in hues of old gold and royal blue. An ice-cream cart must have come by recently. The sweetish scent still lingered on the air. It was a little early for ice cream, but I guess everyone was eager for the warmer weather. Willing summer to come by acting as though it were already here was a bit of claypicken mojo. Sometimes, Dad had told me, it even worked.

The ground in the back of the house was spring-squelchy, loam-dark. It was going to be a bitch to get the mud off my boots. I rang Brie's number again.

"Hello?" said a man's voice, and my heart triple-hammered.

"Brie?"

"No, it's Hallam. Who's this?"

"It's Makeda. You know, I just moved into the unit across from Brie's?"

"Oh, right! Listen, I'd call him to the phone, but we're in the middle of a rehearsal, and he's in a bitch of a mood. The others sound like shit today, and I swear, I've suddenly grown two left feet."

"Oh. Uh, okay. But you guys will be all right, won't you? I mean, frankly, you sounded like shit during practice the other day, too. But the show rocked."

He laughed. "You're onto us already, huh? But something's really off this time."

In the background, Brie's voice yelled, "Hallam! Get your frigging lazy ass over here, or you're out of the band!"

Hallam said to me, "See what I mean? Gotta go. I'll tell him you called."

He hung up before I could say goodbye. I wished I could have kept him on the phone a little longer, but what would I have asked him? *Do you notice yourself getting a little older and a little weaker after every show? And the people in your audience, too?* I was starting to fear that the mysteriously Shiny Brie and his music were the cause of my high, and the thing that had drained Fleet and that guy Win. How old was Win, really? But how would I explain my suspicions to a claypicken like Hallam? Instead, I just ended the call and went back inside.

Abby was buried in her work again. Still a while to go before our magic carpet ride. I flopped onto the couch in the living room in front of the TV. Caught an episode of my soap, and one of those subtly everybody-phobic cop shows that zooms right on past ridiculous until it somehow bumps into fascinating. When it was done, Abs wasn't ready to go yet. I could check online for more Dad sightings. My laptop was over at Cheerful Rest, but Dad's computer sat on a round café table beside his armchair. For some reason, it didn't bother him much to use a computer, particularly to surf the Web. He didn't love the squared-off edges of the box itself, and touching the keyboard made his fingertips itch. But he said that the way the Internet worked was so jes'-grew and contradictory that it was like dealing with a very large, stubborn animal.

I went over to the computer and turned it on. Abby glanced up briefly when the computer made the *bong* sound that let you know it had booted. Sadly, she said, "I haven't turned that on since Dad went into the rest home."

On the screen, a message flashed in a small window. I read it. It made no sense. "Abs?"

"Yeah?"

"Can you come over here?"

"Now? I'm working."

"A calendar reminder just popped up."

Abby looked up from her marking at me, her face stricken. "What's it say?"

"It says, 'Cora, two a.m.'"

"What? Our mom? Is it her birthday today, or something?" Abby reached for her cane and pulled herself to her feet.

"At two a.m.? Who has a birthday party at two in the morning?" I clicked on the icon. "It's not just today. It's a recurring entry. The same day every month."

Abby came and hung her cane off the edge of Dad's round desk.

She leaned on me with one hand on my shoulder for support. She peered at the screen. "That's weird."

"The previous one was only a few days before I checked him into the home."

Abby said, "Maybe Uncle Jack knows what this is about."

I didn't want to talk to Leggy John right now. No need for him to find out how liberally I was interpreting his tacit approval to ride the rug one more time. "What happens if you click on the day before?"

I did so. Maybe that'd distract Abby from the idea of contacting Uncle Jack. The note that popped up read, "Buy oranges, 31." It also recurred every month. "The hell?"

Abby peered at the note. "Why oranges, of all things? And why thirty-one of them?" Abs and I didn't like oranges, and Dad refused to eat any of the "paipsey excuse for oranges these people have over here."

"You really think that number is the amount of oranges he was reminding himself to buy?"

"Yes," she replied, "and I think Mom liked oranges a lot. I vaguely remember Dad telling us something like that."

"So once a month he would buy thirty-one oranges that no one in this household would eat... and then he'd do what with them?"

"And what did it have to do with Mom?"

I had an idea. "Holy shit." I checked the time on the computer. Twelve fifteen a.m. "Wanna go find out?"

"What? Where?"

"I think I know where. Does that all-night deli at the bottom of Woodbine still have a fresh fruit section? And can I borrow enough money to buy thirty-one oranges?"

Abby took her hand off my shoulder and slid the hook of the cane off the desk. "So long as I don't have to eat any of them."

"Come on, then!" I grabbed her jacket and mine, snatched her car keys off the kitchen table and tossed them to her, and whistled to my rug. Obediently it leapt up to shin height, its wings whirring. Butter, napping on the couch, sprang to her feet, all a-bristle and a-hiss. Abby made a yowly, gargly noise at her. Butter looked at her and obediently de-bristled, but she kept a distrustful eye on the floating rug. Abby said, "Butter's right, that thing's creepy. I can't believe that Uncle let you keep it."

"Don't you listen to them," I cooed at the rug. "Mama loves you. And I'm sorry, but you're only going as far as the car for now. But I promise you'll get to stretch your wings soon after that."

Abby asked Butter to stay in the house. "See?" I said. "It's like you have your familiar, and now I have mine."

Butter made an offended noise that didn't need to be translated. I stepped outside the house and ducked. A small rain of acorns pattered down onto the rug floating beside me. "Abby, can you please get them to stop trying to feed us?" I brushed the acorns off the rug.

Abby was trying to see into the foliage of the oak tree. "Persistent squirrels, to be up at night."

The scent of our supper ginger puddings was stronger out here than in the house. And too sweet. Next time less sugar, more ginger. I got Abs to open the back door of the car. "In you get," I told the rug. It zipped into the backseat and settled.

Abby grumbled, "If it tries to put its head out the window so its ears can flap in the breeze, I'm kicking it out of the car."

"You're just jealous."

"Says you."

I heaved the two white plastic bags of oranges off the counter of the deli store. I huffed at Abby, "Thirty-one oranges are heavier to carry than I reckoned they would be."

"You could let me carry one of the bags," she pointed out. "I'm disabled, not unable."

"We're only going as far as the car." I put the bags on the floor of the passenger side and got in.

Abby slid in behind the wheel. "You're still not going to tell me where we're going?"

"Just start the car. I'll show you."

"It's so dark out here." Abby flicked her flashlight on and shone it on the ground, searching for the path.

"Turn that thing off!" I said. "It's like a beacon to the cops." We'd been fighting about the flashlight ever since we got out of the car and slipped around the gate.

"But I can't see anything," she grumbled. "I don't want to trip."

"You won't trip! You'll be flying."

She looked doubtfully at the rug lying on the ground, with me and the bags of oranges sitting on it. "I guess. But why did we have to come here? I didn't know you were going to trespass on the Leslie Street Spit in the dark at oh-God o'clock in the morning, carrying thirty-one oranges!"

I hissed, "If you're going to yell at me, do it in a whisper, okay?"

She whipped around, trying to see in a full circle all at once. The flashlight traced a giddy halo. "Why? Will something follow the sounds of our voices?"

"Yup. And it'll arrive in a car with the words 'To Serve and Protect' written on the side, and we'll probably be fine, 'cause we can just zip away. But the claypickens here who're making out or trying to get some sleep won't. Come on, Abs. Turn the light off and let your eyes get used to the dark so you can see better. And get on already, will you?"

Resignedly, she stepped over the birds ringing the rug and sat down. "There are other people here?"

"In a city full of homeless people, what d'you want to bet that a few of them are squatting out here?" I was panting just from the effort of loading the bags onto the rug. First I spaz out for a whole night, and now I couldn't catch my breath. Not to mention the headaches and the queasy tummy. Is this what Fleet had been going through?

Abby was still looking around. "It'd really suck if your haint decided to show up now."

I smirked and patted the rug. "I'm safe on this baby."

"Are you sure? How do you know your haint can't fly?"

I hadn't thought of that. Quickly, I asked the rug to put us about fifteen feet in the air. Abby squealed when it rose, and grabbed for my arm. "It's okay," I said. "Just relax." I told the rug to take us into the trees.

Abby hissed, "Make it slow down!"

"Fine." I told the rug to head for the beach, andante. It slowed to an ambling pace, the perfect speed for enjoying this trip. It was a very still night, and spring-cool. The water was making quiet lapping noises, like a cat drinking from a bowl of milk. From the lake came the occasional sleepy honk of geese. I could smell the blossoms of green, growing things, and the sludgy scent of goose dung. I could smell living happening, and it was good.

"Maka?"

"That's your wheedling voice. What do you want?"

"You think you could come and hang out with me while I'm writing a piece that the Nathaniel Dett Chorale commissioned from me yesterday?"

I couldn't believe what I was hearing.

"I'm calling it 'Unholy Racket.' It's an Easter arrangement for large gospel choir, blues guitar, timpani, and solo female voice."

I turned and stared at her. Uncertainly, she continued, "I'll be exploring the notion of 'breathing new life' into what had apparently ceased to breathe and why're you looking at me like that?"

"When will you let me the hell go? That's just another excuse to get me back living in the house."

"But things are so much better when you're there!"

"Except for the constant squabbling, you mean? Besides, I've only been away one day. One lousy, stinking day, Abby! You haven't had enough time to figure out what it's like to live without me."

"It isn't the first time you've gone away, though. Remember that trip you took to hike in BC? Two weeks. And the whole time, I couldn't get anything right, couldn't do anything right. When you're home, I can think clearly. I know where stuff is. I know that the theremin should come in right at the first bar." She fake-grinned at me. "Hey, maybe that's your mojo."

"Being your security blanket? There's a name for that: codependency."

"Well, just listen to the psychologist. Who died and crowned you Dr. Phil?"

"Look, I know it's hard. But we can't go on living like this. I can't. It's killing me."

A tear escaped from the corner of one of her eyes. "I need you, Maka."

"Not really. Not any more. Look, we've reached the beach."

She'd kept her nails dug into my arm the whole way. She looked over the edge of the rug. "Tell this thing to sit down, or set down, or whatever it does. I'm not going down there perched atop an oversized doily."

"Come on, Abby!" I'd been looking forward to that part.

"Make. It. Lie. Down."

She was really scared. I sighed and got the rug to put down at the top of the cliff. Abby said, "Thank you. And I am never riding on this thing again."

"Well, how're you going to get down to the beach, then?"

"I have the better part of two good legs, and I know how to use them." A little unsteadily, she clambered outside the protective circle of the rugs' wings.

I handed her her cane. "You are such a spoilsport."

"Bite me."

I got off the rug and ordered it to airlift the oranges down to the tiny beach and wait for us on the sand there. It obeyed. In the dark, its piebald colours blended well with the beach sand and the shadows of the rocks. I turned to Abby. "Okay, now it's our turn."

"I've been to the Spit before—remember when Dad used to take us? But I haven't been down there, ever."

"But you won't take the easy ride down."

"That thing is *wrong*, Maka! Can't you feel it?"

It was only the shortest climb down to the strip of shore, barely five feet. "Look, it's easy to climb down."

I scooted over the side of the incline and scrambled down the rocks and chunks of embedded concrete slab. "See? Nothing to—" A rock shifted under my foot and I stumbled a little, but I was practically all the way down already, so I didn't sweat it. At the bottom, I straightened and looked up at Abby. "Tah-dah!" I spread my arms. "Now you do it. I'll be down here to catch you if you slip. But I bet you won't slip."

Abby eyed the decline doubtfully. "I don't know," she said. "If I tripped like you did just now, I could break my leg."

"Well, so could I have! So could anyone."

"It just looks steeper now than it did when we were floating above it."

"So all that talk about being able to do it yourself was just fronting? I knew it!"

"Maka, please don't—"

"Aw, come on, Abs! Don't ruin the adventure now, before we've barely even begun it. At least get down to the shore."

She stared with longing at the ground below. "I really want to."

"You can do this. It'll be a blast!" I held my hand out to her. "Here. Just give me your hand."

"Wait a sec, okay? Take this." She handed her cane down to me. I took it and rested it on the ground.

Abby sat on the ground above and slowly worked her way forward until her legs were hanging over the edge. "Don't hold my hand," she told me. "It'll only make me more scared to have you pulling me."

"Okay then. So first, put your foot on this whitish rock here." I patted the head-sized rock that gleamed a little with reflected light. "See it?"

"Uh-huh."

"Then step on this piece of concrete, but watch out for that rebar that's sticking out. I'm right here. I won't let you fall."

"You don't know that. I'm a lot heavier than I used to be as a kid, you know."

"You weighed a little less than me then, and you weigh a little less than I do now. Besides, who hauls your gear when you do a show? *Moi.*"

Abby worked her way forward a little farther.

"Watch it," I warned. "Look at where you're putting your feet."

She didn't. She half pushed herself, half slid over the edge, her fingers splayed out in front of her with a childlike, graceless grace. Her foot thudded onto and then slid off the first rock. Her other leg didn't quite hold her when her foot hit the piece of concrete, and over she went. I was ready. I stepped forward and yanked her into my arms before she got too close to the jutting rebar. Whoops. It was harder to hold her up than I'd thought. I thumped down onto the sand on my back with Abby on top of me. The sudden pressure of an adult body on my chest shoved so much air out of me that I couldn't even cry out.

"Whoa there," said Abby cheerfully. I had my arms around her. She'd put her hands up to cradle the back of my head. "Wouldn't want to crack your stubborn head open on these rocks, would you?"

Then we were both laughing, spurred on to greater hilarity by the juddering of our giggling bodies against each other. Abby rolled off me, still chuckling. She stared into my eyes. She leaned forward and planted a soft kiss on my lips. Hers tasted of ginger. "You goof," she said tenderly. "You were always the eager one leading the way, begging me to join you. You made me want to push myself a little bit more, try a little bit harder, just so I could keep up with you."

"I was? I did?" I sat up, trying to suck air in quietly. I didn't want her to see how winded I was from climbing down to the beach and cushioning her fall.

"Maka, for real. You're the reason I mostly walk with a cane instead of needing crutches all the time. You're the reason I can stand up in front of an audience of a thousand people. Don't you remember how scared I was to sing for anyone but you and Dad?"

"I remember you being a little hesitant, but you got over it. You were made to be up onstage."

She swung herself into a sitting position. "A little hesitant? Girl, I was just about peeing myself with terror. You were the one who told me I could do it. Same way you did just now." She patted my cheek, then reached for her cane and got up. "Now, let's try this crazy idea of yours, shall we?"

"My crazy idea? I thought we both came up with it." I rocked myself onto the balls of my feet and creaked into a standing position. Doing so made my knees hurt.

"Nah-a-ah," she replied, shaking a finger at me. "Crazy ideas are always yours, you know that. That's the deal between us. That's our thing."

Oh, my sister. I smiled, shaking my head.

She said, "You laugh now. But just you be figuring out how the rass I'm going to get back up off this beach."

"You'll manage. I know you. Up was always easier for you than down." I didn't bring the rug up again. I upended each of the plastic shopping bags, rolling the oranges out onto the ground. I tied the empty bags around the legs of one of the bigger rug birds.

Abby and I contemplated the pile of oranges. Abby said, "What do you figure we do now? Burn them, or something? Eat them? Juggle with them?"

"They're wet. They wouldn't burn. Besides, Mom's not one of the big guys. Burnt offerings won't summon her."

"You really think he used to meet her here once a month?"

"I don't know. I'm going on a hunch here." I got to my feet, worked a kink out of my back. "I suspect you weren't serious about juggling them."

That earned me a little laugh. "Nah. This is silly," she said. "I don't think anything's going to happen. We should just go home."

She was giving up just like that, without barely having tried anything. Oh, but she could get my goat so easily! "Face it," I snapped, "you're just not interested in anything that might have to do with our mother."

"Face it," she replied, "she has nothing to do with us and never will. We're out here at two in the morning with thirty-one oranges and a lot of egg on our faces."

Of course that led immediately to bickering, which turned into arguing about which one of us was the more selfish, which became a fight about me moving out, which degraded rapidly into yelling and name-calling.

"Oh, yeah?" I said. "Well, if you weren't so bloody stubborn—!"

"*I'm* stubborn? *Me?*"

I honestly don't remember which one of us first picked up an orange and slung it at the other. But since I'm quicker on my feet than Abs is, my best guess says it was me. Anyway, whichever of us it was, we ended up winging oranges at each other. A few landed in the water. Abby got me full in the chest with one. A few more split on nearby rocks. One slammed down onto the rug, which undulated to roll the orange off, then crawled to hide behind a sheltering rock. I didn't know about Abby, but I was nearly peeing my pants from trying to squeal and laugh quietly. We got closer and closer to each other, mock-glaring. I started peeling the orange in my hand. Abby did the same with hers. She began whistling the famous Morricone stanza from the saloon showdown scene in *The Good, the Bad, and the Ugly*. Our grins got broader and fiercer the closer we got to each other. Just before we were within arms' reach, Abby rushed me. Caught by surprise, I nearly dropped my orange. In seconds, we were smushing our oranges on each other's clothing, on each other's faces, crushing the oranges in our fingers until they dripped juice and pulp and filled the air with the sweet citrus smell.

"No!" Abby said between giggles. "Not the hair!"

"Too late! No quarter given, none asked."

"Oh, yeah?" She jammed the remnants of her orange against my mouth. "Eat it. Eat it!"

I shook my head and kept my mouth closed as she smeared sticky juice all over my lips and cheeks.

Abby said, in a soft, hollow voice, "Eat my orange of doom!"

I laughed, and got myself a mouthful of orange pulp. "Hey," I said, licking it off my lips, "This doesn't taste so bad."

"It doesn't, huh?" She reached down and grabbed another orange up from the ground. "Let's just see how you like one with the skin still on!"

"Hey!" I tried to wrestle it from her. She tried to reach my face with it. Neither one of us was trying very hard. "You're the one who— Abs, wait, shush. What's that noise?"

"Oho! You can't fool me like that, you sorry excuse for—"

"Hush, I said! Can you hear it?"

She must have twigged that I was serious. She held still and listened. It was a steady dripping, like rain falling on the surface of the lake. "Did your rug fall into the lake?"

"No, it's over there. Is there a rain shower coming, maybe?"

"It's not rain. It's more like water falling from the leaves of a tree after a hard rain. Except this tree is getting taller and taller..." She dropped the orange and grabbed my forearms. "Makalook-behindmeIthinkthere'ssomethingbehindme."

The hairs on the nape of my neck prickled. I looked over her shoulder at the vast blackness of the lake. I couldn't see the horizon point where it merged with the sky. "I don't see—"

Abby hissed, "Look up, damn it!"

I looked up. There were two silvered circles floating above our heads. Whatever they were, they were pretty. They reminded me of something. And they were dripping water on us. Abby looked up and moaned, "Oh, gods..." at about the time that I wonderingly reached a hand up, trying to gauge how big the circles were.

They blinked. "Holy shit!" They were the size of dinner plates, they were right on top of us, and they were eyes. I grabbed Abby, tried to hustle us out from under the thing. That silver shine; Butter's eyes glowed like that in the dark.

Abby fought me. "No! Wait, Makeda! We did it! I think it's Mom!"

I stopped and turned back to look. Now that I sort of knew what I was looking at, my eyes could discern it more easily. The creature was some dark colour; black or maybe midnight blue. Its body was streamlined; fat in the middle, tapering at the neck end. It was about the size of the pleasure yachts that people sailed on this lake in the summer. Two paddle-like feet in front. Its back was still in the oil-black water, so I couldn't tell what that end looked like. Longish neck. Its head looked too small for its body, but that didn't mean it was a small head. Right now, the creature was bending that head down towards Abby, who'd stretched her hand up to meet it. I tensed, ready to rush in and elbow that thing in the snout, if need be. But it didn't strike. Instead, it slowed its movement down as its head came closer to Abby. Abby touched its nose. "Mom?"

It shied away, snorted. Paddled its two front flippers on the rocks of the shore.

"Try that again, would you?" said Abby. "Can you even understand me?"

Big, it was too big. I backed up against a boulder. That rubbery, slimy thing that smelled of wet algae wasn't the mother I'd dreamed of. That thing couldn't be anyone's mother. "Abby," I said weakly, "come away!"

She turned a joyous face to me. "She says we should stop squabbling like children! She thought we were Dad. She says he hasn't visited her in almost a year."

The creature butted her gently with its snout. Abby threw her arms around its neck. "Mom!"

It was really our mom. "Fine, then," I muttered. "Tell her you started it."

Abby laughed. "She says she heard that."

"Does she know what happened with Dad and the kudzu?"

"She says she can understand you, so you should talk directly to her."

I looked up at the two glowing saucers. "Do you?"

There was a longish silence while Mom answered.

"She says yes, and it broke her heart that she couldn't be at the burying. But she knows that Dad isn't really dead. Hang on; I'm going to try to talk back to her the way she's speaking to me."

I sat on a cold slab of crumbling concrete and watched the miracle as my sister and my mother, one on land and one in water, one stumbling for lack of balance and the other wheezing for lack of breath, danced with each other at the shoreline.

◊ ◊ ◊

Abby and I were maybe nine years old. It was a perfect and rare summer morning; sunlight the colour of tea-stained white cotton. The light kissed the skin softly, like a blessing, and there was just enough of a breeze that you were neither sweating nor chilly. I was lying on my stomach on the front porch, head propped up on my hands, reading a book. I don't remember which one. I think it had a magical goat in it, and maybe two children, and a mountain. I had put the book down to watch a tiny green inchworm measure its way along the porch floor. From inside the house, Abby kicked open the screen door, used one of her crutches to hold it open, and swung through out onto the porch. "Hey!" I called. "Come see this!" I figured that Abby would either really like the inchworm, or she'd think it was gross. Either way, her reaction would be entertaining.

She frowned at me. "No, don't tell it to me, stupid. It's ugly that way. Sing it to me."

"How?"

"Sing it with your body. Like this."

And my crippled sister threw down her crutches and began to dance. She ceased being a little girl constrained by braces and crutches. Her body moved in its own language. Suddenly, her shorter leg wasn't disabling her. It was the crook of a comma, the illustrative pause in a devastatingly meaningful statement spoken in movement. It was the length and shape it needed to be. She made a clicking noise, punctuating her body's gestures and flourishes. Abby had some serious mojo. In the weeks, months, years to come, she would demonstrate it to me. You know that song that goes "You can dance if you want to"? Even sitting mostly still, Abby could dance. The mere flick of an eyelid was articulate; the slightest quirk of her lips. Abby sang tenses with her voice, danced sentences with her body. Abby spoke volumes. But that day, the first time she danced for me, her body was saying the simplest, most childish thing, "I'm bored, Makeda. Come and play with me." I understood it as clearly as if she'd spoken the words. Even the language that only she and I shared was clumsy next to the grace that was my sister.

Locomotion. The one thing I'd thought she needed my help with. The only use I was to anyone in this world, she took away from me. She and I used to get on each other's nerves a fair bit; just the usual squabbling and jockeying for position that happens between siblings. Before that, we'd done so as equals. But the day that Abby danced was when I first understood that I was something lesser than she was.

◆ ◆ ◆

"She says you have Dad's mouth more, but I have his eyes more. Or maybe she's saying she's glad I *have* eyes. Either way, I think it's good." She laughed out loud at some gesture from Mom that I couldn't see, or that I couldn't perceive as communication. "Mom! Stop teasing!"

I'd had enough. "Oh, this is some bullshit!"

Mom and Abby both swivelled to look at me. "What's gotten into you?" asked Abby.

I stood and confronted the bulbous, long-necked, yacht-sized lump that had beached itself on the shore, halfway out of the water. "Okay, okay, we get it. She looks like Dad, and I look like Dad, and we both look like you used to before you got turned into a cross between a plesiosaur and a beached whale—"

"Makeda!" Abby, in full-on mommy mode, actually stamped her foot at me.

"—and it's all blah, blah, blah. What I want to know is, where have you been all these years?"

"Sis, she can't stay on land for very long."

"So we could have had picnics, right here on the shore. At night. I bet she would have brought the freshest salmon ever. She's been meeting Dad here once a month forever. Couldn't she have dictated a note to him for us, or something?" I turned to Mom. "Anything we could have gotten to know you by?" I found I'd sat down on a nearby boulder. "You don't even look like the picture we have of you! That beautiful Mom-lady with the puffball hair and the cute little red dress…" I was blubbering. "Look at what Granny Ocean did to you! Look at what she turned you into."

Through Abby, Mom said, "*I am beautiful. Your father knows it. I am a living thing, and therefore beautiful to him. Your uncle knows it. I am a being that will know death, and therefore I am beautiful to him.*" She'd moved her head closer to me. "*Hey, I'm lecturing you, like a real mother! I've wanted to do that for decades.*"

"Mom, I'm sorry."

"*Besides, the original kingstie is mad jealous of my fat, round tummy.*"

Abby said, "Wait; there's an original kingstie? I thought that was a hoax!"

"*She's real, but I don't see her often. We're not very sociable creatures. Maka, I know everything about you two that your dad and your uncle could tell me. With all the tears I cried from missing you, I'm surprised the lake level hasn't risen.*"

"You cried for us?"

"*Nearly every day. Still do, sometimes.*"

"I came down here a lot as a kid," I confessed grudgingly. "I would comb along the beach, looking for, well, messages from you." I made my eyes meet hers. "I kinda thought that if I arranged pieces of driftglass and other stuff I found just right, I'd be able to read what you were trying to tell me."

There was a strangled laugh from Abby. She saw me glaring at her and tried to compose her face, but that just sent her into another fit of giggles. Eventually she was able to stop laughing long enough to translate Mom's reply:

"*No, sweetie. I never sent you any magical messages. I'm not magic. I was just made this way by magic.*"

I hung my head. "Yeah, I know it was childish of me."

"There is one little thing…"

"Yes?" I reached out to touch her head. Her skin was raspy, like sharkskin, only more so.

"One time, I was missing my girls so terribly, wishing I could hold you and be part of your lives…"

Abby said, "Oh, Mom."

"And—" It took Abby a couple tries to get the next word right, probably because she didn't realize at first that it was a nickname—*"Legs would tell me stories about what you two would get up to, what tricks you'd try to play on him and Boysie."*

"'Legs' is Uncle Jack?" I asked Mom.

"Yes. So that day, after I finished eating some shellfish, I took one of the shells and whispered something to you into it. Then I threw it back into the water."

My mouth dropped open. "I knew it! I knew it! What did you say into it?"

"It's silly."

"Mom, just tell me!"

"I said, 'Makeda, eat your peas.'"

"Yes! Yes!" I did a jubilation dance. I stuck my tongue out at Abby. "In your face! Didn't I tell you that Mom had sent me a message in a shell?"

Abby looked bewildered. "Yes, but how did it…?"

"Who cares? Maybe a tree never talked to me the other day, but I did hear Mom in that shell! I did!"

Abby didn't translate what Mom said next. She just hung her head and said, "Okay, okay. Makeda, I'm sorry I laughed at you just now."

"Wow. You apologizing to me. Mom, there's no way you can hang around, is there?" I rubbed an itchy spot at the back of my head.

"I have to go soon. Girls, I miss your two dads. Now only one of them

comes, and now he's started avoiding me out of shame that he lost Boysie's soul. The three of us love each other to the ends of the earth and back. Without Boysie, Legs and I are like a stool with one leg chopped off. We're toppling. Please find him for us. Find Boysie."

"Son of a gun," I breathed. "You got Uncle Jack, and you kept Dad, too. Mom, if you could high-five, I would so throw one up to you right this minute! It almost makes it worth it that I'm carrying around Dad's mojo."

Mom's head jerked upright. *"What?"*

Abby's eyes went almost as wide as Mom's. "Oh, crap. I think she doesn't know what happened."

"Tell me."

So we told her. A kingstie in a rage is a terrifying sight. "I can't translate that," said Abby, watching the splashing and writhing happening in the water. "I don't know what half those gestures mean, even if she weren't doing most of them underwater. And there are concepts I can't catch. I think there are patterns of bubbles involved."

Mom surfaced. She opened her mouth scarily wide. Hard to be sure in the dark, but I think kingsties have three more pairs of canines than most creatures need. Abby said, "No, Mom. Please don't do that to them! I'm not even sure you can tie a knot in a leg like that. Oh. You don't mean a leg."

"I can't do anything to them! They are gods to us! I sent them across the border to give Makeda breath, not to turn her into a...perch with a lamprey attached to it!"

Abby said, "I think she means something like—"

"Mule. I know. Mom, maybe it's for the best. I came back with my brain fixed, after all."

Her tail slapped the water. *"I didn't care what condition your brain was in!"* She heaved herself out of the water and humped, walrus-like, over to where I stood. She touched her forehead to mine. She opened the lamps of her eyes. There were worlds afire in the depths of them. Such glory. *"You are my daughter. I was happy that you had come to me alive."*

"Mom, it's not that simple. Looking after me as I was, it would have been exhausting."

"Nevertheless."

"Sometimes you would have hated me."

"Nevertheless."

"And then hated yourself for hating me."

"I know. I knew it then. But looking at you, in that moment, I did not care."

Something in me broke open. The next breath I took was sweeter than air had ever tasted to me. I kissed my mother's raspy forehead and closed my eyes against the brilliance of her. I still saw a circle of red on each closed lid. "Abby, how in the world did you manage to translate 'nevertheless'?"

"You think that's hard, you should try everything she put into the past perfect. And now she's laughing at me."

She didn't seem to be doing anything different to me. Maybe it had to do with patterns of bubbles in the air.

My phone rang. It was from Brie's number. "Sorry," I said. "Gotta get this."

She and Abby continued their odd dance at the shoreline. I wandered a little way away from them. Deliberately cheerfully, I said, "'Sup, dude?"

"You haven't been here." Brie's voice was sullen.

"For one whole week, yes. Charmed you noticed. What's it to you?"

"Last night's show sucked. Plus you find Fleet's body, you don't even tell me, then you just leave?"

"Hey, I'm sorry. I know you liked her." Or he wanted to know whether she'd told me anything.

"Makeda, Fleet used to be in my band."

Oh, shit. I swallowed around the sudden lump in my throat. "And she was only in her twenties."

His voice got guarded and sullen. "Did Fleet tell you that?"

"No, my uncle did. He knows stuff like that."

"He a cop?"

"He's a firewall." Mom dipped her head into the water and came back up. That was my mom over there! "Brie, was there something you wanted to tell me about all this? That's why I've been phoning you."

"No." The single, bitten-out word carried more than its weight of anger. "I don't want to tell you shite." I heard his exhaled breath. "But could you come over anyway? You're the only one I know who I can talk to about, you know, what I do."

"I'm not going to end up like Fleet, am I?"

"No! God, no. Never again."

My skin prickled. "Oh, that's reassuring."

Over by the water, Abby did a pirouette. What were she and Mom talking about?

Brie said, "Really, you'll be fine. It's been years since anything like this has happened. I figured out how to stop hurting people."

"Again with the reassurance." I thought for a second. "Okay, I'll come." But I would bring reinforcements. I rang off and walked back to the water's edge. I said. "Mom, Abby and I have to go and do a thing."

"We do?"

"*I have to go soon, too, my darlings. I need to be deep in the belly of this lake before the fishing ships come out, and if I descend too quickly, the bends are murder.*"

"All right," Abby replied. "But Mom?"

"*Yes?*"

"You and Dad and Uncle Jack…"

"*I'm pissed at your Uncle right now. But I do love him. He's messed up and he or somebody better fix it. But he helped save Makeda's life, and he continued to look after you both, and he's one of the hottest honeys in this world, and probably in the next.*"

"But what about Dad?"

Did she still not understand? "Abs, get with the programme here, will you?"

Abby continued, "Dad saved Makeda, too. It wasn't just Uncle. And he looked after us every day. Uncle didn't. And he loves you like air. I don't know so much about the…the other thing."

"*Don't you worry; when he comes back to me and Legs, I'll find out whether he still has his knack for…the other thing.*"

She asked, "Are you saying that you're…with…both of them?"

"*And you two girls would know nothing about anything like that, would you?*" Mom raised a vast tail and slammed it against the surface of the water. I jumped at the loud crack the impact made.

"Abs, I think that's Nessie for 'Stop talking shit.' Yeah, Mom, we had a four-way a few times with the Bejis. Big whoop. Aunt Cathy and Uncle Flash used to be married to each other, and they're brother and sister."

Abby said, "I have no intention of marrying you, just so you know."

"And I am way relieved to know that." I smiled at her. She smiled back.

"Mom, do you miss being human?" Abby clearly wasn't ready to let Mom go just yet. I knew how she felt.

"*Why should I? Especially now that I have my girls in my life. I'll just snag some of those oranges for the road, shall I? Thank you, dears.*"

We watched her paddle out deeper, until her skin blended into the skin of the lake and we couldn't see her any more. "Fuck," I said. "I forgot to show her my rug that I made."

"You sound like a little girl bringing home a finger painting for her mother to tape to the fridge."

"Shut up." Despite the words, I sounded happy. I was. Spring flowers were breathing their perfume into the air, and I knew that life was good.

"So what's this thing that you and I are going to do?"

"I want to go to Cheerful Rest, but you remember Brie?"

"Yes."

"I think he's some kind of scary hoodoo master, and I want to go and ask him about it. Will you and Lars come with me?"

"Yup, you're really living the dull claypicken life, all right. Do we have to ride on that wretched blanket?"

"Aw, come on, give my ride a chance. She's pretty cool once you get to know her."

"I don't know…" Abby stared down at the rug, which had hunched its way over to lean against my leg, cooing softly.

"You know you want to. Didn't you feel like a queen, flying on a magic carpet high above the world?"

"A terrified and somewhat motion-sick queen." She smiled. "But yeah, it was kinda cool. I could stand to do that again."

I kissed her cheek. "Thanks, Sis."

"You realize it's nearly three in the morning?"

"I'm afraid that if I wait, Brie might freak out and run away."

"Well, I wasn't sleepy, anyway. Too jazzed. As for Lars, he never sleeps. And he keeps complaining about how things were more interesting when Jimi was around. Maybe this talking-to-Brie affair will be interesting."

"I'm really hoping not."

She went and sat on the rug. "Either way, I'm in. Start this thing up."

◊ ◊ ◊

Barking, mewing, hissing, mocking,
Tore her gown and soiled her stocking,
Twitched her hair out by the roots,
Stamped upon her tender feet,
Held her hands and squeezed their fruits
Against her mouth to make her eat.

Abby clicked her cell phone shut. "Lars is going to meet us there." She let her cane go to put her cell into her handbag. I caught the cane before it could roll over the side and tumble to the ground below. We were coasting along the wooded Lower Don Trail, threading our way through the branches of the tallest trees. I'd spotted a family of foxes and a skunk. Other than the animal people, the trail was pretty deserted at this hour of the morning. The rushing cold air made my cheeks feel rosy and crisp as fall apples. Abby was lying on her back with her head in my lap. "I could get used to this," she said.

The rug took us along the raised overpass that was the Gardiner Expressway. There were cars on it, though not as many as there would be come rush hour this morning. Abby rolled onto her stomach to peer over the side of the rug. Just in case the rug took a sudden dip, I hooked my fingers through one of the loops on the back of her jeans. She patted my hand. She said, "How come more people aren't seeing us up here? The sky is full of cameras nowadays."

"I don't know. Maybe Dolly took me literally when I told her we didn't want to be visible."

Abby twisted round to look at me. "Dolly?"

"The rug."

"Dolly the doily?"

"Something like that, yeah."

"Goof." She turned back to contemplate the highway.

"Control freak."

"Can it really make us invisible?"

"I have no idea."

Abby rolled to a sitting position, her two legs stuck out straight in front of her. She scowled and crossed her arms. "She never sent *me* a message in a shell."

"Who, Mom?"

She pouted. "Yes. How come you're so special?"

"I'm not, and you know it. Maybe that's why Mom sent me the message. In compensation."

She didn't have anything to say to that.

We took the corridor of rail lines running along just north of the highway, keeping close to the trees on the northern embankment of the tracks. The track sloped down to a narrow, paved alleyway, shielded by the embankment to the south and the windowless backs of the co-ops and housing projects to the north. And then we were on Sherbourne, just south of where we wanted to be. As we got closer, Dolly deked right to take us through a strip of parkland. I guessed we probably weren't invisible; she was sure taking a lot of care to not be spotted.

We startled a raccoon rappelling down a maple tree trunk, and a bunch of worn, shabbily dressed people sitting on and around a park bench, talking and sharing something from a bottle wrapped in a brown paper bag. We were gone from there before they had time to do much more than call out in alarm.

Abby asked, "How come they could see us?"

"Maybe Dolly turned off the onboard cloaking device. Maybe you need to be under the influence. Or a raccoon. The real question is, why were they drinking liqueur? Doesn't that ritual usually involve cheap vodka?"

"Ritual?"

"The ritual of 'If we all share what little money we have, we can afford to buy one bottle of buck five come alive.' Whatever they've got smelled so sweet I think my blood sugar level tripled just from inhaling it." I ducked to avoid an overhanging branch. We'd be there soon.

"You could smell it? But we were yards and yards away from them."

"I can still smell it. It's like somebody diluted candy and then added grain alcohol to it."

A stinging hail pelted us. Abby cried out. The lumps made a hollow tapping sound where they hit the rug. I yelped in pain as something small and hard hit me on the cheekbone. "Ow! What in sweet blue blazes?"

That wasn't hail. The roundish pieces on the rug looked faintly green in the dark, not luminescent as hail would have been.

Abby pulled one of them out of her hair. "They're acorns."

"That damned squirrel is tailing us!" I yelled out into the darkness, "You almost took my eye out!"

"Maka, not so loud."

"Tree rat!" Squirrels hated to be called that.

Abby said, "I've got acorns in my bra."

I got to my knees and started brushing acorns off Dolly. "They didn't hurt you, did they, sweetie?"

Abby responded, "No, I'm fine."

I decided not to tell her that I hadn't been talking to her. She lay back and put her hands behind her head. She closed her eyes.

I sat back down beside her, but I couldn't get rid of the cloying candy smell of the hooch those people had been drinking.

Something was tickling the back of my brain. Something to do with acorns and squirrels. "Hey, Abs, when we left the house tonight, what did you say about the squirrel in the oak tree?"

"Lemme think...I said that squirrels aren't usually nocturnal."

That wasn't good. "And I was smelling flowers down on the beach when there are no flowers there. And ice cream and dessert where there aren't any. And acorns don't ripen till the fall." I had a bad feeling about this. "Dolly, can you go faster, please?" The rug obligingly sped up. It dodged and swerved through the treetops. The speed of our flight sent a crisp wind rushing through my hair. I wished I could just relax and enjoy the ride. Instead, I tried to keep my eyes peeled into the darkness surrounding us. Because the sweet scent that had been dogging me all day was back, and stronger than the free samples section at a perfume counter. And I wasn't smelling ice cream, or spring flowers, or ginger pudding. It smelled like grape hard candies.

Abby had opened one eye to look at me. "What's wrong?"

"I think maybe a tree has been trying to talk to me after all."

"Trees talk slowly. It can take one an hour to say good morning."

"Hear me out. Those unseasonal acorns aren't coming from oddly nocturnal squirrels. I think the oaks have been trying to get our attention. I think Dad and Quashee are nearby. Maybe they've been following us for a while."

"Oh, but that's great!" Abby rolled to a sitting position. "We should land, so they can find us!"

I shook my head. "I'm not so—"

A tapered, boneless shape writhed up in front of us. It whipped around the rug, me, Abby, and dragged us, screaming, out of the air. We thumped onto the ground. The rug squawked, then lay still. The massive vine tendril slid loose from around us and pulled away. Too winded to do much else, I followed its movement with my eyes. In the dark, the kudzu bush was difficult to make out clearly. It was an amorphous, ever-shifting mass. A giant hairball, a twelve-foot-tall mare's nest of writhing vines and roots and restless leaves. Its purple blossoms, usually the size of a fingernail, were swollen as large as cabbages. The grape candy stench from them was so strong, I feared I'd never again be able to smell anything else. I propped myself up on my elbows.

Abby was curled up beside me, making a noise halfway between a pant and a whimper. I asked her, "You okay, Sis?"

"Yes. Just had all the air knocked out of me."

"If you think the fall left you breathless, have a gander at Quashee."

Abby turned her head to look. "Holy gods. And what's that nasty smell?"

"Now you notice it. It's the kudzu flowers."

She made an *ew* face. "It's like an explosion in an air freshener factory."

We both struggled to our feet. Abby winced. "I think I sprained my ankle."

Dolly wasn't making a sound. Was she broken? Quashee's roots plucked at the ground longingly, but kept pulling away. Even as I watched, blossoms and leaves withered and fell away from the body of the plant, to be replaced by new ones growing in as quickly as the old ones died. Lengths of vine alternately bulged and thinned. That was some crazy combination of flora mojo and auxins that Quashee was calling on to cradle Dad and to remain ambulant. "Dad?" I said. "You in there?"

A flight of broomstick-thick tendrils shot out from the body of the plant, headed straight for me. I backed up. "Whoa, not so fast."

The reaching tendrils stopped a few inches away from my head. Looked to be easily twenty of them. They undulated, waving, like sea anemones feeding.

Abby put a hand out in the direction of the tendrils. "Dad?"

"Careful, Sis. I'm not sure that Dad even has a mind to be out of right now."

She touched a couple of the tendrils. They jerked a little way away, then wove themselves back towards her fingers. They twined into a fat paw and patted the back of her hand. Abby smiled. "See? He wouldn't hurt us."

"He yanked us out of the treetops onto the ground."

"He had to get our attention, right, Dad?"

Our conversation was punctuated by the soft thumps of dead kudzu blossoms hitting the grassy earth. Poor Quashee was growing, dying, blooming, climbing, creeping, and seeding, all at once. What looked like vigour was more like death throes.

I reached to touch the tendrils floating in front of me. Lightning-quick, they shot forward and grabbed my head. Abby screamed, "Makeda!"

I tried to tear the tendrils off me, but they didn't give. They pulled me off my feet and yanked. I heard the joints in my neck pop as I crashed headfirst into the springy, wriggly mass of Quashee. I gagged on the concentrated essence of synthetic grape. Lengths of vine whipped around my arms and legs and pulled me spread-eagled. The joints in my shoulders and thighs twanged like elastic bands.

"Dad!" yelled Abby. "Stop it!" I managed to turn my head enough to see Abby swinging at the kudzu with her cane. "Let Maka go!" She landed some solid blows on the lianas of Quashee that had thickened to the point of being branches. Quashee grabbed her cane and it disappeared amongst its thrashing leaves. Even in the dark, I could see Abby's glare. What was she, nuts? She couldn't protect herself against our ravening dad with a mere cut-eye! Whipping the air, Quashee advanced on her. The motion made me dizzy.

"Abby, go! Get out of here!"

I choked on a mouthful of leaves that Quashee crammed into my mouth. Abby shouted, "Hold on! I'm coming back!" Then I couldn't hear anything but the swish and crash of Quashee. I fought, but Quashee was implacably cocooning me in leaves. I tried to yell, "Dad, please!" Another fistful of curled leaves jammed into my open mouth and turned the words into a gargle. More vines curled around my limbs and tugged. A tearing ache blossomed in my joints as Dad tried to pull me apart like a boiled chicken. He was going to get at his mojo if it killed me.

And maybe it should. I'd carried Abby until she could carry herself. I'd held Dad's mojo until he needed it back. He was a deity, and I was a lump of mud that had served its function. Time to break open the clay vessel and pick out the meat inside. I stopped fighting. Dad yanked my shoulder out of its socket. I screeched in agony. In horror, I realized that he wasn't going to make it easy to go gently into that good night.

At my scream, Quashee stopped moving. Leaves unpeeled from my eyes. Small tendrils snaked towards my gagged throat. Leaves slapped them away. The tendrils wrapped around the leaves and tore them to shreds, then reached again for the plug of leaves in my mouth. Defiantly pushed itself deeper in so that my breath could only come in wheezing sips of scant air. The fucking thing was going to choke me! Desperate to yank it out, I struggled violently against the vines swaddling my arms.

A thud reverberated through Quashee. The vines released me, the plug of leaves popped out of my mouth, and I fell to the ground. The unspeakable pain of landing made my vision go grey. It seemed like an eternity before I could suck a much-needed breath in through my unstoppered mouth. The breaths were little sobbing moans of distress. My shoulder sang so I could scarcely think of anything else. The slightest movement amped the pain to ear-ringing levels.

Above me, a whirring flurry of a shadow was beating Quashee away from me. Dolly! It was she who'd thumped into Quashee! Like a sparrow harrying a hawk from its nest, Dolly flew at Quashee, then darted just out of its reach to come at it again and again. Compared to her, Quashee was big, but slow. Slapping at Dolly and missing, Quashee backed away until I was clear of it.

"Here, come out of that," said Lars's voice. He grabbed me under the armpits. Something ground in my shoulder and I screeched.

"You're hurting her!" said Abby. She thumped down onto the ground beside me.

I groaned, "Leave me here. Go help Dolly."

"Dolly?" asked Lars.

Abby pointed. "That thing. She made it."

Lars's eyes widened, and he was off and running. He was holding something thin and flexible. He set about slashing at Quashee. Leaves and chunks of vine began falling. I called out, "Lars, don't kill him! That's our dad!"

"Maka," said Abby, "Dad tried to kill you."

"I'm not so sure."

Before I could say more, a third being joined the fray. A tall, broad-shouldered man with an unmistakable Shine to him. Uncle Hunter, in cutoff army fatigues and a black sweatshirt. He shoved Lars aside. As Abby and I screamed at him to stop, he lit into Quashee, literally tearing it limb from limb. Lengths of vine dropped to the ground and went still. When he was done, the ground was covered in pieces of Quashee. I had gone cold all over in shock. Just like that, he'd shredded our dad. Abby was gasping over and over, as though she couldn't get any air.

Uncle Hunter picked up armloads of the kudzu at a time and flung them into the air, where they vanished.

There was one piece left, a root-ball with a torn piece of root hanging from it. I don't know how Abby managed to move that quickly, but she dashed over to it and picked it up just before Hunter could get to it. He straightened up and gave the three of us an unctuous smile. "Well," he said, "I bet you guys are glad to see me."

With a terrifying calm, Abby replied, "You tore your own brother limb from limb." I began to shake.

Hunter replied, "And not a moment too soon. Saved my dear niece's life"—he nodded at me where I was lying on the sidelines—"you're welcome, and cleaned up the environmental disaster that Boysie had become. Gotta thank you, Abby, for tromping your way through transit like that in your hurry to fetch your"—he sneered at Lars—"instrument. Just like kids, running through the living room and tracking mud on the carpet. Quite disruptive to the rest of the Family. I just had to follow you to see what was up. And I discover that you're socializing with a made thing. Abby, Abby, Abby. We had such high hopes for you."

There. The knot of root that Abby was holding twitched. Hunter hadn't noticed. Her body was shielding him from the sight. She had, though. She shot me a brief glance and opened her mouth. I sisterspoke at her, the chopped-off cry that meant, "Shut up." It did sound like a cry of pain. Go figure.

Hunter said, "You know, Makeda, I could fix that shoulder for you. Part of my new portfolio and all."

"No. Thank you."

"As you wish, short-lived niece o' mine. I'll just dispose of the rest of this mess." He strode over to Abby to get the root from her.

I said, "Don't." I lifted my head, grinding my teeth against the pain in my shoulder. I looked Hunter full in the face and put all the authority I could into my voice. "He's dead. You've done more than enough."

He smirked. "That's no way to talk to your adoptive father, *burrito*."

I twitched at the hated nickname. "It's the last piece," I said. "We'll burn it."

A green shoot lengthened from the root-ball and curled around Abby's wrist. She pulled it into her body and set up a torrential wail of fake sobbing. Especially when her tears were crocodile tears, Abby's crying was something to hear. Hunter grimaced and put his fingers in his ears. "All right, all right! You two dispose of it." Abby's sobs abated a little. "Wow," Hunter said to me. "All this fuss. I'd think you'd be glad you got to keep your wits about you tonight." He laughed at his own joke. "Laters, pets." He flicked out into transit.

Abby snickered. The waterworks were completely gone. "Oh, my God, could that god be any dumber?"

"Abby, goddamnit, you let Hunter follow us!"

"How could I know that?" she barked back. "I was just trying to save your sorry ass."

"All right, never mind that. Is it really alive?"

Triumphantly, Abby held her hand out to show me. The rootball was cradled in her palm. The single green shoot braceleted her wrist. "Saved Dad and Quashee both."

"Yeah, and you'd better get it off you soon, before it tries to make you into a dolma."

Abby looked at her wrist in dismay. She picked at the tip of the kudzu shoot. It came up easily. She uncurled some more of it. It writhed between her fingers like an earthworm. "It's all right," she said. "I think it only wants to hurt you."

"Well, keep it the fuck away from me, then. But take care of it, okay?"

"Of course I will! He's my dad, too."

Lars said, "Fucking elitist prick piece of shit. Goddamn, I hate those guys." Without any warning, he grabbed my arm and yanked my shoulder back into place. I was too stunned to even scream, and then the pain was mostly gone. He said, "We should get the kudzu into some soil. Poor thing's starving."

I nodded. "Maybe put him near his roses, Abs? You know, for company."

"Like hell," Abby replied, contemplating the kudzu. It had put out another tentative shoot. "He's not going back into open soil. It's a pot for him."

"Couldn't we plant him by the lake? Mom could visit him then."

"Listen to you, talking about introducing an invasive species into a fragile ecosystem! Dad would give you many kinds of hell for that."

"I know." The tip of one of the shoots was investigating Abby's skin. I shuddered.

"Maka?" Abby's voice was soft.

"Yeah?"

"The way I see it, we gotta keep Dad trapped in this form so that you can live out your natural life before giving him back his mojo."

"How can you say that? It's Dad!" A tear escaped down my cheek.

"Who has all of eternity. You only have a few decades."

Lars interjected, "If you guys are going to do that, you should probably get it into some soil soon. And give it some water. It's dehydrated."

He was right. It was the time of day that Dad called "'fore day morning." In the predawn light, I could see that Quashee was wilting.

My eyes were stinging, and I was running hot, then cold. I was just about perished from fatigue and the shock of watching Hunter viciously attack Dad, and we hadn't even talked to Brie yet. "Just don't give it enough soil for it to Hulk out on us again." I didn't actually agree to Abby's plan, but I wasn't fighting her on it, either. Some loyal daughter I was.

Suddenly my right leg jerked painfully out to the side. I cried out. Abby jumped. "What was that?"

"Nothing. Leg's gone to sleep." At least, I prayed that it was nothing. It'd been years since the last time! But the trembling only got worse. Both legs spasmed. The familiar, dismaying light-headedness took me. A powerful full-body contraction slammed my head back against the ground. Warm urine soaked my thighs as my bladder let go. I had time enough to say, "Abby!" as the world went away. My last thought was, *Fuck. Now she'll never let me out of her sight.*

❖ ❖ ❖

> ... *Watch'd by her,*
> *Counted her pulse's flagging stir,*
> *Felt for her breath,*
> *Held water to her lips, and cool'd her face*
> *With tears and fanning leaves.*

❖ ❖ ❖

I came to in Lars's arms. He was carrying me up the stairs in Cheerful Rest. It was a jerky business that did nothing to help me feel less queasy. My feet banged limply a couple of times against the railing. I felt the impact, but not the pain. I couldn't quite focus, and my tongue and lips weren't working right. Abby? Where was she? I must have made some kind of sound, because a warm hand stroked my head, and Abby's voice said, "It's all right, Maka. I'm here."

Lars rumbled, "I still think we should take her to the hospital."

"No," Abby replied. "They'll shoot her full of sedatives. She hates being helpless like that."

Oh, God, I could smell the piss on myself. Which meant that Lars could, too. And I'd probably gotten some on his jacket. Mortified, I tried to beg him to put me down. The words came out garbled, guttural. My hands thrashed weakly against his chest. I wasn't parsing the fact that I couldn't walk on my own. I just wanted not to have strangers see me in this condition. I just wanted Abby. The body contractions started again. One flailing arm caught Lars across the face. My eyes rolled sickeningly back in my head. Lars swore as he fought to hold on to me. I heard Brie's voice say, "What's going on?" before I went out again. I stayed semiconscious this time, enough to hear snatches of anxious conversation.

"Lay her down, I said! She's having a seizure! She hadn't had one this bad in years."

"We need to put a spoon in her mouth so she won't swallow her tongue!"

"No, we don't! Nobody does that any more!"

My body came to rest on a firm, padded surface. My bed?

"Is she dying? Does anybody know CPR?"

"She's not bloody dying! Let me deal with it. I know what to do." There was someone beside me, her head level with mine. She said, "Easy, Maks. Don't worry, I'm here." Abby. She smelled like Abby. I tried to focus on her face, to sit up. The room spun. Abby's voice said, "No, girl. You remember how to do this. Lie back down. Look, I'll cover you." A warm softness gathered around me, hiding away my wet jeans, the pee smell. Tears of gratitude rolled down my nose. Abby stroked my arms. "You with me, sweetie?"

I managed to grunt, "Uh-huh." My eyes kept slipping in and out of focus. My hands were trembling. There was a fierce itch between my shoulder blades. And I was crankier than a bull moose in mating season. A seizure? Really? Why now?

Brie's voice asked, "What's happening to her?"

Abby answered, "Myoclonus. Muscle contractions she can't control. She used to get them when she was a kid."

I'm right here, I thought. *Stop talking about me as though I weren't in the room.* With a head full of cotton wool and a mouth full of rocks, I managed to gargle out, "Why...Brie...here?"

Brie replied, "They couldn't find your keys. I let them into your unit."

"Uh…"

The effort of talking set my head spinning again. I reached my hand out. Abby took it. She murmured soothing noises. I felt the mattress sink and shift. She was climbing into the bed beside me. "You'll be okay," she said. "I'm right here. Lars, would you put her so that I can hold her, please?"

Though Lars was gentle and brief, the movement left me dizzy. But now I was in Abby's arms, safe. She cradled the back of my head and rocked me the way she knew I liked being rocked when I was coming out of a seizure. The dizziness lessened a little. "Dad?" I asked, relieved that the word had come out more or less clearly.

"He's here, too," Abby replied. "Lars found a discarded yogourt tub. Don't worry; Dolly's making sure he stays put." That was good. Dolly would make sure that Dad wouldn't try to break me open again.

Brie's voice said, "Uh, which one of you is Dolly?"

Lars answered, "The afghan. Long story."

Abby began to hum a simple, wordless ditty in four-four time. I remembered it, but not quavery and thin the way she was singing it now.

Abby stopped. She gave me an apologetic smile. "I'm afraid for you," she said. "You can hear it in my voice."

I whispered, "You and Dad…" My throat felt as though someone had rubbed it with sandpaper.

Abby finished the thought for me. "Yes, Dad and I used to sing it to you. And even Uncle sometimes joined in, remember?"

"Uh-huh. Not the same without Dad's voice." That was the longest sentence I'd managed in a little bit. It exhausted me.

"He can't exactly help right now, I'm afraid."

"Abs," said Lars, "try again."

She didn't hesitate for a second. "Okay, Love." The way she spoke to Lars brimmed over with tenderness and trust; even I could hear it. Gentle as breath, Abby started the tune again. Five notes into the first phrase, Lars closed his eyes, opened his mouth. Like taking the lid off a pot of popping corn, his voice exploded into impossible scales of sound, ran righteous riffs around, with and through the tune. Abby's voice grew stronger, buoyed up by his. She smiled at Lars as though she were a cat and he were cream. The smile made her notes into burnished brass. She started scatting a counterpoint to the tune that she was somehow sustaining the while. Brie laughed the way you laugh when you just can't believe that something is happening. Lars echoed the laugh, wove it into the melody. Now Abby was laughing, too; small, bright starbursts of merriment. She nodded at Brie, as though giving him permission. He looked stricken. He shook his head. Lars jerked his head to one side in an *aw, c'mon* gesture. Brie's face went soft with longing. Of course; on the phone he'd told me that he'd been crap last night. Maybe he was a claypicken after all. They had off days, right?

Then Brie seemed to come to a decision. He leapt into the jam with both feet, literally. He stomped out a syncopation, clicked his fingers to punctuate the beats, slapped out the counterpoint on the drum of his chest, punched a rhythm on the walls with his fists; anything except his voice. Backed by all that rhythm, Abby and Lars hollered and whispered and jook-jointed. The tune was both like and unlike any version of it that my family would sing to me. Abby *doot-doot-doot*ed, a shout-out to the daily joys of just plain living. The music welled up, made me feel safe and strong. It was bigger than three beings and one tune. It was beauty. Together, the three of them were raucous, raunchy, angelic, sweet. Gradually my body's twitching stilled. My breathing began to come more easily. Lars's sound ramped down into a cheerful, chunky backbeat. Abby swanned into the rich, buttery tone that was her trademark. Brie stopped his gumboot stomp, instead tapping out a beat against his thighs with his hands, softer and softer, until it was little more than a pulse beat. Lars began to climb again, his notes ascending higher and higher, but quieter with each one. Then I couldn't hear him any longer. Now it was just Abby and Brie, and gods, it was practically orgasmic. Brie's face was alight with wonder. So was Abby's.

Brie and Abby wound down to a quiet finish, and only then did he sit down hard on the floor and say, "Holy fuck, that was amazing! Have you all got the zimzam?"

"The what?" asked Lars.

I scowled. "Is that what you call it?" My voice was returning. "Look at him," I told Lars and Abby. "He's Shiny. I think he's some kind of too—" I glanced at Lars. "Instrument. And he's doing some scary shit to people in this building."

Abby frowned. "He's not Shiny."

"What do you mean? Of course he is." I lifted my head to look at Brie. But no matter which way I turned my head or squinted, there was no green aura flash around him. I sat upright, ignoring my swimming head. "How'd you do that? Where's your Shine?"

He narrowed his eyes at me. "I lost it. We tanked so badly last night that the band's talking about breaking up. And I am not hurting anybody."

We all jumped at a loud caterwaul from outside my door. Brie looked exasperated. "Ignore him. It's just Yoplait."

The caterwaul warped into the eerie, almost verbal yowl that a cat can do when it's pissed at a human. The sound broke off suddenly. Then there were three sharp raps at the door. The little hairs on my arms stood up. "Lars, would you get that, please? I have to change out of these clothes." I got out of bed, my blanket wrapped carefully around my lower half, and went to the bathroom to peel out of my pissy jeans. While I was in there, I heard Lars call out, "There's no one there!" His voice was puzzled. "Just the cats. Hey! No!"

I opened the bathroom door in time to see Yoplait bound into the room, Butter hard on his heels, with Lars after them. Abby cried out, "Butter! You're supposed to be at home!"

I made it back into the main room just as Yoplait evaded Brie's grasping hands. I said, "Wait. Let them be."

The two cats sniffed cautiously at Dolly, who whirred peaceably at them. They genuflected to Dad, who had already sprouted enough shoots and foliage that I could no longer see the battered yogourt container of dirt into which Abby and Lars had transplanted him.

Butter and Yoplait shot me a look. Then, together, they grew and stretched and transformed until Beji and Beji were standing there. Brie made a squeaking sound. Lars and Abby went openmouthed in astonishment.

"You fuckers," I said. "You've been spying on us all this whole time!"

"Nah, not on you," replied Beji.

"Well, sometimes on her," said Beji. He winked at me. "You're fun to spy on."

"The thing is," continued the other Beji, "we've been watching Brie for years."

"Me? Why? And what the hell are you guys?"

Abby answered that. "Godlings. And our cousins."

Beji blew her a kiss, then turned to Brie. "You haven't lost your zimzam."

Abby said, "Will someone tell me what in blue blazes zimzam is?"

Brie brightened up. "I haven't lost it?"

"No," Beji replied. "You lost Makeda's mojo. Twice now."

My skin was prickling all over. "My mojo? Brie had my mojo? But I thought I didn't have any!"

Lars said, "Told you I could smell it. You're a creature of mojo."

Abby snarled, "Will everyone just stop telling her she has mojo? At this rate, I'll never hear the end of it from her!"

I rounded on her. "See? I was right! You just want to keep me powerless and under your thumb!"

We were each trying to yell over the others. Brie was telling the Bejis that it was his fucking zimzam, thank you very much. Lars was shouting at Abby that she was not the boss of him. I was accusing the Bejis of being voyeuristic pervos. The Bejis were accusing each other of handling this all wrong.

Abby put her pinkie fingers to her lips and whistled, probably with only a twentieth of her sound-making power. The cups on top of my fridge rattled, along with my back teeth. I clapped my hands to my ears. Everyone fell silent. Abby glared at us all. "That's better. Now, we're going to do this one at a time."

I said, "Let's start with the Bejis."

"Fine, let's do that." Abby nodded at them to begin.

"So," said Beji, "our job as celestials is to look after twins."

Other Beji continued, "Then you guys were born, and not only were you twins, you were kin. We've been very protective of you from the start."

"And very interested in everything to do with your lives."

"We followed Uncle Boysie and Uncle Leggy John when they went to do the operation on you, Makeda."

I shook my head in bemusement. "I keep forgetting that you guys are older than us. You look like teenagers."

"We're millennia older. And yet with all our experience, we still can't figure out why you decided to stop dating us."

"Oh, hush. That was just a bit of booty-call fun."

Brie boggled at me. "You had sex with your *cousins*?"

Beji smirked. "And you decided that dating shouldn't be fun any more? Never mind, don't answer that. As we were saying, we were there, hiding, when you got operated on."

"When Uncle Legs tossed away that tiny piece of unformed mojo, Beji here snapped it up."

Abby grimaced. "Ew, gross."

"Wore it in a locket on a collar around her neck."

Brie gasped. "You're really the cat I found injured on the road when I was a kid?"

"I am. That car would never have hit me, but I was distracted. Because the locket was wriggling. Something was trying to get out of it. Never did find out what, since I got smushed by a car and my original cat body died. Had to grow myself a new one. And then I discovered that you'd taken off with the locket."

"But I don't even know where that is any more!"

"It's here somewhere, in Cheerful Rest. Probably slipped behind something when you were moving in. I've been looking for it for years."

"But you know the weirdest part?" said Beji. He turned to me. "The other night, when your haint attacked you and I fought it off? It came out of Brie's unit. That's when Beji and I figured it out; whenever your haint comes to you, Brie's Shine disappears. We think your haint is your mojo. Somehow it developed. But it's unattached. It's desperate to be part of you again."

I boggled at them. "That thing can't be my mojo! It's been trying to kill me for years!"

Wonderingly, Abby said, "It's trying to get inside you, where it belongs. All this time, that's what it wanted."

"By climbing in through my *mouth*?!"

Beji shrugged. "It doesn't understand why that makes no sense. It's your mojo, not your brain."

"Fine, but Brie says it's gone now. So where did it go? Did it die?" Heaven help me, but I half-hoped it had.

Brie burst out, "It can't be dead! It's my talent, I need it! If you don't have it, where did it go?"

Beji said, "It won't die. Not as long as Maka is alive."

Something was weird. "Beji," I said, "if you're Butter, how come you and Butter were at Dad's interment at the same time?"

Beji shrugged and pointed to himself. "Demigod."

The kudzu whipped a length of vine in my direction. I stepped back just as Dolly slapped it away with one of her corners. Brie watched Dolly with a thoughtful, covetous look on his face. "Hang on," he murmured. "Makeda, you recently did some mad powerful zimzam, right?"

"Mojo, not zimzam." Then I understood. "Oh, my gods." I pointed at Dolly. "It's in there. My mojo's moved out of the locket and into the rug."

As one, everyone turned to look at Dolly.

Brie said, "So you do have it!"

"Dude, as far as I'm concerned, you can have it back. I'll make do." I shuddered at the thought of having that creepy, shifty thing living inside me. What was it, anyway? The power to be nasty, violent, and malevolent?

"But what if it won't come back to me, now that it's found you?"

"I'm telling you I don't want it!" I pointed at Dolly. "You. You listening to me? I don't want you!" My skin crawled at the memories of trusting my body—and my sister's!—to that nasty, stupid thing whose only purpose was to do me violence. "You go back to Brie. You belong to him. Leave me alone."

Dolly seemed to shrink in on herself a little, like someone pulling a shawl tighter around their shoulders to keep the cold out.

"Hang a mo," said Lars. "No need to be rash about this." He turned to Brie. "You don't need Makeda's mojo in order to perform."

"My mojo, you mean. Shouldn't I have squatting rights, or something? She doesn't even want it."

"You jammed with us a few minutes ago, and you weren't half bad."

"You don't get it, do you? 'Not half bad' isn't good enough. I couldn't lead. I could only follow. And I sure as hell didn't dare vocalize. I stuck to percussion."

I saw Abby square her shoulders and I knew he was in trouble. "First of all," she said, "I'm daughter to a celestial, my mojo is music, and Lars here used to be one of Hendrix's axes, so when we say that you weren't half bad next to us, that means you were pretty fucking good."

Brie boggled. "Hendrix? As in Jimi?"

Lars smiled. "Damned straight."

"Second of all," Abby continued, "you have a problem with percussion? It's just as brilliant a means of making music as any other, and older than most."

"Third of all," I added, "what the hell are you? You're not human, but you're not Family, either."

Beji said, "He is human."

Brie said, "Of course I am. Abby, I'm not hating on percussion. I played tambourine enough years to learn that there are skills to playing even the simplest instrument. But suppose somebody took your cane away?"

Abby was unimpressed. "I'd get another one, or find a way to make do without it."

Brie looked as though he'd just been told about a death in the family. "Suppose I can't? Suppose I need Maka's ugly-ass mojo in order to be a musician at all?"

"Hey! Don't you insult my magic!" I'd just tried to give Dolly away, but now I was feeling all ownerish again.

Abby smiled. "And yet," she said to Brie, "you've already begun remaking yourself. We all saw that a little while ago. You're a musician, whatever your instrument."

Yoplait Beji said, "She's not lying."

Brie moved very slightly away from her. "I can't get over it that you're Yoplait."

"Sure. But Beji and I could hear you from outside the door. You were as good as when you have a zimzam going on."

Abby said, "I can prove it to you, too. I have a show coming up."

I asked, "The Nathaniel Dett one?"

"No, before that. A small performance at the Music Gallery. Brie, headline with me."

Brie's eyes got round as moons. "For real?"

"For real."

Something delightful was happening. Or rather, something wasn't happening, and that was delightful. Because I wasn't feeling it. The envy, the shame, the lack I would have expected to feel at my mojo-master sister recognizing mastery in another.

Abby pulled one of her cards out of her handbag and handed it to Brie. "Come and rehearse with me tomorrow. After we all wake up, I mean. Damn, I could sleep for a week."

"Abs," I said, "isn't Lars your band lead for that gig?"

"Sure, but Brie won't be taking his place, or anything."

"They'll still have to work together. That okay with you, Lars?"

"Totally fine, ducks. Nice to be asked though, you know?"

Abby shot me a curious look.

Brie shook his head at the address on the card. "Guys, I don't belong in someplace so high-toned."

Abby replied, "All the more reason to do it, don't you think? Throw it in their faces."

Lars chuckled. "Too right."

"Jesus. Okay, I'll do it."

Abby clapped Brie on the shoulder. "Attaboy." She had to reach up to do so.

"But," said Brie, "I'm going to want to rehearse all day every day between now and then."

I leaned over and stroked Dolly and grinned like a fool. They could do whatever they wanted. I had my mojo.

7

◆ ◆ ◆

Must she then buy no more such dainty fruit?
Must she no more such succous pasture find,
Gone deaf and blind?

H E REALLY WAS AWFUL in rehearsal," said Abby. I had
my cell phone open on my workbench. I didn't even need to
put her on speaker. Her voice over the cell phone always sounded as
though she were standing right beside me. She probably didn't even
realize she was doing it. "Maybe I'm wrong about him," she continued. "Maybe he does need supernatural aid in order to make music."

"Don't worry, he'll come through this evening." I wasn't really
sure that he would, not without my haint working for him. But I
didn't need to stress about it. That was Brie's problem; Brie's and
Abby's.

"I almost asked him not to perform tonight after all."

"Abs, that would probably have broken his heart."

"I'm not even sure how I came to invite him to gig with me."

"It made sense at the time, right?"

"Yeah. You were there with your head in my lap, and it just
felt right to make the offer."

"Then trust your instinct."

"Maybe. But I'd rather perform without him than crash and burn onstage because of him. I just didn't want to make any trouble between the two of you."

"The two of who?" I asked, only half listening. I'd swivelled my chair over to where my laptop was on my worktable. I typed "kudzu" into the search engine.

"You and Brie. You sounded pretty hot for him."

"I was. Not much feeling it nowadays, though. Dunno why not."

"Did you ever find out what he wanted to tell you the other night?"

"Not yet. Seems like whenever I try to talk to him, he's either about to leave to rehearse with you so he doesn't have time or he's just come back from rehearsal, so he's too tired. It can wait. How's Dad?" I was all shivery. I'd thought it'd be hot in my place, but I was always cold. I shrugged into the cardigan I'd hung over the back of my chair.

"Dad's climbed completely up the tall standing lamp in the living room. I'm not turning that lamp on, 'cause I don't want to singe his leaves."

I winced at the thought of letting Dad get burned.

"And I will never eat anything grape-flavoured ever again. The organic waste is overflowing with those giant blossoms. I'm living on allergy meds. Plus Dad's almost covered his favourite armchair. I'm afraid that if Butter falls asleep anywhere in the living room, I'll come home to find a cat-shaped lump covered in kudzu."

"All that in just a few days? Can't you prune him back, or something?"

"Truth is, I'm afraid of him."

"Yeah, well, imagine how I feel. I'm not going to come visiting for a while."

She sighed. "I suppose that makes sense."

I noticed something on the web page I was scrolling through. "Says here that the leaves make good pesto."

There was a shocked gasp from the other end, and then a yelp of laughter. "I am not making Pappy pesto for dinner!"

"Dad would probably think that was hilarious. But I guess it's time to let Uncle Jack know that we found him."

"Would you do that, Maka? Uncle kind of intimidates me."

"You?" I replied, astonished. "What in the world could intimidate you?"

"Uncle Jack isn't exactly in this world most of the time."

"Yeah, but you know what I mean. You're the Family's golden girl. You don't have any reason to be scared of a single one of them. Well, maybe Hunter. But Dolly and I can keep you safe from him."

"They expect so much from me, even Uncle Jack. You can tell how much he hates it that I'm seeing Lars."

"He's a fine one to talk, trying to hide the fact that he and our claypicken mom are an item. At least you're not in the closet."

"They want me to prove that I deserve their favour. I'm supposed to be the compensation prize for Dad's indiscretion. I'm the new celestial, the golden girl."

"Except for that little problem of your eventual death."

"Everyone on Dad's side of the Family used to be mortal once, too. Maybe mortality's curable."

"But they have to think you're worth it, I guess." Jealousy turned like a worm in my belly. I'd thought it was gone for good. But I knew our family would never see me and Dolly as anything but abomination.

Abby replied, "The way they tell it, that's not their decision. The Big Boss made them what they are. Hey; you're getting really attached to that afghan, huh?"

"I think I am. So long as my haint—my mojo, rather. Gods,

doesn't that sound good? My mojo. But so long as it stays in the afghan and doesn't pop out as something nasty with too many teeth and hands that's trying to climb down my throat, it and I are cool."

"But don't you wonder what your mojo would be like if it were fully part of you?"

"And how would I find that out? Ask Uncle Jack to operate on me again? No, thank you. Not after the back-alley mojo-ectomy he gave me and Dad the last time. No, I'm content like this. Now that I have Dolly, I can fly. I can fight off marauding kudzu daddies. And I'll always have someone to sing me to sleep at night."

Her voice small, Abby said, "That used to be me."

"Don't sweat it. You can harmonize with her sometimes, okay?"

"I guess. There's a tremble in your voice. You sick?"

"I think I'm just coming down with a cold. No biggie."

"I'm heading for the Music Gallery in a minute. Should I wear the green velvet?"

When Abs was jittery like this just before a performance, she had a hard time making small decisions. "No, it's too warm out today. How about the tan linen pantsuit?"

"That sounds good."

"All right, I'm gonna ring off. I'll summon Uncle Jack and tell him we found Dad."

"You have the white rum?"

"Come on, Abs! As if I'd forget. There was lots left over after we interred Dad's body."

"True 'nough. Say hi to Uncle for me."

"Yup. See you in a bit."

Overproof white rum? Check. Matches? Check. Fire extinguisher? Check. I poured a shot or three of the white rum right onto the cement floor of my unit. It began spreading immediately. I bellowed, "Uncle Jack!"

"Busy! Oo, you brought me a treat!"

He hadn't materialized, so I watched the puddle of white rum carefully. Yes, it was growing smaller. I lit a match and tossed it into the puddle. The rum burst into licking blue flames.

"Ow! Ow! I was drinking that!" He was there, and he looked none too pleased. His suit jacket and shirt were open, exposing a very well-defined chest for such a skinny-ass being. His pants were at half-mast. He wasn't. But when your dad is pretty much the doctor for all living things (albeit currently without portfolio), and your uncle is the crown prince of sex, birth, and death, you pretty much couldn't be embarrassed by such a piffling thing as the gallant response.

Putting himself back together, Uncle grumbled, "I was busy, damn it!"

"Yeah, so I just heard. You can get back to her later."

He grinned, of course. "Back to *her*? You know better than to make assumptions like that."

"I just figured you might be with Mom."

"No, but I'm going to see her"—I saw him put two and two together mid-sentence—"tomorrow. Or maybe last week. So you've been talking to your mother, have you? And you might want to put that flame out. There's nothing about the future that can't be changed by a foolish act in the present."

I used the extinguisher. Stinky, messy things. "What did you do with my mojo?"

He glared back. "This is why you disturbed my assignation?"

"Did I really interrupt you, though? Rumour has it that you can be in more than one place at the same time."

He smirked. "Yes, and to delightful effect, I might add."

"Gah. TMI, Uncle."

He got himself properly dressed. "Like I told you, you didn't have mojo. There was no seed inside to grow. It was an empty lump of stuff. Offal. A flap of waste ectoplasm. I'm sorry, Niece, but that's the way it was. Would you mind pouring me a fresh dram of that stuff? Thank you."

I did. He sucked it back like it was water. I said, "We found Dad. He's at home. Abby's home, I mean."

The brotherly joy that lit his face made him almost too bright to look at. "Boysie? He's all right?"

"He's still riding Quashee."

It was as though someone had put the sun out. "Of course. Then he doesn't have much longer." He folded himself up and sat, dejectedly, on the floor. "Looks like Hunter's got himself a new job."

I sat beside him. "I tried to let Dad have his mojo back."

Uncle went alert. "What do you mean?"

"He attacked me and Abby. Pulled us down out of the sky into a park."

"Out of the sky, Makeda?"

I was too busy trying to tell my tale of botched self-sacrifice. I didn't notice at first how his tone had changed. "Yes. We were cruising on Dolly. Wee hours of the morning. Only a few people saw us."

Uncle looked around my room and spied Dolly, lying in her preferred place under my worktable. "Makeda," he said, his voice dangerously low, "didn't I tell you to stop using that thing?"

"Well, sure you did. But you were all 'nod nod wink wink' about it, so I knew you didn't mean it."

"I meant for you to use it once more, just so you could show it off to your sister. Not for you to go jaunting about on some malevolent piece of made thing and endangering Abby's life into the bargain. I meant for you to stick it in a corner and leave it there until I came back for it."

"It's not malevolent. It's the house for my mojo. Besides, you didn't come back for it."

"I'm busy, child. I was going to get around to it. And it's the what for your what?"

"Beji says. My haint; it's my mojo, all grown up."

I told him about my haint leaving Brie and taking up residence in Dolly. He shook his head. "No, no! What in the seven perfect circles has gotten into you? Letting the Bejis fill your head with stories like that. They're the reason that Boysie's a haint in the first place! Setting his soul free without a body to house it; what were they thinking?"

"Wait; Dad's a haint? Like my haint?"

"No, like a real haint. The thing that hounds you isn't a ghost of anything. I would know if it were." He gestured at the blue-painted ceiling. "This trick was never going to keep you safe from that monster. It just kept you from being paralyzed by terror all the time."

I couldn't believe my ears. "Holy fuck, Uncle. Is there anything you've ever told me the truth about?"

He smiled sadly. "Believe it or not, most of it was the truth. Any lies I told you were the symptom, not the problem. I'm guilty of trying to cushion the blow of what your dad and I did to you. Now I see that it wasn't a mercy. It's only allowing you to delude yourself with fancies. Like this notion that you have mojo hiding somewhere, if only you can find it."

I scowled at him. "Yeah. Great. Makes me feel so much better. You were saying about Dad?"

Sorrowfully, he replied, "Your father is currently a soul without a body. That's a ghost, Makeda. A haint."

"Don't say that! It's like he's dead."

"Not yet. But he will be if I can't find a way to fix this."

"When he grabbed me and tried to tear me apart, I tried to let him do it."

Uncle Jack turned and took me in his arms. "Why would you do something like that?"

"It's Dad's, and he's important. He should have it back. I think he tried, but part of himself wouldn't let him. Uncle, Beji said she had to grow herself a new cat body when her old one died. Couldn't you grow Dad a replacement body?"

"I can't. Only he can do that for himself. I could give him a loaner, but it's inconvenient. There's always some part that's not working, and he'd have to trade it in for a new one every few days. Else they draw flies. Don't you go relaxing, little niece. I'm still pissed at you." He held me away from him. "That rug has to go."

"But my mojo is in there!"

"IT IS NOT!"

The sheer force of his negation made the building shake. My glasses and tools clinked from the sound wave, and Dolly set up a resonant humming. Uncle Jack swung in the direction of the sound. He shuddered when he looked at Dolly.

"So then what is my haint?"

He shook his head. "For all I know, it's a corrupted file. Probably damaged by your rug there."

"Before the rug existed?"

"Sure, why not? Time's not linear, no matter what your senses tell you." He stood up and went over to my workbench.

"Please, Uncle."

"No." He bent over and reached towards the rug, then swore and pulled his hand back. His palm was smoking. He blew on it. "Makeda, what did you do? How did you give that thing its own firewall?"

I looked at his hand in awe. "What could hurt you?" Truth was, I kinda felt good about it. Dolly could defend herself!

"Nothing should be able to hurt me." He glowered at Dolly. "This is bad." He straightened up. His face was both sad and stern. "Nothing can be allowed to exist on this plane if it can defy death. It's like a cancer. And if you're right and a human's using it sometimes, that's infinitely more dangerous. Maka, honey, I'm sorry, but if I can't destroy your creation, you have to do it."

"No, Uncle!"

He crossed his arms. "Yes. You must. And this time I'm going to make sure it happens. I'm going to stay right here and watch you."

Uncle was implacable. His face stern, he perched on my bed and oversaw the whole thing. With my body, I hid the pair of scissors I was holding. I tailor-sat beside the rug. "Hey, sweetie." I stroked it. Tears steamrollered down my cheeks.

I looked at Uncle, hoping for a last-minute reprieve. He only raised an eyebrow and nodded at me to continue.

The rug shifted uneasily to and fro. It could sense my distress, as a pet can. "Shh," I said. "It's okay, baby." The slow passes of my hand along its uneven surface soothed both me and the rug. Slowly, I calmed. So did it. When it was relaxed, stretched out luxuriantly on the floor with its birds whittering in pleasure from the petting, I picked up the pair of scissors. In order to get at my mojo, I had to unmake it. I snipped an edge of the crochet. The rug jumped. The birds squawked in a painful range of frequencies. The clipped knot unravelled. The rug tried to get away, but I was holding it tightly. I pulled on the loose end of yarn, and more of the rug came undone. One of the birds snapped at my hand. I hissed at the pain, but held on. The bird's strike bruised two red triangles into the skin of my wrist. The rug jerked frantically at my hand. "I have to do this," I sobbed. "I don't have any choice."

At my words, it stopped struggling so hard. It had fought off the Dad-kudzu and zapped Uncle with a touch. It could easily have gotten the better of me. But like a dog being savaged by its own dear human, it submitted, and did its best to squash its own instincts to fight back. I yanked more and more of the yarn free. It was like pulling my own guts out of my belly. The rug lay on the floor, twitching. Its birds made gulpy, clucking sounds, like whimpers. Uncle was making similar noises. He wasn't enjoying this. I didn't care. He wasn't suffering like Dolly was.

The yarn went taut. I'd reached the rows where I'd affixed the birds, many of them with epoxy. To my horror, I realized I would have to cut around the places where the glue had welded the strands of yarn together. "Oh, gods." I picked the scissors up again. When I dug the jaws of the scissors into the fabric, the birds screamed and the rug went stiff and flat as a piece of board. Then it slumped. I wailed, "I'm sorry, I'm sorry" at it as I cut and tore its birds away. Each bird I removed went silent, then dulled immediately into a clumsily wired-together assemblage of artificial scraps. The part of the rug where the birds were too tiny to see was a subtle thickening that curved around the edge of the rug. I cut it away. Now there was no sound but my weeping. The quivering flap of material lying on the floor was the only thing left. Uncle said, "Finish it."

I picked it up and began doggedly picking the stitches out.

When I was done, I was left with a crinkled pile of waste yarn scraps, and another of metal and glass junk, no more coherent than the refuse swept up off a metal shop floor every evening. Uncle sighed. "Thank you, my dear."

"Bite me." My voice was hoarse.

He sighed. "Time to go visit with my brother. And Makeda, since you're determined to live here, you should know; that child I took across the border the other day? Fleet? She used to be in that Brie person's band."

"I know that. You need to go."

"This was the right thing to do, Niece."

I let him leave without telling him goodbye. My ears were

ringing. There was snot drying on my upper lip. My head felt swollen and tender, but I was cried out. I creaked to my feet. My joints hurt like I was carrying the weight of the world. I dragged myself over to my kitchen area and got a couple of garbage bags and my dustpan and broom. I had to sweep Dolly's remains up and trash them.

I crouched over the carnage I'd created. Wearily, I leaned over to sweep it up.

A form guttered into existence on the pile of disassembled bits. Shocked, I yanked my hands away. It was an ugly toddler with hands too big for its body. Then it was a writhing, snaky thing with too many fangs. Then a cross between a massive toad and a soft-boiled ostrich egg, wearing flashing baby runners on three of its four splayed feet. It bled a sickly green light from scissors slashes all over its body. One of its eyes had been slit open. With the remaining one, it glared hurt and hatred at me. My haint! Exulting, I reached for it to cradle it to me, to bandage its wounds. It slapped me away with man-sized hands. I fell backwards onto my ass. Quickly the haint shovelled up as much of Dolly as it could in its arms. The cuts I'd made in it scabbed over as I watched. "Please," I begged. I reached for it again. It snarled, baring ragged ridges of yellowed fangs.

My door banged open. Brie came rushing in, wild-eyed. "Brie! Help me!"

Brie looked at the tableau in front of him: me sprawled on the floor, my haint glowering over me, its too-long arms full of broken birds and scrips and scraps of yarn. He growled at me, "What are you doing to it? Leave it alone!" He pushed himself between me and my haint.

"I can explain," I said. "Uncle made me do this."

"Don't. You don't deserve something this wonderful." Brie turned to embrace the haint. That was when I saw that it had a large scaled and feathered tail. It walloped Brie sideways with it. He crashed to the floor. I heard his head hit the concrete. Then it hissed at me and was gone, leaving me bereft and so, so cold.

◆ ◆ ◆

Brie hissed as I touched his head with a towel I'd soaked in cold water and wrung out. "Damn, that hurts."

"Let me have a look." I moved closer to him on the bed and parted his 'fro. "Bit of a bruise, but no swelling." I checked his eyes. They were tracking fine. "You feeling confused? Or sleepy?"

He scowled. "Bitch of a headache, is all."

"You should probably get checked out, but I don't think you have a concussion. What the hell was that about? And why were you even home? Shouldn't you be at the concert hall? You're on in a couple of hours."

Sullenly, he replied, "I just needed to pick something up first."

The bastard. "As in my haint?"

"I can't perform without my zimzam! I'm gonna look like a fool up there!" He pulled his head out of my hands. "But clearly, now that it has you, it doesn't want me."

"Yeah, you see how badly it wanted me."

"Well what do you expect? You destroyed its home!"

"My uncle says that it's not a mojo."

"I don't know what you guys would call it. But it's my zimzam. I feel it like I feel my left arm attached to my left shoulder. I don't have to look to know that it's there, or to reach out with it. Only time I couldn't feel it was when it was wrapped up in that rug of yours. And I guess when it was out looking for you."

"I dunno, Brie. All this time I thought it was dangerous."

Brie looked at his feet. In a small voice he said, "It is."

My heart did a fear-flop. "Go on."

He turned towards me, his face a picture of misery. "You gotta understand," he pleaded. "I never meant to do it the first time and I haven't done it since!"

The creeped-out feeling was crawling up my spine, vertebra by vertebra, from the inside. "What the fuck did you do?"

"I had to take care of them! I never meant to hurt them!"

Slowly, the story came out. "My zimzam, or hoodoo, or whatever the fuck you want to call it, if I'm not careful, it hurts people. Like any drug, I guess. It gives you a buzz, but it takes something from you, too. It took me a while to work out that that's what was happening."

"That's what happened to Fleet?"

"Oh, God. Faith. My sweet Faith." He put his head in his hands. "Fleet and I used to date. We met at one of my gigs. She came up afterwards and said she wanted to play with us. She could make a flute do things it wasn't meant to. And she was gorgeous. When the cops came and told me the other night that she'd died, I locked myself in my room and cried for hours. I only came out because you knocked on my door. I'm not quite sure what it is that happens. But my band members started to look really tired."

"What, the Soul Chain guys?"

"No, the first Soul Chain."

"Crap! What happened to them?"

"You saw Fleet."

"So everyone who comes to your shows starts to age prematurely?" I fought the impulse to check the backs of my hands for liver spots.

"No, no! Jesus. Just the band. I swear, when I realized it was happening, and I realized it was me, it made me sick."

"What'd your band members think about it?"

"It was like they didn't notice. They kept saying they felt great, they didn't know what their friends and family were worrying about. Then the first one dropped dead. And then another. This building was a godsend."

"How come?"

"Milo, he's an under-the-table kinda guy. People in his building out of work? He gets them to put him down as their landlord when they apply for pogey. Rent money comes directly from the government to him. He didn't say boo when I moved Fleet and Win in, and then filled up the other units with the new members of Soul Chain."

"Win, too?"

He hung his head. "Yeah. I make sure that Fleet and Win and those guys..."

"And what're you doing about your new band? 'Cause I don't think there's any such thing as just using a little crack."

He replied, "You know what? I'm done with all this."

He stood up. I leapt up to bar his way. "What the hell do you mean by that?"

He backed towards the door, his hands held up to ward me off. "I can only deal with so much weirdness, okay? Your family are gods—"

"Demigods."

He stopped. "Whatever. Sometimes they're cats. They can control the fucking *weather*. You're being chased by some kind of scary goblin thing that turns out to be one of your organs, then you work some far-out mojo that seriously makes my zimzam look like baby spit-up, and you've been excuse my French fucking your cousins the cats. The twin cats—"

"Not while they're cats!" I protested. "That would just be creepy." The Bejis had been right, though; why had I decided to stop dating them? Maybe I could ask them out next time I saw them.

"And now your sister, the princess royal of music, wants me to jam with her in public without my zimzam? Don't you get it? I couldn't do it on my own. I needed your goddamned goblin mojo thing. But clearly, it doesn't want me any more."

"Brie—"

"Don't. You know, I thought maybe there was something between you and me."

"You did?" I'd hoped there could be, too. But for the past few days I hadn't been feeling it so much.

"Yeah, but there can't be. It's all too much. I can't keep up with you guys."

"With us guys? You mean with Abby. She's the sister with the power."

He glowered at me. "Sister, you have some power of your own, and it just clonked me on the head and fucked off."

A horrible thought occurred to me. "Shit. Where'd it go?"

He shook his head. "Dunno, but it's not in the building. I can sense it when it is."

I went all over goose bumps. "Oh, gods above. Abby. It's gone to try to get rid of Abby. It's jealous of her."

"How do you know that?"

"Because it's a piece of me. I gotta help her!" I grabbed my phone off my worktable. "Looks like you're going to be at your gig after all. You're coming with me."

He looked really unhappy at that. "Why? What can I do?"

I was trying to call Abby while shrugging into my jacket. "I don't know, but I can probably use all the help I can get."

My cell phone rang. It was Abby's number. Had my haint already reached her? I didn't want to scare her if I could help it. Maybe today could still go off smoothly. I answered the call. "Hey. Don't worry, I'm on my way with Brie. He just had a bit of cold feet."

"Maka, Abby needs you over here right away." It was Lars's voice.

"Crap. Did my haint get to her?"

"No." He sounded puzzled. "But she's lost her voice."

"She got a cold, or something? But she knows a bit of anaesthetic spray will—"

"No. I've never seen anything like this. She can't speak above a whisper, and nothing works. She thinks it's overexposure to Quashee. She can't go onstage like this."

"That's the least of her problems right now. Get her somewhere safe, okay? Behind a locked door, out of sight. I think my haint's after her."

"What? Why?"

"I'll explain later. Don't tell her what's up." I had a glimmer of an idea. It was a terrifying one, but it might solve everyone's problems. I slipped my cell phone into my pocket and shrugged the rest of the way into my jacket. "Come on," I said to Lars. "You can warm up in the cab."

"Can't I just stay here? Abby doesn't need me."

I thought of the skunk that used to fetch and carry for Dad; of all his animal supplicants, in fact. They served him if and when they wanted to, because they wanted to. He never compelled them, never took their love for granted. A real lord knew that his subjects were his equals. "Well, maybe I need you."

"What're you going to do?"

I said the words I'd never thought I could utter. "You should have your zimzam, not me. I don't want it. Especially if it tries to hurt my sis."

He brightened up. "You'd give it back to me? Wow, Maka. That's . . . wow."

"And that right there is the problem. You're acting as though it has no choice in the matter. It's not your slave, Brie. You are not the boss of it."

He frowned. "I don't understand."

I said, "I want you to thank it for everything it's ever done for you. Then I want you to ask it to please come back to you."

"Ookay," he said doubtfully. "And if that doesn't work?"

I took my Super Soaker down from its hook on the wall. "It'd better work. 'Cause if it tries to do anything to Abby, I'm gonna do my best to destroy it."

◆ ◆ ◆

Lars met us when we arrived at the gallery. He gave Brie a measuring look. "So you finally decided to show, huh?"

Brie sighed and pointed at me. "She made me."

Lars nodded. To my surprise, he said, "She can be fierce."

Could I? "Where's Abs?" I asked.

"In the greenroom. She should have gone onstage ten minutes ago."

Brie touched my arm. "It's nearby. I can feel it."

"Fine. You go and try to reason with it." He nodded. He looked scared, but he went anyway.

Lars asked, "What's going on?"

I replied, "My haint's gone rogue. It's pissed at me, and I think it's looking to get back at me by hurting Abby."

"Shit. I gotta get back to her, then!"

I took his wrist. "Brie might be able to stop it."

But when Lars and I rounded the corner, we found Brie leaning against a wall with a fresh shiner on one eye. "That thing packs a wallop," he said. "I'm just glad it didn't use those four-inch talons it's grown since we saw it a few minutes ago."

"You should go to Emergency."

He pulled away from the wall to stand straight. "No, I'm going to keep trying." He stumbled off. Lars and I rushed to the gallery's greenroom. An ashen-faced Abby flew into my arms. She was safe! I hugged her back. She said not a word. She just looked at me with lost, frightened eyes. She coughed. She put her hand to her throat and grimaced. In a hoarse whisper she said, "Nothing works. I can't sing!"

I stroked her hair, kissed her forehead. "Poor Abs." I meant it. For her, being unable to channel her voice would be like losing all her faculties at once. "I think I can fix it. But I need a little time."

Lars said, "No problem. She was only due to go on ten minutes ago. People will just think she's getting her diva on. The band will play in the meantime. I'll go get them started. Just don't take too long."

I moved to let him past me. I clicked the door shut and turned the latch to lock it.

Abby was still standing just in front of me. "I'm bombing." Her voice crackled like old potato chip bags. Her face was slick with tears. "The show's a complete failure. We have to give people their money back."

Something banged on the door, thrice. It came from too low down, and it wasn't the right cadence for a knock. I gulped. "Probably the stage manager." I prayed Abs would believe me. I was running out of time. "Have you put on your makeup yet?" I asked her, edging her closer to the dressing room. It had a door with the right kind of handle. I prayed that it opened to the inside.

She shook her head. "Why would I bother with makeup?"

She coughed again. It looked painful. The haint tried again to bang the door down. This time Abby realized that it wasn't the stage manager. "What—?"

I hustled her into the dressing room. I was in luck for once; the door did open inwards. I shoved Abby in the direction of the old couch that was in there. It broke my heart to see her stumble, but she caught herself and sprawled onto the couch. "I'm sorry, Abs." She was still struggling to turn to face me, trying to ask me in a whispery shout what was going on. I grabbed her outfit up off the chair she'd hung it over and snatched her cane from the dressing table. I dashed out of the dressing room and slid the cane through the door handle.

A massive blow from outside the greenroom cracked the frame of the outer door. It held, but it wouldn't for much longer. I tossed Abby's clothing down and braced myself, holding her cane like a club. I was all flop sweat, but I would go down fighting.

The next sound was a knock. Two raps, quiet and civil, about halfway up the door. "Abby? Makeda? It's Brie."

"Yeah?" I replied. "Prove it." Abby banged on the dressing room door and rattled it.

The voice from outside the greenroom said, "Oh, come *on*! What am I going to know that my zimzam doesn't? Just let me in, while I can still control the damned thing."

"Fair enough." He sounded tired. I let him in. He looked tired. And as though he was still fighting. I asked him, "Did it agree to come back to you?"

"Not exactly." He took in the jammed dressing room door, the angry thumping from behind it, me stripping down to my undies and getting into Abby's clothes. "Let's just say that we're having a battle of wills at the moment, and I'm not sure who's winning. I don't know how long I can hold on to it. What're you doing?"

I pulled on Abby's jacket. "I'm being Abby." At that, Abby's noises got louder. Sounded like she was throwing herself against the dressing room door. I called out, "Relax, Sis. I'm trying to protect you." If this worked, I could fix everything in one fell swoop. Abby would be safe, Dad could have his mojo back, and Brie could have his precious zimzam, if he could convince it to stay. And me? I'd cross that bridge when and if I came to it.

Brie said, "You're not going to get up onstage, are you?"

"I may not get that far if you can't talk some sense into your zimzam. Crap, I really haven't thought this through, have I? Listen: It'll come after me, thinking I'm Abby. It's not very smart. When it does, you grab it. Try to convince it to come back to you."

"Jesus. It nearly took me out the last two times I tried." He twitched. "Holding on to it now's like riding a bucking bronco. And I've never ridden a horse."

"If you and it can't come to an agreement, I will do my very best to beat it to shreds. Hear that, haint o' mine?" I sounded about as brave as I felt, which wasn't much.

"Okay, okay. How much time do I have?"

"How would I fucking know?" I had a thought. "Hey; can you sing, now that you've roped yourself to your zimzam?"

Abby tried to shout. All I could hear was squeaky hissing. I said, "Stop it, Abs. You're going to ruin your voice."

Brie shook his head. "Don't dare try to sing. I'm just holding it still so you can do what you have to." He looked close to tears. "I'm really going to miss it. And the band. And being a musician."

"It's not like I want to do this!" I truly did mess up everything I touched.

"Hang on," said Brie. "Maka, sing something, would you?"

"In a pig's eye. I sing like someone's freezing the balls off a brass monkey! Plus I don't have any training."

He replied, "Just try it. Sing 'In Anyone's Home.'"

One of Abby's pieces. I gulped. This was going to be horrible, I was going to squawk like a chicken in a blender. But Abby needed me. I took a breath, opened my mouth, and softly tried the first few words of the song:

Mm, mm, mm, mm
In anyone's home we are lost.

God, I was even worse than I'd feared. I clamped my braying mouth shut. But Brie waved me on. "Keep it up," he said. "Those last few notes were better. I guess I was, like, calibrating."

"Come again?"

"I'm not strong enough to force my zimzam to help me sing, but I can draw energy from it and pass it on to you, if I concentrate hard enough. Go again."

Damn it. I threw myself at the next couplet:

Mm, mm, mm, mm,
We are lost in anyone's home.

He and I stared at each other, openmouthed. That had sounded good! "Was it right?" I asked him. "I don't know from pitch."

"It was perfect." He pumped his fist in the air. "Yes! I can fucking do this! Who knew?"

"But why do you want me to sing?"

The rattling of the dressing room door grew frenzied.

Brie sighed. "Maybe you can get the zimzam to latch onto you permanently. I'd rather it be alive than dead, even if that means I don't have it."

My eyes brimmed over without warning. "Now who's being noble?" I hugged him.

Someone rapped loudly on the greenroom door. "Come on, folks, let's go! People are getting restless out here." Finally, the actual stage manager.

Brie grabbed my hand. In a strained voice, he said, "You can do this. I'll be helping you, sitting right out front where you can see me."

"Ms. Joli!" yelled the stage manager.

I called, "I'm on my way!" Kinda sounded like Abby. Kinda.

Brie said, "We need to hurry. I'm not sure how much longer I can control this thing."

I hadn't done this in ages, not since Abs and I were both kids. I'd grown a few inches taller than her. Her pants were too short in the crotch for me, and her shoes pinched. She walked differently nowadays, too. More strongly, and I didn't quite have the hang of it. As I moved towards the door, I pulled my leg up a little to mimic her shorter one, tried for her characteristic gait. "No," said Brie. "A little more limp, but a little more attitude, too. You need to work the whole diva thing. And pull your shoulders back. No singer would choke up on her diaphragm like that. At least Abby doesn't."

There was polite clapping from the audience outside. The band had finished the song.

"Showtime," I said. "Let's go." I called out, "Abby, I promise this'll work out!"

She threw herself against the door a couple more times.

I stepped out into the performance space, Brie behind me. My heart was a jackhammer in my chest. Head up. Shoulders back. Attitude.

We were approaching the steps to the stage. The audience broke into applause when they saw me. I jumped about a foot at the sudden sound. And oh gods above, Beji and Beji were in the audience! They waved at me—or rather, at Abby. I felt like I was going to hurl. Brie squeezed my free hand. I concentrated on his touch, the realness of it. He leaned in close and whispered, "Don't get too close to the mike. If this works, you could blow it out."

He stood beside me and gave me his arm. Huh? Right; Abby would be helped up the short, railing-free stairs. I took his arm, leaned on it like I needed it. Actually, I did. I was shaking so badly that my teeth were chattering. "Ready?" he whispered.

"No. I mean, yes."

He glanced at me nervously, but escorted me up the stairs without another word. Thank heaven the audience was mostly in darkness, but for the people closest to the stage. From his place with the band, Lars looked at me suspiciously. I shrugged at him. He raised a single, elegant eyebrow. Brie escorted me to centre stage, where the stool and the mike were. He made sure I was seated. I nodded my thanks at him. He turned the mike away from us and whispered, "Wait till I get down in front. When you're about to begin, give me a nod."

"Sure." My mouth was as dry as the Sahara. Brie turned the mike back towards me and got offstage. I took a sip of water from the glass. My hands were shaking so badly that I spilled a little of it on Abby's pants.

I'd lost sight of Brie. Frantically, I searched the first few rows of people with my eyes until I saw him; there, a little to my left.

There was a set list on the small table by Abby's stool. The silence had stretched on too long. I needed to get going. I glanced at the set list, and went blank. I couldn't make the words make sense. I closed my eyes in panic.

"'In Anyone's Home'?" It was Lars, prompting me with his soft voice. Bless him. I nodded. They began the opening bars of the song. Crap! Was Brie ready?

Brie's eyes were shut. Did he know when I was supposed to come in? He opened his eyes, thank heaven, just in time for me to give him my signal. A split second late, I croaked out the first few words.

Mm, mm, mm, mm
In anyone's home we are lost.

It was frightful. Creaky, too soft, nowhere near on key. It wasn't working! People at the front of the house frowned. Frantic, I looked at Brie. He mimed, *Pull your spine up straight. Keep going.* I couldn't let Abby fail. Through gonging terror, I took a gasping breath and launched into the rest:

Mm, mm, mm, mm,
We are lost in anyone's home.

My voice boomed out so loudly that the mike squealed. Feedback. But I'd been on key, just too loud. Remembering Brie's instruction before I went onstage, I lifted the mike stand and moved the mike farther away from my face. I winked at the crowd. A few people laughed. I sang, and it was good. It was like Brie was holding me up, singing through me, but with Abby's voice. When I ran out of air, the last note I'd sung would somehow continue until I caught my breath again. I belted. I grooved. I wailed. Once I blanked on the words to the second verse of "Women of Other Worlds," and I freaking *scatted*! Just for a few seconds, but I did! My eyes adjusted to the darkened crowd enough that I could see a few people dancing. By the fifth song, I was swinging along with the band like I was one of them. I was flirting with the crowd, cracking jokes, twitching my shoulders in time to the music. I. Was. Making. Could Abby hear me? Was I doing good? Brie sure looked proud of me.

I glanced at the set list. Sixth song was a cover, slower tempo, change of gears. A pang of sadness cut through my elation. Dad used to sing this to us and now, for the first time, I'd be able to sing it, too. I beat out the tempo against my thigh, the band started in to my direction, and I sang, sweet as honey in the rock:

Go to sleep, you little baby,
Go to sleep, you little baby,
Your momma's gone away, but your daddy's gonna stay
Didn't leave nobody but the baby.

People were swaying in time. A man down in front blinked tears out of his eyes. *Dad*, I pleaded silently, *come back to us!*

Go to sleep, pretty baby,
She's long gone with her red shoes on.

She was gone, or she had been. Abs and I had never known a mother, just Dad and Uncle Jack, whom so many claypickens hated and misunderstood. But now we had Mom back. And most of Dad, if we could just get all the pieces together. There had to be a way.

I knew which verse was next. Dad used to change it sometimes when he sang it for us. On the word "you," he would point at us both. For Abby, for Uncle, for Dad, I opened my throat and sang Dad's version:

Don't you weep, pretty baby,
You and me and the devil makes four,

Don't need no other lovin' baby.

One or two people looked startled when I broke the rhyme, replacing "three" with "four." I heard Lars say, sotto voce, "That's right, girl." Other than that, most people didn't seem to notice the switch. I sang the song through to the end, then immediately leapt into the last one, a blazing version of Hendrix's "Room Full of Mirrors." That was a new one for Abby. She'd put it in for Lars. I'd only seen her rehearse it once. The terror pounced again. But as the band lit into the tune, Brie laughed and threw both thumbs up. He jumped to his feet. Taking his cue, so did everyone else who'd remained seated till now. Brie mouthed at me, *I know this one!* He began pumping his head in blissful time to the music. His lips moved, soundlessly feeding me the lyrics; I started singing, and then the whole audience was dancing, stomping, clapping, so loudly that it didn't matter when I flubbed the occasional line. The band and I fucking rocked the house. The crowd went nuts. Holy shit, what a rush this was! Now I understood why Abby loved performing so much.

But where was my haint? Brie looked like shit on a bun from fighting to control it. And I couldn't feel any sign that it had tried to come for me. What would I even feel? Brie's description hadn't helped. As we boogied full force towards the end of the song, I closed my eyes and sang to my haint that love would shine on my baby, then I'd know she was for me.

That should have been the end of the set, but the crowd was calling for an encore. Sure, I could do that. Abby had a list of possible songs in case an encore was in order. I scanned the list. Ah. There was one of my favourites. I told the band "Branch Down." They started in on the opening notes. The audience quieted in anticipation. Brie was clearly exhausted, but he squared his shoulders. I gave him the nod, he gave me the thumbs-up, and I threw myself into the song—

*   *   *

—and sprawled flat on my metaphorical face. The notes came out as some unholy offspring of a squawk and a screech. I clamped my mouth shut. Brie looked about ready to collapse. He mouthed, *It's gone. Do you have it?* Frantically, I shook my head. The band kept gamely playing. Brie looked thoroughly confused. He motioned me to jump back into the song. I tried, I really did. If anything, it was even worse. Then, to my abject horror, people in the audience began to boo.

I felt the rush, like an oncoming wave. Power, of a type I'd never known before. My haint! I stood ready to receive it, not knowing whether it would bond with me or strike me down.

And I sensed it slap against me and bounce off, repelled. Something green and growing inside me stirred, wormlike. Something not a part of me. While I carried Dad's mojo, I had no room for my own.

The greenroom door banged open. Abby'd managed to get free. She came out with her back to us, step-clump, holding a chair that she was using to fend off her attacker. "Get away!" she yelled at it.

It was my haint. It was the least human-looking I'd ever seen it, like an orangutan and a snake had spawned a kid. Think furry, four-legged centipede the size of your average dog. Snarling. The people in the crowd who were nearest started hollering in fear. They tried to run, but the people who couldn't see that there was danger were pushing in close for a better view. I jumped down off the stage to try to help Abby. My haint reared onto its hind legs and came at us. Lars barrelled towards us, holding a two-four over his head. He managed to slam it down on the haint's skull. Glass and beer exploded from the flimsy box; Lars had used one with full bottles in it. The haint howled in pain from the liquid as the beer began to drain down through its fur. It backhanded Lars, who went down with a whuffing sound of air being pushed out of his lungs.

The Bejis leapt into the fray. The haint boxed them away easily. Brie tried to get between the haint and Abby. The haint grabbed him around the middle, and they began to tussle. I rushed to Abby's side. I took hold of the back of the chair she'd been holding. "Get out of the way!" I yelled at her. "It's me it's looking for!"

Her eyes widened as she realized what her attacker was. "Then let's both fight it!" she said. She wouldn't let go of the chair. She shouted at the fast-dispersing crowd, "Douse it with water! It can't stand water!"

"Give me the damned chair!" I said.

"No way."

Brie and the haint were down on the ground and rolling. Something covered in fur shouldn't have been shaped like that, shouldn't have been able to writhe like that. There was blood. I could see gashes on Brie's face. "Brie!" I shouted.

Abby released the chair to me. "Go!" she said. "I'll get some freaking water!" I was already rushing the haint with the chair. But suppose I hit Brie? I hesitated. With an arm that seemed entirely too long, the haint reached out and grabbed a leg of the chair and pulled it easily out of my hands.

An earsplitting guitar wail had us all crouching and covering our ears, even the haint for a second. Someone's hand grabbed me around the middle and yanked me out of the way just as the haint leapt to where I'd been. I didn't see it land. The music was waves of vertigo, spinning me into the giddiness of transit.

That had to be Lars beside me, that wriggling giggle of summer-midnight black and banana-popsicle yellow. He smelled like the steam off superheated sidewalks when the first drops of rain hit. Underneath that a whiff of naphtha.

My vision normalized. We were on some kind of open plain,

Lars and I. Red dirt as far as the eye could see, in any direction. Daylight, but with no sun. Further observation would have to wait until I was done being sick onto the red dirt.

"Sorry 'bout that," Lars said. "Couldn't think of another quick way to get you out of there." He was astride his motorbike.

I spat to get the taste out, and wiped my mouth on the sleeve of Abby's beautiful green silk blouse. "Where's Abby? Didn't you bring her out, too?"

"I guess she decided to stay." He didn't look too happy about it.

"And what about Brie? And all the people in there! It'll go after them!"

He shook his head. "Have a feeling not. Have a hunch it'll be coming after you, any second now."

Great. And me without my water gun. "So you brought us to the driest place you could find? How's that going to keep me safe?"

"Didn't have time to think it through. Brought you to the first place I could get to. And I wasn't only trying to keep *you* safe, but all the claypickens in that room. Hop on, wouldja?"

"Well, thanks a whole fuck of a lot! You take me back there, right now!"

"Can't. I'm sort of lost. And you need to get on this bike, like, yesterday."

"You're *lost*?!"

"Yup. And keeping on the move might be our only chance," he said quietly. "Look up."

I did. Far away, high up in the not-sky, a V-formation of angular shapes was headed towards us. "Gods fucking damn," I muttered. I hopped on. He gunned the bike into life. We zoomed over open ground. I looked over my shoulder and up. Already, the birds were closer. A silvery needle flashed at the leading tip of each one. Needle-sharp beaks, catching the light. I knew where I'd seen those birds before. Last time I saw them, they'd been aluminum patio lights and bits of worn glass glued onto a clumsily knitted rug. Hard to tell at this distance, but the birds seemed to be feathered. I was pretty sure that all their feathers would look like the one I'd knitted into the rug. The birds' heads had a frosty, translucent gleam, like beach glass held up to the light. What the hell had I done?

There was a small lump on the horizon, getting larger quickly. Greenish. "Gonna head over there!" said Lars.

"Is it the courtyard?"

"Dunno, but there might be some shelter."

The birds began to angle downwards. I shaded my eyes and tried to make out the thing on the horizon. "I think it's a woods!" I said.

"What?" shouted Lars over his shoulder.

"Nothing. Go faster!"

"Giving her as much as she's got!"

The birds massed into formation in the airspace above us. They were manoeuvring to get between us and the trees. "Grab my lance!" yelled Lars.

"You wish." I was only half paying attention, mesmerized by the V-formation diving down towards us.

The lead bird plunged, a flurry of iridescent black feathers powered by heaven knew what. Its body was the size of a badger, each wing about two feet outstretched. Its beak was definitely metal, and it was aiming for Lars's eyes. Pinions slapped my face in its passing. Lars turned his head. The bird slammed into the side of his helmet, cranking his head to the side. He grunted. The bike slewed. I screamed his name. He canted the bike into a deep, angled circle; either deliberately or because he'd been hurt. I didn't know which. Somehow, I managed not to fall off. The bird, built more for soaring than for quick changes of direction, missed its next strike and flopped off to one side. We spun out of the turn. Lars leaned forward and gunned 'er. He was still with me, then.

We headed for the trees again. The attack had sent us backwards a few yards. The other birds were dropping down to attack now. Lars punched at them one-handed, making the bike wobble. I wasn't wearing a helmet. I gripped the bike with my knees and tore at the birds with my hands. They smelled like algae-clogged lake water and sunbaked goose guano. Their claws raked our arms. "My umbrella!" yelled Lars. "Fucking get it, already!"

"All right! Cripes." I reached around Lars and grabbed his umbrella out of its holster. Good thing I bent my head just then, too; a claw strike missed me by centimetres.

As I withdrew the umbrella, Lars took hold of the tip and pulled. It came away in his hands. It was a sheath. Beneath it, the end of the umbrella was a blade a good foot long; slim, sharp, and flexy. It was the rapier he'd used when he was battling Dad in the park. "You fight them off!" he said. "I'll get us there."

Tentatively, I stabbed at a bird. The jolt sang its way up my arm and numbed my fingers. I gave a little scream as the bird impaled itself on the blade. Puce blood, yellow-flecked, stained the fabric of the brolly. As I tipped the blade downwards to shake the bird off, two more came at us. More from intuition than common sense, I clubbed them away with the handle. I barely managed not to gut myself or Lars with the blade. The bird slid off its tip and tumbled onto the ground, left behind us as we sped forward. From then on, I held the brolly rapier so that I could use either business end: one sharp, one thuddy. I only whacked Lars once, luckily with the thuddy end. Banged myself in the head about three or four times and put a slice across the top of one of my shoes before I got the hang of it. "Can't you buffet them with a wall of loud music, or something?"

"In this wide-open space? You got a Jimi-sized bank of amps? 'Cause I sure don't!"

We were close enough now to see that the woods were wrapped

in kudzu, which was growing thicker as we watched. My heart sank. "It's Dad!" I yelled into Lars's ear.

Lars only grunted. He was busy dodging raptors as they dove for us, talons outstretched. "Lars, we can't go in there! He'll kill us!"

"Where, then?"

A bird raked the back of my neck. I screamed and fought it off. A part of me could sense the gouges in my skin, feel the blood trickling past the collar of my shirt. But I was too hyped to feel any pain. Yet.

We zoomed up over the top of a ridge. From there, it was clear that Dad covered the horizon, as far as spirit eyes could see. There was only one choice to make. I said into Lars's ear, "Dad was trying not to hurt me that night! Head into the kudzu!"

"Yeah," grumbled Lars, "the very model of loving parenthood, he was." But he aimed for the kudzu anyway. He zigzagged the bike. The birds, like evil, could only travel in straight lines. I was leaving a trail of dead and dying birds behind us, but more were coming. Abby said I'd made thousands and thousands of them, and she must have been right, because they were massing so thickly in the air that they looked like a thunderhead bearing down on us. I concentrated on leaning with Lars when he banked into turns, on swinging his goofy rainbow umbrella sword at the birds that came too close, on stabbing them when I could.

As we approached the edge of the woods, the kudzu flowed and locked us out, like an eye snapping shut. Lars growled and plunged the bike right into the thick of it, snapping tendrils of vine as he went. The smell of torn green things rose all around us, and the stench of grape candy. I turned and swung at a bird that had plunged into the tunnel we'd created. The blade connected with a satisfying thud. The bird fell to the ground. Its beak made a metallic twanging noise as it connected. The bird flopped about.

The bike whined to a halt halfway into the vegetation, then

stuck. "Keep going!" I shouted at Lars. He gunned the motor, revved the engine. The wheels spun, kicking up shredded kudzu leaves and lengths of vine in its wake. The front end of the bike caught air, dumping me off the back. I thudded down onto my behind. The brolly rapier went flying. Lars clutched at it and managed to catch the handle, then had to swing it immediately at a volley of three birds.

"Dad!" I shouted. "It's me, Makeda! Let us in!"

Was the kudzu pulling back a fraction? A flurry of feathers and glinty beak flew at my face. I punched, hard. Bastard got a good slice at my forearm before I connected. "Ow!" It came at me again. I stomped it to the ground. Its body gave with a crunch under my boot in a way that would have made me sick to my stomach a few minutes ago. A lifetime had passed between then and now. I lifted my boot. On the ground under it was a lumpy smear of feathers, blood, glass shards, and small gears.

Lars jumped off the bike. "We're going to have to go on foot! Come on!" He took my hand and yanked me forward. There was the smallest open wedge in the wall of kudzu, around the front of the bike. We shoved past it. The lead bird slammed in behind us. The space had already shrunk so much that it was a tight fit. The bird pushed and paddled with its clawed feet, squirmed on winged elbows, its daggered beak still aimed at us, its pinprick red eyes narrowed meanly at our faces. I tried to back away, came up against a solid tree trunk. My skin prickled as I watched the kudzu vines embolize the bird into a chancre of flesh with the smallest tip of silver peeking out. The bird gave a quiet, hopeless squawk. The kudzu sealed the opening completely. For a few seconds more, we could still hear the muffled concussions as other birds thumped into the wall of kudzu, but failed to find a way in. Then nothing. Lars and I were left standing in the cold, green dark. "Whoa," he said.

I looked around, up. Foliage clustered so thickly around and above us that it created an artificial twilight. I could scarcely see my hand in front of my face. There was one source of light, though; Lars had sheathed the sword and opened the brolly. It fluoresced in a lazy flow of muted, shifting colours with the occasional glittery sparkle. "God, that's so gay," I said.

Lars held it erect and bowed slightly. "Thank you, milady."

I tried to peer through the semi-dark. "Dad?"

No answer. "Well," I said, "at least we're still alive."

Lars glanced around nervously. "For now."

By the pied, ever-changing light of the brolly, I tried to make out some details of where we were. Not much use, really; I couldn't tell for sure what other vegetation there was, because everything was covered in kudzu. The tall, standy-uppy things were trees, but what kinds of trees? Whatever they had been, they were now, for all intents and purposes, kudzu trees. The bushes? Kudzu bushes. I sat on a fallen kudzu-clad log, trying to think what to do now.

Lars snapped the brolly shut. It kept up the light show, though muted. He rested its tip on the ground, and I saw that it'd make a creditable cane, too. "Handy for hiking," he told me. "What the hell were those bird things, do you know? I've never seen anything like them."

"Yes, you have," I replied glumly. "I think I made them."

"You are shitting me!"

I shook my head. "Kinda wish I were."

"Those were Dolly's birds?"

"Yup. My haint's pulling out all the stops. It's seriously pissed at me for trying to destroy it."

A small black snake wriggled out from under the log. I recognized it. "Hey, little one. Got away from that nasty, bitey haint, huh? Well, I'm afraid I brought it to you. I'm so sorry." I put my palm flat on the ground in front of it. It crawled onto my hand, its scutes dry and raspy against my skin. It spiralled around on my hand for a couple of turns, then tried to crawl off my palm. I put it down on the ground so it wouldn't fall. It slithered off a little way, then stopped. It turned its head and looked back at me. "Okay," I said to it. I stood and brushed off the back of Abby's pants. Not sure why I bothered; the fabric was powdery all over with the dust it'd picked up on the hell ride here. I pointed to the snake. I told Lars, "I think we're supposed to follow that little guy."

He peered through the rainbow-lit gloom. "That snake? How d'you know?"

"It's a melanistic garter snake. You only find them on the Leslie Street Spit. Dad was very fond of them."

He gave a grunt of laughter. "You Joli sisters, never a dull moment with you two, is there?"

"'Scuse me? You used to live with Jimi Hendrix."

"Well, put it that way…"

"C'mon." I reached for his free hand. He clasped mine. His was a warm mitt of a paw, with calluses in interesting places. I held on, and we began following the little snake's twisty trail, deeper into the tulgey wood. I was all nerves. "Lars, don't keep quiet, okay? This light is making my head spin. I can barely make you out. If you stop talking, I won't know whose hand I'm holding."

"Shall I turn the brolly off?"

"Gods, no! Then there won't be any light at all."

"True that. What d'you want us to talk about?"

"Are you the guitar that Hendrix set on fire?"

I could hear the smile in his voice. "Everyone asks me that. You want my life story, is that it? Shall I start with my birth in a crossfire hurricane?"

"No, I want you to tell the truth, not recycle old rock lyrics. Besides, that's the Stones, not Hendrix."

"Yeah, well it's kinda private."

"I'm sorry. I didn't mean to get too personal. Gods, I can be such a dolt."

To my chagrin, he replied, "Yeah, people can be. You guys are mercurial. Instruments are simpler. We are what we are. We don't go changing our minds or our natures every five seconds."

"That must get dull," I muttered.

He laughed. "If you ever tell one of the others I said this, I'm going to deny it. But yeah, some of us...for example, trying to have a conversation with Lucy?"

"Lemme guess: B. B. King's axe?"

"No, not Lucille; Lucy. John Henry's hammer. She's all thud, thud, thud. That chick gets a topic in her head, she'll run it right into the ground. What a voice on her, though. You know that beautiful, brassy clang you get when a hammer hits the sweet spot? It's like that. She says even just a simple hello, and it's like angels shouting the length and breadth of the universe. It's like Michael's trumpet. Which is wild, seeing as Michael's trumpet is just a made-up story."

"I—" I was too dumbstruck by what I'd learned from his last few sentences to say anything intelligent. It wasn't just musical instruments. "Is Stagecoach Mary's coach one of you guys?"

"Luvvie, both of that fearsome woman's pistols and her rifle are enspirited. But not her stagecoach. Though I did once meet an enspirited flatboat. Big River's Daughter, her name was. But the stagecoach that Mary drove wasn't a thing she loved and toiled with and worked on and handled till you could see her finger marks worn into it, and till it had raised calluses on her hands that fit to its shape like a glove and its hand. Her stagecoach wasn't the thing that people talked about and gossiped about and legendized in their own minds. Her guns were."

"Huh. That's wild." I was getting used to seeing by the coruscating effect of Lars's rainbow-casting brolly. I could see the snake more easily. I stepped over a fallen log in the split second before I would have tripped on it and gone sprawling onto the forest floor. "Where'd you find the two-four that you clonked the haint over the head with?"

"I can't really remember. Maybe it'd been in the wings somewhere. All I could think of was getting to Abby. And you, of course."

"Lars, are you and Abby going to last?"

It was a second or two before he answered. "I don't know. She's amazing, but—"

"But she can get a little bossy?"

He chuckled. "Yeah, I guess you would know about that. But that's not really the problem. I'm an instrument, yeah? It's kinda hot for me when someone knows how to take the lead."

I held a hand up. "Okay, TMI."

"Nothing's TMI with you lot. It doesn't bug me that Abs is a leader. But it's really getting up my craw that she always assumes I'll follow."

"She forgets to ask you first."

"For her, there's nothing to forget. It just doesn't occur to her that it's important."

Lars and I walked in silence for a few paces. Then he said, "You don't, though. You treat me like an equal. How come is that?"

I sighed. "You're not my equal, though."

He stopped and looked at me. "Come again?"

The snake flicked its tongue impatiently at us. We got going again. I said, "I mean, you're better than me. You have everything I've ever wanted. A soul *and* mojo. A sense of purpose. Independence."

"And Abby?"

I thought about that. "Actually, I'm finally figuring out that I do have Abby. Always will."

"Yeah. Glad I don't have to tell you that."

A forest is never really quiet, but this one was, except for our footsteps and the scritchy sound of the snake's movements. No wind in the trees, not even the sound of gargantuan kudzu blossoms falling. Looked like Quashee had licked that overgrowth problem—in spirit space, at least. Pretty soon, I couldn't stand the silence any more. "Did you know it was me?" I asked Lars. "Impersonating Abby up onstage?"

"Sure. And I figured you had some help from Brie, doing his thing. But girl, you were on fire!"

"I was?"

"Given what you had to work with? Yeah."

"Great. Thanks a lot." Given what I had to work with. Sheesh.

"Don't you think Maka deserves better than that?" asked a quiet voice beside us.

I leapt about a foot. "Beji! What are you doing here?" I went and hugged him. I'd forgotten how good he smelled.

"We followed you." He pointed to the forest floor, where Yoplait was pacing beside us. Still walking, she transformed into Beji.

I said, "Not quite what I'd planned for our first date in forever."

They looked confused. Suddenly my tummy itched so fiercely that I had to scratch it. The Bejis went on the alert. They watched me dispassionately. Catlike.

"How're you feeling?" Beji asked.

"Think I'm getting a cold," I replied. "Plus there's that armada of scary birds chasing us."

"They can't get in here, nohow," Beji pointed out.

"Contrariwise," Beji added. "There is no illness in spirit space." All I could see was his grin.

"Aren't you confusing the Cheshire cat with Tweedledum and, uh, Wheedledee? No, that's not it." I was kind of unsteady on my feet, I realized. "Why is it so hot in here? And where's the snake taking us?"

"What snake?" asked the Bejis.

There was no longer a snake in front of us.

Lars stopped. He looked around uneasily. "Uh-oh. The kudzu's moving in."

It was. The vines were visibly getting closer. In amongst the leaves of one of them hung the little snake, its spine clearly broken. Mesmerized, I watched the vines pull in. "Dad?" I said.

"Maka, get down!" said Lars. He pushed me down to crouch at his feet. I heard his rapier sing as he swung it around in the air.

A vine as thick around as a thigh lashed out at me. Lars chopped it away before it hit me. He didn't get a chance to do it a second time. The kudzu crashed in and cocooned us all in ropes of green.

"Uncle Boysie! Stop it!"

"Please, Uncle Boysie! She's almost ready to slough it off!" The Bejis crouched beside me, cradling me on either side.

The kudzu withdrew from us a little space, and I could breathe freely again. Lars rolled out of the kudzu hug and lay there coughing.

Beyond that space, the kudzu thrashed and twitched like something in agony. I asked, "Is Dad dying?"

"He needs his mojo," said Beji.

"I can't give it to him!"

"You've been itchy and feverish for days, haven't you? And headachy?"

"Yeah."

"We figure you're rejecting Uncle Boysie's mojo."

"But I won't be me without it!"

"Then maybe you'll be someone new. We can help."

Kudzu vines started slapping the ground near us. The Bejis didn't give me time to think. Yoplait and Butter leapt at me in deadly silence. They dug their claws into me, one on either shoulder. "What are you doing?" I screamed. I tried to pluck them off. I found I was lashing out at Beji and Beji, both tugging at my clothing. Or maybe not my clothing. Something tore away from me with a soft *pop* and a little pain. Beji and Beji were holding it in their hands, and it was so Shiny that I had to look away. "Why are you doing this?" I cried. "You're killing me!"

"We don't think so," replied Beji.

"At least, we hope not," said Beji.

I whimpered. I curled up and waited to lose my faculties.

Instead, I felt blessedly cool. The fever I hadn't been aware of had broken. The low-level headache that had had me chewing painkillers for days was gone. My head was clear enough for me to finally realize how foggy it had become. I took my head out of my hands and looked around. Beji and Beji smiled protectively at me. I said, "I'm still here."

"Good," Beji replied. He looked worried. He asked Beji, "That's good, right?"

She nodded slowly. "I hope so."

I squealed, "You *hope* so? I may be about to go brain-dead because of you two, and all you can say is that you hope it won't happen?"

A thigh-thick rope of kudzu yanked Dad's mojo out of their hands. Dad pulled it up against the mass of his body. I sat up. I was more scared than I'd ever been, but part of me didn't want to miss the miracle. If I could just see Dad whole again, just for a second, before I lost myself.

But when the vines let it go, Dad's mojo just hovered there, not touching him. A tremor went through the main body of Quashee. It flopped to the ground, twitching. The kudzu that had been covering the forest began to withdraw, to shrink in on itself. And except for a few rotting tree trunks, still rooted in whatever passed for soil in this place, there was no forest there. The kudzu had choked it all to death, creating a vast vine barren. "Dad!"

Lars wheezed, "He can't work his mojo with the kudzu body, remember? Quashee has his own mojo."

The Bejis looked at each other in dismay. "We forgot about that part."

"Oh, gods," I muttered. I really was going to have to watch my dad die twice.

There was a whistling from the air above us. Once more, I looked up. My heart plunged. With Quashee shrunken and the forest denuded, Dolly's birds had a clear shot at me. Vaster than all outdoors and shot through with glints and flashes of colour, a grey-black cloud of mechanical raptors was bearing down on me. When I failed, I sure didn't fail small. It never rains but it pours.

Rain. As in thunder and lightning. Free-flowing electricity. Electricity was power, was amplitude. And Abby'd said you could sing anything to smithereens if you hit the right note.

"Can't you buffet them with a wall of loud music, or something?"

"In this wide-open space? You got a Jimi-sized bank of amps? 'Cause I sure don't!"

Maybe I did have something like that. My mojo, if I had any; wouldn't it be some amplification of a skill I already had a natural talent for? Didn't Abby's life go smoother when I was around? Didn't I have a knack for making my big failures bigger and my small achievements insignificant?

I yelled, "Lars! Go fetch Abby!"

"Sure thing. If I can find my way back."

"That'll have to do."

He nodded, tottered to his feet and headed for his bike. He was a little wobbly, but he was on the move.

"Bejis, I want you to brew up a storm, like you did last time."

"You're sure about this?" asked Beji.

"No, I'm not! Fucking do it, already!"

They joined hands. Fluffy little white clouds started dancing around above the haint birds that gyred deathwatch circles in the air above me. "I need more than that!" I yelled at the Bejis. "Give me storm clouds, damn it! Lots of them! Water slows the bastards down."

The Bejis closed their eyes tight, their brows furrowed. Slowly the clouds drew together. As clusters of them joined, they took on anvil shapes. Their undersides were greying up with the weight of moisture in them. "Yes! Like that! More!" Had Lars been able to find his way back to Abby? I couldn't do this without her. I probably couldn't do this at all.

The clouds vomited rain onto the birds. They screamed. A few tumbled out of the air. But the rest kept going. In arrow formation, they dove down, heading straight for me. It was all on me. Despairing, I threw my arms wide and my head back. "Please let this work," I prayed, though I didn't know to whom. Dad couldn't help me, and Uncle wasn't going to take the risk twice of messing around with life and death.

And in that moment, I knew to whom I should be praying. "Abs, I don't know whether I'll ever find my mojo, and I'm not even sure what my mojo will turn out to be. But I know this; as long as I have strength to do so, I can carry you wherever you need to go. And I need you to go with me right now."

The birds were so close that I could hear the wind whistling through their pinions. The sound was louder than the pounding of my terrified heart, louder than the crash and smash of thunder from multiple lightning bolts. The rain was too far away to touch us, but the buildup of electricity crawled along my skin, erecting the short hairs on my arms and legs.

"Maka, I'm here!" cried Abby's voice from somewhere behind me. Even through the cacophony, I heard her loud and clear.

I whipped around. "Everyone get out of the way! Now!" I turned back to face the killing flock. I shouted, "Come on, then!"

And they were upon me. They struck. They pierced my body, sharp as a million needles, but didn't come out the other side. It hurt like fuck. With a fierce joy, something seeded in me, became part of me, filled me so full I couldn't hold it. And still more and more birds came. Their metal parts attracted lightning from the mountainous thunderheads above. Lightning arced towards them, followed them sizzling as they dove into my skin, in through my eyes and mouth. I felt my body shuddering and jerking with the power of it. I could do nothing but take it. I couldn't inhale, couldn't scream, couldn't even fall. The storm surge danced through me, transfixed me in its eye, that pregnant, lowering calm before the raging resumes. My legs wouldn't hold me. I thudded down onto the ground. I didn't feel a thing.

Abby screamed and ran, transit-limber, to kneel by my side. "Maka, what're you doing?"

Consciousness was fading quickly. I tried to explain. "I...it..." But I couldn't find the words. English wasn't coming to me.

English wasn't the first language I'd learned.

"*Trying to free him,*" I said in sisterspeak. "*You...sing the right vibration. Destroy...kudzu.*"

"*Me? But I can't sing low enough!*" she protested.

Deep breaths, deep breaths. I wasn't dying, not yet. I was just receiving my haint, that had been trying to get back into me all my life.

My mojo. "I think I can help," I said hoarsely to Abby. "Bejis, would you guys prop me up, please?"

The kudzu was still twitching, but oh, so faintly! Dad's mojo hovered just outside it, as close to the other part of itself as possible. The light from the godlike mojo hurt my eyes. "Do it, Abby. Just sing."

She took my hands and began, a keening note that soared rapidly down towards the bottom of her range. As she did, something unfurled in me like steel-bladed flowers blooming, like shatterglass exploding, like muscles I hadn't known I had. Somewhere in the flesh world, my head jerked and slammed against a concrete floor. I grunted with the pain of it. I could feel my body reeling me back in, away from Abby.

She stopped. I felt the flow of power dip to zero, as though someone had put a crimp in a fire hose. "*What's wrong?*" she asked fearfully.

I was barely there at all, but I managed to respond, "*Sing.*"

She started again right away. It was like landing on soft grass. In this space, her gesture of unquestioning trust in me was more than an abstract. It literally broke my headlong tumble towards my cage of flesh. Now I understood how faith sustained the lives of gods. I *couldn't* let her go. I aimed my awareness in her direction, and I reached out. I don't know how else to describe it. I stretched out and caught the something that was Abby's pure, beautiful sound. I cradled it safely, and I carried it down, down. She slipped lower than her range and kept going down. Elephant subsonic deep. Leviathan deep. I held on to Abby's sound even as it was expanding in my arms, even as the place where we were began to resonate with the impossible vibrations of it. I couldn't hear it any longer, but I could feel it shaking every atom. Abby's voice descended to somewhere impossible, then lower, and lower, and held. My new-found, unpracticed talent sliced at me with razor-blade roses. My mind was slipping. My new mojo wasn't enough to hold it. I didn't have time to lament. Just before I went, I wrapped my arms and legs around my precious sister-burden. I couldn't let go, I couldn't. Beji said in my ear, "The kudzu's just kinda going liquid. You guys are doing it!"

And it was killing me. I gritted my teeth and held on as I ripped Quashee away from Dad's soul so that Dad could reclaim his mojo. I thought, *I'm sorry, Quashee. This is no way to repay you.*

And then I couldn't make sense of the world any longer. Regretfully, I felt myself going. The last thing I remembered was a flash of green bright enough to show through my closed eyelids, and Abby's gleeful voice exclaiming, "Daddy!" It could have been wishful thinking, though.

◆ ◆ ◆

Would tell them how her sister stood
In deadly peril to do her good,
And win the fiery antidote.

So I guess my mojo is to be some kind of amplifier? To whom was I speaking? Where was I?

"Not really, but it was clever of you to work it that way."

Well if not that, what is it, then? What's my gift?

"You still think it's something you get, don't you? Something you own?"

Isn't it?

"Honey bun, no. It's a service you give to others, not the other way around. Some of your kin still haven't grasped that. I love them to pieces, but a couple of them can't tell shit from Shine-ola, even after all this time." It snickered at its own pun. "You, now; you're learning how to give."

And what, exactly, am I giving as I'm learning to do this giving thing? I was trying to be sly.

"Nukka, please."

Five-cent fine! I crowed.

"No, not for me."

I briefly wondered again who I was speaking to, but I was too intrigued by the conversation to distract myself by trying to figure it out.

"I'm way too old a dog to fall for your tricks. You'll fashion your mojo into something way more interesting than if I tell you what I think it is."

Spoilsport.

"Not usually. I generally don't interfere once I've set the machine in motion. Invalidates the experiment. But you were a highly entertaining result, so I thought I'd stop by and chat a bit. You won't remember, anyway. Tell you what, I'll give you a little clue to your mojo. Your kin, the ones you call celestials, they each govern a range of tensions between a particular set of related dualities."

Say what now?

"Life and death, for example."

You mean Uncle Jack?

I received an impression of a smile. "You learn quickly. Wilderness and civilization."

Dad.

"Salt and sweet."

Granny Ocean.

"Oh, this is a fun game! Joie de vivre and fear."

Huh? I reflected on that awhile. *Uncle Jack again?*

"Clever child. Just keep being yourself, and the two poles of your mojo will become clear."

I'm going to have to think about that.

"You do that."

But right now, I'm going to nap for a while.

Nothing. Nothing for the longest, most peaceful while, as the planets whirled in their orbits and stars burned out.

It was the tiniest thread of sound. Sometimes I wasn't even sure I was hearing anything. Curious, I strained to hear better. There! Yes, it was a tune. I could make out a note or two. Pity. I'd been doing just fine lying here, resting.

Where was here, anyway? And where was I? As in really; I didn't seem to have a body.

There it was again, like a mosquito in the ear; such a tiny noise, but piercingly difficult to ignore. I cast about for a little while, searching for the source of the sound, sometimes getting a little closer, sometimes a little farther away. A few times I gave up and tried to go back to my rest. But every time, there the bloody tune was again. I needed to find it, if only to turn it off. And then I did find it, and it wasn't a whiny little stinger of sound. It wafted like the scent of something delicious that your dad's cooking on the stove, and you can't quite tell what he's cooking, but it's making your tummy rumble, so you follow that tantalizing smell, getting closer with each step:

Mm, mm, mm, mm,
In anyone's home we are lost.

Lost? Was I lost? Wait; hadn't someone said something to me recently about being lost? The voice came again:

Mm, mm, mm, mm,
We are lost in anyone's home.

I knew that song. Maybe I even knew that voice, though I was too far away to be able to tell for sure. I tried, and managed to drift closer. I was getting the knack of it.

Mm, mm, mm, mm,
In anyone's home we are lost.

Someone had dreamed those words. Had dreamed about little ghost girls, playful with their sticking-out braids and their summer dresses, trying on their mothers' clothing and tottering around in high heels four times bigger than their own little feet, and laughing for the silliness of it, then going parading through the house, singing:

> *Mm, mm, mm, mm,*
> *We are lost in anyone's home.*

Closer. Closer. I was moving faster now. Someone had told me about her dream the second she opened her eyes. Couldn't wait to tell me what she'd dreamed, how cheerful the girls had been, though the song was slow and the words sad, how she'd even remembered the tune *and* the words. She'd sung it for me, in a child's voice already showing the promise of the power it would have:

> *In anyone's home we are lost,*
> *We are lost in anyone's home.*

Abby! I was rushing now, hurtling towards the sound of my twin's voice.

I opened my eyes. I was in a hospital bed. Sitting beside it, crooning the dirge lullaby, was—

"Abby."

She gasped and hurried over to touch my hand and kiss me and kiss me. "A minute longer," she said, "and Uncle was going to have to do his job."

"His jo— Oh, shit."

"He said you were seconds from dead, but Dad said you weren't ready to go yet."

"Dad?"

She nodded. "Dad wasn't willing to mess with the natural order of things any more. But I told him that he might have rules to follow about these things, but I don't. And I sang and I sang and I thought you weren't hearing me, but you came back!"

I said, "I'm not lost any more. You brought me back."

"You've always been the one carrying me. It was my turn to carry you for a little while. Hey; when we brought you out of transit, you were clutching Quashee's root crown. It's the only part of him that was left, but it was exactly what he needed to regrow. Dad mended the hoodoo tree, and he's back climbing it. At normal speed this time."

I kissed her hand. I was still so weak, it took all my strength. I laid my head back down on the pillow.

An irreverent voice said, "Out of the way, there, Abs. Gotta say hi to my other niece."

"Uncle."

His hug was as enveloping and Shiny as the satin lining a coffin. It was the sweetest welcome. "Decided to come back, did you? And brought a passenger with you?"

"I have mojo, Uncle."

"I know that now. I'm sorry I gave you the gears."

I kissed his bony cheek, inhaled the sweetly decomposing scent of his cigar. My life stretched before me, balanced between freedom and responsibility. "When do I get to see Dad?" I asked.

> *"For there is no friend like a sister,*
> *In calm or stormy weather,*
> *To cheer one on the tedious way,*
> *To fetch one if one goes astray,*
> *To lift one if one totters down,*
> *To strengthen whilst one stands."*

ACKNOWLEDGMENTS

This book received support from the Toronto Arts Council and from the Ontario Arts Council via publishers' recommendations to the Writers' Reserve Program. Profound thanks to Bear and Ishai for keeping me and mine fed in the final few weeks before the deadline, when I could do nothing but eat, breathe, and sleep this book. May your own words flow freely. Appreciations for my agent, Don Maass, for my patient editor, Lindsey Rose, and for the team at Grand Central Publishing. And, as ever, deep gratitude to an international community of friends and family who literally sustained me through the past five years as I struggled to return to health and independence. I give thanks for you all, every day.

READING GROUP GUIDE

Discussion Questions

1. Makeda and Abby are twins, yet they have very different personalities. In what ways are they similar and in what ways are they different? How do you think their individual challenges and experiences have shaped their personalities and their relationship with each other? How do you think Abby's physical dependence on Makeda during their early years shaped their relationship?

2. What do you think of the bargain Cora made for the lives of her daughters? Did she make the right choice? Would you have done the same in her place?

3. If you were born conjoined to a twin, would you want the doctors to try to separate you, even if it might mean one of you could die? Or would you rather not take the risk, and live permanently connected?

4. Do you like Uncle John? Do you think he knew what he was doing to Makeda? Why does he insist that Makeda's rug isn't her mojo? Is he lying to her?

5. This book is full of unconventional relationships: Abby/ Makeda; Cora/Boysie/Uncle John; Abby/Makeda/the Bejis. Do these relationships feel realistic and true to you?

6. How do you think the poem extracts sprinkled throughout the book relate to the text? Do they deepen your understanding of it?